Bound to Him
—by Love and Lies . . .

"What are you  questioned softly.

Leah's ago_____ r head. "I can't tell y_____

"Has it to d____

"Y-yes—no._____ng as though she were dying inside, Leah pulled her hand from Ian's. "Oh, God! Please just leave me alone."

Ian was on Leah the second she bounded from the settee. "You'll not escape me—not until you've told me what's troubling you."

Her lips pressed tightly together, she refused to answer.

"Has acknowledging my love upset you? Damn it, Leah! Look at me!" he demanded, shaking her. "Does it have to do with your Irishman?"

"Yes," she lied, hoping he'd let her go.

"Are you in love with him?"

What was another lie after so many? "Yes."

He continued to study her. "Your eyes say otherwise, Leah. You're not in love with him. Desperately, fully, wildly, you are in love with me, just as I am in love with you, Leah, and I shall prove it." Wet and hot, his mouth covered hers. . . .

Books by Charlene Cross

Masque of Enchantment
A Heart So Innocent
Deeper Than Roses
Lord of Legend
Almost a Whisper

Published by POCKET BOOKS

Charlene Cross

Almost a Whisper

POCKET **STAR** BOOKS

New York London Toronto Sydney Tokyo Singapore

An *Original* Publication of POCKET BOOKS

A Pocket Star Book published by
POCKET BOOKS, a division of Simon & Schuster Inc.
1230 Avenue of the Americas, New York, NY 10020

ISBN: 0-671-79431-0

First Pocket Books printing April 1994

10 9 8 7 6 5 4 3 2 1

POCKET STAR BOOKS and colophon are registered trademarks of Simon & Schuster Inc.

Cover art by Lina Levy

Printed in the U.S.A.

For

Eric and Shirley
Glenda and Jim
Shirley, Jeanie, and Sonja
Cecil, Sue, and Jodi

and

Ruby Massey,
the best Grandma ever.
This one is yours.

Almost a Whisper

CHAPTER
1

York, England
April 1841

Destitute.

The word tolled inside Leah Balfour Dalton's mind like a death knell.

She stared across the paper-strewn desk, carefully measuring the solicitor's sober expression. Though he seemed to be telling the truth, she refused to accept his declaration. Her gloved hands clutched the chair's arms as she prayed she'd misunderstood.

"Surely, Mr. Kingsley, there must be something left of my father's estate—even a small amount on which the children and I might subsist."

"I am sorry, Miss Dalton, but as I said, your circumstances can be described as none other than destitute. I wish it were otherwise, but, alas, it is not."

The solicitor's shoulders dropped from what Leah considered to be an indifferent shrug.

"But Balfour was sold," she said of the estate that had been her home for nineteen years. "There must be a remainder from its sale."

"The place was auctioned, Miss Dalton, the winning bid

most disappointing. There was only enough profit to settle your father's debts. Not a farthing more."

Positive that Terence Dalton's assets had far outweighed any liabilities, Leah spurned the man's statement. "Are you quite certain?"

Clearly affronted that she'd presumed to question his integrity, Mr. Kingsley snapped, "Yes, I am *quite* certain, young lady." He sighed. "I sympathize with you, Miss Dalton. I know it has been a difficult time for you and your siblings—"

"Difficult?"

Leah came out of the chair and slammed her palms on his desk. The violent action sent the solicitor sinking back into his seat.

"You dare cast it off as 'difficult'!" she accused, trembling with pent-up fury. All that had happened during the past five weeks whipped through her mind and body like the winds of a tempest. "My parents are dead—first my mother, then my father. Barely a fortnight had passed when the next blow struck—cruelly, I might add, for we were tossed from our home, much like slop from a bucket! Hope, Kate, Peter—you are aware, Mr. Kingsley, that Peter has weak lungs and has been ill since birth. Then there's little Emily, who is only five. They are in a foundling home, a dreary, horrible place, unfit for tender young hearts such as theirs, and certainly unsuitable for Peter's condition."

"Your siblings are fed and attended to," Kingsley stated.

"So are sheep in a pen before they are slaughtered," she bit back, then rushed on. "I thank the Lord young Terence escaped the orphanage, yet he, too, is suffering. He was torn from his beloved studies, his tutor dismissed. Now he is reduced to mucking out stalls and firing bellows in Leeds for the smithy Jones just to feed himself. As for myself, I have been unable to find a suitable position with a decent wage—one that would allow me to bring my family together again."

Beneath her gloves, Leah's hands were badly chafed. To be close to the younger children, she had taken a job as a

2

scullery maid, earning two shillings a week. If her pay hadn't included a daily meal and a sleeping cot beneath the kitchen stairs of the inn, she'd be living on the streets of York.

Pride prevented her from relating this or the abuse she continually endured from her lecherous employer. As though Leah's situation weren't bad enough, her bottom bore a multitude of bruises, painful and colorful reminders of the innkeeper's insistent pinches, delivered whenever his wife was out of his sight.

Her thoughts again focusing on the issue at hand, Leah noticed the solicitor seemed unaffected by what she'd told him. Never would she allow this man to know just how low she'd sunk. Taking a deep breath, she attempted to sound composed.

"Unless you plan to help us, sir, you may keep your sympathy. The emotion alone does us little good. Surely the many years my father employed your services has meant something to you?"

John Kingsley peered at Leah over his wire-rimmed spectacles. "I am fully aware of your circumstances, Miss Dalton. It is a tragic situation, but unfortunately I am unable to offer you assistance. I think it would be best if you leave."

Leah's mouth flew open, but he waved her off. "If you hadn't noticed when you first burst through the door, unannounced, I am otherwise occupied. I have a letter to finish and a strong-willed niece to see to, both of which I hope to deal with inside of a quarter hour.

"Where is the chit?" he grumbled, viewing the wall clock. "She was to be here twenty minutes ago." His gaze returned to Leah. "If you have it in your mind to seek me out again, I should inform you that tonight I set sail for India in the queen's service. I shall be gone a very long time, Miss Dalton. As you can see, I am packed and anxious to be on my way."

Leah glanced around her and realized the place indeed was in disarray. Folio cabinets lay open, files bulging from their shelves, Mr. Kingsley's assistant quickly setting them in order. An assortment of luggage was stacked in one corner, while the outer office also held a collection of trunks and hatboxes, which undoubtedly belonged to his niece.

Her attention shifted back to the desk top. By the solicitor's left hand lay a bank draft, the amount indecipherable from where she stood. Pen poised over the letter he'd been framing when Leah had first launched herself into the room, he scrawled the words: *I remain your most obedient servant, John Kingsley, Esq.*

Throughout Leah's perusal of the room, Mr. Kingsley had been ignoring her, no doubt impatient that she leave. Feeling suddenly drained, she instead sank back into the chair. "I suppose it is utterly hopeless, then," she whispered across the way. She fought back the tears which threatened to gather and spill. "I just cannot believe my father would leave his six children without means of support. We were not overtly wealthy, but certainly we prospered more than most. Dear Lord! There is so much I don't understand . . ."

Leah's feelings of dejection must have somehow evinced themselves, for John Kingsley looked up at her. Slowly, he lifted the blotter away from his signature and set the thing aside.

"Miss Dalton," he began on a far gentler note. "I presume you realize that your father hadn't intended on any of this happening. Your mother's sudden illness, his horrible accident as he rode breakneck from the south of England—" He swallowed the rest, Leah's gaze having shot to his face. "I apologize for my choice of words. Terence's death was indeed a tragedy. It is all a tragedy . . ."

The last of his words, along with his inflection, unnerved Leah. Her father's death wasn't all that troubled her, but his life as well. Mystery surrounded the late Terence Dalton, and because it did, questions abounded in Leah's mind. She'd not rest until they were answered.

"Why is it, Mr. Kingsley, on the few occasions we needed to hastily contact my father, our messages were always relayed to him through you?" At Leah's inquiry, his expression grew stoic. "Likewise, sir, why have you refused to respond to my written queries, requesting to know where he is buried?" The man remained silent. "I am certain you know far more about my father than his family ever did," she remarked, "including my mother."

"Terence Dalton was a good man. I both knew and liked him. We were old friends."

Leah noted how he'd hedged her questions and dismissed her statement. "Yes, he was a good man, but he absented himself from his family far too much."

"His business was in London. For it to function effectively, he had to remain there."

"While his family remained in Leeds? Strange, don't you think, that he'd prefer to keep us so far north?"

"It was my understanding, Miss Dalton, that he wanted to spare you from the rot and decadence that is London. The place teems with prostitutes and pickpockets. Black smoke hangs heavy over the city, blocking out the sunlight. The stench from the Thames is disgusting, while the threat of disease plagues the population continuously. London is not the ideal place to rear a family."

"Perhaps you are right, Mr. Kingsley. But I am certain there are areas close by that are quite acceptable."

"Did your mother ever complain about her husband spending so much time away?"

"No, but—"

"If your mother didn't object, I'd say you have little reason to question your father's motives."

Leah disagreed.

Elizabeth Dalton had been a gentle soul, unassuming, sweet, given to an easy smile. Leah resembled her physically: flaxen hair, tilted green eyes, and full pouting lips. But that was where the similarity ended, for Leah was far more independent than her mother could ever have hoped to be. In fact, because of her mother's timidity, Leah had been forced to become the stabilizing factor in her siblings' lives. That her mother hadn't objected to *these arrangements* didn't mean they were acceptable, but more likely that she dared not object to them.

"Mr. Kingsley," Leah began just as he pulled out a clean sheet of paper from his desk drawer.

"Miss Dalton," he countered, taking hold of his pen. "You say you cannot find suitable employment, correct?"

"Yes, that is correct. But—"

"I assume it is because you lack a proper reference," he interrupted.

"That, and the fact that I don't have any experience."

"You helped rear your brothers and sisters, did you not?"

"I did. About my father—"

"And you helped them with their lessons, I suppose?"

"Yes," she said, exasperated.

"You are well educated, correct?"

"I am fluent in French and Latin, have studied all the classics, including Shakespeare, and I cipher exceedingly well. My sewing is acceptable. I am an expert gardener, not only with growing roses, but also with vegetables and herbs. I've even assisted with the lambing when the ewes were in labor at Balfour. In fact, Mr. Kingsley, there isn't much I don't know about running a household, inside and out."

"Excellent," he said, scrawling the salutation *To whom it may concern:* across the top of the page. "There is a family I know just outside York who is in need of a governess. This letter of introduction should allow you the opportunity of securing an interview. I hope it will afford you that which you seek."

As his pen continued across the paper, Leah knew his sudden desire to assist her was nothing more than an evasive maneuver. So far he hadn't answered any of her questions. "What I seek, Mr. Kingsley, is the truth. Why was my father buried elsewhere than the churchyard at Leeds?"

The bell over the outer door jangled stridently; the solicitor's attention fired toward the sound, as did Leah's. A portly little man, his faced flushed, rushed into the room, a letter in hand.

"Fields," the solicitor sharply admonished his coachman, "do have the courtesy to enter without making such a commotion." He peered around the man. "Where is Miss Kingsley? The two of you were to be here sometime ago."

"Sir, your niece—she's disappeared," the harried man

responded. "The house staff searched everywhere. This letter is all we found."

Accepting the missive from his man, Kingsley set his pen aside, then ripped through the seal. A dark frown settled across his forehead as he quickly scanned the contents of the note. "Damnation!" he erupted, his fist pounding the desk. "The ungrateful chit has eloped!"

Startled, Leah watched as he sprang from his chair, his gaze casting about the desk's littered surface. Shoving aside her unfinished letter of introduction, he grabbed hold of the paper that he'd set his signature to, just minutes before, crumpled it between his hands, and tossed it down. The thing skittered across the desk, dropped to the floor, and settled at Leah's feet beneath her skirt's hem.

"She is much like her father," he snarled between his teeth. "A bad seed." The wall clock began striking the hour. "We're late," he said, having fully noted the time. "Farnsworthy, we must leave at once! Help Fields load our luggage in the coach."

"Yes, sir," his assistant replied, locking the last of the folio cabinets lining the rear wall. The man scurried to the corner, the coachman at his heels. "What about Miss Kingsley's luggage, sir?" Farnsworthy asked, his hands and arms brimming with his possessions. "The private conveyance is past due. When the driver arrives, there won't be anyone here to tell him your niece won't be needing passage."

The bank draft was snatched from the desk, stashed into the top drawer, and quickly locked away. "Damn the girl for the problems she's caused me," the solicitor ranted, the key disappearing into his pocket.

Red-faced, he strode from behind his desk and headed toward the wall rack. A light-weight wool cloak was lifted from the hook and swung around his shoulders; a polished beaver top hat met his silvery head. Leah realized he intended to desert her.

"But Mr. Kingsley!" she cried, leaping from her seat. "My letter of intro—"

"I have no time to waste, Miss Dalton," he said, eyeing

7

her from across the room. He walked into the waiting area; Leah sped after him. "If Mr. Farnsworthy and I are to make our eight o'clock departure in Hull, we must leave this instant." Slipping his wallet from his pocket, he extracted several bank notes. "I shall employ you to take charge. When the hired coach shows up, you are to instruct its driver to load this gaggle of trunks and hatboxes, then have him disburse with them."

"But are they not your niece's?" Leah asked, confused.

"They are, Miss Dalton, but she is no longer in need of their contents. She has made her choice, and I have made mine. The coachman is to take her possessions to the nearest charitable institution where they are to be distributed to the poor." He placed the bank notes in her hand. "The man has been paid his fee. Don't allow him to convince you otherwise. You may tip him for his trouble. The remainder of the money should help alleviate your financial difficulties somewhat. I trust, Miss Dalton, you will make certain what I've asked is thus executed."

The outside door opened, the bell clanging loudly, then the panel slammed to, the window rattling from the force of Mr. Kingsley's exodus. Through the etched-glass pane, Leah watched as he climbed into his coach and seated himself next to his assistant. With a snap of the whip and a shout from the driver, the vehicle rolled away.

Leah's fingers curled around the bank notes, her shoulders slumping. Glancing at the mound of luggage, she made her way back into the inner office.

Beside her vacated chair, Leah stared at the ball of paper that had landed at her feet. As she stooped to retrieve the thing, she briefly pondered the solicitor's quick burst of temper. A feeling of hopelessness enveloped her when she finally sank back into her seat.

Her impromptu visit to Mr. Kingsley had produced none of the results she'd hoped for, her many questions remaining unanswered. He'd compensated her nicely for such a simple task as delivering a message, but his sudden generosity wasn't enough to reunite her family, something she desired with all her heart.

Resentment welled inside Leah. How could her father possibly have been so remiss with his finances as to leave his children impoverished? Her mother's face flashed before her eyes; Leah's indignation surged. And why hadn't he been at his dying wife's side when he was needed most?

True, it was said, his own life had ended as he rode north to Leeds, his horse stumbling on a pitch-black road between London and Balfour, the tumble he'd taken breaking his neck. Yet, why had his family not been informed of his accident until over a week after its occurrence? And why did his resting place remain secreted from his children?

There were too many mysteries for Leah to simply let the matter rest. As she centered her attention on the line of folio cabinets against the far wall, each marked by a letter of the alphabet, the *D* beckoned to her. Placing the money and crumpled paper on the desk, she rose from her chair and made her way to the cabinet where she jiggled the latch only to discover it was locked.

A letter opener lay within reach, and Leah quickly retrieved it. After sliding the thin blade between the abutting doors and slipping the lock, she shuffled through the folders until she hit on the one she sought. Inside, she found a single sheet of paper, a solitary line written across it.

"Eighteen Hanover Square, London," Leah whispered, committing the inscription to memory.

The address was unfamiliar to her, the letters posted to her father from his family being directed to a point on St. James's Street. But she suspected the missing pieces of his life, along with a hidden legacy, lay in London on Hanover Square. Unfortunately, she had no means of getting there to discover if this were true.

Dejectedly, Leah placed the file back with the others, then sealed the cabinet doors. Seated again, she stared at the crumpled ball of paper resting atop the desk. Wondering over its contents, she seized the thing, smoothed it across her lap, then read:

My dearest Madeline,
It is with deep regret I must decline your invita-

tion to join you at the end of next month to close out the Season. I have so enjoyed this arrangement in the past, but in a few short hours, I will be sailing to India—an unexpected and sudden request from Her Majesty. I doubt I shall return to England until possibly the latter part of November or early December, weather and business affairs permitting. Perhaps we will be able to spend Christmas together at Kingsley Hall—if, of course, Huntsford does not object.

If the young woman standing before you has properly introduced herself, you are aware that she is my niece, Miss Anne Kingsley. I am in a fix, dearest Madeline, and must ask the greatest of favors from you. The girl is my ward, her guardianship a responsibility I took on to myself two months past. A mistake, I fear, for she has been a thorn in my side ever since. Anne cannot travel with me to India, yet I fear leaving her alone, especially when she fancies herself in love with an Irish bounder who followed her to York from Ulster. My late brother and I had been estranged for over a quarter century, therefore you heard not a word from me about James or his family—mainly because there was nothing good to say about any of them. As it is, considering my niece's lowly upbringing, she is in need of a firm, yet charitable individual to guide and watch over her. I could think of no one except you, dearest Madeline. Your patience is renowned, as is your ability to tame the most brutish of creatures who have managed to stumble into your path. Therefore, I am certain you will be able to instill in my irascible niece the proper social behavior, as well as keep her from the arms of her Irishman.

I know I am causing an imposition, but I saw no other way. A bank draft has been allocated in your name for Anne's care. From the remainder, you may issue her a weekly allowance. A modest sum will do,

*for she tends to be a spendthrift. Should you find this
task too cumbersome, I shall fully understand. In
such case, please use a portion of the money to hire
the girl a chaperon, then ensconce her in a hotel
until my return.*

*Thank you, Madeline, for your understanding
and care. I hope my request does not tax our special
friendship. If you cannot assist me, do not fret. Take
the easiest course. In fact, a chaperon might be the
wisest choice of all.*

My regards to the earl.

I remain your most obedient servant,
John Kingsley, Esq.

Her curiosity piqued, Leah came to her feet and searched
through the papers piled on the desk top until she unearthed
an envelope. Turning it over in her hand, she eyed the
inscription: *The Right Honorable, the Countess of
Huntsford: 7 Berkley Square—*

"London." Leah uttered the last word aloud.

An idea formed.

Mr. Kingsley wouldn't be returning for seven months,
possibly longer; his niece's luggage was sitting in the outer
office; a hired coach was on its way to collect the errant
Anne Kingsley, its driver none the wiser she'd eloped.

Leah knew her intentions were risky; she could fail
miserably, and at great cost. Before she lost her courage, she
rounded the desk, retrieved the letter opener again, and
forced the drawer's lock. The bank draft in her possession,
she gasped at the amount, knowing it would take her an
eternity to earn even a pittance of this sum as a scullery
maid.

Still debating whether she should cry off or forge ahead
with her plan, she stared at the smooth envelope, then the
wrinkled letter. A marked difference, she decided, her hands
quickly crumpling the former, knowing she had no other
choice but to proceed. Then she attacked the bank draft,
making it appear equally as shabby. Lighting a candle with a

match from a nearby holder, she dribbled wax on the envelope's flap, sealing the letter and bank draft inside.

Satisfied with her efforts, Leah snuffed the flame, then continued reviewing her strategy.

The countess was to give Anne Kingsley a modest allowance from the funds sent to her. Over the next several months, while Leah investigated Terence Dalton's secret life in London, posing as the solicitor's errant niece, she hoped to save the needed fare to book passage to America, she and the children being well away from England's shores before Mr. Kingsley returned. In the meantime, were Leah's duplicity ever to be discovered, she knew she'd be branded an imposter and a thief. She'd never see her siblings again, the rest of her days being spent in a dank prison cell. That's if she wasn't hanged!

Turn back, before it's too late, her conscience admonished.

Inside Leah's soul, wickedness wrestled with virtue. The letter weighed heavy in her hand as she thought of Hope, Kate, Peter, and little Emily languishing in that dismal orphanage—and Terence, who was given to scholarly pursuits, now reduced to a manual laborer. Reckless her plan might be, but no other option existed, not if she wished to find the answers she sought, and bring her family together again.

The consequences be damned. Her decision was made.

The faint sound of wheels lumbering along the roadway snapped Leah from any indecisiveness she might have felt. Quickly, she snatched her reticule from the chair, stuffing the bank notes that Mr. Kingsley had given her within. The letter, requesting that the Countess of Huntsford take the ill-mannered Anne Kingsley under wing, held firmly in hand, she dashed into the reception area. A wagon rolled by the office door, traveling on down the street. Leah's shoulders dropped when she saw it was not the coach. If she had to wait much longer, her conscience would begin to belittle her again.

She searched about for something to occupy her mind, finally catching sight of the trunks and hatboxes stacked near the door. Leah's own meager wardrobe would never suffice for her intended masquerade. Yet she was uncertain if Anne Kingsley's clothing fit her.

Unstrapping and opening a trunk, she pulled a lavender day dress from inside, then draped it against her body; a pair of shoes fell next to her feet. Relief washed through Leah as she decided she and Anne wore nearly the same size.

Again the sound of rolling wheels drew her attention. Glancing out the window, she noted a coach heading her way. Hastily, she folded the dress, stashing it and the shoes back into the trunk, then rebuckled the straps.

Thou shalt not steal.

. . . he that speaketh lies shall perish.

The Biblical passages trumpeted inside her head just as the bell jingled over the outer door; Leah drew a deep breath, attempting to steady herself.

"Missy," the coachman said, doffing his worn hat, "did someone here hire a coach to the south?"

"Mr. Kingsley did," she answered truthfully, the excerpt from "Proverbs" still ringing in her mind.

"Sorry I'm late, but one of the horses threw a shoe. These here things yours?" he asked, motioning toward the luggage.

"Everything is to be loaded."

As the man began shuffling cases, hatboxes, and trunks through the doorway, Leah again fought with her conscience.

Beware the loss of your immortal soul, the dogged voice needled within her.

The last of the collection stowed in the boot and atop the coach roof, the man came inside. In the dim light, he eyed her closely; Leah swallowed hard, her guilt and trepidation nearly choking her.

"You look a mite peaked, Missy. Are you sure you're up to traveling such a long way? The road ahead is difficult, if not downright hazardous."

Her siblings' forlorn faces, as she last remembered seeing them, leapt to mind. Leah felt her determination renew itself. She'd readily walk through the fires of hell if it meant putting an end to their misery and suffering. "Hazardous, yes," she replied, sweeping through the opening out onto the step, her chin high. "Since I have no other choice, this is the avenue I must take."

The door to Mr. Kingsley's office closed behind them, and the driver checked his manifest. "Where to, Missy?" he asked, assisting Leah into the coach.

"Seven Berkley Square, London."

CHAPTER
2

Berkley Square, London

Under Leah's hand, the ornate brass knocker fell against the door for the second time. Footsteps sounded on the other side of the panel, and she quickly reminded herself to behave as the ill-tempered Anne Kingsley would. The latch was released, and Leah drew a deep, calming breath, knowing her deception was about to begin.

The door opened to reveal an elderly gentleman, impeccably dressed in butler's livery. "Yes?" he intoned, peering down his long nose at her.

Leah lifted her chin a notch. "Inform the Countess of Huntsford that Miss Anne Kingsley wishes to see her," she stated imperiously.

Cold eyes examined her from head to foot, then the man looked at the stack of luggage littering the sidewalk outside the elegant terrace house. As he did so, the hired coach noisily rounded the corner onto Charles Street, disappearing from sight.

In response, one furry white eyebrow arched inquisitively, but the butler remained steadfast, his tall form blocking the entry. Leah's insides quivered, but she refused to be intimidated by the man's condescending manner.

"I insist you deliver this to the countess," she said firmly, extending her hand toward his. "It is a letter of introduction from my uncle, Mr. John Kingsley."

The butler accepted the tattered envelope. "Wait here." Then the door slammed in Leah's face.

Forced to stay on the stoop, she wondered if the countess was as inhospitable as was her pompous butler. But then Leah hadn't been very congenial herself.

She nibbled on her lower lip, considering the man's cool reaction to her. The old adage about a drop of honey versus a tun of vinegar came to mind, and Leah quickly rethought her strategy. Perhaps it would be wise to deemphasize Anne's abrasiveness, at least until she had the opportunity to fully measure the countess's temperament. Far and away, Leah would prefer to keep her own personality than adapt that of the shrewish Anne. But how could she possibly convince the woman that John Kingsley had erred in his assessment of his own niece?

Of equal concern to Leah was that the countess would see through her masquerade. The fear of discovery sent a rush of dread spiraling through her body. Why had she so foolishly followed this deceptive path?

Knowing it was too late to change things now, Leah turned from the door to gaze at the small park directly across from the elegant four-story stone house. Tranquil and green, the setting reminded her of the gardens at Balfour. How she longed for their serenity and the life she once had at her home near Leeds. Someday she and the children would return to Balfour. "By hook or by crook," she vowed adamantly, "it will again be ours."

"My pardon, Miss," the butler declared from behind her, the door having opened on silent hinges; Leah spun toward him. "If you are through mumbling to yourself, the countess will receive you."

Leah's relief offset her embarrassment as she stepped into the foyer. Squaring her shoulders, she followed him up a flight of marble stairs, across the gallery, and into the sitting room, where she gaped at her new surroundings. Exquisite furnishings dotted the area, fine artwork lined the walls, and plush Oriental carpets cushioned the floors. Lady Hunts-ford's tastes were irreproachable, and Leah realized she'd entered a world far above her own.

"Miss Kingsley," a woman's voice addressed from the doorway; Leah turned toward the soft, lilting sound. "Please forgive any inconvenience you may have suffered. Simmons is quite protective about allowing strangers into the house. I hope he hasn't given offense, especially since you are my dearest friend's niece. Please," the countess said, a gentle smile playing on her lips, "make yourself comfortable." She motioned toward the settee. "I imagine your journey from York was a long and tiring one."

Tall and statuesque, the countess was most striking, a wealth of silver hair crowning her head. Virtually unlined, her face beamed with good health, her once youthful beauty still shining through. No wonder Mr. Kingsley called her his "dearest Madeline." He was undoubtedly enamored of the woman. Briefly, Leah considered how the earl responded to the solicitor's obvious adoration for the countess. Then she wondered if the poor man was even aware he had a rival.

Positioning herself on the settee, Leah smoothed her hand over the lavender day dress she'd procured from Anne Kingsley's trunk and donned that morning at the small inn where she'd stayed the night. The fit was a bit loose, but she still looked presentable. "The journey was certainly long and tiring, as you've said," Leah responded at last, "but I fear my sudden appearance on your doorstep has placed you at a disadvantage. I know my uncle has requested that you look after me while he is gone, but I do not wish for you to suffer any imposition on my behalf. If it is more satisfactory for you to find me a chaperon, as my uncle suggested, I shall understand fully."

"You know the content of his letter?" the countess asked, sitting beside Leah.

"He informed me of the particulars," Leah fibbed, then wished the woman would cast her out so that she'd not have to continue the falsehoods. "I shall be as equally comfort-able in a hotel."

Leah felt ill at ease being held under the woman's

assessing blue gaze. Certain she'd been found out, she fought not to squirm on the settee. For the hundredth time, she silently castigated herself for stupidly rushing into this sham, a farce that would surely lead to her ruin.

"I hadn't known John had a brother or any other family, for that matter. What happened to your father—uh, Giles, wasn't it? No . . ."

As the countess searched the letter, Leah's brain quickly scrambled for a name. *"James,"* she blurted out, startling the woman; Leah nearly dissolved through the threads of the blue-and-white silk-covered cushion.

"Yes, James. And your mother's name?"

"Anne." Leah offered the first name that came to mind, then realized it was supposed to be her own. "I am her namesake," she added in haste.

"As I am my grandmother's," she apprised Leah. "My Christian name is Madeline."

"Yes, I know," Leah said, then saw the query in the countess's eyes. "Whenever my uncle speaks about you, he says your name almost reverently."

Two dots of red stained the countess's cheeks, and she looked away in embarrassment.

There was definitely more to their relationship than mere friendship, Leah surmised. Not knowing why, she sought to prove the assumption correct.

"Uncle was most disappointed he couldn't join you in London," she commented, playing out the game, seeking a confirmation. "I'm certain he'll be quite eager to see you and the earl upon his return. He would so like to spend Christmas with you. He's mentioned such several times."

"I would enjoy that," Madeline said, a hint of longing in her voice. "I do hope his business doesn't keep him through the Yuletide. I shall be most disappointed if it does."

Leah studied the woman carefully. Yes. *Dearest Madeline* was in love with John Kingsley. For some reason, the knowledge annoyed Leah, possibly because of the deception being served on the woman's hapless husband. Then again, it seemed inappropriate for Leah to pass judgment on the countess when she herself was no better than a liar and a thief.

"Should it come to pass his business keeps him beyond Christmas," Leah pressed, "you could always spend the holidays with the earl."

"Ian?" The countess sounded surprised.

Leah nodded, acting as though she knew the man's name.

Light laughter flowed from Madeline's throat. "I sincerely doubt that, my dear. If all goes as planned, he'll be doing his own entertaining at Falcon's Gate."

"Falcon's Gate?" Leah asked, visibly confused.

"Our home near Selkirk, Scotland. No, he shan't wish to have me around with Veronica there. If John has not returned from India by then, I shall spend the holidays with friends here in London. Of course, you will join me."

An unseemly lot—Madeline and John, Ian and Veronica —when they all became bored with one another, did they switch off partners and start anew? Who entertained whom was actually none of Leah's concern. If all went as she planned, by Christmas, the children and she would be far from England's shores. Lord and Lady Huntsford could do as they wished, with whomever they liked. Then a thought struck.

"Does that mean you have agreed to honor my uncle's request and act as my guardian in his stead?"

"No."

Leah shot the countess an astonished look.

"I'll not act as your guardian. Instead, you shall be my guest. However, I must insist you promise to adhere to your uncle's wishes. You are not to attempt any communication with this young man who has followed you from Ulster. Should he somehow appear on my doorstep, I shall send him away. Is that understood?"

Leah turned her attention to her gloved hands and fought to keep a straight face. The interview was going far easier than she'd expected. "Yes, I understand," she whispered, pretending disappointment.

"Good. Then we should get along quite well."

The countess assessed her guest momentarily, then smiled. Gentle fingers coaxed Leah's face toward hers.

"I know it will be difficult for you, my dear, but if you are truly in love with this young man, and he with you, the time you are apart will not weaken the feelings you have for each other. The effect will be just the opposite. Your emotions will be far stronger than they are at present."

"If you say so."

"I know so." She patted Leah's folded hands. "Now, let's see if we can agree on a suitable allowance. I shall expect we will be attending several parties in the next few months, so I shall need to withhold the appropriate amount for your new gowns and accessories."

Following a quick mental calculation, she named a figure that nearly toppled Leah straight to the floor.

"Oh my, isn't it enough?" the woman asked, misinterpreting Leah's expression.

Leah resisted the urge to leap from the settee and dance about the room. "It shall do," she croaked, trying to catch her breath.

"Should you find you are coming up a bit short each week, we will renegotiate the sum."

"I expect to be most prudent with my expenses," Leah said, not wishing to be *too* greedy. As it was, she didn't know how she'd repay Mr. Kingsley, but she intended to do so. "Since it is my uncle's money, I feel I would be taking unfair advantage of his kindness were I to spend extravagantly."

The countess frowned slightly, then glanced at the letter, and Leah immediately realized her slip. Then just as quickly, she recognized that this might be the opportune moment to plant a seed of doubt in the countess's mind.

"I know my uncle harbors a low opinion of me. Other than a heated argument over . . . over . . ."

"Your Irishman?" the countess supplied as Leah attempted to come up with a name for Anne's lover, only to fail.

"Yes, my Irishman," she said, nervous fingers plucking at her dress. The lies were mounting, Leah's guilt along with them. Still she had no choice but to forge ahead. "We argued once about my father, too. I never was able to learn what had caused the rift between them. My father never spoke of his past. I didn't even know he had any living relatives until after he'd passed on. Whatever the source of their disagreement, it seems my uncle still carries a grudge. But I fear his wrath is now directed at me—sins of the father, as it were."

Hesitating, Leah glanced at the countess to note the woman's sympathetic expression. But did that mean she believed Leah's fabrication about Anne's relationship with her uncle over the word of her trusted friend? Leah was unable to tell.

"I do so want to mend the ill feelings between us," Leah continued. "I know he thinks I am a spendthrift. When I first came to him, I'll admit I took advantage of his generosity, probably because I possessed nothing as fine as what the shopkeepers offered. I simply couldn't resist. But now, I am determined to change his opinion of me. What better way is there for me to start than by proving to him I can manage money wisely?"

"By what you say, I take it you have no funds of your own?"

Since the countess had circumvented the first of Leah's statement, latching on to the latter part instead, Leah assumed she'd failed to convince the woman that Anne wasn't the ill-mannered shrew John Kingsley had painted her to be. Truly, she needed this woman as her ally, not as her enemy, especially if she wanted to avoid the constant threat of suspicion. A drop of honey, she reminded herself, certain her actions would in time override Kingsley's words.

"I am what is termed as destitute," Leah replied finally, and truthfully. "I have no inheritance on which I can rely."

"Your parents," the countess said, coming back to the original question that somehow had been skirted during their conversation. "What happened to them?"

With the question, the dark moments of the recent past swirled up inside Leah. Again she experienced the pain of her loss, the pain of being separated from the children; her eyes filled with tears. "A carriage accident," she said weakly, her gaze falling away from the countess's. Finding it far easier to mask her hurt behind another persona, she willingly continued the lie. "It overturned. They were killed instantly."

Tenderly, the countess's fingers pressed Leah's hands as they still rested in her lap. "I am truly sorry that you have suffered such a tragedy. Come," she said, rising, "you must be exhausted. I'll show you to your room where you can rest until supper."

"My luggage—"

"It has already been attended to."

Nodding, Leah followed the countess from the sitting room, across the wide gallery overlooking the entry foyer, toward another flight of stairs. As she passed the ancestral portraits ranging along the wall between the doorways, she briefly glanced at each. At the base of the steps, one painting in particular caught her eye. *Handsome* was how she described the lordly figure who had been set on canvas, his larger-than-life image hanging from ceiling to floor. Intrigued by the man within the frame, Leah promised herself to study the portrait more closely later on.

Soon standing at the entry to her room, Leah saw that Anne's trunks were nearly unpacked. The last dress had just been placed into the wardrobe, the young maid shutting the garments away.

"That will be all, Milly," the countess said, stepping into the bedchamber. "Miss Kingsley would like to rest. You may store her trunks later." With a bob of her head and a slight curtsy, the maid withdrew. Madeline turned back toward Leah. "Welcome to Sinclair House, my dear. I do hope these accommodations will be satisfactory."

As she took in her surroundings Leah thought they were more than satisfactory. Decorated in soft shades of blue, green, and lavender, with a smattering of yellow, the chamber reminded Leah of an English garden. "Sinclair House?" she asked, eyes still agog with the room's beauty.

"That is the family name," Madeline informed. "Huntsford is the title belonging to the earldom. Well, Anne, how do you like your room?"

While the countess spoke, Leah had moved to the window, where she gazed down at the park. Children, accompanied by their nurses, played among the flowers and trees. One small girl, her blond curls bobbing in the light breeze flowing through the shade-dappled haven, reminded Leah of little Emily, the youngest of her siblings. Emily was the most confused by all that had happened, by why her family had been torn apart.

When Papa comes, he will make everything better again. He'll not leave us here in this smelly old place. You'll see, Leah. You'll see. When is Papa supposed to come?

Emily's words, uttered while Leah had last visited the orphanage, tore through her heart. A sob caught in her throat as tears stung her eyes. Her emotions teetered on the edge of a great precipice. One small nudge and she'd be spinning helplessly toward the inky void that always seemed a hairbreadth from swallowing her.

A hand fell upon her shoulder; Leah blinked. Fighting down the hysteria threatening to consume her, a result of the hopelessness she faced, she turned from the window.

"What is it, Anne?" the countess asked. "I called your name several times, but you didn't respond. Are you feeling ill?"

Deeply engrossed in her thoughts, Leah hadn't heard the woman addressing her. But of course she'd been hailed as *Anne.* To adapt to another name wouldn't be easy, and her repeated failures to respond when summoned was bound to raise suspicion, so Leah came to a decision. "I apologize, but I must confess I'm not accustomed to being addressed by my given name. Because my mother's name was also Anne, it became quite problematic for everyone in the house. Whenever my father called for my mother, we would both appear, and vice versa. So it was decided I should be called by my middle name. In fact, I cannot remember ever being called anything else. If you don't mind, I would prefer to keep the name most familiar to me. It is Leah."

Apparently the countess believed Leah's tale, for the woman's light laughter filled the air.

"I had a similar problem whenever my grandmother and I were together. However, your alternate name is far lovelier than the one I was saddled with. It may not appear so now, but I once had deep auburn hair. In the sunlight, it glowed like fire. Because of its russet color, my grandfather deemed me *Fox*. I allowed it simply because I adored him so. Thank goodness, he was the only one bold enough to call me that. Had anyone else taken the liberty, I would have trounced him. Leah is a beautiful name, and if that is what you wish to be called, Leah it is."

The issue resolved, Leah breathed a sigh of relief. For the present, she felt safer in her role as Anne *Leah* Kingsley.

"Supper is at eight, so I'll expect you in the sitting room by a quarter to. We can visit a bit before we eat. Until then, you really should get some rest," the countess said, moving toward the large wardrobe. After searching through the assortment of dresses hanging inside, she pulled one into view. "This should be most suitable for the occasion. I shall ask Milly to press it for you. By your attire, I assume you are no longer in mourning."

Either the real Anne didn't adhere to the practice or some time had elapsed since her parents' deaths. Leah preferred to think it was the latter. "It has been just over six months since their passings," she quickly supplied, for that was the proper time to outwardly show one's grief over the loss of a parent. "I could no longer abide being draped in mourning. The colors are so depressing in themselves," she said of the black crepes, to be replaced later on by shades of gray, ornamented by purple or lavender. "Other than the one dress, I gave the rest away."

"Our customs can be so very stringent," the countess remarked. "As you say, the colors do nothing to help lighten our moods. However, tomorrow we shall pay call on my couturière, where we shall be surrounded by bright silks and satins. Madame Lejeune carries the latest in prints, too."

"Is it necessary?" Leah asked. Spending money on something as frivolous as the construction of a half dozen new gowns seemed such a waste, especially when she could put the funds to use elsewhere, such as in her savings. "I mean my uncle might not agree with the expenditure."

"Nonsense. I know you want to make amends by proving

you are not the spendthrift he has accused you of being, but John has given me permission to use the bank draft he sent for your care in whatever way I see fit. New gowns are a must."

"But—"

"I'll not hear another word," the countess said.

Leah knew any further discussion on the topic was useless. The countess had made up her mind.

"In my opinion," the woman continued, for she must have caught the dispirited look on Leah's face, "the right gown can make all the difference in attracting the proper young swains. Your uncle will have to accept it and so will you."

"But I'm not interested in attracting young swains," Leah said.

"I know you think you are in love, Leah, but I very much imagine your gentleman friend is the only beau you've ever had. Allowing yourself the opportunity to meet other men will either strengthen your resolve about your current relationship or cause you to realize you were about to make a mistake. Whatever your future decision might be, no harm will be done by your experiencing the excitement of a few parties." She draped the gown she'd selected from the wardrobe over her arm and headed toward the door. "I shall leave you alone so you can nap. Should you desire anything simply ring." She pointed toward the blue silk bell cord adjacent to the canopied bed. "It is good to have you at Sinclair House, Leah. I hope you will enjoy your stay."

Long after the door had closed, Leah's mind still spun. Never would she have conceived that dupery could be this easy. *Too* easy, she decided, positive she'd eventually get caught. She was a thief, an interloper, and a cheat. The tags fit well, and because they did, Leah's guilt continued to mount. The countess had been most kind to her, undoubtedly because she believed Leah was Anne Kingsley. But woe unto her if Madeline Sinclair discovered the truth. Newgate Prison, with its rats and vermin, would quickly become Leah's new home.

The horrible thought pushed aside, Leah studied her current surroundings. Mindful of her siblings' bleak environment, she took little pleasure in the beauty and comfort that was presently afforded her. Until the day her family was reunited, Leah doubted she'd find much joy in anything. As though to punctuate her prevailing unhappiness, Leah's heavy sigh echoed throughout the room.

For now, Anne's allowance was her only hope, and Leah meant to save every penny. If all went well, in a few short months, the Daltons would be planning a new life far from England's shores. Soon, if she could manage it without drawing suspicion, she intended to seek out the address she'd committed to memory, certain it was there she'd find her answers about her father's mysterious past.

When first reaching London, she'd called up to the coachman, asking him to take a turn by St. James's Street, then to travel on to Hanover Square. He'd refused, stating his manifest strictly forbade any detours. Berkley Square was her destination, and Berkley Square was the only place he could take her. Thwarted, Leah knew she would have to find the places on her own, Hanover Square in particular.

Leah prayed that a legacy indeed awaited her there, the bequest hidden even from Mr. Kingsley. Gladly, she'd end this ruse, fully aware of the severity of its consequences. Yet Leah knew that until she was assured of her family's livelihood, she had little choice but to continue her masquerade.

Weary from her trip, plus the sleepless night she'd spent at the inn somewhere between York and London, Leah stripped down to her shift, slipped beneath the silk comforter, and sank into the feather mattress. Breathing deeply, she tried to let her mind float free. But one question kept badgering her.

What would she find at Eighteen Hanover Square?

"You are charitable to a fault, Madeline Sinclair," the ninth Earl of Huntsford said, then shook his head. Sighing, he dislodged his arm from the mantel where it was propped and ran his fingers through his hair. In the other hand, he held John Kingsley's letter. "I suppose if a cat dropped one of her litter on our stoop, you'd snatch it up, posthaste."

"Doubtlessly, I would," the countess responded from the settee. "Since I've been deemed the champion of the downtrodden, what else would you expect?"

"If you remember, *I* am the one who termed you so. And I would expect a bit more prudence from you, madam. You cannot forever be taking in every stray that lands on our doorstep."

"I'd hardly call the girl a stray. Heavens, Ian! She is John Kingsley's niece. What was I to do? Slam the door in her face?"

"From what I've gathered from Kingsley's letter, it might have been far wiser if you had. Apparently, his niece has nearly run him ragged since he took guardianship of her. And this young man with whom she fancies herself in love—if he is truly that eager to wed and bed her, don't you think he'll find her? I cannot be forever poking about the gardens after dark, watching for a ladder to swing against the house."

"She has agreed neither to communicate with nor to see him while she's in my care." The countess smiled pleasantly. "Besides, she's in the front bedroom, two doors from yours."

The earl rolled his eyes, for he saw himself constantly bounding from his bed at the tiniest noise, to check through his window for signs of an intruder. "You are most thoughtful," he said dryly. "I assume you will also expect me to introduce her into London society by escorting her to the round of balls and social events scheduled these next few months. If so, I doubt Veronica will be too pleased with another party tagging along."

"Veronica would survive," Madeline insisted. "However, I plan to escort her myself. Were she on your arm, none of the young gentlemen would dare approach her."

Ian chuckled. "It is a match that you're after, isn't it?"

"Maybe. At the very least I hope to present her with a choice. So far she seems not at all like the person John described in his letter. Normally I trust his judgment, but I cannot help wonder if this split between John and his brother hasn't automatically colored his opinion of his niece. Yes, a new suitor is a possibility. She can make up her own mind who it is she loves."

"How old is she?" Ian asked, finding himself curious, for the letter never mentioned such.

"Eighteen, nineteen—no more than twenty, I'd say. She's far too young for you."

Blue eyes netted blue. "Did I say I was interested?"

"No, you didn't. But the girl needs someone closer to her own age. Definitely not a father-figure."

Stung by her words, Ian came away from his position near the fireplace. "I wouldn't exactly describe myself as an old codger."

"Nor would I," Madeline said.

"I'm still in my prime."

"Agreed. But time *is* slipping by."

"When is it not?" he queried, then focused on the issue needling him. "Why do you think the girl wouldn't be interested in a man my age?"

"I didn't say she wouldn't be. I simply mentioned that a man closer in years to her own might suit her needs better. I didn't mean to give insult, so calm yourself. Leah should be joining us shortly. I'd like very much for your first meeting with her to go well."

"Leah?" he asked. "I thought her name was Anne."

"Both are correct. Since her mother's name was also Anne, *our* Anne was called Leah to avoid confusion. She prefers the name she's most accustomed to, so we are to call her Leah."

Ian fought the urge to shake his head, thereby clearing the muddle from his brain. "Leah—Anne—whichever she desires, so be it," he said, then glanced at the mantel clock. Seven-thirty. A brandy—that's what he needed to ease the tension inside him. For some unexplained reason, he felt the girl's presence was going to wreak havoc in their lives, especially in his. "If you don't mind, I will retire to the study for a few minutes. I'll not be long."

"Don't imbibe too much, Ian," the countess said as he

strode toward the doorway. "I wouldn't want Leah to get the wrong impression about us."

Coming up short, he turned around. "Had you not the most peculiar way of throwing disharmony into a man's life, I wouldn't presently be deserting you for the soothing effects of a brandy."

The countess sighed heavily. "Your father always said the same thing. But from the day we married until the day he died, he was never gone from my side for more than five minutes at a time. Oh, Ian, I do hope you will soon find that special someone so you, too, can experience a love like the one your father and I shared."

Ian's gaze softened on the woman who presently held his heart. Adrian Sinclair had been dead for well over six years, and even though she tried to hide it, his father's beloved Madeline still mourned his passing as if it were yesterday. "Not everyone is as fortunate as were you and Father. It may be, Mother, that I shall never find that 'special someone.' I might have to settle for a pleasing companionship instead."

"Veronica?"

"Yes, Veronica. We are well-suited in temperament and share many of the same interests. I am thinking about asking for her hand, possibly by the end of next month."

"I caution you not to act in haste, Ian. Veronica is a delightful young woman, but I doubt you will be happy with her. Mark my words. Your special someone is out there, somewhere, waiting for you to come into her life."

Ever optimistic, his mother believed in storybook endings, but Ian was a realist. At one time, he thought he had found the right woman for him, but to his chagrin, she turned out to be his best friend's wife. Alissa and Jared Braxton resided at Hawkstone, the estate next to his own near Selkirk. Their joy in each other seemed to grow day by day, and Ian wished them well.

"And how, pray tell, will I know she is the one?" he asked, doubting such a woman existed. At thirty-three, he'd yet to find her.

Madeline smiled up at him, confidence showing in her gaze. "You'll know, son, the moment you see her."

"Should I encounter the lady you speak of, Mother, I'll let you know. Right now, I want nothing more than to seek out that brandy."

Having descended the steps only a moment ago, bathed, coiffed, and dressed in the gown the countess had selected for her, Leah inspected the portrait she'd seen earlier that day. Her head tilted to one side, then the other as she assessed the virile figure standing inside the gilt frame.

Thick, auburn hair crowned his noble head, and her fingers itched to feel its texture. An impossibility, she knew.

Her attention affixed itself to the man's face, with its angles and planes, each perfectly positioned to form a striking effect. Exceptional. The word came to mind as she studied his shapely lips.

The eyes drew her.

Magically, the artist's hand had captured the glint in his subject's deep blue gaze, and Leah wondered what could be the root of the man's mirth. Informally posed, his arm resting on a pedestal, his flowing white shirt open halfway down his broad chest, he seemed to be boldly flouting propriety, and enjoying every minute of it.

Tight black breeches molded to his narrow hips and sinewy thighs. Impressive. She concluded such, for very little had been left to the imagination. Or had it? Fire burned her cheeks, and her concentration quickly skipped back to the man's face, and his laughing eyes. It was now *Leah* who had become the source of his merriment! Or so she believed. Mortified, she wanted to kick herself for her daring appraisal and the fantasy it evoked.

Leah demanded her fluttering heart to behave, then stepped forward to read the nameplate attached to the ornate frame. "Ian Sinclair," she mused aloud, "ninth Earl of Huntsford."

"At your service, Miss Kingsley."

Leah spun around, nearly colliding with the man who had crept up behind her. *"You!"* she cried, glancing at the portrait, then back at him. A grin played on his lips. He appeared to know what she'd been thinking. Her embarrassment flamed anew, and Leah nearly groaned aloud, for this deep chuckle stated he was aware of that, too.

"Yes, we are one and the same," Ian said, his amusement sounding in his voice. "Since I am here in the flesh, you may inspect me more closely." He stepped around her and centered himself beneath the huge portrait. "Which do you say? Of the two, who is the more handsome? Me or my likeness?"

Why, the real man, of course, Leah admitted in silence, for she appreciated that the artist hadn't done him justice. Finding herself caught under his remarkable blue gaze, glee dancing within, she felt herself melting. His grin grew wider. He sported with her, she realized; Leah sobered. "There are flaws in both," she said, tilting her chin up a notch, trying to quell the strange quivering in the pit of her stomach. "Although each is acceptable, neither is singularly impressive."

His pride being stung for the second time in less than ten minutes, Ian was now the one to sober. Why, the little snob. He studied her from head to foot. Swathed in green silk, which complemented her fascinating dark-lashed eyes, she stood up to his scrutiny, her gaze never wavering.

Oddly, Ian found himself intrigued—had been so, in fact, from the moment he'd spied her after leaving the sitting room, searching out his brandy. But his increased interest, he surmised, stemmed from her rejection of him, a rare incident with most females he met. That she should rebuff him nettled greatly. By her mutinous stare, apparently she considered him a cad. She had drawn a conclusion. But on what basis?

"My vanity is crushed. You have wounded me, Miss Kingsley," he teased, feigning an injured expression. "And we have just met." He turned, facing the portrait. "I had thought it was a rather good likeness of me. Look at the pose. It bespeaks—"

"Arrogance," Leah interjected.

Frowning, Ian looked back at her. "I was under the

impression that it illustrated my zest for life. Arrogance, you say?" He viewed his image again. "No, Miss Kingsley. You have misread the artist's depiction of me. Something else must have given you such a notion, false as it is. Since we've just set eyes on each other, I cannot imagine what it might be. Did your uncle caution you against me?"

The countess certainly bagged herself a young one, Leah decided. But then she remembered her own conjecture that no man, whatever his age, could resist the woman. His youth didn't trouble Leah. What irritated her was that the earl had the unmitigated gall to flirt with her, Lady Huntsford being under the same roof. "My uncle never spoke about you at all," she returned, aloofly turning her head.

Ian again chuckled. "Hardly surprising, since it is my mother who holds his attention where the Sinclairs are concerned."

Leah's gaze bounded back to his face. "Your mother? But I thought . . ." Realizing her near slip, she swallowed her words. Certainly Anne Kingsley would have known the Earl of Huntsford was the countess's son, *not* her husband. And, she, Leah, should have conceived the very same on first seeing him. Spying his confused look, she quaked in her shoes. Dear God! How would she get out of this one?

"Thought what, Miss Kingsley?" Ian asked. "Didn't you know he is in love with her?"

"N-no, I-I didn't," she whispered, relief washing through her, for he'd saved her himself. "By the admiration in his voice whenever he spoke about her, I suppose I should have recognized the fact, but I was engrossed in my own concerns. Hence, my ignorance."

"By 'concerns,' I assume you mean the young man whom you fancy yourself in love with?"

"Yes, of course," she lied readily, finding the task easier with each untruth that passed between her lips. Her conscience had been stilled, but one day it would attack her with a vengeance, she knew. Until then she'd not fret over the consequences of her actions; she'd simply play the game.

"The death of my parents has also claimed my attention," she admitted openly, tears once again stinging her eyes. "The recent turns in my life have not been easy, but I'm learning to adjust. I consider myself a survivor, so whatever it takes to come through, I'll do."

Liquid green eyes stared up at him, and Ian's heart lurched. Tempted to enfold her in his arms, allowing her to expel her grief, he fought off his sudden desire to protect her, wondering over the emotion altogether. As his mother had indicated, she seemed not to be the irascible, ill-mannered girl John Kingsley had described in his letter. However, a quick shift in personality, thereby winning his mother's trust, wouldn't surprise him, for she appeared intelligent enough to use the ploy as a means to an end. Unsure of her true character, Ian felt compelled to let her know exactly where they stood.

"My mother explained your situation to me, and your cares are understandable, considering what you have suffered. May I say I admire your fortitude. Such strength is commendable, but I must caution you that doing 'whatever it takes to come through' may not be the wisest course to follow, especially if you are referring to the young man who has pursued you from Ulster to England. You are welcome here, Miss Kingsley, but do not seek to trick my mother while under her care. It will bode ill for you if you do."

"That you distrust me is apparent," Leah stated. "I have given my word to the countess that I'll not contact him while at Sinclair House. It is a promise I intend to keep. Besides, my uncle's fears are premature. I do not plan to marry for quite some time. Not until I'm assured I have found the right man."

"Then you're not certain you love him?"

"I'm not certain of anything at present," she declared. "My pledge to your mother being the exception, of course."

Ian studied her intently. "I can forgive almost anything, Miss Kingsley—apart from lies and deceit, that is. Remember such, and we'll get along remarkably well." He looked at the standing clock against the wall opposite him. "I believe we will soon be called to supper. My mother awaits us in the sitting room. I would consider it an honor if you would allow me to escort you there."

Leah viewed his proffered arm, then looked at his hand, his long fingers curling lightly against his palm. Strength resided in each. Suddenly certain her neck would snap like a twig under their combined force, she felt a chill run the length of her spine.

I can forgive almost anything . . . apart from lies and deceit, that is.

His words spun through her head, and Leah knew if she had any sense she'd flee this place, the maze of London streets swallowing her in a trice.

"You seem distressed, Miss Kingsley," Ian said, marking how she'd suddenly gone pale. "Have I somehow given offense? Or are you feeling ill?"

"Yes—ill," she said, knowing she'd not survive under this man's scrutiny. He was too astute for her liking. He'd unmask her, expose her for the cheat she was. She had to stay as far from him as possible, for as long as she could. "The journey—I'm simply exhausted. I really must return to my room. Please offer the countess my apologies. I'm sorry, but it cannot be helped."

Certain her claim of illness was feigned, Ian watched as Leah scurried the few feet to the stairs, then up them, the tail of her dress finally disappearing from sight. He'd scared the hell out of her. Only a fool would have missed the fact. The question in Ian's mind was why.

Well past midnight, Leah was wide awake, the carpet suffering because of her sleeplessness.

After she'd fled the gallery to her room, she'd disrobed, then donned a nightdress and wrapper, whereupon she began to traipse the floor, indecision gripping her. Directly, the countess had checked in on her, and only after Leah's assurances that she was well, simply weary from her trip, did the woman leave her. A tray of food had been sent up, but Leah simply picked at the fare, her nerves too jangled to eat.

In the interim, between pacing monotonously and fretting

over whether she should stay or flee, she'd composed two letters, the paper taken from a lap desk situated on the table near the window. She addressed one letter to the orphanage, telling those in charge she was in London, instructing them to contact her brother, Terence, in Leeds, should an emergency arise with Peter, or with the others. She included a note for the children.

The second letter she'd written to Terence, explaining her whereabouts, and that she was seeking answers regarding their father.

> *. . . I cannot explain everything, dear Brother. Trust simply that I have our welfare in mind. Should an emergency arise with you, or with the children, then, and only then, are you to contact me at the aforementioned number on Berkley Square. The letter is to be addressed to Miss Anne Kingsley. When I see you next, I shall explain why the masquerade . . .*

When the letters were finished and hidden away until she could post them, Leah knew she'd committed herself to staying and playing out the ruse. Still, she'd continued to pace the floor, with Ian Sinclair, and how she might evade him, holding her thoughts.

Now, hours later, her feet aching, she still had no answer. God help her if the earl ever discovered who she really was. She imagined his temper, once fully aroused, was equal to a raging tempest. Pray she never felt its force.

Footsteps sounded along the corridor, and Leah froze in her tracks. Momentarily, the firm tread stopped just outside her room, the light flowing from beneath her door having attracted attention. The strides continued on. A door opened and closed not far from her own. The trapped breath rushed from Leah's lungs.

For one who had pleaded illness, she should have been asleep long ago. Removing her wrapper, she tossed it at the bed, then headed toward the lamp sitting atop a table near the window. The wick turned down, she blew out the flame.

In a second's time, she was under the silk coverlet, sinking into the feather mattress.

As Leah stared through the darkness at the canopy over her bed, she felt certain the footfalls she'd heard belonged to Ian Sinclair. She trembled uncontrollably as she lay there thinking about him.

"Precious Lord, don't let him discover the truth about me," she whispered fervently.

Because of her deceit, Leah doubted her prayer would be answered.

Standing at his window, Ian watched as the rectangular light, falling on the street below, faded into blackness.

Off to bed, was she? For one who claimed fatigue, she certainly kept late hours.

As before, he was certain she'd fled to her room for one reason, and one reason only: fear.

"Hide if you will, Miss Kingsley," he said. "Soon enough, I'll discover what it is that has you quaking in your shoes."

CHAPTER

3

❧❧❧

Just over a week later, Leah was descending the stairs toward the gallery when she again caught sight of *him*. As she neared the lifelike image of the present Earl of Huntsford, she purposely averted her gaze. Whether on canvas or in the flesh, the man positively unnerved her.

So far, and much to Leah's relief, she contended primarily with his portrait, seeing the actual man only in passing, and only fleetingly, for she quickly scooted from sight. To her chagrin, his deep laughter always chased her through the house, its masterful owner obviously aware that he alarmed her.

While glad he was hardly ever around, Leah had still wondered about his numerous absences, and on casual inquiry as to his whereabouts, she was informed by the countess that the earl and the Lady Veronica Whitcomb were off to the races; attending a soiree; or had gone to a ball.

The two, it seemed, were continually together, and Leah had assumed they were betrothed. On Leah's mentioning such to the countess, Madeline, her voice suddenly sounding lackluster, confirmed a marriage appeared imminent. Leah could only surmise that the countess wasn't overjoyed with her son's choice of a mate. As for Leah, she cared little where he went or with whom, just as long as he stayed away from her.

Leah's feet met the marble floor, and she aimed herself toward the sitting room where the countess waited. They were to leave shortly for the couturière's, a final fitting required on the gowns selected the day after Leah's arrival.

On her first visit to the shop, Anne's allowance settled on her beforehand, Leah had pulled a young helper aside and asked the girl to post the two letters she'd written, offering her an added shilling for her trouble. By now, Terence should be aware she was in London. Her heart constricted with sorrow, for she wondered how he and the children fared, Peter and Emily especially. Soon, Leah vowed, they would be together again, never to be torn apart.

Two steps from the open doors, Leah quickly skidded to a halt. Agitated voices sounded inside the sitting room. Leah recognized them as the countess's and—God help her!— the earl's. She listened closely as the countess's words filtered out to the gallery.

"I see no reason why we cannot give Leah more freedom," Madeline insisted. "Over this past week, whether here or in public, she has always demonstrated the proper behavior. She's promised not to contact this young man, and I accept her word as being true. Besides, we both have our own lives to lead. I cannot be forever dragging the poor girl along with me wherever I go."

"You should have considered that before you took her in," Ian snapped.

"It's not that I don't enjoy her being with me," Madeline returned. "I do. But having tea with a group of women who are nearly twice, and in some cases, three times my age would not be to my liking if I were Leah. I'm sure she's miserable. Likewise, she cannot be forever in your care. You have business appointments, your club, then there's Veronica—really, Ian, your schedule is as full as mine. For both our sakes, as well as for Leah's, I think we should stop breathing down her neck and allow her some independence."

Anticipation filled Leah when she heard those words. She'd bemoaned her lack of freedom only once to the countess, but apparently Madeline remembered it, hence the discussion. Dared she hope?

"We?" Ian questioned. "Other than the back of her dress as she invariably dashes off to her room, I've hardly set eyes on our guest. As I recall, Mother, John specifically asked that she be watched, yet you seem intent on doing the opposite. If she's given more freedom, what's to say she won't rush back to York, straight into her Irishman's arms? I imagine she's behaved exceptionally well while in your company. But did you ever consider that it is all an act? I sincerely doubt John would have packed her off to London if his concerns weren't valid."

"I realize that, Ian. John is usually very sensible. Still, knowing Leah as I do now, I keep coming back to the same thought."

"What thought, Mother?"

"That John's disappointment with his late brother has somehow fallen onto his niece. All things considered, I say we should offer her our trust."

"And I say you've been bamboozled."

At the earl's response, Leah bristled. He was right, of course. But that wasn't what concerned her. To crack the mystery about her father's past she needed some latitude. As it stood, she'd learn nothing, for she was guarded continuously. Deciding it was time she faced Lord Huntsford, Leah entered the room, then announced, "I hope I'm not interrupting anything."

"Miss Kingsley," Ian greeted. "Been eavesdropping, I take it?"

By the way he'd looked her over the instant she'd marched through the doors, Leah should have known she'd been found out, possibly because of her too bright smile. "Actually, I was," she said, "but when one hears her own name in the course of a conversation, one is likely to become interested in what is being said."

"Forgive me, Leah," the countess declared upon rising from the settee. "It was improper of me to have entered into a discussion about you without your first being present. I had hoped to persuade Ian that you need not be constantly tied to either of us."

"I do not fault you, Lady Huntsford," Leah responded. "I know you meant well, and that you were acting in my interest. Obviously your son remains unconvinced as to whether or not I can be trusted. What amazes me is that I traveled to London on my own, a private coachman my only companion. Had I wanted to escape back to York, I could have done so virtually anywhere along the way. With my uncle off to India, and with you being ignorant of my existence altogether, who would have known that I hadn't arrived at my original destination? That I am here should attest to the fact that I can be trusted. Or at least one would think so."

The countess's gaze shifted back to her son. "She does have a point, Ian."

Leah held her breath as he appraised her.

"You may have your freedom, Miss Kingsley," he said finally. "But with a stipulation."

The excitement that had first rippled through Leah suddenly stilled. She watched as he strode to the open doors where he shouted for Milly. In an instant the young maid appeared.

"You called, sir?" she asked with a quick curtsy.

"Come, Milly," Ian ordered. "I have a job for you." The maid now inside the room, he said, "Whenever the countess and I are unavailable, and Miss Kingsley wishes to go out, you are to go with her and act as her chaperon. She's not to leave Sinclair House without you. Understand?"

"Yes, sir. I understand."

"Is this really necessary?" Leah asked. "It seems Milly has enough to do without the added burden of acting as my chaperon. I am perfectly capable of going it alone."

"Where you come from it might be thoroughly acceptable for a young woman to be out on her own," the earl said. "But here, in London, it is not."

"Ian's right, dear," Madeline stated. "It's highly improper

40

for a young woman of your station to be seen about town without a chaperon or her maid. It's simply not done."

Whether by Milly, Madeline, or the earl, Leah was still trapped. She couldn't possibly unearth any information about her father. Unless . . .

"And, Milly," Ian said, "while you are out with Miss Kingsley, should she do anything in the least untoward, anything that draws your suspicion, you are to report it to me immediately."

"Y-yes, sir. I'll report it, sir."

"You may go, Milly."

Leah's hopes were now completely dashed. She'd thought perhaps she could befriend the girl, the two making a pact, Leah's movements kept secreted from the Sinclairs. Clearly, the earl had anticipated such. And though the words were left unsaid, the message was unmistakable: If Milly failed in her duty, she'd be dismissed from her position. It was unlikely Milly would go against her employer. Nor would Leah ask her to do so.

"Well, since that's all settled," Madeline stated, "I believe we have an appointment to keep. The carriage is out front, is it not, Ian?"

"Both the carriage and Ferguson await us."

"*Us?*" Leah cried as her gaze again snagged the earl. Twinkling blue eyes perused her as his shapely lips twitched. He appeared to be fighting back a grin.

"Ian has an appointment with his business agent," Madeline explained, coming up beside her, drawing on her gloves. "Since we are all headed in the same direction, he has offered to drop us by the couturière's and pick us up on his way back."

Leah's heart nearly stopped. "Oh," she whispered, feeling strangely lightheaded.

"Do you object to the arrangement, Miss Kingsley?" Ian inquired. "If so, I shall see to hiring a cab for myself."

Please do! her mind shouted, the spinning sensation ceasing. "No, certainly not," she declared instead. "As it stands, it will save us all time."

41

Ian shot her an engaging smile. "It will also allow us the opportunity to become more fully acquainted." He stood aside. "After you, ladies."

On stiff legs, Leah followed the countess from the sitting room and across the gallery, the earl trailing after them. Once outside, Ian stepped around Leah and offered his hand to assist her.

Idleness was not his vocation, she decided, studying his slightly callused palm. Then his hand, warm and gentle, gripped hers. Leah's fingers tingled beneath her glove as she climbed inside the carriage. Confused by her reaction, she quickly pulled free, seating herself next to the countess.

Her fast retreat apparently wasn't lost on the earl, for she heard his soft chuckle. Donning his top hat, retrieved from Simmons, along with his gloves, on his way out, he followed her into the carriage. The door thumped to, then he folded himself onto the opposite seat, and continued to stare.

Leah's attention immediately skittered away from Ian. Her trembling hand flowed across the mint green muslin day dress, smoothing out nonexistent wrinkles along her lap. *Damn his eyes.* She wished he'd look anywhere but at her.

When the ensuing silence had stretched her nerves to the breaking point, she finally blurted out, "The day is most lovely."

The carriage rolled away from the curb. "Most lovely," he echoed, heeding her still.

Leah spotted the houses along the street as the conveyance passed quickly by them, then she looked skyward. "I had been told black smoke continually hangs over London, but obviously that isn't true. The heavens are a stunning blue." The same as his eyes, she thought, remembering how they shimmered like twin sapphires in a face of bronze. That he enjoyed the outdoors was apparent.

"It depends on which way the wind blows," Ian responded. "If it blows at all. But the skies over London pale in comparison to those over Scotland. Is it the same in Ulster, Miss Kingsley?"

She again attended him. "Since I've not been to Scotland,

I cannot say. But I imagine they are similar in nature. After all, at that point, Ireland and Scotland are only a short distance by sea."

"From what part of Ulster do you hail, Miss Kingsley?"

"County Antrim," she said, thankful she remembered her geography.

"What town?"

"Near Larne," she blurted out, for it was the first name that came to her.

"I suppose you were born there?"

"I was."

"Strange, but you do not flaunt an Irish brogue."

"You must remember, sir, Ulster contains a mixture of Scots, Welsh, English, and Irish, therefore the accents vary. Besides, my parents were English," she snapped.

"You are right, of course. After a time, though, one would think the dialects would mesh, giving the citizenry a distinct vernacular of their own." Hers, he decided, derived from the north of England. "But perhaps I err in my assumption."

Examining her delicate profile, for she'd once again turned away from him, Ian felt certain he was being hoodwinked. He wished now he hadn't consented to give her more freedom.

True, as asserted, she could have run off before reaching Sinclair House without anyone knowing she had. Still, it seemed odd that she so readily agreed not to see her young Irishman. She claimed she was undecided whether or not she loved him, but John Kingsley was of a different mind, his letter making that quite plain. If no concern existed, as she contended, why, then, would her uncle have shipped her off to London?

He wouldn't have, Ian conceived.

Kingsley was astute and levelheaded, not given to forming irrational conclusions about people. Likewise, his business acumen was unmatched. The two facets conjoined, there was little question as to why he'd been called into service by their queen. Victoria trusted him, and so did Ian.

However, Miss Kingsley was another matter. For all Ian

knew, her disavowed lover was an Irish insurrectionist, she an avid supporter to his cause. Her entire family may have been anarchists, hence the Kingsleys' estrangement.

"What happened that your father decided to leave England and settle in Ulster?" he asked, again drawing her attention. "And why, Miss Kingsley, is your uncle so adamant against your seeing this young man whom you claim no longer holds your interest?"

Frantically, Leah's mind clambered for an appropriate response. "As to your first query, my father never discussed it. As to your second, I cannot say. Should you want to know the answer to either question, you'll have to ask my uncle."

Ian heard the irritation in her voice, and apparently so did his mother.

"Enough, Ian! You have overstepped the bounds of propriety. Subjecting Miss Kingsley to such interrogation is not only rude, but brash. Henceforth, please show more decorum."

Ian spied his mother's condemning look. Were he to continue badgering the girl, he'd undoubtedly be set afoot, his mother instructing Ferguson to stop the carriage immediately. Though the day was exceptional, he hadn't planned on spending his time walking the streets of London. Wisely he took her cue.

"I apologize, Miss Kingsley. In my eagerness to become better acquainted, I fear I have acted impetuously. I do beg your forgiveness." By her pinched expression, he knew she thought his words were naught but drivel. They were.

"I am sorry, Lord Huntsford, if my presence at Sinclair House still disturbs you. On the night we first met, I explained my feelings. In your allowing me more freedom, I had hoped your suspicions were put to rest, but I can see that you still do not trust me. That being the case, perhaps it would be best if the countess were to find me a chaperon, as was suggested by my uncle, and I shall willingly take my leave. I do not wish to be a source of conflict between your mother and yourself."

Nor did she wish to be under his watchful eye, Ian surmised. She turned toward his mother.

"Tomorrow, please be kind enough to make the required arrangements," Leah announced. "I cannot stay where I am not welcome."

Madeline's stringent glare pinned Ian to the seat. "That won't be necessary, Miss Kingsley," he stated. "I'll not hound you again with my questions. Hereafter, I shall remain on my best behavior." Uncertainty showed on her face. "A promise for a promise," he said. "You keep yours, and I'll keep mine."

"I agree to your stipulation, Lord Huntsford. A promise for a promise it is."

He smiled. "Excellent, Miss Kingsley. I am happy we could come to an agreement."

"I, too, sir. I would have missed your mother's company had we not done so."

"But not mine, I'll wager," he mumbled under his breath, drawing a confused look from Leah. Until he was assured of her integrity, he planned to keep a close watch over her, something he doubted she'd relish. The carriage pulled to a stop in front of the couturière's just as her mouth opened, doubtlessly to make a query over his murmured comment. "We're here," Ian declared, glad for a shift in the conversation. Stepping down to the sidewalk, he helped Madeline alight, then he turned to Leah. "Miss Kingsley."

She slipped her fingers into his proffered hand, then lightly sprang from the carriage. As before, she quickly pulled free of his hold and scurried behind the countess, where she hid from view.

"Enjoy yourselves, ladies," he said, tipping his hat. "I'll be around in an hour to retrieve you."

"If we are not finished with the fittings," his mother said, "you may wait for us here at the curb."

The countess moved aside, and Leah found she was no longer shielded. Snagged by the earl's amused gaze, she could do nothing but stare at him. He grinned wickedly, then winked. Dumbfounded by his familiarity, Leah stiffened, then with a toss of her head, she spun around and hurriedly traced after the countess who waited for her at the shop's door. A bell jingled as the two women entered the

45

establishment. Forcefully, the door slammed behind Leah, drowning out the deep chuckle that had trailed her inside.

At the noisy disruption, all eyes turned her way; Leah swallowed her embarrassment. "Excuse me," she said. Her own eyes downcast, she chased after the countess toward the back of the shop, silently cursing Ian Sinclair with each step she took.

As Leah recalled their exchange in the carriage, she knew she had no choice but to accept his terms, especially if she hoped to collect Anne's allowance, tucking the majority of it away. She had risked a lot by taunting him. Had he or his mother taken her seriously, deciding to place her in a hotel, the funds for Anne's care would have been quickly absorbed, not a farthing left for Leah.

Besides, the only commitment she'd made was to stay away from this zealous young man who'd supposedly followed her from Ulster. He and Anne were now sharing the joys of wedded bliss, Lord Huntsford and his mother unaware of such, so Leah would have no difficulty in keeping her side of the bargain. As for the earl's, she felt sure he'd be less prone to delve into her past, continually haranguing her at every turn. Life at Sinclair House should be far easier to endure—*if* he observed his pledge to her.

The fittings went well, three of the six dresses being perfectly tailored to her form. Those she could take with her today. The others, she was informed, would be ready by next week. Garbed again in her mint-green day dress, Leah heard the couturière clicking her tongue. "This frock hangs like a sack on you. Hardly an acceptable fit."

"I've lost weight since it was sewn," she quickly explained.

Madame Lejeune gathered several inches of material at Leah's waist. "Have you been ill?"

"No, not ill. My parents died over six weeks past. Since their loss, I have no appetite for food, or anything else."

The woman frowned at Leah. "Should you not be in mourning?" she asked, censure clearly sounding in her voice. "Six weeks—have you no respect at all?"

Too late, Leah realized she'd responded not as Anne

Kingsley, but as herself. "Did I say weeks?" The woman nodded curtly. "Forgive me. I meant *months,*" she corrected. "Still, it seems as though it were only yesterday since it happened. A carriage accident," she offered. "They were both killed instantly. I just did come out of mourning. My clothes, I fear, no longer fit me."

The woman's once harsh look had turned to one of compassion. "Poor child," she said, patting Leah's shoulder. "If you'd like, I could alter your dresses to your current size. But then, if you were to regain your weight—"

"I think we should see what the future brings," Leah broke in, then smiled her appreciation. Considering the enormous cost of the gowns, which the countess had insisted Leah needed, she imagined the couturière's fees for such work would be equally as hefty. Spending precious money on a few seams meant to better enhance her figure seemed exceptionally frivolous. She could look like a frump for all she cared. The money was meant to secure a future for the children, not to salve her own vanity. "As you say, I could regain my weight. Then we would have to start all over again."

"Well, if you do fill out some, there is a triple seam in each of your new gowns. We'll simply remove the stitches as needed." The couturière draped a finished dress, which Leah was to take along with her, over her arm. "I'll box this up," she said, pulling aside the curtain. "When you are finished in here, the countess awaits you up front."

"Thank you," Leah said, donning her gloves. After checking her appearance in the mirror, she stepped from the dressing room and nearly collided with the young helper who was to post Leah's letters. "Were you able to do the favor I asked of you?" she inquired once she'd offered her apologies over their near mishap.

"Aye, I was," the girl replied. "The same day, in fact."

"You had enough money, then?"

"I did," she said, a look of guilt entering her eyes. "Too much, Miss. I owe you two shillings, sixpence, I do."

"Keep it," Leah said, her hand catching the girl's arm as she reached into her apron pocket. "I may ask you to again post a letter or two for me. We'll settle up later, when the time is right."

The girl frowned. "Why can't you post your own letters? It sure would save you the trouble of lookin' me up each time you wanted to send one off."

"I find myself in a fix, uh, Miss, uh—"

"Foster," she responded. "But Sally will do."

"My uncle sent me to London for fear I'd elope. I am constantly being watched. To post a letter myself would be impossible. Were anyone to discover I was writing Terence, I'd be in more trouble than I presently am."

"So you want me to get your letters safely away to Terence, no one bein' the wiser."

"I thought you'd understand, Sally. You are, after all, a romantic at heart, are you not?"

The girl blushed. "Aye, Miss. I have a beau myself, I do. No one on God's green earth would keep me from him either."

"Leah, dear," the countess called from the front of the shop. "Are you ready to leave?"

"Then do we have an agreement, Sally? You'll post my letters for me?"

"Aye, Miss. Whenever you need a favor, just come round and ask. Good luck to you."

"There you are," Madeline declared, just as Sally scurried back into the workroom. "Ian is awaiting us. Are you finished here?"

"I need only to gather my packages," Leah said, smiling brightly. "Of the six gowns, three were a perfect fit. We are to come around for the others next week."

"Wonderful," the countess returned. "There is a party tonight I'd very much like for you to attend with me. Once we are home, I'll help you select the right dress for the occasion. If you don't mind, that is."

"Of course, I don't mind. Since this will be my first party in London, I welcome your expertise," Leah said, wishing she could skip the function altogether. The countess, however, had made it clear that Leah would be attending many of the same balls and soirees as did her hostess. It would be rude of her to show dissension at this late date, especially after the gowns had been purchased. Besides, refusing to comply might draw more suspicion, this time from the mother, not the son. "I'm a country girl and am not as astute as you. The moment we return to Sinclair House, I shall become your willing pupil. You may teach me the fashionable way to dress."

Madeline laughed lightly. "With or without my tutelage, my dear, you are certain to draw a man's eye. A few hints are all you'll need. The rest you've mastered on your own."

Before the two women left the shop, the Sinclairs' coachman was summoned inside where he gathered the packages, containing the three gowns, a matching pair of shoes for each, gloves, fans, and assorted accessories. Presently, he stowed the lot inside the carriage.

"Excuse me, sir," Ferguson said, all available space beneath the driver's seat now taken.

Ian shoved himself aside as a large box settled on the seat next to him. "You seem to have cleared out the store," he commented, eyeing the package.

"Hardly," the countess responded from the seat opposite him, another parcel falling on top of the first. "There is still more to come next week."

"The carriage will be at your full disposal when it is time to retrieve them," he stated, knowing, if he thought to combine their trips, he'd be walking home. There would be no room! He turned his attention to Leah. "I take it you enjoyed your outing?"

"Very much."

Ian noted how she refused to look his way. Forever cool, he decided, considering what it would take to break through her icy facade.

He knew the answer.

His suspicions set aside, his actions toward her had been abominable. And if he hoped to have her warm to him, he needed to be less abrasive and far more soothing in his approach. The truth was, the aloof Miss Kingsley intrigued him as no other woman ever had. Because she had spurned him, he supposed it was the challenge of the chase, but Ian vowed that, whatever it took, he would somehow capture her notice.

His gaze drifted to her mouth. Full, pouting lips beckoned to him, and he wondered how they would taste beneath his own. Sweet as honey, he determined, certain he could quickly melt the frigidness from her veins with just one kiss.

Another package hit the seat beside him, and Ian fairly jumped from his skin. Coming to his senses, he shifted in his seat and looked to his coachman. "Ferguson, once we are finally on our way, head for St. James's Street. You may drop me by White's. After the ladies are safe at home, the carriage unloaded, you may come back for me."

"Aye, sir," the man said, the last parcel leaving his hand for the seat.

"White's is on St. James's Street?"

Surprised to hear Leah's voice, Ian turned her way. "It's been at the top of the street for some time—unless they packed up and moved out since I was there last."

"And when was that?"

"Yesterday," Ian responded with a grin. "Why the interest, Miss Kingsley?"

"I had heard of the place," she explained, not wanting to give herself away, "but I never knew its location."

"You'll be able to see it, firsthand, but from the outside only. Ladies are not allowed. Sorry to disappoint you."

"Do you perchance have the street number at White's?" she asked, hoping she didn't sound too eager in her desire to know.

"Are you planning to write a letter protesting their policy against women being permitted on the premises?"

"No, I am not. But I am meticulous for detail, sir. When I enter this day's event in my diary, I shall want to include every bit of information I can glean about it." A plausible lie, she thought, then hoped he would respond with the truth.

Ian eyed her at length as the carriage pulled away from the curb. The horses broke into a fast trot. "Thirty-seven," he said finally.

Leah's heart sank the moment she heard the number. All

the letters posted by her family over the past years had unknowingly gone to her father at White's, the oldest gentlemen's club in London. For him to have received his mail there meant he had to have been a member. And to be a member, Leah felt certain, one had to be extremely wealthy, if not, in fact, a titled gentleman. To her knowledge, Terence Dalton was neither of these. Still, there was a lot she didn't know about him.

The sharp call of her assumed name broke Leah from her trance. "Y-yes?"

"I asked, Miss Kingsley," Ian pronounced, "if you hoped to write a book someday?"

"Excuse me?" she inquired, the meaning of his query escaping her completely.

"You said you were meticulous for detail and that you entered your experiences in a diary. I wondered if you were keeping such a journal in hopes of one day having it published."

"As commonplace as my life is, I sincerely doubt anyone would wish to read about it. I keep a journal for my descendants, for they would be the only ones interested in what has happened to me. However, I want to be accurate for my posterity's sake. Dates, times, places—they are exceptionally important to me."

Leah saw that Lord Huntsford attempted to fight back a yawn. Excellent. She wearied him with her explanation, false as it was. Perhaps he'd learn never to question her again.

"Have you not read an historical account where the author has offered a year, but not a precise date for the event he is writing about?" she continued, desiring to destroy him with tedium. "I, as the reader, am given to wonder if the happening occurred in the spring, the summer, the autumn, or the winter. When something is so poorly documented, I cannot help but marvel at whether the writer has done the proper research required to support his facts. That is why I am so meticulous, sir. If one gives an accounting, I believe it should be *completely* accurate."

"Well, Miss Kingsley," Ian said, uncrossing his arms from

where they hugged his chest, "I suggest you sharpen your pencil and take fastidious notes, for we have arrived at White's." The moment the carriage had stopped, he fairly leapt to the sidewalk, then tipped his hat. "I shall see you later on, ladies."

"Leah and I are going to the Carstairses' party tonight," the countess said, "so unless you intend to stay home, I shall tell Cook not to prepare supper."

"I won't be in this evening either," he replied. "Tell Cook she can have the night off."

Absently listening to the exchange, Leah weighed her options. Within White's were the answers she sought about her father's life in London, but she had no way of getting inside to pose the questions. To even risk such an attempt would end in disaster. Either through Milly or through one of his peers, the earl was certain to learn she'd been snooping around his club. Eighteen Hanover Square now seemed to be her only hope. If she could just search out the address without drawing suspicion. . . . Unfeasible, she decided, for she was positive Milly would tattle on her.

On a sigh, Leah watched as the earl bounded up the steps toward the club's entrance. He stopped short, another man having stepped through the doorway into his path. Briefly, they spoke, then after patting the other man's shoulder, Lord Huntsford walked inside White's.

Leah's gaze was at once riveted to the newcomer who now stood in full view. Tall and slender, he descended the steps in a what appeared a familiar gait. Studying him intently, she felt her heart race, then as he drew closer to the carriage, it nearly stopped. A black armband encircled his left sleeve, and Leah wanted to shout her objection, but her mouth refused to open. At the countess's nod, he tipped his hat, exposing a wealth of sandy blond hair.

No, her mind screamed, needing to deny what she saw was true. *It cannot be!*

The carriage jolted as the reins were slapped against the horses' rumps. While she and Madeline rolled by the young man, who now strode up the sidewalk, Leah felt she might faint. "W-who is he?" she asked the countess.

"That's Arthur Covington—Viscount Covington, now,"
Madeline said. "As you can see by his armband, he is in
mourning."

"Are you saying he lost his father?" The countess affirm-
ing such, Leah demanded: "When and how did he die?"

"Six, almost seven weeks ago. Are you certain you want to
hear the details?"

"Very certain."

Leah's adamant stare prompted the countess to continue.
"I see no harm in telling you the story. Since you've lost
your own parents, I know you will be most sympathetic. His
father was killed on the road north, somewhere just south of
Leeds. Such a tragedy. Lord Covington left behind a de-
voted wife and four children, Arthur being the oldest. The
man's death seems so senseless. No one is quite certain why
he was bent on such a perilous trip—at night, alone, and on
horseback. He was found the next day by a passing mail
coach. His neck . . ."

As the countess rambled on, Leah's mind closed itself off
from the rest of her story. She already knew what Madeline
would say. Her father's life in London was a mystery no
more. Fate had intervened, conveniently tossing the answer
straight at her face. Though she wished otherwise, the truth
could not be denied.

Arthur Covington was her brother by half.

CHAPTER

4

That night, in the Carstairses' ballroom, Leah occupied one of the many chairs bordering its walls. Potential suitors eyed her, but the vigorous wagging of her fan warned them off. As she absently viewed the waltzing couples, one word played a litany over and over in her mind.

Bigamist!

Anger at her father's duplicity roiled inside Leah like a churning volcano. How could he have done this to her mother, to her brothers and sisters, to her? Callous and selfish, he'd considered no one except himself, the repercussions, once the truth was discovered, be damned.

Catch colts—that was what she and her siblings were, for she'd learned from the countess that Arthur Covington was a full year older than Leah. Two wives, two families—both loving him as though he were exclusively theirs.

His betrayal was unforgivable. Not another tear would she cry over his loss. Her heart, wounded by the knowledge that her father was not the person she'd believed him to be, had closed itself off. Fond memories of the man she'd once lovingly called "Papa" were now banished forever.

Leah continued to survey the whirling throng with growing distaste. Garbed in their costly finery, priceless gems sparkling in the candlelight, stilted smiles gracing their haughty faces, these gentlemen and ladies of quality appeared unconcerned about anything except themselves. From the conversations she'd been privy to after the countess had introduced her around, she doubted any of them were aware of the abject poverty and hopelessness in which the masses lived.

In contrast, the Daltons—at least those who lived in Leeds—had always cared for their neighbors, sharing even when they had little to share. Chiding her, her father had once called Leah a bleeding heart. Now she understood why.

Did they even care? she wondered, still staring at her father's peers. She decided they didn't, racehorses, fashion, and games of chance being uppermost in their thoughts. In her estimation, they were naught but a showy lot, their collective wits being no more than that of a covey of peafowl!

Though Leah felt disdain for the women, it was mainly the men who fostered her scorn. Besides being of the masculine gender—which in itself was enough to draw her contempt!—they stemmed from the aristocracy, the same as did her father, making them all untrustworthy in her mind. As for the ever discreet Mr. Kingsley, Leah no longer felt any guilt about filching his money. He'd been a willing party to the deceit played on Leah's family, stealing their birthright, leaving them destitute. He *owed* the Daltons every penny she took, and then some.

Briefly, she considered Arthur, an amazing match to their father, and wondered if he knew about their sire's bigamy. If he did, could he have joined forces with John Kingsley, the two then conspiring to ruin the Daltons? Still, Arthur could be unaware of their father's deceit, the solicitor having acted solely on his own. Leah didn't know what to think, but somehow she had to discover the truth.

Oh, if she could only get free from the vigilant eyes of both Sinclairs, and their watchdog, Milly, she—

"E-excuse me, Miss K-Kingsley."

Torn from her thoughts, Leah looked up at the timid

young man who had addressed her. She recognized him, for he'd extracted an introduction from the countess upon her and Leah's arrival.

"L-Lady Huntsford suggested I should approach you and request a dance."

Having noticed how very nervous he was, Leah took some pity on him. "I'm certain the countess meant well, but I prefer the solitude of my own company at present. Thank you, but no thank you, Lord Miles."

At her cool dismissal, he struck a sharp bow, then turned on his heel, aiming himself toward the opposite side of the ballroom.

"That's the third young buck you've managed to refuse within the past fifteen minutes," the elderly woman sitting beside Leah said. "Were I you, my dear, I'd be less tempted to chase the next one away. You may be missing out on an excellent match as a result."

Earlier, after the countess had excused herself, desiring to speak to an old friend she'd seen across the way, the woman had taken Madeline's seat, polite preambles quickly made. Leah now settled her attention on the old duchess, whose full title escaped her at the moment. Feathers jutting from the crown of her head, the loose skin beneath her chin jiggling whenever she spoke, she resembled a Cornish hen garishly garbed in purple satin.

"I'm not interested in making a match, Your Grace," Leah said finally, wondering if the woman realized what a ridiculous sight she was. "In fact, marriage is the *last* thing on my mind."

A multitude of jewel-studded bracelets jangled as the woman lifted her hand to inspect Leah through her lorgnette. "Surely you jest. It is the only way for you to take a step up in society. Marriage isn't that difficult to endure, considering the benefits. Of course, there is the problem of children. However, I managed to find a simple solution, which forestalled a great deal of injury to my nerves.

"When they are born, you immediately hand them over to their nurse, then on to a governess, and when they are old enough, you ship them off—the boys to Eton, the girls to a proper finishing school. They are never to be underfoot. *Never*.

"Once they have been civilized, only then do you take them in hand, presenting them to society, making certain they marry into the right family. Take my advice, and you shall save yourself a lot of trouble and worry." The duchess came to her feet and tapped Leah on the arm with her fan. "I'd not reject another young suitor if I were you, and so coldly, too. In the end, you may find that you will have to marry down."

"I shall keep your recommendations in mind, Your Grace," Leah said politely.

"Do that, dear girl. When I catch up with my son, Rupert, I shall send him your way. He is yet unattached, and I expect you to dance with him. Who knows? If you are to Rupert's liking, one day soon, you may very well become part of my family."

The woman turned. Feathers bouncing, broken barbs floating around her like snowflakes, the duchess appeared to be molting as she ambled off.

Staring at the comical figure, Leah decided to find another spot to sit before Rupert came seeking her out. Quickly, she stood, then noticed a glimmer near her feet.

Sapphires and diamonds encased in gold weighed heavy in Leah's hand after she'd retrieved the article. Recognizing it as one of the duchess's many bracelets, Leah knew it was worth a small fortune.

At first she pondered the idea of withholding the information about her find. No. It was John Kingsley's pockets she hoped to empty. He deserved to be fleeced. But robbing some pompous old woman of a family heirloom, even if she was a member of the peerage, had never been part of her scheme. Before the temptation became too great, Leah rushed after the duchess.

"Your Grace," she said, catching up to the woman, "I believe you dropped this."

Her lorgnette met her face. The woman blanched at seeing the bracelet, then she snatched it from Leah's hand. "Oh, my dear, thank you! I cannot imagine what I would have done had you not found it. The thing is worth at least five thousand pounds, if not more. You have saved me. Truly you are forever in my gratitude. I must tell Rupert of your magnificent deed. Wait here. He shall want to thank you himself." The duchess quickly meshed with the crowd.

Rupert. Even his name sent a sickly chill down Leah's spine. Deciding she'd better not tarry, she spun around, then froze.

"Most noble of you," Ian said, smiling down at her. "The duchess, however, does have a tendency to inflate the value of her jewels. Cut the price by half and you'll have its actual worth."

Leah frowned. These people had no concept of what it was to be poor. That one bracelet, whether it was worth the amount the duchess had quoted, or merely a fraction of the price, would have quickly solved Leah's dilemma, she and the children living comfortably for many years to come. "No matter what the cost, I'm certain, to her, the thing is priceless."

"And to her son," Ian stated, his attention fixed on the man as he came toward them. "If you are eager to escape him, I suggest we make a hasty retreat." Not waiting for her reply, he pulled Leah into his arms and swept her onto the dance floor, into the waltzing crowd.

"What do you think you're doing?" she demanded, stumbling over his feet while fighting against his hold.

Ian knew they looked an ungainly pair, but he continued to spin her around. "I'm attempting to save you from Rupert's grasp." His foot trod upon hers; the air hissed through Leah's teeth. A soft curse slipped through his lips. "Will you at least allow me to lead? Unless, of course, you'd rather have old Rup as your partner."

Leah spotted the man standing on the fringes of the dance floor beside his mother. Squat and round, his hair but a handful of strands strategically positioned to cover his balding pate, he looked to be at least fifty years of age. Mother and son appeared cut from the same plate, not only in physical aspect, but in their dress as well. Foppish was too masculine a word to describe him. Enshrouded in lace and ruffles, a bright blue coat covering his portly body, he gazed at Leah through a lorgnette, identical to his mother's.

"I would rather forgo his company altogether," Leah confessed, her feet finally finding the right rhythm. Briefly, she marveled at what an exceptional partner the earl was. "I thank you for your intervention, my lord. He may be a very nice man, but I am in no mood to dance—with him or with anyone else. If you'd just lead me across the way, I'd be most appreciative."

Ian grinned knowingly. "How appreciative, Miss Kingsley?" he teased, then felt her stiffen in his arms. He chuckled. "After all, I did save you from one of the most notorious lechers in all London."

"Rupert?" she asked in disbelief.

"Yes, Rupert," he replied. "By your expression, Miss Kingsley, I'd say you doubt my word. Or am I the one whom you believe is the lecher?"

"A lecher, no. A knave, yes."

An auburn eyebrow arched inquisitively. "I assume I should take that as a compliment."

"You may take it as you wish." They were drawing close to the French doors that stood opposite the spot where he'd spun her onto the floor. Leah desperately wanted to be free of him, for his nearness affected her in the strangest way. "You may release me now," she said, only to feel his warm hand tighten at her waist. "What are you doing?" she cried as he twirled her out one of the openings onto the darkened balcony. They came to a stop in a secluded corner, behind a potted tree, the stone balustrade at Leah's back.

"I am hoping, Miss Kingsley, to have a private word with you," he said, his body blocking her only avenue of escape.

Fearful he'd somehow discovered her deceit, she fell back against the barrier, gripping it for support. She measured him carefully. "What about?" she asked nervously.

Dim light filtered through the lacy branches concealing them, to slightly illumine her upturned face. As Ian studied her, he thought she resembled a frightened rabbit collared by a hungry wolf. She might have good cause to be alarmed. An erratic pulse fluttered just above the black lace banding her slender throat. Spotting it, Ian was instantly tempted to press his lips to the rhythmic point, inspiring it to flitter even more rapidly. Then his gaze fell lower. Mesmerized, he watched the satiny tops of her breasts rise and fall above the low neckline of her gown as she drew breath unevenly. Envisioning what might lay hidden beneath the rose-colored silk, he swallowed a groan.

Amazed by the intensity of his sudden, unexplained passion for her, he fought to control the fire that had erupted in his loins, fearing it might become a raging inferno. *Unexplained?* All one had to do was look at her to know why he desired her. A rare beauty, she held him spellbound.

"You have nothing to fear from me," he reassured, then counted on his words being true. "If you wish to leave, I'll not detain you." He retreated a step, not simply for her benefit, but for his also. "I merely wanted to offer my apologies for my poor behavior. You called me a knave, and that I've been. I'll not fault you if you cannot forgive me. But know this. Presently, unlike earlier today, my regrets are genuine. I hope, Miss Kingsley, we might attempt to become friends, especially when we'll be so close at hand over the next few months. What do you say? Shall we give it a try?"

"Close at hand?" she asked.

By the wary look she cast his way, Ian surmised that if they were presently at the opposite ends of the world from each other she would still consider it too close. "Sinclair House is not *that* large," he said. "We will have the occasion to meet from time to time. It will be the same during the Season. As tonight, my mother and I do manage to attend the same parties. Again, it is inevitable we'll meet." Conveniently, he'd precluded the fact that he'd purposely chosen this party over another, simply because he wanted to keep an eye on her. Much as would an overprotective father, he thought drolly, understanding his interest in her wasn't the least bit parental. "Inside, when we nearly collided," he said after observing her closely, "by the expression on your face, I presume you hadn't expected to see me at all this evening, correct?"

"I hadn't realized you'd be here."

"Hadn't realized? Or were *hoping* I'd not be here—which is it?"

"If you must know, in all honesty, it is the latter. Do you blame me for feeling so?"

"No. Your reaction is quite natural, considering how I've treated you, Miss Kingsley. It was ill-conceived of me to go on the attack as I did. My conduct toward you has been less than fair. My only excuse is that, on first reading your uncle's letter, I felt as though my mother had been unduly put upon. Myself, as well. You were described as a brutish creature, lacking the simplest of manners. Added to that, you were accused of possessing a beastly temperament. I had formed an opinion about you without first getting to know you. Then there was my concern over this *Irish bounder*, as your uncle termed him. Whereas you have denied a serious involvement with the young man, your uncle seems to think otherwise. It became a matter of whom to believe."

"Are you saying you now believe me instead of him? Is that why you are so eager to make amends?"

"I'm willing to give you the benefit of the doubt. And I'm desirous of making amends so we might have a favorable and receptive coexistence while we are both in London."

"But you still don't fully trust me, do you?" she asked.

"Would you be offended if I said I didn't?"

How could she be when she played him false? A family trait, she decided, knowing she'd not be in this fix if it were not for her father's duplicity. "No, I'd not be offended. Likewise, you shouldn't be offended when I grant that I don't fully trust you."

"Me?" he asked, obviously surprised by her confession. "Why would you not trust me?"

"You have offered a truce between us, but I suspect you still plan to keep watch over me as a hound would a bone."

"Since you are under my care, it is a given I'd seek to protect you."

"I am under your mother's care," she said, correcting him.

"That is neither here nor there. While at Sinclair House,

or any other residence I own, you are *both* under my protection."

Leah stared at him, not agreeing in the least. After a long moment, he shook his head.

"Did it ever occur to you, Miss Kingsley, that I watch you as I do, simply because I find you exceptionally attractive?"

At his admission, Leah's knees nearly gave way. Thank goodness she still held on to the balustrade. Then she marked the teasing light in his eyes. "You're jesting," she accused.

"Am I?" he asked, moving a step closer to her. He lightly caught her arm. "Despite what you might think, you are quite lovely, Miss Kingsley. A man cannot help notice your refreshing beauty. I do not lie when I say I find myself intrigued. That is why I forever gaze at you."

Immediately Leah wondered whether her father had acted in the same flirtatious manner. Perhaps that was how he became involved with two women—falling in love with both, too weak to make a choice. Or maybe it was simply a quirk of the aristocracy. Whatever the answer, she planned to put a stop to this outrageousness—now. "Were your betrothed to hear of your roguish conduct, Lord Huntsford, I'm certain she'd have much to say. If you do not wish for her to learn of this, I suggest you unhand me at once."

"Betrothed?" he queried, his brow wrinkling. "What betrothed?"

"Lady Veronica Whitcomb," Leah snapped. "Now loose me or I'll call out for assistance."

Deep laughter rumbled from Ian's throat; Leah stared at him as though he'd gone mad.

"I suppose my mother told you we were engaged to be married. If so, she has jumped the gun."

"What are you saying?"

"I'm saying, Miss Kingsley, I'm not betrothed to anyone. The Lady Veronica and I are well-suited, but I've yet to ask for her hand. I'm not fully certain I will. With your knowing as much, is my *roguish conduct* now less offensive to you?"

Her arm tingling from his touch, Leah wanted desperately to be free of him. At the moment, she despised the masculine gender, Ian Sinclair included. Or so she told herself. "You are too familiar, sir. Loose me, or you shall sport a bruise on your shin."

Ian bit back a grin. "What happened to your threat to shout for help?" he asked, purposely baiting her. Wide eyes flashed green fire while her lips pouted petulantly. God, she was beautiful, angry or otherwise, he mused. "Thought better of it, did you? A wise choice. For had you drawn attention to the fact that we are secreted away out here behind this tree, Veronica's hopes of becoming a countess would surely be dashed. The next Lady Huntsford would be you, Miss Kingsley."

"Me?"

"Alone together, a young woman who is presumed to be a virgin and an experienced man—we are in what many would call a compromising position."

"Presumed?" Leah shot at him.

Like an enraged wolverine, she appeared ready to tear at his throat. Still Ian decided to press the point. He had to know. "Then you have not been intimate with your young man?"

"I have been intimate with no man, sir. Nor do I plan to be—not until I marry. Which I doubt I'll do anytime soon."

Relief washed through Ian as he decided she told the truth. "Your wedding may not be that far off. As I said, we are in a compromising position. Draw attention to the fact, and the scandalmongers would destroy you, along with my family name. Considering such, do you think my mother wouldn't insist on our immediate marriage?"

"Let the clacks say what they will. I'd never marry you—never," she avowed.

So, she was still smitten with her Irish bounder, was she? The thought stung Ian. "Never say never, Miss Kingsley, for it is certain to come true." His free hand moved to her face, and gentle fingers trailed alongside the curve of her cheek. His thumb lightly caressed her lips. "And if by chance it does come to pass, I promise you'll not be sorry."

Enthralled by his words, his touch, Leah went weak. Quickly she fought to regain her senses. Her vow against marrying wasn't meant just for him, but for all his gender. How, after her father's deceit, could she trust any man again? She couldn't. To Leah, all men were liars and cheats. *The same as you,* a little voice needled, letting her know she wasn't to be trusted either.

"Lord Huntsford—Ian?" a woman's voice called; quick footsteps followed his name across the balcony. They stopped, and the woman pivoted in several directions, searching him out.

"Stay here," he ordered, releasing Leah's arm, then he turned away from her.

Leah sank back into the shadows, watching as he rounded the tree. His long strides carried him across the slate, and as she peeked through the feathery branches hiding her, she realized that he intentionally headed the woman off. Leah questioned whether he did so for her sake or for his own.

"Veronica," he said when he was nearly upon her.

"There you are," she declared, spinning around, smiling. "Why on earth are you out here? The party is inside."

"I stepped out for a bit of fresh air," he responded, taking her arm and guiding her toward the French doors.

"Is that the only reason, Ian?" she queried.

"If it wasn't, would you become angry with me?"

The light flowing from the ballroom spotted the Lady Veronica's face. Leah noted she was an exceedingly attractive brunette, probably four or five years older than herself. By their conversation, she now knew why he'd been so intent on his steering the woman away from the secluded corner. Had Veronica caught them, a heated quarrel would have ensued. Of that Leah was certain.

"That depends on what the other reason is," the brunette said just as they passed through the doorway.

Her words confirmed Leah's theory about a probable argument. Coward, she silently berated him, positive the Lady Veronica meant more to him than he'd initially let on. For one brief moment, Leah had allowed herself to believe he might be different from her father, that he could possibly be trusted. But the moment had passed.

Pulling herself away from the balustrade, she made her

way into the ballroom. Her eyes searched the dance floor as she walked around its perimeter, looking first for the earl, then for Rupert. Were she to spot either one, she intended to bolt to the other side of the room.

The anger she'd held inside her all afternoon and into part of the night had taken its toll. She felt suddenly weary. Leah fought to hold on to her fury, fearing if she let it go, another emotion would take its place. She could ill-afford to be brought down by her tears in front of all these people. No more confrontations, she prayed, wishing she could just dissolve into the walls.

"Leah, dearest."

Hearing her name, she pulled up short, then noticed she'd nearly walked straight into the countess. Beside Madeline stood the Lady Veronica Whitcomb. To Leah's relief, Lord Huntsford wasn't with them.

After the countess made the proper introductions, she turned away and began chatting with another of her peers, allowing the two younger women to become acquainted.

"You are from Ulster, I hear," Veronica said, making the first move at conversation.

"Yes."

"With your coming from such a backwater, I imagine you are quite caught up in the excitement of the London Season. This is your first party, is it not?"

Leah bristled, for in a roundabout way she'd just been called a bumpkin. "It is my first party, and most likely my last."

Surprise showed on Veronica's face. "I thought you were to remain in London until close to Christmas."

"I am."

"Surely, you'll be attending more parties, then?"

"Not if I can avoid doing so," Leah said.

"Why not?"

"For all its sparkle and color, I find this affair to be exceedingly dull. The atmosphere is stuffy and the attendees are ostentatious. Call me provincial, but I prefer genuineness to showiness any day."

"I hope, Miss Kingsley, you aren't likening me to the

pompous boors you've just described," Ian said from directly behind her. She whirled toward him, and at spying her startled look, he grinned down on her. Having gone for some refreshments, he passed Veronica her glass, then extended his own toward Leah. "Would you enjoy some wine?"

"No, I wouldn't." Leah glanced at the brunette. "Excuse me, please."

From over the rim of his glass, Ian watched as Leah rushed to his mother's side. Soon, he surmised, the pair would be leaving the party.

"You heard her remarks, I assume?" Veronica asked.

Ian swallowed the wine he'd sipped. "I did."

"She's certainly a curious creature," Veronica commented. "I cannot imagine what has occurred to make her so hostile to everyone here."

"I suppose she thinks we are an arrogant lot. For the most part, she's right."

"By the look she threw you, I'd say she considers you to be the most arrogant of all."

"I imagine she does." Although he felt Veronica's questioning stare, he didn't elaborate, his attention remaining fixed on Leah.

"If she abhors you so, life at Sinclair House will become unbearable for you. Isn't there some way for you to gain control of the situation so you might find peace?"

He quaffed the remainder of his wine, his gaze resettling on Leah. "I guess I'll just have to change her opinion of me."

CHAPTER
5

"You're exceptionally quiet this morning, dear," Madeline stated across the breakfast table. "Are you still not feeling well?"

The spoon in Leah's hand stilled above the stewed fruit she had been aimlessly shoving around her bowl during the past ten minutes. Last night, wanting to flee both the Carstairses' party and Ian Sinclair, she'd pleaded a headache. The countess had taken pity on her, and they'd left early. While Leah slept, her anger had dissipated, but since she'd awakened, mental misery had been her closest companion. Still she knew she must hide the truth.

"I'm fine," she said, managing a weak smile. "Just a little sluggish. The aftereffect of too much excitement, I suppose."

"Then you weren't the least disappointed in your first London party?"

From her continual talk the previous afternoon about the festive London Season, it had become apparent to Leah that the countess had truly wanted Leah to enjoy her first gala. She couldn't very well ruin the woman's expectations.

"Other than when my head began to throb, I relished every moment of it."

"I'm so happy to hear that," the countess said, beaming. "Week after next, we'll be attending another party, far grander than the one the Carstairses gave. You will be quite impressed with . . ."

Her heart weighing heavy, Leah closed out the countess's words, thoughts of her siblings claiming her attention. The burden of knowing they were all illegitimate had become hers alone to bear. To disclose what she'd learned about their father would utterly destroy the others. Desperately wanting to protect them, for her family had already suffered enough, Leah vowed to keep Terence Dalton's betrayal a secret. With the pledge, her determination renewed itself. Only she could reunite her family. Whatever the risk, whatever the cost, she'd see them together again.

". . . the Delderfields' gardens are set aglow by the flames of a thousand candles, young couples strolling along the paths, the light of love reflecting in their gazes," Leah heard the countess say, again conscious of her surroundings. "The setting is quite romantic. A spectacular sight to see."

"I'd think if they were truly in love," Ian proclaimed from behind Leah, the sound of his voice making her jump, "they'd be seeking out a darkened spot, away from inquisitive eyes, where they could express their desires fully. A stolen kiss is not really stolen if everyone is allowed to see."

As he spoke, Ian had come around the table stopping at the countess's side. She offered him her cheek; his light kiss fell upon it.

"Good morning, Mother." He regarded Leah. "Miss Kingsley," he greeted as he moved into his chair. His linen napkin snapped against the air before he settled it on his lap, his attention never leaving Leah. "You look a bit fatigued this morning. Too much party?"

Too much of you, she wanted to blurt aloud. With great effort, she kept the words sealed behind her lips. "Since I'm not accustomed to keeping such late hours, it was rather tiring," she said instead. "As time goes on, I expect I shall become used to it all."

"I noticed you left early," he commented.

"I was suffering from a headache," Leah lied.

Knowing he had been the true source of her ills, Ian felt tempted to let loose a chuckle. Quelling the urge, he somehow managed to exhibit the appropriate amount of sympathy. "I am sorry you were so stricken. I hope through sleep you were able to recover from the attack."

"It bedevils me still."

"Such as now, I suppose?"

Leah spotted the mirthful twinkle in his eyes. "Yes, such as now," she bit back at him.

"Dearest child," the countess interjected. "You should have said something when I asked about your health a moment ago. You may have refused to take something last night, but I'll not allow the same from you today. There's no reason for you to suffer needlessly." She turned toward the butler. "Simmons—have Milly stir up some of my special remedy for Miss Kingsley. When done, bring it here at once."

"That won't be necessary," Leah said. "The pain is intermittent. I'm certain it will be gone shortly."

"Nonsense," Madeline declared. "My remedy will relieve whatever ails you. I promise your pain will be gone inside of a few minutes."

If that were only true, Leah thought, wishing there was a quick cure for despair and hopelessness. "You're making too much out of this," she insisted, knowing the only medicine that could possibly help was to again be reunited with her siblings, their cares and worries a thing of the past.

"I shall hear no further objections," the countess returned. Again she looked to her manservant. "Do as I've requested, Simmons."

The butler settled a bowl in front of the earl. "As you wish, ma'am," he said, then headed toward the connecting door, leading to the kitchen.

"Had I been you, Miss Kingsley," Ian announced, retrieving his spoon, aiming it at a plump prune, "I'd have put up more of a fight. But since you allowed my mother to win out,

I shall offer you this advice: Before you swallow the stuff, hold your nose, for it has a most disagreeable bite."

"Thank you for the warning," Leah muttered, understanding she'd have no choice but to ingest the bitter herbs once they were set before her. One lie too many and she would now suffer for it.

Madeline's harsh look fell upon her son. "My remedy managed to cure many of your ailments, sir. You never complained before."

"That's because my lips were pursed and my tongue was paralyzed from the effects. It is hard to speak under such conditions. However, I'll not deny your remedy works, albeit with a hard kick."

"Something you fully deserve, now and then," his mother quipped.

Ian chuckled. "Admitted, madam. Perhaps I'll swallow the remedy meant for Miss Kingsley. That should prove I am sincere in my wish for us to become friends."

"You need not martyr yourself for my sake," Leah said.

"Oh, but I must," he replied with a wide smile.

Leah's heart did an odd little flip-flop, his grin the cause. She gritted her teeth, angered by her reaction.

"Really, Ian," his mother declared, her attention all the while focused on her houseguest, "you make it sound as though my remedy were formulated from arsenic. You've managed to frighten Leah nearly out of her wits. If you no longer wish to try my cure, dear, I shall excuse you from doing so."

Leah caught Ian's conspiratorial wink. He'd saved her from the ordeal of having to ingest the medicine. Then she wondered at his purpose. "I think I shall forgo the cure, especially since I am no longer suffering any pain."

"As you wish," the countess said just as the butler reentered the room. "Never mind, Simmons," she said, waving him off. "Miss Kingsley is no longer in need of my remedy. Dispose of it, please."

The glass balancing on a silver tray, the butler turned and retraced his steps, the door swinging shut behind him.

Madeline's attention settled on her son. "I was surprised

to see you at the Carstairses' last night. You've always expressed dissatisfaction with their parties. I believe you called them *dull.*"

"They are—usually." Last night was different, he silently acknowledged. "But then, no matter whose party it is, they all have a tendency to become tiresome."

"Did you not enjoy yourself, then?" his mother asked.

"For a time I did." Until the intriguing Miss Kingsley had departed, he admitted silently.

"I know you despise the Season, Ian. But for Veronica's sake, I'd think you'd at least show some enthusiasm toward these affairs. She appears to thrive on the round of parties and balls."

"Then perhaps she should attend the remainder by herself," Ian countered, weary of hobnobbing with the likes of his peers, most of whom he could barely suffer. "My tolerance is nearly at an end."

As Leah chased a prune with her spoon, she quietly listened to the exchange. She'd have thought he would take pleasure in these lofty functions, but apparently he didn't. She wondered why he hated them so.

"The extravagance for such pageantry is insupportable," he said, unknowingly answering Leah's unspoken query. "Instead of giving parties, they should be investing their time and money in more rewarding pursuits. God knows there is enough suffering to be had in London alone. Collectively, they could change many of the ills plaguing our society. But no. They'd rather primp and preen, trotting out for each other."

"Many are involved in charitable endeavors, Ian. They are not wholly niggardly."

"The cost of one party alone, Mother, could feed several dozen families for a full year, possibly more. That is why I do not allow such events at Sinclair House. The money we save is put to better use."

"I know you are exceedingly generous to those in need, son. And I agree with your position. But you must realize the Season has become a way of life for those within the peerage."

"They are too caught up in themselves," Ian barked.

"You are undoubtedly right, but you must remember," Madeline countered, "the majority of them have been insulated from the realities of human suffering, therefore they cannot appreciate the extent of the problem."

"Well, it is time they open their eyes and see it fully. Else the misery will overrun them as it moves northward from the Thames."

"You have no need to convince me," Madeline said, then looked at the clock on the mantelpiece. "Goodness. I shall be late for my meeting." She turned to Leah. "I'd ask you to go along with me, dear, but I fear you will become quite bored by the proceedings."

While Leah sat silently heeding the dialogue between mother and son, she was astonished by his stated concern for the masses. She'd automatically lumped him in with the rest of his peers, but apparently she'd misjudged him. Maybe he wasn't such a knave after all. "I shall be fine here," she answered, deciding to use her time alone to again write Terence. "Go along to your meeting. There's no need to worry about me."

"Where are you off to, Mother?"

"To the Westovers'. The duchess is planning a charity auction, all proceeds to go to the orphanage she supports."

"A fine woman," Ian announced. "At least *she* fathoms the extent of the problem." He looked at Leah. "As for you, Miss Kingsley, you'll not be staying in this house by yourself. You'll be coming with me, so finish your meal."

"With you?" she asked, eyes flying wide. "Where to?"

"It is May Day, Miss Kingsley. We are going to Kingston-upon-Thames to join in the celebration at the marketplace," he responded with a smile. "Veronica and her brother will be coming by for us within the hour."

"How thoughtful of you, Ian," the countess said.

Leah's mind raced. With mother and son both gone for the day, this might be her one opportunity to sneak from the house and find her way to Eighteen Hanover Square. She simply had to learn more about the Covingtons. Leah prayed when she uttered her next words that Madeline would support her.

"Thank you, Lord Huntsford, for your offer," Leah said, "but I feel as though I'd be intruding. Besides, I had planned to spend a quiet day here at Sinclair House, so I'd really rather not go."

"Nonsense, dear," her hostess announced. "There is no reason for you to sit in this house and miss all the fun. The Whitcombs won't mind in the least if you join them, and the festivities at Kingston-upon-Thames are always such a delight. I know you'll have a wonderful time."

"It has been decided, Miss Kingsley," Ian declared, his grin growing wider. "You are going with me." He nudged the hand in which Leah held her spoon. "Eat up, or we'll be late."

An unappetizing bit of prune finally found her mouth. Dear God, she thought, in total dismay. Of all times, why had the countess chosen to desert her now?

"You are exceptionally quiet today, Miss Kingsley," Veronica said. "Are you not feeling well?"

Leah stared at the woman whose words had nearly mimicked those uttered by the countess at the breakfast table. For the past hour, as the carriage rolled smartly along toward Kingston-upon-Thames, the Lady Veronica Whitcomb had done little else but talk about the Season's upcoming events, none of which held any interest for Leah. Ian had responded to Veronica's queries about what party they should attend, while beside Leah, Lord Whitcomb had remained nearly as silent as she.

Directly opposite Leah, Ian caught her vacant look. "I believe Miss Kingsley is still suffering the effects of a headache that came upon her last night."

"I'm so sorry," Veronica returned. "I have some powders in my reticule should you desire relief from the pain."

"Thank you," Leah said, feeling as though she'd played this scene before, "but their use won't be necessary. I'm quite fine."

"Should you change your mind, just let me know," Veronica stated, then immediately began discussing the Delderfields' ball.

Leah tuned out Veronica's words. As she transferred her gaze, her eyes caught the earl's. His suggestive look sent a spark of excitement whisking through her. Fire burned her cheeks, embarrassment claiming her.

She quickly dipped her parasol, its canopy blocking Ian from her sight, only to find a pair of hazel eyes were fastened upon her. Shaken by Lord Jonathan Whitcomb's studious appraisal, Leah again shifted her parasol, shutting out both men. Absently, she viewed the scenery.

Lord Whitcomb was an attractive man with dark hair and faultless manners. Other than the polite exchange of greetings when they'd been introduced, nothing of consequence had passed between them. Nevertheless, he made Leah exceedingly nervous, for he continually watched her.

The cadence of the horses changed. Hooves sounded hollowly as they trotted across the bridge leading into Kingston-upon-Thames. Before they'd left London, the earl had promised Leah a picturesque journey back in time. As she looked around her now, she found she was not the least disappointed in what she saw.

Apart from a few modern structures, the village retained a distinct medieval flavor. The ancient buildings sported a fresh coat of whitewash, while in May Day tradition, spring flowers burgeoned gaily from both windowsills and doorsteps. As the carriage drew closer to the marketplace, the narrow streets grew more congested. Finally they came to a standstill, the way ahead clogged by pedestrians and vehicles.

"It appears all of London has descended on the village, the same as we," Ian commented, viewing the snarl in front of them. "Instead of sitting here, waiting, why don't we proceed on foot? We'll make the marketplace a lot faster if we do."

Both Veronica and Jonathan agreed, while Leah kept silent.

"Three ayes and one abstention," Ian said. "I guess we walk."

Once they had all descended from the carriage, Leah was astounded when Ian offered her his arm. Then she saw Veronica had already latched on to her brother's sleeve. Leah had no choice but to allow the earl to escort her. After the driver had been instructed on a familiar locale where he should park and remain, the foursome set off toward the center of town.

After Leah lowered her parasol, for safety's sake in the crowd, Ian guided her around the throng of carriages blocking the street. "Are you enjoying yourself, Miss Kingsley?" he asked.

The day was bright and cheery, the mood of the crowd surrounding them quite gay. Leah could not help being caught up in the excitement. "Very much so," she replied, her anticipation of seeing the marketplace escalating. "The place is much like a fairy tale come to life. When we crossed the bridge, I halfway expected to see a knight and his squire riding alongside us."

Ian chuckled. "You still may get your wish."

"My wish?" she asked, gazing up at him.

"Your knight and his squire," he replied.

They were passing behind a carriage, when suddenly the vehicle jolted backward. Leah felt the reflexive jerk of the earl's hand as she was pulled against him, away from danger. Apologies were offered to the couple from the driver at Ian's barked command that he control his horses. The incident over, her heart racing slightly from the scare, Leah found herself still held snugly to the earl's side.

"Thank you," she offered, trying to put some distance between their bodies, but he kept her firmly beside him.

"Until we have made our way out of this crush, I want you close," he explained. "Another occurrence such as the one we just experienced and you might not be so lucky."

Even if she wanted to, Leah discovered she was unable to move away from him. The crowd had funneled into a tight alleyway. Like sheep being herded through the gate of a pen, the multitude squeezed together, their progress slowing even more so.

"If fate allows, we shall yet make it out of here alive," Ian said.

He eased Leah in front of him. Her waist tingled where his hands still lingered. Warmth radiated through her clothing as his chest pressed solidly against her back. While his body protected her from behind, his broad shoulders absorbed the shocks from either side. Unbelievably, even in this crush of bodies, his own particular scent stood out above the rest. Clean and fresh, a hint of spicy cologne enveloping him, his masculine aroma wafted into her nostrils. Affected by his nearness, Leah suddenly felt giddy. She breathed deeply, hoping to clear her head.

Soon the congestion broke loose, and everyone streamed from the narrow alleyway out into the open. There in front of Leah stood the marketplace. Mesmerized, she gaped at the spectacle playing out before her.

Jugglers performed for children and adults alike; strolling minstrels sang while strumming on their lutes. A beggar or two shook tin cups, halfpennies jingling inside. Brightly colored tents and awnings covered row upon row of tables lining the funnel-shaped area. As Ian had said, all of London must have descended upon the town, for the commonality stretched far and wide.

"Well, what do you think?" he inquired.

Leah looked up at him. "It is everything you promised it would be."

A vivacious smile lit her face, and Ian's breath caught in his chest. Exceptional, he thought, his heart behaving most oddly. "Not quite everything," he said, then nodded toward a distant corner of the marketplace.

She looked in the direction he'd indicated. "A maypole!" she cried, having spotted its top over the tents. She turned toward him, childlike excitement glistening in her eyes. "Might we go see?"

A deep chuckle rumbled from his throat. "Whatever milady wishes, I shall gladly do."

Their gazes held. Around them the hum of voices quieted;

strangely, the world stood still. Slowly their smiles faded, and each searched the other's eyes.

Ian felt himself take a step nearer to Leah. She remained steady, unafraid. Light and airy, her name slipped between his lips; his hand reached out to her.

Leah wondered if he'd spoken at all, then his fingers touched her arm. Gently, he drew her closer; she didn't resist.

"There you are!"

Leah blinked as Veronica's voice broke the spell. She pulled free of Ian's hold and quickly stepped away from him. Turning around, she riveted her attention to the top of the maypole. Mercy! Confused by what had just occurred, she fought to control her wildly spinning emotions. Then Leah vowed, that whatever the cause, such a thing would never happen again.

"I was afraid we had lost you," Veronica said on reaching Ian's side.

"We were about to head over to the maypole," Ian announced, his voice sounding oddly tight. "Miss Kingsley said she wanted to see it."

"How delightful," Veronica returned, taking hold of Ian's arm. "Shall we go, then?"

Having noted Veronica's sudden possessiveness, Leah shuffled along behind the newly paired couple, Lord Whitcomb at her side. He'd extended his arm, but she'd politely refused. His constant scrutiny of her set her on edge, and after what had just transpired between Lord Huntsford and herself, her nerves were jangled enough.

Determined to take her mind off Ian Sinclair, she thought about the children and how they would so enjoy Kingston-upon-Thames and its marketplace. Practically anything one desired was offered here. Glancing at the booths as she passed them, she promised to buy each of her siblings a small gift, in hopes of lifting their spirits. Her savings would be lessened a little, but the expenditure was well worth the joy it would bring. Next week, with the excuse of needing a dress altered, she'd seek out Sally Foster. The young woman could post the packages for Leah.

By the time they reached the maypole, a large crowd had gathered around it. Rising on tiptoes, Leah attempted to peer over shoulders and around heads, but she found her view totally blocked. Disappointed, she settled back on her heels.

"Too short, are we?" Ian asked, apparently having noticed her dilemma. "Wait here. I'll be right back."

A moment later he returned. In hand, he held an empty packing crate, purchased for a shilling from a vendor at a nearby booth. Placing the wooden box on the ground, open side down, he tested its sturdiness with his own weight. The crate held him easily, and he hopped free, assured it was safe.

"Ladies," he said, extending his hand first to Veronica, for the device was large enough to hold both women.

"I think not, Ian," she said. "It would be indelicate of me to climb onto a box. What if it tipped over?"

"As you wish." He turned to Leah, offering her his hand. "Miss Kingsley."

Eager to see the event unfolding around the maypole, Leah held no such compunction about appearing indelicate. If the crate supported the earl, it would certainly bolster her. Her fingers met his hand, and she stepped aboard the box.

Head and shoulders above the crowd, Leah viewed the dancers garbed in peasant dress, chains of flowers decorating their heads and necks. Held in their hands, gaily colored streamers weaved in and out, braiding against the tall pole, as the troop ringed round and round it.

This commemoration of spring, Leah knew, was said to have stemmed from Roman times, when Britain's conquerors honored their goddess, Floralia. Others claimed the celebration originated with the tree-worshipping Druids. By medieval times in England, the ritual had become the villagers' favorite holiday. Spring carols were sung, gifts given and received, a king and queen crowned. What better place to celebrate this occasion than in the quaint little town of Kingston-upon-Thames?

Keeping close to Leah, just in case she should slip, Ian ignored the festivities, beholding her instead. Delight etched her face, her cheeks flushing with excitement. Strange how the simplest of things seemed to give her the greatest of pleasure. To Ian, her innocence was refreshing.

Were all woman as unpretentious as she, he'd have settled down long ago. He pictured himself at Falcon's Gate, a half-dozen flaxen-haired children scurrying through its large rooms, happily at play.

His brow furrowing, Ian suddenly remembered the conversation he'd shared with his mother moments before he'd first met the errant Miss Kingsley. Vividly, the words replayed inside his head:

"Mark my words. Your special someone is out there, somewhere, waiting for you to come into her life."

"And how, pray tell, will I know she is the one?"

"You'll know, son, the moment you see her."

Like a mule's kick, the realization struck Ian. Then just as quickly he questioned its verity. Was it possible? Had he found that special someone his mother had spoken of?

CHAPTER
6

"Ian, must we stand here all day? There is so much to do. Can we not be about it?"

Veronica's exasperated tone snapped Ian from his trance. "Do *you* wish to see more?" he asked Leah. "If so, we can stay."

A huskiness had sounded in Ian's voice, drawing Leah's notice; she looked down on him. Instead of the familiar bedeviling light she was accustomed to seeing, his eyes shimmered with genuine warmth, and something else she couldn't quite fathom. Leah's fascination grew, then she realized she was again falling under his spell.

"I'm ready to go, if everyone else is," she announced, looking from Ian toward Veronica. The woman seemed annoyed by the attention the earl was paying his houseguest. The last thing Leah wanted was to provoke the woman. Nor did Leah wish to be the source of her pain. Thinking the earl should be more considerate of Veronica's feelings, Leah ignored his tendered hand and leapt from the box.

"Ready?" Veronica asked, quickly latching on to Ian's arm. "On the way over, I spotted a booth with the most interesting jewelry." She took hold of her brother's arm as well. "Let's see if we can find it."

"Coming, Miss Kingsley?" Ian inquired over his shoulder. He noticed how she trailed behind them, purposely keeping her distance. Veronica's abrupt possessiveness, he decided, his attention again on her.

Normally, Ian overlooked those parts of an individual's personality that tended to vex him, but in the last week, Veronica's were beginning to wear on him. Right now, it was her sudden show of jealousy.

The Lady Veronica Whitcomb might have a different view of things, but from the very start, friendship was all Ian had ever offered her. True, knowing it was time he married, and believing Veronica might be an acceptable mate, he'd mentioned to his mother that he was thinking about asking for Veronica's hand. But *that* was before he had met Leah.

Never once after being introduced to Veronica by Jonathan, both men being members at White's, had Ian overstepped the bounds of propriety, not even in an attempt to steal a kiss from her. Certainly, he'd escorted her to several balls, but he'd done so at her request. Other than last night, Jonathan was usually in tow. What annoyed Ian now was that she was beginning to act as though she owned him. What chafed him even more was that he allowed such behavior.

Ian was in a quandary. He liked the Lady Veronica, but he certainly wasn't in love with her. Leah was the one who fascinated him. So why didn't he just break off his relationship with the Whitcombs and be done with it?

"Here we are," Veronica chirped.

Yanked from his thoughts, Ian saw they had reached the booth Veronica sought. As she rifled through the sparkling pieces on display, he pretended interest. An item selected, she held it up for Jonathan's and his appraisal. With a nod or a quick shake of his head, Ian gave his opinion. Always, he watched Leah from the corner of his eye.

She stood to one side, browsing through a collection of

brooches and pins. One item in particular caught her fancy. With the vendor's permission, she picked it up and examined it closely. Slim fingers traced the brooch's delicate craftsmanship. Her perfect teeth played along her lower lip as she turned it in her hand. With a smile at the vendor, she shook her head and placed the brooch back on the table.

Ian's attention jumped back to Veronica the moment Leah swung his way. In a few steps, she stood beside him. "If you don't mind," she said, "I'm going to move along down the line. I won't be far."

"We'll catch up with you," he said, then again pretended interest in Veronica.

Free from the others, Leah proceeded along the booths, quickly scanning the sellers' wares. In short order, she selected the gifts for her siblings.

Tortoise-shell combs for both Hope and Kate, pink satin hair ribbons for Emily, and a small tin soldier for Peter. Each favor was wrapped in brown paper and tied with string.

Having made her final selection, a book of poetry for Terence, Leah turned to see the others converging on her. Dropping the change from her purchase inside her reticule, the smaller packages already hidden within, she jerked the ties, retrieved Terence's present, and walked toward the threesome.

"What did you buy?" Veronica asked, a long finger tapping the paper wrapping.

"A book of poetry," Leah responded. "The binding is a bit tattered, but the pages are still in very good condition."

"Oh," Veronica commented. "How practical." Straight away, she began showing off the jewelry she'd acquired.

"They are all lovely," Leah said of the half-dozen articles. "I'm certain you'll enjoy them."

"Considering they have little monetary value," Veronica's brother said, surprising Leah, for he'd hardly spoken a word all day, "I doubt they will hold her interest for long."

"Jonathan," Veronica admonished, "you make it sound as though I were a spendthrift."

"I do so because you are, dear sister. But what irks me is that it's my money you're always spending."

"Oh, tosh, Jonathan," she said, playfully swatting his arm. "I've not shorted you yet, have I?"

"No, but your debts are mounting. If you don't pay up soon, I shall have to charge you interest."

"Look over there," Veronica said, obviously desiring to change the subject. "Isn't that the most beautiful shawl you've ever seen?"

She moved toward the booth, and Jonathan rolled his eyes. "She's your sister, Whitcomb," Ian proclaimed, noting the man's disgust.

"If you're smart, Huntsford, she won't become your wife."

Veronica? Not likely, Ian thought, his vision centered on Leah. She stood between the two men, attending to neither one. "The notion of marriage has crossed my mind," he said, wondering again if Leah were indeed his special someone.

"You could always reconsider," Whitcomb returned.

"Reconsider? That's doubtful," Ian countered.

"Jonathan!" Veronica called from across the way. "Will you come here, please?"

On a mumbled oath, Lord Whitcomb strode toward his sister, pulling his wallet from his inside coat pocket. The shawl paid for, he lingered beside Veronica while their purchase was wrapped.

"A book of poetry, hmm?" Ian asked Leah as they waited for the pair. "Whose verses do you favor?"

"Lord Byron's," she responded, refusing to look at him. From his conversation with Veronica's brother, it was apparent to Leah that, unlike what Lord Huntsford said last night, he *did* plan to marry. He'd lied to her. Still she didn't understand his purpose in doing so. Men—they were all untrustworthy.

"Good old George, is it? An excellent choice," Ian said.

"You sound as though you knew him."

"Hardly. I was a mere lad of eight when he left England,

never to return to her shores. When he died several years later, he wasn't very much older than I am now."

"Had he not led such an unseemly life, he might still be writing his poetry."

"Ah, you refer to those dark rumors about him," Ian said, then noted the look she shot him. "Then you are aware of the gossip about Byron having committed incest with his sister. If so, then you are also aware that those rumors led to the failure of his marriage, and his ultimate exile from his homeland. Of course, there is also his liaisons with a married woman or two. Exceptional men, Miss Kingsley, are sometimes known to be morally weak."

In many ways, Leah considered her father to be an exceptional man. Because he was, that didn't automatically give him the right to act in such an unprincipled manner. "There is no excuse for behavior of that sort," she said, thinking more of her father than of Lord Byron.

"No, there is no excuse. It is only to say that, like all men, he also was human—maybe too much so. We all carry our own personal demon inside us. Perhaps the larger the demon, the more we are driven by its force. Despite Byron's improper conduct, you still enjoy his work, don't you?"

By what the earl had said, Leah recognized the demon residing in her, understood why it had come into being. Admittedly, she was driven, her siblings' welfare giving impetus to the evil force. Yet she blamed her father for its existence. Had he been strong enough to exorcise his own demon, she might not have been encumbered with one of her own. "I cannot deny Byron's words have meaning for me," Leah replied, wondering what sort of wickedness lived inside Ian. The thought must have shown on her face, for she heard him chuckle.

"There's no need for you to speculate about me, Miss Kingsley. Let it be known, I am demon-free. As for Byron, there is one poem of his I particularly enjoy. I'm not certain I can remember it fully though. May I?" He took the small book from Leah. The wrapping and string fell away as he began quoting: "'*She walks in beauty, like the night of cloudless climes and starry skies; and all that's best of dark and bright meet in the aspect of her eyes; thus . . .'"* Opening the cover, he frowned. "This is Shelly, not Byron."

"I know." Leah retrieved the book and discarded wrappings from his hand, then noted his confusion. "You asked who was my favorite poet, not whose poetry I purchased."

"So I did." He saw the Whitcombs were headed their way. "Are you through shopping?" he asked Veronica once she gained his side. "If so, why don't we find the carriage, collect the food, and make our way to the Fairfield? We could have our picnic there."

"I cannot believe you are hungry this soon," Veronica countered.

"If Huntsford isn't, I am," Jonathan piped in, shifting his sister's newest purchase under his arm. "Besides, you've nearly depleted my funds. I say we head for the carriage before my wallet has been completely emptied."

"For that comment, dear brother, I should refuse to depart the market," Veronica said with a pretty pout. Throaty laughter rolled from her lips and brightened her eyes. "But, since you say you are famished, I shall relent. To the carriage it is."

"Excellent," Ian announced and motioned everyone on ahead of him. Wending toward the area where the carriage awaited them, he kept a stride or two back from the others, then he suddenly stopped. "Go on without me," he called, attracting their attention. "I'll catch up with you shortly."

"Where are you going?" Veronica asked, but received no reply. "I know what he's up to." A self-assured smile crossed her face. "Come along. Let's not spoil his surprise."

Jonathan frowned down on her. "Surprise? What surprise?"

"He's gone back to get me those earrings you refused to buy. Unlike you, brother, Ian is most willing to part with his money."

"Unlike me, sister, he still has some money to be parted from. Come. Let's get out of this crowd," he said, having been bumped and jostled, for they were blocking the path. Catching hold of both women's arms, he ushered them away from the marketplace.

Still a distance away from the carriage, the trio heard Ian's shout. Stopping, they waited. As he caught up to them, an obviously confused Veronica eyed the large package in his hand.

"What do you have there?" she asked while fingering the paper.

"Mince pies," Ian said, grinning.

"Pies?"

"Yes, I thought we could enjoy them with our picnic. Had you expected something else, Veronica?"

"Actually, I did. However the pies will do."

Seeing the high arch of Lord Whitcomb's eyebrow, for he looked surprised by her admission, Leah fought to keep from laughing out loud.

"Then let's find the carriage so that we can head on over to the Fairfield," Ian said. Balancing the pies in one hand, he waved the other before him. "After you, ladies."

As they walked on ahead, Leah cast a glance toward Veronica. *Spoiled* described her best. She thrived on attention, desiring it constantly, receiving it always. Her brother, though obviously annoyed by Veronica's foolish handling of money, acceded to her every whim. That he adored her was quite apparent.

Lord Huntsford puzzled Leah, however. He didn't appear the sort to tolerate self-indulgent behavior. His statements at the breakfast table that morning, expressing his impatience with his peers, seemed to bear out her judgment of him. But Leah no longer understood the workings of the masculine mind. Stunning, yet superficial—perhaps that was what a man of his caliber desired in a mate. If so, the earl would certainly find his fulfillment in Veronica. For some unknown reason, Leah hoped he'd be appropriately miserable.

Spotting his family's carriage, Jonathan directed his companions toward it, where they stowed the packages, afterward gathering blankets and a picnic basket from the boot.

Ambling onward, they were soon at the Fairfield, just east of the marketplace.

Activity stirred on the expansive green. What appeared to be a grandstand caught Leah's eye. Colorful pennants and banners flapped in the afternoon breeze. "A tournament!" she cried. Smiling brightly, she faced Ian, anticipation shining in her eyes.

"Milady desired to see knights and squires, and so she shall," he said, returning her smile.

They began walking toward a large oak near the edge of the field. "Are they really going to joust?" Leah asked, certain she'd taken another step back in time.

"It will be done more for sport than for the sake of settling disputes. Even so, a man is sometimes injured. The event will be real enough once the contestants begin tilting at one another."

"I could never understand the fascination over a joust," Veronica declared, stopping beneath the tree. "Grown men, suited in armor, riding pell-mell at each other, a lance in hand—all foolishness, if you ask me."

"Strange," Jonathan commented, dropping the blankets on the ground. "I recall, when as children, you had a grand old time playing the fair maid, while Arthur Covington and I rode our ponies along the fence, sticks waving in a play joust." His hand met his arm. "I still bear a scar where he jabbed me. In fact, as I recall, you demanded I get back on my pony and fell the knave. Something about defending your honor, wasn't it? The only foolishness, dear sister, was that I obeyed you, for he managed to unseat me again."

At the mention of her half-brother's name, Leah's gaze had marked Lord Whitcomb fully. Apparently he felt her stare, for he now turned her way and searched her face. Then the light of dawning awareness appeared in his eyes.

"Arabella," Jonathan said, smiling broadly.

"Who?" Leah asked.

"Arabella Covington—Arthur's sister. I've been trying all day to think who it is you resemble." His attention shifted to his sister. "She looks like Arabella, don't you think, Veronica?"

The woman peered around his shoulder. "Her nose and chin, perhaps. I don't know, Jonathan. I haven't seen Arabella in ages. If you want to eat, help spread these blankets."

Hearing she had a half-sister who resembled her slightly, Leah grew extremely nervous. Lord Whitcomb might be the inquisitive type. What if he discovered the truth about her? Sure disaster, she thought.

"You never did pay much attention to Arabella," Jonathan grumbled, shaking out one cover, then another, overlaying the ground where the four would sit. "Given that fact, I doubt you'd remember anything about her."

"Because of your ages, you, Arthur, and Arabella were a threesome," Veronica defended. "Being older, I seldom tagged along with you. Ian," she said, turning to him, "do you remember what Arabella Covington looks like?"

"Leave me out of this," he said, placing the picnic basket and pies at the edge of the blankets. "I'm older than all of you and am mostly in Scotland. Besides Arthur and his father, I don't believe I've met anyone else in the family. If so, I don't remember."

"I still say she resembles her," Jonathan insisted, flopping onto the blanket.

"Ignore him, Miss Kingsley," Veronica said, kneeling beside the picnic basket. "Jonathan still fancies himself in love with Arabella. They were involved in a most torrid affair. Ever since she bounced him, he's been carrying a torch for her."

Jonathan snorted loudly. "Since she was eight and I ten, I'd hardly call the episode torrid." He looked to Leah. "Veronica caught us by the stream at Oakbrook, our family's estate, sharing a quick kiss behind a tree. She has never let me forget the incident from the moment it happened."

Leah knelt at the corner of the blanket between Veronica and Jonathan. Ian settled down opposite her. "Then you and the Covingtons lived close by one another?" she asked, finding herself interested in her father's first family.

"Our estates at one time bordered. The late Lord Covington suffered some financial difficulty and had to sell his property—I believe Arthur and I were about thirteen at the time. The family moved to Hanover Square, where they now stay year-round. I don't think Arthur ever got over the loss of Covington Court."

The estate's sale, Leah determined through quick calculation, fell about the same time Peter was born. His premature birth had nearly drained the Dalton family's finances, the medical bills soaring as specialist after specialist had been summoned from Edinburgh, from London, even from Paris. Miraculously Peter had survived, his lungs however remained weak. A small sniffle could turn into a life-threatening illness, and Leah worried about him continually.

Though she hailed her father's unrelenting attempts to save Peter's life, she denounced his method of doing so. By what Lord Whitcomb had said, she was positive 'the late Lord Covington' had robbed one family in order to secure the welfare of the other. The situation had reversed itself though. It was now Leah and her siblings who'd been ousted from their home. Terence Dalton was the cause of everyone's misery, the Covingtons and Daltons alike.

"Have you seen Arthur lately?" Veronica asked, unpacking the basket, passing the napkins around first.

"Not since the funeral," Jonathan replied, taking hold of the linen square. "I should go round and visit. But by what I've heard from others, I hesitate to do so. He's reported to be in a dour mood."

"I saw him the other day at White's," Ian said. "His father's death and the responsibility of his now being head of his family must be weighing heavy on him. He didn't act himself. As you say, Whitcomb, his mood was dour."

"I'll make it a point to visit him this week and discover what this *mood* is all about." Jonathan looked at Leah. "Are you certain you aren't related to the Covingtons?" he asked.

"I know none of them," she said, then rose from the blanket. "Excuse me, please."

Ian watched as she opened her parasol. Shielding her face with it, she took off across the green toward the grandstand.

"Did I say something to upset her?" Jonathan asked.

"I don't know," Ian said while bounding to his feet. "But I'll soon find out."

Leah fought back her tears to no avail as she stumbled onward across the field. All this talk about the Covingtons had been too much for her. Arthur's dour mood—did it stem from his discovery that their father was a bigamist? If so, he undoubtedly fought to keep what he'd learned secret, the same as did she. Should word of their sire's deceit ever get out, it would mean ruin to his family's name. The Covingtons would be ostracized.

Then Leah wondered if Arthur, having discovered the truth about their father, had, with John Kingsley's help, set the groundwork meant to destroy the Daltons. Anger and hurt roiled inside Leah at the prospect. If that were the case, she vowed to cause both men as much misery as possible. It was only fair that they suffer as much as she.

Preoccupied, Leah paid no heed to her surroundings. A horse's whinny pierced her ears. Jolted by the sound, she looked up and froze. A racing phaeton skidded toward her, its driver frantically trying to stop. A quick prayer drove through her mind, for Leah knew she was about to die.

Hands gripped her shoulders, instantly jerking her from death's path. Unbelievably, the vehicle slid past the spot where she once stood. A curse exploded above and behind her; she was spun around. Her parasol flew from her fingers.

"What the hell were you thinking?" Ian thundered, his hands biting into her arms. "You nearly got yourself killed!"

Staring up at the earl, Leah blinked. His dark scowl appeared forbidding. He looked as though he might thrash her. "Let go of me," she demanded, a sob catching in her throat.

Tears brightened her eyes and stained her cheeks, and as Ian regarded her, his once-pounding heart twisted with compassion. "You've been crying, and your tears are not because of what just happened. What's wrong, Leah? Tell me."

His voice had softened considerably while concern

showed on his face. Leah wanted to dissolve against his chest and cry out her sorrow in his arms. "Nothing," she said, fearing if she spilled out her misery along with it would come the truth. He'd reject her, she knew.

"I don't believe that. You dashed off heedlessly. Something made you do so. Tell me what it was."

"I needed to be alone. That's all."

Ian snatched her parasol from the ground, then taking hold of her hand, he pulled her around a line of vacated carriages parked beside the green's makeshift thoroughfare, away from the Whitcombs' view. "Have Veronica and her brother in some way caused you distress? Or am I the one who sent you chasing across this field?"

Drawing a shaky breath, Leah realized he wouldn't be satisfied until she answered him. "All of you have been most courteous to me. It was the talk of your friend's father's death that upset me, for I couldn't help thinking about my own father. My mother, too."

Sadness marked her face, and Ian's heart wrenched upon his seeing it. His hand rose. If he could only smooth the pain away, he thought, gentle fingers brushing her cheek. "It was callous of us to discuss such things, especially when your hurt is still so new. I apologize for our insensitivity, mainly my own. It's my fault."

Light tremors ran through her from his touch. Again he wove his spell. This time, Leah didn't fight against his masculine appeal. She felt safe and protected being near him, something she truly desired right now. "Your fault?" she asked, surrendering to the man and the moment.

"Of us all, I am most aware of your situation. Veronica was told, but may have forgotten. Jonathan may be ignorant altogether. I should have put a stop to such talk the moment it began. I blame myself for helping to remind you of your loss. Will you forgive me, Leah?"

As her name passed through his lips for a second time, it sounded even more magical than it did the first. Staring up at him, Leah became mesmerized by what she saw. No man could possibly be as handsome as he was. But it was his tender regard that captured her completely. No one had ever looked at her with such profound caring. Unbidden, her heart swelled with emotion, and Leah realized how very easy it would be to fall in love with him.

The revelation shook her to her core. She had no time or interest in romance. Her siblings were and always would be her first priority. Besides, she was uncertain if she could trust any man—even Ian. Especially Ian. By his own words, it was quite plain that the Lady Veronica was his choice.

"I hadn't meant for you to suffer any unhappiness," he said, addressing her continued silence. "But your expression says you believe otherwise."

"You are not the source of my unhappiness, Lord Huntsford," she said, drawing away from him, wishing he hadn't followed her. Then again, she wouldn't be here had he not tracked after her. "By allowing me some time alone, I'm certain I'll be able to regain my composure. Will you grant me such?"

A trumpet sounded by the grandstand. "Better yet, the tournament is about to begin. Why don't we wander over and watch the first joust?"

"I'm afraid my heart is no longer into seeing the tournament."

"No knights and squires for milady?" he asked, a coaxing smile playing on his lips. "I thought you were enthralled by the prospect of returning to the romantic past."

"It is the stuff of fairy tales, sir," Leah said, the realities of what she presently faced having nearly destroyed her girlhood dreams. "I imagine even then happy endings were rare. Excuse me, but I desire a moment to myself."

"As you wish," he said, and she turned away from him.

Just in case intervention again became necessary, Ian kept a close vigil over her as she strolled along the line of carriages.

Something troubled her beyond her parents' deaths. Though possible, he doubted it had anything to do with her Irish bounder.

The fear she'd initially exhibited whenever he drew near had now vanished, yet intuitively he knew she still hid from him. She kept something secreted away in her heart, something that caused her great worry.

Concerned eyes fast upon her, Ian was determined to discover the source of her torment. His future happiness, he was now certain, depended upon it.

An hour later, the Whitcombs' carriage rolled to a stop in front of Sinclair House.

"Supper is at eight, Ian," Veronica said, releasing his arm. "We shall expect you by seven."

Ian rose from the seat. "I'm afraid I won't be coming by this evening." Stepping down from the vehicle, he extended his hand toward Leah. "I've decided to stay in. Please offer your parents my regrets."

As Leah slid across the leather, reaching for Ian's proffered hand, she felt Veronica's hard stare upon her. At a glance, she verified the sensation. Veronica's eyes sparked with displeasure. Trouble brewed. And Leah knew why:

After her brief walk alongside the carriages, the quiet interlude allowing her to calm her emotions, she'd returned to Ian's side, whereupon he guided her back across the green. Reaching the picnic site, he'd related Leah's near mishap to the Whitcombs, insisting they pack up and head back to London. Both brother and sister acceded to the earl's wishes, Veronica's assent coming with less verve than did Jonathan's. That the woman blamed Leah for this new shift in plans was most apparent.

"A bit late to be begging off now, isn't it?" Veronica asked, her tone showing annoyance.

"One dinner guest more or less won't throw havoc into the arrangements," he returned, steadying Leah as she descended from the carriage. "I apologize, but tonight I'm in the mood for solitude."

"Is that what you call it?"

With the innuendo, Ian felt Leah stiffen beside him. He smiled coolly. "Alone, in my study, attending to some financial matters, which I've neglected while here in London—yes, Veronica, I'd call that solitude. I'll see you in a day or two."

Tipping his hat, he turned and loped up the steps. Leah was already at the entry. "I fear she believes I am the reason you have changed your plans for this evening," Leah said, the carriage moving away from the curb.

Ian reached around her, his hand aiming for the doorknob. "Well, she's right."

CHAPTER
7

Leah stumbled over the threshold; deftly Ian caught her arm. "Easy does it," he said.

Again steady on her feet, she gaped at him as he directed her toward the stairs, then up them. "I don't understand why you would change your plans because of me."

"You don't?"

"No."

"I did so," he said when they reached the gallery, "because I'd rather spend my evening alone with you."

Leah blinked. "Your mother will be here, won't she?"

"Once she becomes immersed in one of her charitable activities, she has a tendency to lose track of time. So, I doubt she will."

Footsteps sounded in the sitting room across from where they stood. Certain the light taps belonged to the countess, Leah breathed a sigh of relief. She turned around, waiting for Madeline to appear. Her hopes plummeted when the butler loomed in the doorway, a potted plant in desperate need of water in his hands.

Noting the slump of her shoulders, Ian fought back a

chuckle. His mother wouldn't save her. No one would. "Simmons, has the countess returned yet?" he asked, wanting to prove his point.

The man peered around the drooping fronds. "No, sir, she hasn't. I believe she will be dining with the duchess."

"Then tell Cook to prepare a supper for two." Simmons nodded, and Ian looked down on Leah. "I'll see you at eight, Miss Kingsley."

"I'd rather take my meal in my room," she said to his back as he strode up the stairs.

"In the dining room at eight."

Her eyes narrowed on him. "I shan't be there," she insisted, moving to the first tread.

"Then you'll go hungry."

His words streamed down on her just as he disappeared from sight; Leah stamped her foot in frustration, then looked to the painting beside her. Dancing sapphire eyes perused her from inside the gilt frame. "What are you laughing at?" she snapped.

Lifting her skirt, she marched up the steps, vowing the portrait's subject would eat alone.

At a quarter past eight, Ian sat in the dining room, staring at the clock.

Stubborn little minx, he thought, certain by now her hunger would have driven her to the table. She'd picked at her fruit this morning, had eaten not a bite of their picnic, and now she refused supper. Did she abhor him so much that she'd rather starve than dine with him alone?

The clock continued to tick. Five minutes. Ten. Sighing heavily, Ian was about to relent and order a tray to be sent up to Leah when he saw a flash of color near the edge of the doorway. Grabbing hold of his wineglass, he struck a nonchalant pose. "Ah, Miss Kingsley," he said, saluting her once she stood fully in view. "It appears I've won out."

"My stomach won out," she grumbled, walking into the room. "Otherwise, I'd not be here."

Ian laughed, then rose from his chair. "Either way, you'll soon be savoring the very best."

His double-entendre must have escaped her, for no response came forth. Had she caught the dual meaning, she'd have bitten his head off.

Ian surveyed her as she moved toward him, the skirt of the green chiffon she wore rustling softly. Her unbound hair streamed past her bare shoulders and down to her waist, like waves of golden silk. *Stunning* was the word that came to mind. He wished they could always be thus—alone, together, wrapped in the glow of candlelight. One day he hoped it would be the flame of love enveloping them instead, but for now he'd settle for this.

Reaching Ian's side, Leah spied the warm glint in his eyes. Another message lay hidden in their marvelous depths, but as before, she was unable to catch its meaning. Nervously, she slipped into the chair he held for her.

"Wine?" he asked, lifting the bottle from the table.

"Please," Leah responded, then watched the rosy liquid flow into the crystal glass.

As he stood close beside her, looking the very image of his portrait, his clean masculine scent spun around her, then stole into her head, its effect making her dizzy. This would never do, she decided, then wondered why she'd been foolish enough to join him. But another look into his compelling eyes told her the answer.

An opiate—that was what he'd become to her. No matter how hard she fought against his magnetism or tried to deny the implication, she found she couldn't resist him.

His nearness left her feeling euphoric. That's why she'd stopped pacing the floor in her room, why she'd rung for Milly to assist her in dressing, and why she was now seated in the dining room. He'd become a *habit* she couldn't escape.

Leah vowed that Ian Sinclair would never know the full extent of her fascination with him. She prayed it was a promise that she could keep. To hope for anything of meaning to blossom between them was fruitless. The children were her primary concern. Her main focus must remain on their futures, not some fanciful daydreams about a man she barely knew. Besides she was a liar and a cheat, something he couldn't abide; while he, being part of the aristocracy, the same as her father, was someone she didn't know if she could fully trust.

Then there was the Lady Veronica.

The earl's affiliation with the woman, or his lack of, had Leah completely baffled. Did he or didn't he intend to marry Veronica? If he did, Leah felt it was very callous of him to be toying with her while all along being committed to another.

Still, if he were obligated, why then would he have broken off his supper engagement with the woman, moments later stating he'd done so because he preferred to spend his evening alone with her?

"Forgive the informality of my attire," Ian said, shifting from Leah's side and into his chair. He placed the wine bottle on the table. "I was in my study, attending to some book work. When I noticed the hour, there wasn't enough time for me to change."

Leah had the answer she sought. The earl's desire to stay in tonight had nothing to do with her. He'd said as much to Veronica. Financial matters—that had been his excuse.

"Perhaps I am the one who is dressed too formally," she said, masking her disappointment at learning the truth. Just why the knowledge bothered her, she couldn't say, especially when she knew there was no future for them. "The occasion, after all, is of no special consequence."

Ian eyed her a moment. Something nettled her, he decided. "Perhaps, Miss Kingsley," he countered, "the significance of this occasion is yet to be unraveled. Give it time, and maybe you'll discover its true purpose."

"Purpose?"

"Yes. Everything under heaven has a purpose, does it not?"

"I suppose."

Catching her questioning stare, Ian chuckled. "And right now, you're probably wondering about mine, correct?"

"It has crossed my mind," Leah said. "Should you care to tell me what it is, I'd be most grateful."

"Guessing games don't intrigue you, then?"

"Not in this case."

The connecting door to the kitchen swung wide. Pushing a serving trolley, Simmons angled himself toward the table.

"You'll discover the answer as to my purpose soon enough," Ian said, his man stopping beside him. Covered plates were placed atop the white linen tablecloth, first before Leah, then the earl. The butler lifted the silver domed lids, and a delectable aroma wafted into the air. "At present, we shall enjoy our meal," Ian finished, noting the faint rumble that emitted from Leah's stomach.

As soon as her napkin settled onto her lap, Leah retrieved her fork and quickly speared a succulent piece of lamb. Ian watched while she worked her way around her plate. Delight showed on her face as she relished each new taste.

After a few minutes, his laughter rolled forth. "And here I thought *I* was the one who enticed you down to the dining room. But from the looks of it, you *were* actually hungry."

The fork in Leah's hand stilled as she attended him. "I had said as much, didn't I?"

He feigned a wounded expression. "You did, but you could have pretended otherwise. A man doesn't like to think a woman prefers food above him."

"Her choice would probably depend on who the man is," she returned.

A silent curse rolled through Ian's mind. She referred to her Irish bounder no doubt. *Damn!* He'd make her forget him yet. "I guess it does. But, remember, Miss Kingsley, a determined man can always change a woman's mind." With that, he swilled his wine, then lifted his fork and attacked the food on his plate.

Studying him, Leah wondered at his swift change in mood, then she reviewed their last exchange. Anne's Irish lover—that's what set him off. Stunned, Leah believed his flare of temper stemmed from jealousy. Impossible. Veronica held his heart. If not his heart, then at least his promise they'd be wedded. Certain she'd misread him, she again began picking at her food.

The meal was finished in silence, their deserts hardly touched. Wine poured into their glasses, Ian insisting Leah imbibe. "Enough," she cried finally, her hand covering the crystal rim after her fourth glass.

The bottle settled on the table, and Ian leaned back in his chair. Rolling the stem of his own glass between his fingers and thumb, he stared at Leah. Damn, how he wanted her.

While they dined, he'd managed to calm himself. He'd been surprised by his quick display of anger. Not like him at all. Admittedly, though, no woman had ever excited his emotions as did Leah. Acting like a pouting schoolboy certainly wouldn't win her heart. Slow and sure, he needed to chip away at her reserve, retaining his composure as he did so. Else all would be lost.

"It won't be easy, old boy," he muttered under his breath.

"What?" Leah asked.

"I asked if you wanted to withdraw to the sitting room now that we are through here."

"I'd rather go up to my room."

His glass met the table. "The night is still young, Miss Kingsley," he said, rising from his chair. "We shall adjourn to the sitting room." He urged her away from the table. "Once there, we'll enjoy a quiet chat."

Leah's head swam a little as he escorted her from the dining room, along the gallery, and into the sitting room. Rightly, she blamed the wine. A giggle bubbled forth as she flopped down onto the settee.

Mirth sparkled in Ian's eyes as he stared down on her. She was soused, and with only four glasses. He watched as her cheeks suddenly flushed with color.

Leah waved her hand in front of her face, then bright green eyes looked up at him. "It's terribly warm in here, don't you think?"

"Not at all. However, if you are uncomfortable, perhaps some fresh air will help." He took hold of her hand and pulled her up from the settee. "Come along."

Once at the French doors, Ian drew them wide. The cool night air swept over Leah as she stepped onto the small balcony. She inhaled deeply while moving to the balustrade.

Partially closing the doors, Ian came up behind her. "Better?" he asked.

"Much," she said, feeling his presence at her back. She shivered slightly.

Ian noted the tiny tremor. "Now you're cold."

Separated by mere inches, the heat of his body radiated into her own. "Hardly," she replied. Nevertheless, his hands settled on her shoulders. Gently, he massaged them. Leah fought down the soft moan trembling in her throat, for his touch was magic. Swallowing hard, she looked out over the gardens, the area bathed by the light of a three-quarter moon. "I haven't had a chance to view your mother's flowers," she said, seeking to dispel the odd tingling inside her. "I imagine they are spectacular by day."

The sweet scent from the garden graced by a multitude of spring blossoms wafted up to the balcony. Above their fragrance stood Leah's own special womanly perfume. Ian's head was filled with her bouquet. "And by night, too," he uttered softly, his breath fanning her hair. He was surprised she allowed him so close. While he could, he meant to savor the moment. "You enjoy tending flowers, I suppose?"

Leah thought of the gardens at Balfour, where as a child she'd chased around the plants and shrubs, her siblings doing the same as each grew old enough to run and play. She missed the beauty and serenity of her home. But even more so, she longed to be with her brothers and sisters again. Tears gathered. She resisted their spilling over. Her throat clogging, she couldn't respond.

Instinctively, Ian knew something was wrong. "Leah?" He turned her toward him. Liquid eyes glittered up at him in the moonlight. "What is it, sweet? What troubles you so?"

Unable to withstand his gentle query or the tenderness in which he gazed down on her, Leah blurted out: "I'm homesick. Oh, God, how I miss them so." Then she fell against his chest to finally cry out her misery.

Sheltering Leah in his arms, Ian held her close. Light kisses rained atop her head as soothing words flowed from his lips. "Hush, little one," he rasped, his throat tightening as his heart absorbed her pain. "Time will heal the wound.

It's not easy to lose someone you love. I know this for a fact. You have your memories, Leah. Through those remembrances, you'll always be close to them, and they you."

Leah's sobs soon subsided. The once crisp curls peeking through the V of his shirtfront lay damp against her cheek. His skin felt warm and steamy. Drawing her head back, she noticed she'd soaked his chest. Embarrassment rippled through her. "I'm sorry. I didn't mean to drown you out."

An understanding smile played on his mouth as his hand met her jaw. Lightly his thumb wiped the remaining tears from one cheek. "There is nothing to be sorry about. You needed someone to hold and comfort you. I'm glad it was me." He tipped her chin a notch higher. "Feel better now?"

Her hands still rested against his solid chest, and she could feel the steadiness of his heartbeat. Gazing into his wondrous eyes, she was again mesmerized by this extraordinary man. "Yes."

As her answer came forth, his thumb brushed softly against her lower lip. "No more tears, then?" he asked.

She felt herself drawn closer to him by the arm that still held her. "No more tears."

"Is there anything else you need?" Her shoulders lifted a bit, indicating she didn't fully know, then Ian noticed how her attention had dropped to his mouth. "How about this?"

Leah saw his head move. Her eyelids fluttered closed. Briefly, tenderly, his lips touched hers. She was at once all hot and tingly inside. The feathery kiss over, Leah stood spellbound.

"Anything else?" he asked, reining in his masculine urges. *Say there is,* his heart begged.

Whether it was the wine or the man, or a combination of both, Leah found she couldn't resist his question. "Do that again."

Her name whispered around her, then his mouth covered hers fully, eager and searching. Leaning into him, Leah surrendered to his mastery. A soft moan rose from her throat as his tongue slipped lightly between her lips. On his gentle probe, she trembled against him.

Her body pressed so closely to his own, Ian felt the quivers running through her. Guilt racked him, yet his loins ached unmercifully. Plied with wine, her inhibition had fled. He'd taken advantage of her, but it couldn't be helped. God, how he wanted her. Still he feared her retribution.

Tearing his mouth from hers, his lips tracked across her cheek to her ear. "Are you sure this is what you desire, Leah? If not, tell me to stop."

Stop? Never, she thought. This was where she wanted to be, in his arms, so close to him, feeling safe and protected. The words telling him what she desired formed in her mind. They nearly met her tongue, when unbidden a picture of the orphanage, drab and cold, flashed through her mind.

"Will we ever leave this place, Leah?"

"Will this always be our home?"

Hope's and Kate's questions tore at Leah's heart. What had she been thinking? The children were her first concern, not her own frivolous wants.

Coming fully to her senses, she shoved against Ian's chest. "Let go of me," she demanded.

Frowning, Ian pulled back. "What's wrong?"

Leah noted his sudden confusion, but she cared little. She had to get away from him. "How dare you ply me with wine, then misuse me this way," she accused. With a final push, she stumbled away from him.

Ian reached out to her. "Leah, I assumed by your response that you wanted—"

"You assumed wrong," she snapped, cutting him off. She was now at the doors. "I know what I want, and it has nothing to do with you."

Light streamed onto the balcony as she pushed inside the sitting room. She gathered her skirt and ran to the opposite doors, Ian watching as she disappeared.

Closing his eyes, he sucked the night air into his lungs, trying to calm himself. What she wanted, he decided on releasing his breath, was her Irishman.

Upstairs, Leah slammed her bedroom door behind her.

Leaning back against the panel, she drew a cleansing breath to steady her nerves. The lamp burned low on the table near the window, and she looked about the room, searching for something to do. Anything to take her mind off what had just happened. Anything to erase Ian Sinclair from her thoughts.

There, in the center of her bed, she spotted a small package wrapped in silver paper and tied with green ribbon. In a few steps, Leah stood next to the offering, studying it closely. Finally, she snatched it up. The ribbon and paper fell away. Inside, she found the brooch she'd been admiring earlier in the day while at the marketplace. A card was enclosed with it.

Affectionately, Ian.

Both card and brooch in hand, Leah sank onto the mattress where she read the inscription again. What did this all mean? The card, the gift, and yes, the kiss—it was as though he were courting her.

Impossible.

Trying to make sense of it all, Leah warred with her own feelings. Surely she misread him. Veronica was to be his bride. But maybe not.

He'd denied his betrothal to Veronica, intimated that she may not be the next Countess of Huntsford, had even broken his supper engagement with the woman. But to what purpose? Leah wondered. So he could simply toy with her?

Thinking of her father, Leah knew she could never abide a man who played two women false. Still, where Ian was concerned, she didn't know what to believe.

Just now on the balcony, and while on the green at Kingston-upon-Thames, his concern seemed genuine as he'd consoled her, prompting her to confess her troubles. And his kiss—it bespoke a tender yet fervent passion that not only confused, but frightened her.

Admittedly, Leah feared that her father's deceit had ruined her ability to put her faith in any man, freely, wholly. But whether or not she could trust Ian wasn't the issue.

The children were her first concern. Because they were, her destiny was set. She had seen to that the moment she'd left York.

Fingers tracing the delicate craftsmanship of the brooch,

Leah blinked back her tears. She preferred to think that Ian's heart wasn't involved. Nothing good would come from his loving her or her loving him. She had deceived him, and in a few months, she'd be slinking off into the night, her ill-gotten savings tucked close. When he discovered her betrayal, his love—if he loved her at all—would fast turn to hate.

Regret filled her at the idea that he would someday despise her. Then an odd sensation settled in her chest. The feeling, Leah decided, was one of loss. Surely her own heart wasn't becoming involved. Tormented by the notion that she might be succumbing to Ian Sinclair's charms, she vowed not to yield any further. Somehow she had to keep him at bay.

With one last look, Leah closed her hand around the brooch, a replica of the twelfth-century Scottish original. He'd gone back for it, masking his purchase with mince pies. By doing so, Leah felt certain he was unsure of his own feelings. Still his kiss said otherwise.

Her teeth worried her lower lip as she rethought her decision. No. There was no future for them. She wrapped the brooch and card back in the paper, then bounding from the bed, stored it with the few pieces of jewelry belonging to the real Anne Kingsley. Afterward, Leah readied herself for bed.

Lying in the dark, she kept reaffirming her decision, repeating it over and over in her mind: *no future, no future, no future.*

Why then, did she feel so miserable at knowing there wasn't?

CHAPTER
8

A week later, a frustrated Ian sat in his study. Steepled fingers patted lightly against his lips as he leaned back in his chair. His brow shadowed, he thought about Leah, something he did continually. Since their shared kiss, she had made it clear: She wanted nothing to do with him. Totally, fully, she'd rejected him.

At breakfast, just hours after she'd fled the balcony, he had entered the dining room, wondering what her mood would be. Her reaction was just as he'd feared. Leah was distinctly cool.

On his attempt at conversation, she'd answered politely, but reservedly. By dinner she'd ignored him altogether, opting to speak to his mother exclusively. Supper had been a complete disaster. Afterward, when he caught her at the foot of the stairs, and wanted to question her, to apologize, she'd brushed past him to seek the privacy of her room, her firm "good night" ringing in his ears.

And so the days went. Aloof silence now greeted him at every turn. Nothing he said or did could crack her icy facade. Ian cursed himself, knowing he'd moved too fast.

She'd accused him of taking advantage of her at a time when she'd been most vulnerable. In actuality, he had.

Damn his luck! Had he tempered his desire and taken things more slowly, Leah might still be speaking to him, even warming to his subtle overtures. But no. He had to charge her as though he were a bull in rut. Not surprisingly, she'd bolted.

Still, something troubled him.

At first, he believed Leah's dash from the balcony was because of her Irishman. But, as the days had passed, one question kept running through his mind: Why would a woman who was in love with one man respond to another's kiss as freely and as eagerly as Leah did to his?

Likewise, one response kept coming forth: She wouldn't. Not if she were really in love.

Something else made her run. But what?

A knock sounded on the door. "Come," he said, sitting forward. The panel opened, and Milly's face appeared. "Close it." He inclined his head toward the door once she stepped into the room. The latch clicked to, the maid walking toward him. "The gift for Miss Kingsley—are you certain you did as I had instructed?"

"Yes, sir," she said, stopping in front of his desk. "But I already told you that."

"Well, tell me again," he snapped, then watched as the maid's eyes widened. "Just repeat what you told me, Milly. I want to make certain I understood you correctly."

"Like I said before, I placed the package in the center of her bed, the way you told me I should."

"Do you know if she opened it?"

"I don't know for certain, sir. It's been a week. I haven't seen it since. She's got it tucked away somewhere, I guess. But I'll tell you again the same as I did when you first questioned me: The next morning, I found a green ribbon on the floor by her bed when I straightened up her room. It looked like the one tied around the package you gave me. I suppose she opened it."

"Thank you, Milly. That will be all."

With a quick curtsy, the maid retraced her steps, the door closing behind her as she left the study.

Maybe not all was lost, Ian thought, promising himself he'd not question Milly again. At least Leah hadn't tossed the brooch back in his face. Not yet, anyway.

Leaning back in his chair anew, he rested his head against the rich leather. With splayed fingers, he massaged his forehead as he pondered the rare beauty whose reservedness constantly tormented him. Bright, witty, independent—this was Leah. Soft, innocent, alluringly feminine—this, too, was Leah. She was totally unimpressed with his title and his wealth, just as she was totally unimpressed with him.

Damnation! He'd waited all his life to find a woman such as her, only to discover she didn't want him.

Untrue, he decided, remembering again her ardent response to his kiss. She felt the same stirrings of desire as he. She must have. Wanting her as he did, Ian refused to believe anything less.

Another light rap sounded on the door. Ian viewed the panel in anticipation. "Enter." Disappointment streaked through him as his mother's face peered around the wood.

"Are you busy?" she asked, coming into the room.

"No—not at the moment."

"I was wondering if you planned to use the carriage anytime soon."

"I have a business appointment at one-thirty."

"Oh."

"If you need the carriage, Mother, use it. I can always take the phaeton."

"It's not for me, but for Leah."

Ian frowned. "And why does Miss Kingsley need the carriage?"

"She has asked to go to the couturière's. She has a dress she needs altered, and I believe the last of her gowns are ready, too."

"I take it you won't be going with her."

"I have some things I need to attend to," his mother said.

"Then send Milly with her."

"I need Milly here," Madeline informed him. "I thought

since Leah is only going to Madam Lejeune's that it would be perfectly all right for Ferguson to accompany her. It will be just this one time."

"As long as he keeps an eye on her, and doesn't take her anywhere but the couturière's, I see no harm."

"I had hoped you'd say that."

Madeline continued to linger; Ian noted her meditative look. "You seem pensive, Mother. Is there something else you need?"

"Actually there is." She sat down in the chair opposite him. "I've just received word from your great aunt Augusta. She's taken a nasty fall. At first, the doctor feared that she'd broken her leg, but apparently she'd simply wrenched her knee."

As the words came across his desk, Ian grew wary. "So?"

"So I'm very concerned about her."

"God only knows why."

"Ian! Hold your tongue," his mother admonished. "She is a blood relative."

"I apologize. But she is not exactly a favorite of mine."

"I know she can be overbearing at times."

"An understatement, madam."

Exasperation showing on her face, Madeline drew a deep breath. "Nonetheless, I'm most concerned about her. She has managed to outlive all her loyal servants. Those who are now in her employ don't appear very eager to stay with her for long."

"Given her disposition, can you blame them?" Ian eyed his mother. "Just what is it you're asking?"

"Considering her age and condition, plus the fact that I'm not certain she's being cared for properly, I believe we have two options here."

Madeline's gaze fell from Ian's. He watched as her fingers played with a crease in her skirt. "I'm listening, Mother."

"Either we can send round for her and have her come up to London for a while, or I can go down to Bath for a week or so."

"As I see it, Mother, there is only one option. You may begin packing immediately."

"I knew that would be your response."

"Then why did you ask?"

Blue eyes snared him. "My leaving creates another problem, sir."

Ian's eyebrow shot up in query.

"You and Leah shall be alone in the house," she said.

He'd been so determined to keep the cantankerous Augusta away from Sinclair House, Ian hadn't thought about his being solely with Leah. Reminded of such, he nearly leapt from his chair and sprang hand-to-foot around the room. "We are a bit short-staffed, but with just over a half dozen servants running about the place—Simmons, in particular—I'd hardly say we'd be alone," he declared, containing his excitement. His mother off in Bath, he felt certain he could break through Leah's frigid veneer. There would be no one to interfere.

"But there will be talk, Ian."

"Then don't tell anyone outside this house you're leaving."

"I suppose that might work. But Leah and I are expected at the Delderfields' next week. I doubt I'll be back by then. I'd managed to finagle an invitation for her—you know how difficult they are to come by—and I've already sent word we'll be there. If Leah were to show alone—"

"She can arrive with me," he interrupted. "The Whitcombs and I are planning to attend. Our acceptances have already been sent. I see no reason why we can't make it a foursome. As for your not making an appearance, I'll simply tell anyone who asks that you've taken to your bed with a minor malady of some sort."

"Then you don't mind Leah's coming with you?"

"Certainly not, Mother. She is more than welcome."

"Thank you, son," she said, rising from the chair. "I knew I could count on you. I'll tell Leah that I will be leaving on the morrow."

Ian surveyed her as she headed toward the door. She suddenly turned.

"You will keep watch over her for me?" she asked.

"Should this young man, whom John abhors, so much as makes an appearance—"

"I'll guard her even unto my very last breath, Mother. Have no fear, she'll be kept under my closest care. I promise." Ian thought his mother looked hesitant, but then, with a smile, she left the room. "The very closest care."

The countess was deserting her.

In utter misery, Leah traveled inside the carriage as it wended along the streets toward the couturière's. How on earth was she going to continue to fend off the earl with his mother away in Bath?

As it was, she didn't know how much longer she could hold on. Whenever he approached her, she was purposely cold. So far the tactic had worked. But one sultry look, one warm touch, and her shield of ice would melt. Without Madeline there for her to hide behind, she'd be left completely vulnerable.

"Miss?"

Pulled from her preoccupation, Leah saw Ferguson standing beside the carriage. They had arrived at Madame Lejeune's. Surprised by the fact, she lowered her parasol and clutched Anne's dress close. Hidden inside its folds were her siblings' gifts and letters, all wrapped and addressed, for Sally to post.

"Thank you," she said, once she'd stepped out onto the sidewalk, Ferguson's steadying hand aiding her. "I shouldn't be too long."

"I shall wait for you here, Miss," he returned.

"I expected as much," she fairly snapped, then felt instantly contrite. It wasn't Ferguson with whom she was angry, but his employer.

While Leah headed toward the shop's door, she remembered how Lord Huntsford had loped down the steps at Sinclair House just as Ferguson was about to guide the carriage away from the curb.

"I know you were already given your instructions, Ferguson," he'd said, pointedly looking at Leah. "But I thought I might repeat them, so there won't be any mistakes. Miss Kingsley is to be taken straight to the couturière's and straight home. There will be no detours along the way. You will also wait for her in front of the shop. Is that clear?"

"Yes, sir," his coachman had responded. "Quite clear."

"Good," the earl had announced. He then grinned. "Have a pleasant little journey, Miss Kingsley."

After a slight bow, he loped back up the steps and into the house.

Where did he think she'd dash off to? Leah wondered as she opened the door. The bell jingled, announcing her arrival. With Madame Lejeune inside the shop, and Ferguson at the front door, there would be little chance of her escaping the premises without one of them seeing and reporting it.

"Ah, Miss Kingsley," the proprietress declared in her familiar French accent, "you have come for your gowns. And I see you have brought a dress to be altered. You've changed your mind then, no?"

Madame Lejeune stood only a few feet away from Leah. As she'd spoken, she drew on her gloves. A bonnet graced her head, her reticule dangled from her wrist. "Apparently, I've come at a bad time," Leah said, certain the woman was on her way out.

"No, never. I have an appointment to keep, but Sally is here. She will see to your needs. If you don't mind, that is?"

Leah felt relieved. She wasn't quite sure if she could pass the two packages to Sally, along with the cost of the postage, without Madame Lejeune noticing. "Since you have taken Sally into your employ, her skills can be nothing less than exceptional. Go along to your appointment. You don't want to be late."

"You are most kind, Miss Kingsley. And very understanding. Some of my clients, I fear, are too demanding. They expect me to take every measurement, from neck to hem, then want me to sew every stitch. They do not understand that my talent lies in the designing of the gowns they wear. One would think they would realize I had graduated from a mere seamstress long ago."

"One would think," Leah returned with a smile.

"Sally." At the couturière's call, the young woman came rushing from the back room. "Miss Kingsley has come for her new gowns. She also has a dress to be altered. Attend to her, please. I shall be back in an hour or so." She looked to Leah. "Good day, Miss Kingsley. I hope to see you again, soon."

Once the couturière left the shop, the bell tinkling in her wake, Leah turned to Sally. "I'm glad we are alone, Sally. Again I need to ask a favor of you."

"You want another letter posted, right?"

"Actually, I have two packages that need posting." She slipped them from inside the gown's folds and handed them to Sally.

"This one's to your beau. But the other is to an orphanage," Sally said, frowning. "The last name is the same as your Terence's."

Leah felt she should give Sally some sort of explanation. Still she couldn't very well tell her the full truth. "Terence's parents are both dead. Because of financial circumstances, he was unable to care for his siblings, hence they were all placed in an orphanage. I bought each of the children a gift, hoping to lift their spirits. Only through you am I able to make certain they will receive their presents."

"I understand, and I'll be glad to post these for you." Sally paused, then asked, "Is that why they won't let you see Terence—because he's poor?"

Sally's annoyed tone wasn't lost on Leah. "Yes," she said, feeling more than a bit guilty. Still, she had little choice but to lie. "Terence's social standing is why I am—"

Leah swallowed her words as the door opened, the bell sounding loudly. A rather plump woman ambled into the shop, demanding to see the couturière. When Sally informed her that Madame Lejeune was out at the moment, the woman screeched her dismay. The side-seam of the gown she wanted to wear to a social event that night was ripped, and she needed it fixed immediately.

"With all I need to attend to, I have no time to spare. I must have the repair done now!" the woman shrieked.

Sally hesitated. "See to her needs, Sally," Leah declared, then grasped the packages.

"But you were here, first."

"I am in no hurry. I'll simply browse while I wait."

"Thank you, my dear girl," the woman chimed. "You are most generous."

While Sally assisted the woman, Leah turned toward a rack of fabric. A bolt of black crepe caught her eye. If she were still in York, she'd be dressed in mourning. She'd also be washing dishes, scrubbing pots and pans, and fending off her former employer's lecherous advances. But she was here, in London, in the guise of Anne Kingsley. And she was nearly the length of England away from her siblings.

She thought about Arthur Covington.

How very unfair that he should live so well, his family drawn close to him as he dealt with his grief. Growing resentful, Leah wondered why he should be afforded such comfort while she was being denied the same. What made his family better than hers?

Anger swelled inside Leah. Maybe it was time that she confronted Arthur, told him who she was, then under the threat of exposure, demand he assist the Daltons.

Eighteen Hanover Square.

As the address repeated itself in Leah's mind, the bell sounded again. She glanced at the door. The plump woman, her blue gown draped over her arm, exited the shop. "That was fast," Leah commented when the shop girl had reached her side.

"If she wouldn't try to stuff herself into a size smaller than what she wears, her seams would hold just fine. Now, Miss," Sally said, taking hold of Anne's gown, "let's head on back to the fitting room and see what we can do with this dress."

"Never mind about an actual fitting. An inch less on both sides will do just fine," Leah told her while eyeing Ferguson through the front window. He stood facing the shop, just as his employer had ordered. Promptly, Leah fished in her reticule. "Here is the money for the postage." She handed Sally the two packages, along with several coins. "Tell me, is there a door that leads out the back?"

"Yes. It opens into the delivery yard. Why?"

"Do you know where Hanover Square is?" she asked, ignoring Sally's question.

"Sure. It's only a few blocks from here.

Leah sighed with relief. "I need another favor from you. There is something I must do, and since I'm watched constantly, this might be my only chance. First, I'll need directions from the delivery yard to Hanover Square. Second, should this venture take a bit longer than expected, and should the gentleman by the carriage come inside to inquire about me, I'll need you to intercede. Are you willing to assist me?"

"I don't see no reason why I shouldn't."

"If we get caught, it could mean your job."

"Not if I tell whoever asks that you slipped out the back when I wasn't lookin'."

"You are very wise, Sally. Still, should something happen, you'd be even wiser to act as though you are unaware of anything that has passed between us. I say this more for your protection than mine."

"I understand, Miss."

After receiving the directions, Leah followed Sally to the rear of the shop. "Thank you. You are truly priceless." Then she was out the back door.

Quickly she wended her way through the delivery yard, dodging wagons and horses as she went. Soon she was on a side street. At a fast clip, she made her way to Hanover Square, her parasol shielding her face.

Looking at the resplendent three-story brick structure, draped in black crepe and bearing the number *eighteen*, Leah was well aware that Arthur's life had been filled with far more prosperity than her own. But had he been happy?

That, and a thousand other questions filled her head. Before she lost her nerve, she strode the walkway to the front door, but just as she reached for the knocker, another question flitted through her mind.

What if Arthur refused to be blackmailed and had his half-sister arrested instead?

A man of Arthur's social status had power. An influential

word and a few gold sovereigns from Lord Covington to the gaoler, and Leah might never find her way from the depths of Newgate Prison, not even to stand trial.

Her fingertips skimmed the smooth brass ring, but suddenly she jerked her hand from the knocker as though it had burned her. Leah knew she risked too much by facing Arthur this way. Lifting her skirt, she turned on her heel and rushed from the entry, back toward the street.

In disbelief, she heard the door open behind her, and she wondered if she had accidentally let the knocker fall. "Miss?" a male voice questioned, but Leah refused to look back.

"Who is it, Crenshaw?" another man asked.

To Leah's ears this voice sounded far younger. *Arthur.* She dashed pell-mell toward Oxford Street and the delivery yard behind Madame Lejeune's.

When she reached the intersection, Leah scanned the traffic. Vehicles moved in a steady flow in both directions. At last there was a break, and she hurried to the opposite sidewalk, then down the narrow street, heading for the yard's entry.

Oddly, a niggling sensation followed her all the way to Madame Lejeune's back door. Then Leah remembered the scene on Oxford Street. Among the wagons, hackney cabs, and carriages that clogged the roadway in the distance, a lone phaeton loomed in her mind's eye. Her stomach gripped in fear as she realized what had been troubling her.

In that mass of vehicles, she felt certain she saw Ian Sinclair.

Having returned from the couturière's several hours ago, Leah stood to one side of Madeline's bedroom, thinking about the earl. On her way from Madame Lejeune's back door to the front, she'd informed Sally she had no time to talk. Her new gowns were boxed and waiting, and on gathering them up, she was quickly out the entrance and into the carriage. After arriving at Sinclair House, she'd learned that Ian was indeed out. He had a business appointment and had taken the phaeton.

Pray he hadn't seen her, Leah thought, then doubted he had. Otherwise he'd have been here long ago, his angry accusations raining down on her like hailstones in a summer storm.

As Leah watched the proceedings around her, the countess instructing Milly on what clothing was to be packed for her trip to Bath, she felt not only nervous but dispirited as well. Why did the countess have to leave her?

"Add my black crepe in with the other dresses, Milly," Madeline said, then turned to Leah. "Even after six years, Augusta thinks I should still be draped in mourning." She tapped her finger against her upper lip. "Never mind, Milly. Put the crepe back into the cupboard. If I take something black, my aunt will insist I wear it daily." Her bubbling laughter climbed into the air as she again looked at Leah. "Without the crepe, I can wear whatever I wish."

Leah noted the mischievous sparkle in the countess's eyes. For a moment, she felt as though she were gazing at the woman's son. "Is your aunt really so unconscionable?" she asked, then spied Madeline's surprised stare. "I mean— well, you said the earl won't allow her in the house."

"Ian would definitely call her unconscionable, and he very well might be right. But I prefer to call her quaint. It sounds far more flattering."

"I take it, then, they don't get along well at all," Leah said.

"Get along well?" Madeline asked, appearing stunned. "Let me put it this way, dear. Whenever the two are together in the same room, each sits with a dueling pistol, primed and ready, within hand's reach. Were they in opposite rooms, they'd be firing cannon balls across the hall, attempting to fell the other first. That is why Ian spends most of his time at Falcon's Gate, and Augusta stays in Bath. At that distance, neither one can harm the other."

"And that is why you are going there, instead of your aunt coming here. Are you certain I cannot accompany you? I might be of some help, especially if your aunt is short on staff."

"I'd very much enjoy having you along, Leah. But Augusta is—well, Augusta is Augusta. I fear she might not be very tolerant of a stranger in her home. Besides, you are expected at the Delderfields' next week."

"I'd rather not go since you won't be there."

"Nonsense. Ian has offered to escort you. Veronica and Lord Whitcomb will be in attendance also It won't be as though you don't know anyone. You should have a grand time with Ian and the Whitcombs there."

"I suppose," Leah said, sounding disinterested.

"The Delderfields are very selective in who is allowed at their parties. I was able to arrange this invitation for you, so I shall expect you to attend. Don't disappoint me, Leah. They are expecting you. I know you will enjoy yourself. I want you to wear the amethyst silk. You'll be positively stunning in it."

The woman stepped closer to her, then pulled Leah aside. They stopped a few feet from the open door which led into the hallway.

"While you are out and about, I ask that you don't mention to anyone I'm not at Sinclair House," Madeline said in a low voice. "Should someone discover such, there will undoubtedly be talk."

"Talk?" Leah asked.

"Yes, dear. Talk. Ian and you will be alone in the house. Although I trust my son fully, I hesitated about leaving you here unchaperoned—especially for the length of time I expect to be gone. But considering Augusta's disposition, I have little choice. Just keep quiet about my not being here, and there shouldn't be any gossip."

The magnitude of the countess's departure hadn't fully hit Leah until now. She knew she and Ian would be alone at Sinclair House, but she hadn't actually considered what *alone* meant. With Madeline gone, there would be no one to protect her, no one to act as a buffer between them. She wasn't altogether certain she could continue to resist Ian. Her aloofness might fade into acceptance. Then what? Apparently her misgivings showed on her face.

"Don't fret, dear. I'll be back within two weeks. Besides, Ian has assured me he will watch over you."

"I believe my exact words were 'kept under my closest care.'"

Hearing the familiar voice, Leah whirled around to see Ian lounging against the doorframe. Handsome as ever, he was dressed in evening attire. She stood stunned, for she hadn't known he was home. Quickly, she searched his face, hoping to gauge his mood. No accusation sparked in his sapphire eyes, and she breathed a sigh of relief. Still she remained wary.

"Miss Kingsley," he greeted her, then turned his attention to Madeline. "I'll be leaving for the evening. Is there anything you need, Mother, before I go?"

"I don't think so, son. Everything seems to be under control. Where will you be off to? It's still early."

"Eventually, I'll end up at the opera. But first I plan to eat a light supper somewhere, then stop by White's for a bit."

"I take it, then, Veronica isn't going along," Madeline said.

"No, I'm going it alone. Unless, of course, Miss Kingsley would like to join me? White's isn't a necessary stop."

Trapped under his constant stare, Leah grew quite nervous. "I think not," she blurted out.

"A pity. You'll miss a highly acclaimed opera. It's a wonderful little tale about love and lust, lies and betrayal. I think you'd enjoy it, Miss Kingsley."

At his words, Leah's insides trembled. Had he seen her after all? Again she studied him. Then on drawing a calming breath, she realized anything the earl said might be easily misconstrued, a result of her own guilt. "No thank you," she returned finally, her manner reserved.

"Perhaps it is just as well. The ending is exceptionally bleak."

"Then doubly no. Life is depressing enough without adding to it. Besides, I had planned to help your mother with her packing."

"Nonsense, dear," Madeline piped in. "Milly and I can see to the packing." She looked at Ian. "Isn't there a lighthearted play you could see instead? Perhaps Leah would enjoy that more."

"I'm certain there is something that would give us both a great deal of enjoyment. However, it is up to Miss Kingsley whether or not she wishes to be daring enough to search it out."

By his rapt regard, Leah doubted he'd been referring to the theater or the opera. "I really would rather stay in tonight," she said, then turned to Madeline. "If you don't mind, I'd like to spend my evening with you."

"How thoughtful of you, dear. But I don't want you to stay in if you'd actually prefer to go out."

Ian shoved himself away from the doorframe. "I believe Miss Kingsley has made her choice, Mother. There will be other evenings after you've gone. I'm certain I'll be able to talk her into being adventuresome—at least on one of those nights."

"Well, if you should take her to Covent Garden or Drury Lane, make certain she comes to no harm," Madeline instructed, then viewed Leah. "The criminal element in that area is most appalling. If you go, take nothing of value with you. And watch your reticule. Cutpurses are everywhere. That is what Ian means by being adventuresome."

Leah saw the mirthful challenge in his eyes. Rubbish! That's not what he meant at all.

Ian chuckled. "I've sworn to keep her in my closest care, Mother. And that I shall. Good evening, ladies. I'll see you tomorrow."

Leah listened as his footsteps carried him down the hallway to the stairs. She was now certain he hadn't seen her on the street, but it was obvious that once his mother was gone he planned to seduce her.

Lord Almighty! At once Leah considered falling on her knees and begging the countess to stay. But, were she to do so, she feared the repercussions nearly as much as she feared being alone with the earl.

The woman trusted her son fully, had said so herself. On Leah's entreaty, the question would arise as to why Leah insisted that the countess must stay. She'd have little choice but to reveal the truth about the kiss she and Ian had shared.

Posthaste, a chaperon would be hired, a hotel room let, Leah ensconced quickly within. Undoubtedly, the countess would retain control of the money sent by John Kingsley for his niece's care, paying for the erroneous Anne's expenditures as the accounts came due. Her allowance would be severed. What little savings Leah had managed to squirrel away so far was well below the amount needed to enact her plan. She had no alternative. No matter how much the prospect of being isolated inside this large house with the woman's son alarmed her, she had to keep silent.

Why, she wondered, couldn't good fortune shine upon her at least once?

In short order, the countess finished instructing Milly on what should be packed. With the maid left to finish up, she and Leah retired to the dining room where they ate a light supper. As Madeline regaled her on Augusta and Ian's warlike temperaments, Leah found herself understanding why the earl desired to keep his great aunt at bay. The pair's militant behavior took the form of verbal sparring more than that of hand-to-hand combat. However, according to Madeline, Augusta wasn't averse to attacking with her cane, if the opportunity presented itself. To keep from strangling her, Ian forbade the woman's visiting Sinclair House whenever he was in residence. She was never allowed at Falcon's Gate.

"Have they always been at loggerheads?" Leah found herself asking.

"No, not always. Ian never considered Augusta his favorite, but at one time, he was most civil to her, and she to him. Their feud started when Ian was four-and-twenty. Intent on making a match between her oldest friend's granddaughter and Ian, Augusta had invited both families to her home in Bath. Her plan was unknown to us at first, but it quickly became apparent what she was up to.

"After being introduced to Agnes Crenshaw, the daughter of Sir Robert Crenshaw, with much ado from Augusta about how very charming Agnes was, Ian remained very polite to the girl, but he held no interest in her. I cannot say I blame him. Though she was quite fair of face, her intellect was a bit on the short side. Flighty is how I'd describe her, and her constant giggling nearly drove everyone mad.

"Anyway, as a result, Ian could barely abide her, but Agnes was quite taken with him. Apparently, she had enough sense to know things weren't going well between them. She maneuvered Ian into what is known as a compromising position, making certain they'd be caught. Agnes's father, seconded by her grandfather, insisted they be married at once. Ian refused, and Adrian—that was Ian's father—backed him. Both families were at a stalemate. Then it was decided that Agnes and Ian were to be stringently questioned.

"Ian held to his story, vowing he'd been set up. Agnes, however, could not withstand the duress. She caved in and confessed she'd tried to trap Ian in marriage. Embarrassed, Agnes's family left Augusta's house. Apparently, they blamed my aunt for the entire episode. They've never had contact with her again. Although Ian was cleared of any wrongdoing, Augusta refused to believe he was innocent. She's been on the attack ever since."

"How very awful for your son," Leah said, thinking she understood why he'd been so protective of her while on the balcony at the Carstairses'. Or was it of himself? "Does the earl believe the situation occurred because of Augusta's prompting?"

"I'm not certain what Ian thinks about the matter. He never speaks of it. However, though Augusta may have encouraged Agnes to give chase, I doubt very much she suggested the girl climb into bed with Ian in the middle of the night. Augusta is too straitlaced for that."

Leah blinked. "Climb into bed with him? Didn't he try to toss her out?"

"That's precisely what he was about when her father came storming into his bedroom. His head dulled with sleep, he didn't have enough wits about him to leap from the bed when he found her beside him—which I doubt would have changed anything much. Instead, he tried to shove her off the opposite side of his bed. From what I was told, by the position of his body, it appeared as though he were attempting to make love to the girl."

"I don't understand," Leah said. "If it was the middle of the night, how could Agnes possibly ensure they'd be caught?"

"It was a ritual with her mother to check in on her at precisely two o'clock each morning. Agnes's father burst into Ian's room at five minutes past the hour. Needless to say, none of us got much sleep from that moment on until the situation was finally resolved."

"Perhaps Agnes wasn't as doltish as everyone believed," Leah said. "Had she a bit more mettle, the outcome might have gone the other way. The earl may have been forced to marry her."

"Ian would never have done so. He cannot be *forced* into anything—ever. Believe me. I know my son."

"Whatever happened to Agnes?"

"For the price for her deceit, I understand she is forever repentant. Her father placed her into a convent. She is now an Anglican nun."

Would that the price of her own deceit be just as merciful, Leah thought, certain, if she were ever discovered, her payment wouldn't be a nunnery, but the gallows. "A fitting punishment, I suppose, as well as a lesson learned."

"Assuredly, Sister Agnes won't attempt to trap a man again," Madeline said, her laughter rising. "As for Ian, he has become most cautious. Never will you find him in the company of an unattached female alone. If someone did, it would mean he is exceptionally interested in the young woman, possibly even to the point of wanting to marry her. That is why I cannot understand his and Veronica's relationship. Whenever they are together here at Sinclair House, he has yet to walk with her alone in the gardens. They've never gone onto the balcony, seeking privacy and solitude. It makes me wonder if he's even kissed her." Madeline sighed. "Oh, well, if Veronica is his choice, I shall abide by his decision."

Leah was confused. Surely, his mother was mistaken in her assessment of her son. Cautious, yes, but he was also excessively bold. His kiss attested to a wealth of experience, something a novice could hardly demonstrate. He had to have been alone with the opposite sex to become as adept as he was with his lips. Renewed delight spiraled through Leah as she remembered their supple mastery, and the feelings they evoked. Immediately, she took command of her senses; the warmth inside her faded. As Leah gauged the countess, she felt certain that Madeline's knowledge of her son was indeed limited. Disunity over what the countess had said must have manifested itself on her face, for the woman's next words surprised Leah.

"I don't mean to suggest my son is inexperienced, Leah. We both know that men have certain needs. There are women who are willing to accommodate the male gender in such cases. That type of woman a man seldom marries. It is the kind of woman a man marries who Ian shuns. Because of Agnes, he fears being trapped. Mark my words: Unless he cares for the young lady, and deeply, he'd never place himself in a situation that might be misinterpreted. In that area, he's most hesitant."

With Leah he wasn't the least bit hesitant. Not once, but twice he'd secreted himself on the balcony with her. Had kissed her passionately the second time. Leah questioned whether such actions meant he truly held feelings for her, possibly desired that someday she'd be his wife.

Affectionately, Ian.

The inscription on the card accompanying the brooch again imprinted itself in her mind. If things were different, she'd be more than eager to accept him as a suitor. Even more so as a mate. It was impossible, though. That's why she'd been so standoffish the week through.

Besides, since seeing him only a short while ago, Leah wasn't fully certain Ian Sinclair hoped to court her. He could very well be toying with her. To stroke his vanity, perhaps he wanted to engage in one last flirtation before he married the Lady Veronica. And despite what his mother said, Leah doubted he was averse to doing anything that might be misunderstood. He was too sure of himself, and like Madeline said, he could not be forced. To prove the point, he possibly conspired to secrete himself on every available balcony in London with whatever young virgin was at hand, daring her to cry foul. Leah may have been only one of many.

"I think I shall retire early," Madeline said, their desserts finished. "I need to fortify myself for what is to come. Augusta has a way of reducing my stamina. Are you headed upstairs? Or do you wish to linger in the sitting room for a while?"

"I believe I also shall retire for the night," Leah said, hoping to fortify herself as well. Dreading what lay ahead after the countess had left Sinclair House, Leah followed the woman from the dining room and up the steps. Once outside her own room, Leah hugged Madeline. "I shall miss you."

"And I shall miss you, dear. But not to worry. I am leaving you in capable hands. Ian will be most attentive to you. I'm certain you'll enjoy his company." She patted Leah's hand. "It grows late. I'll see you in the morning."

Imploringly, Leah watched as the countess made her way to her door. Still she managed to keep silent. After the woman disappeared into her room, she entered her own.

Much later, as she lay cuddled in her bed, she stared through the darkness, unable to sleep. She heard the clock in the gallery strike the hour of two. Soon afterward, Ian Sinclair's footsteps sounded along the hallway. As he passed by her room, the countess's words streaked through her head.

I am leaving you in capable hands. Ian will be most attentive to you.

That, Leah determined on a groan, the door opening and closing not far from her own, was exactly what she feared.

CHAPTER
9

By eleven the next morning, the countess was on her way to Bath. A jittery Leah stood on the sidewalk, the earl beside her. As the carriage turned the corner and disappeared from sight, Leah resisted the urge to chase after it. Without the countess to protect her, she felt certain her fate was fixed.

No sooner had one vehicle vanished than another appeared at the entrance to Berkley Square. When it rounded the corner, coming from the opposite direction the countess had taken, Ian swore soundly. Startled, Leah gazed up at him.

"I forgot Veronica and Jonathan were coming by," he said in way of explanation, then smiled at the couple as their carriage stopped at the curb.

"Good morning. Where is your mother off to?" Veronica asked.

"To her couturière's."

"To a friend's."

The answers erupted from Leah and Ian simultaneously. Veronica stared at them. "Well, which is it?"

"Actually both," Ian responded in haste, taking the lead.

"She has a fitting, then will be traveling on to a friend's, where she is spending the day."

"I see," Veronica said, apparently satisfied with the explanation. "Are you ready, Ian? We don't want to miss the first race."

"We'll be with you in a moment." From the corner of his eye, he spied Leah's swift glance. "We shouldn't be long."

Veronica quickly looked at Leah. "I hadn't expected Miss Kingsley to join us."

"Whether or not it was expected, she is doing so."

Leah frowned up at Ian. This was all news to her. "I can easily stay here," she stated, hoping to disengage herself from the group. At the moment, she wanted to be away from them all, the earl especially.

"Nonsense," Jonathan piped in. "You are more than welcome to join us."

"It is settled, then," Ian announced firmly. "We'll be back in a moment." Taking hold of Leah's arm, he urged her up the steps and into the house.

"I don't wish to go," Leah insisted in a low voice, the front door still standing wide.

"But you are," Ian countered, keeping a firm grip on her. "Milly," he said, spotting the maid as she came from the rear of the house, feather duster in hand. "Fetch Miss Kingsley's bonnet, gloves, wrap, and parasol, will you?"

"Yes, sir." Catching up her skirt, Milly scurried up the stairs.

"I can get my own things," Leah snapped.

"And chance that you'll lock yourself in your room?" he asked. "Oh, no, Miss Kingsley. I don't have time to search out the keys, then drag you from your hiding place. Milly can get your things while you remain here."

"I don't see why I need to go along. Your plans were with the Whitcombs. Obviously, I wasn't included."

"You are now."

"Why?"

"I cannot keep an eye on you when I'm at the Bayswater Hippodrome and you are here."

"It's not necessary for you to watch me every minute of the day," she insisted.

"Oh, but it is. I promised my mother I'd keep you in my closest care. And that I shall." When Milly returned, he took the lavender bonnet that matched the day dress Leah wore from the maid's hands. Settling the thing on Leah's head, he skillfully looped the long ribbons around each other. With a tug, a perfect bow lay slanted against her left cheek. "Stop pouting, Leah. I promise you'll enjoy yourself. How about a smile?"

"Stop treating me as you would a child," she said, swatting his hands away from her face. She pulled on her gloves, afterward accepting her parasol, shawl, and reticule from Milly, the last article the maid apparently having remembered on her own. "And I might have something to smile about," she finished.

Ian gathered his top hat, gloves, and walking cane from the stand near the door. "When I treat you as a woman, as I did a week past, you don't seem to appreciate that either." Instant color streaked her cheeks; low laughter rumbled from his throat. "If not as a child, and decidedly not as a woman, tell me how you wish for me to handle you, and I'll see if I can oblige."

"As you would your own sister."

"I don't have a sister."

"Pretend you do."

"Sorry, but I cannot do as you've asked."

They were headed toward the door. "And why not?" she inquired.

"Considering the way I feel about you, like Lord Byron, I'd be fast fleeing England, never to return."

"What has Byron to do with this?"

"Incest, little *sister,* is forbidden."

Leah skidded to a halt. Her mouth worked several times, but her voice was frozen in her throat. He ignored her, and she watched as he continued out onto the front stoop. Once beside the carriage, he lingered, waiting to assist her.

Her head still spinning with Ian's words, Leah collected her wits and followed through the door, Milly closing it behind her. Descending to the sidewalk, she eyed him warily. Surely he didn't mean what she thought. He'd said it plainly enough, though—once he'd spelled it out to her. *Lord have mercy!* With his mother now safely out of the way, he planned to seduce her!

Her legs wobbled at the realization. Just how she managed the last few steps without falling, she couldn't say, but she did. Reaching Ian's side, she dismissed his proffered hand and climbed up into the carriage, where she quickly sat next to Jonathan.

Behind her, Ian came aboard and sat beside Veronica. At the driver's command, the horses were set into motion. As the carriage rocked along, Ian studied Leah, but she disregarded him. Deciding that a Highland frost couldn't be any more frigid, he silently chastised himself for not holding his tongue.

Feeling his gaze on her, Leah attempted to stay calm. Though she presented Ian a reserved face, her thoughts churned almost wildly.

Damn him for being so irresistibly masculine! her mind railed in silence. If seduction was indeed his goal, Leah feared she'd be unable to repel his advances. Her first priority was the children, and she must remain focused on that one objective. To that end, the next two weeks were crucial. If she could only get through them without incident, until the countess returned, she'd be safe. With his mother again at Sinclair House, her son wouldn't dare be so bold. But it was the next two weeks that worried Leah most.

"Planning ahead, are we?" Ian asked across the way. Leah's sharp look speared him, and he chuckled.

"A private joke, Ian?" Veronica inquired.

"Not really," he said. "Miss Kingsley and I had a mild disagreement over whether or not she should come along today. She's angry because I won out. Were she wise, she'd learn, whatever the stakes, I always win."

Thinking he was exceptionally sure of himself, Leah shifted her attention from Ian to Veronica. "My problem, Lady Veronica, is he tends to think of himself as my father."

At that, Ian's eyebrow shot up; Leah noted his reaction. "Given the differences in our ages," she needled, "I can understand his paternal concerns, but I believe I am of an age where I can make my own decisions without interference from Lord Huntsford."

Apparently Leah's underhanded jab at the earl struck a hilarious chord in Veronica, for her throaty laughter bubbled forth. "She has a point, Ian."

"Hear, hear!" Jonathan seconded.

Annoyed that Leah had painted him as having nearly gone to seed, Ian studied her intently. One night alone together, and he'd prove himself every bit as capable as her young Irishman. Even more so. "Age, Miss Kingsley, does have certain advantages over the fumbling ineptness which invariably accompanies youth. Given my years, along with the experience I've gained, I consider myself quite adept—paternally or otherwise."

Ian spied the blush on Leah's cheeks and bit back a grin. His underlying message wasn't lost on her. Satisfied, he addressed the Whitcombs, whose rapt stares had snagged him the instant he'd finished his sentence. "Don't be willing to offer Miss Kingsley your sympathy so easily. If I felt she could be trusted, she would be more than welcome to stay at home by herself," he informed them. "But she cannot be trusted, therefore, she is here with us."

Both Whitcombs looked at Leah as if she were a criminal. That she was, but none of them knew of her offense. Not yet. "Explain yourself, sir," Leah demanded.

"If you like." He turned to Veronica. "I hadn't mentioned it before, but since Miss Kingsley insists I justify my statement, I shall. The truth is: She was sent to London, not simply because her uncle was called into the queen's service, his duty taking him off to India, but because she is being pursued by an avid suitor—an Irish bounder, as her uncle termed him. Kingsley is adamant they not see each other. And even though she has promised not to see the buck should he appear on our doorstep, who knows what she'll do were he to arrive—especially if she's alone. With my mother away for the day, I am obligated to watch over her," Ian explained. "That's why she complains I'm behaving as though I were her father."

Leah noted relief showed on Veronica's face. Apparently, she'd been concerned about Ian's attentiveness to his houseguest. But no more. "Then you are madly in love, are you?" she asked Leah.

"Yes—madly." Leah hoped the falsehood would set Ian back in his seat. But the quick look he flashed her said he didn't believe her.

"A private supper, glasses of wine partaken, the sweet fragrance of flowers floating on a soft breeze, an ardent kiss stolen under a moonlit sky—I suppose, Miss Kingsley, you shared all these things with the man whom you claim you love?" he asked, then chuckled again. "Romance at its best, wouldn't you say?"

The jab had been returned. Leah knew he'd not let her forget their interlude on the balcony. Even if he never mentioned it again, she doubted she could ever erase the memory of his kiss. Its magic would always be with her. Her mood suddenly subdued, Leah could no longer look at him.

"You sound so cynical, Ian," Veronica declared. "I hope this doesn't mean you're one of those men who thinks being sentimental is unmasculine. Surely you believe in romance."

"I never said I didn't. I just wondered if Miss Kingsley was being properly courted, that's all."

"Well, I, for one, am most disappointed," Jonathan interjected, his attention falling on Leah. "I thought I might be able to persuade you to attend the Delderfields' ball with me. I must confess, though, I had an ulterior motive. I had hoped I could become a viable suitor. But now, I find I have no chance at all. To know you have already given your heart to another has wounded me greatly. I shall undoubtedly suffer in my misery forever."

Leah spied the jollity in his eyes. "I'm sorry, Lord Whitcomb, if I've dashed your hopes. But I imagine your alleged disappointment will resolve itself within a few short hours, if not minutes. As for the Delderfields' ball, I had planned to attend with the countess," she said, not forgetting the woman's instructions. "I will, however, save a dance for you, if you'd like."

"You are most kind, Miss Kingsley," he said. "I am eagerly awaiting the moment the orchestra plays the waltz meant just for us."

"As I recall, brother, you told me that your dance card has been filled," Veronica stated.

"Did I?"

"You did."

"Well, then, I shall just have to scratch a name from the list and add Miss Kingsley's in its place."

With Jonathan's jesting, the atmosphere in the carriage had grown less tense. They were now headed north, up Park Lane. At her query, Leah was informed that Hyde Park lay just to their left. Having nearly reached the intersection ahead, Leah saw a crowd had gathered at the park's northeastern corner. A man stood on a box, preaching loudly. Boos and applause met his words simultaneously.

"Speaker's Corner," Ian informed her at her questioning look. "Anyone who wishes to state his opinion on whatever issue chafes him may do so. But he does so at his own risk."

"How so?" Leah asked.

"His audience may not agree with his statements. More than one hapless soul has come away with a bloody nose for failing to choose his words carefully. It is a hazard one faces when speaking his mind."

Soon the driver reined the horses to the left, and they headed westward, out the road to Bayswater. While Leah remained virtually silent, the Whitcombs and Ian discussed the upcoming races at the Hippodrome. Before long, they were passing through the gates, a high wire fence surrounding the vast race course. Again, Ian explained to Leah that the enclosure had been erected to keep out the riffraff. Having received his instructions from an attendant, the Whitcombs' driver parked the carriage near the rail, only a few yards from the lush green track itself.

The group watched as the horses entered for the first race were put through their exercises. "I have my horse," Veronica said, grabbing up her reticule. "Come along, Ian. Let's place our wagers."

"Miss Kingsley, do you wish to gamble on a horse?" Ian asked.

"No. I doubt I'd win, so it would be foolish for me to lay a bet with the 'legs.'"

"So you know the slang for bookmaker, do you?" he asked, surprised that she did. "Apparently you're not a novice at horse racing after all."

Leah had been to the race course at York once with her father. It was there that he'd explained how one placed a bet. "I'm Irish, remember?" she said in answer to his statement.

"That's debatable," Ian mumbled under his breath, still certain her accent originated from the north of England. With a mental shrug, he brushed the thought aside.

"Are you coming, Ian?" Veronica asked.

"You and Jonathan go along. I'll be staying here with Miss Kingsley."

"Why do I have to go?" Jonathan grumbled.

"Because you need to place my wager in the book."

"Is that all, dear sister?"

"Well, I could use a few sovereigns. I know you have some to spare because I saw you tuck some coins into that small black purse you carry. Don't be so niggardly, brother. If I win, I'll pay you back double."

Rolling his eyes, Jonathan helped his sister down, then guided her toward the bookmakers.

"Have you chosen a horse, yet?" Ian asked Leah.

"The bay," she said, still studying the stallion. "He has long legs that are well-muscled. A sure winner, if I ever saw one."

"Well, I've chosen the dappled gray."

"Surely you're jesting. His left front knee is swollen. My guess is he'll pull up lame."

Ian studied the horse. "I see no difference in either knee."

"Then you must be blind. It's swollen, I say."

"Tell you what," Ian said, grinning. "Let's set a small wager between us on whose horse is better. Neither one has to finish in first place. The race is strictly between the bay and the gray. What do you say? Whichever of the two crosses the line before the other is the winner."

Leah's teeth played along her lower lip for a moment. "How much of a wager?"

"Ten sovereigns."

"Too high."

"Five."

"Still too high."

He chuckled. "You don't like taking risks, do you?"

"Not with money I don't."

"Tell you what. If you win I'll give you ten sovereigns. How's that sound?"

"What if you win?"

"You may give me another kiss."

Leah stared at him as if he'd gone daft. "Not on your life."

"There'll be no money out of your pocket. Just a sweet meeting of our lips."

She studied him closely. She could certainly use the money. Besides, she was positive his horse would go lame. "Done," she said, then wondered why she'd been so impetuous. What if she lost?

Ian's eyes twinkled with mirth. "Sure of yourself, aren't you?"

"I wouldn't have wagered if I felt I'd lose."

"We'll see who comes away with the purse." Suddenly Ian laughed at his own pun. He noted Leah's frown. "Never mind. You wouldn't think it funny. Especially if you were to lose."

The trumpet sounded, announcing the first race. Veronica and Jonathan came scurrying back to the carriage.

"That big black had better win," Veronica said, falling into her seat, "or I'll simply die."

"I'll second that," Jonathan said.

"What do you mean?" Veronica snapped.

"I have decided, dear sister, it would be far simpler to be rid of you than to continue paying your debts. Pray your horse wins. Or you'll be in your grave, and I'll be in Newgate."

The gun sounded, and the string of horses vaulted away from the post. The foursome rose to their feet, as did all the other spectators in the carriages and the stands. Pounding hooves thundered past them, ripping clumps of sod from their moorings. As the pack rounded the first curve of the two-mile course, Leah noted the gray was several lengths in front of the bay. She closed her eyes and prayed her horse would pull ahead.

Veronica jumped up and down inside the carriage, urging her horse on, for it was striding into the lead. Three quarters of the way around, she suddenly groaned. "You dim-witted nag!" she yelled, for the gray had overtaken the black. Veronica's horse quickly fell back into the pack.

That's when Leah noticed the bay was beginning to make its move. Now it was her turn to cheer.

Long legs stretched in a bounding stride, cutting the distance between itself and the gray. The pair rounded the last curve, headed for the finish line. The bay's nose was adjacent to the gray's hip, then its withers. "Go!" Leah cried. Two strides from the finish line the gray faltered. The bay shot forward. "I won!" she shouted, then spun around to face Ian. Her face beamed with joy.

His lips quirked into a half grin. "So you did, Miss Kingsley. Do you want your payment in gold or will a bank note due?"

"Either is fine." Leah watched as he pulled a ten-pound note from his wallet. He handed it over to her. "Thank you," she said, stuffing it into her reticule.

"I thought you said you didn't wager," Veronica said.

"She couldn't resist the terms," Ian answered for Leah.

"Well, it's certain *you* won't be wagering again anytime soon," Lord Whitcomb said to his sister. *"This* bank has closed its doors."

"Brother, you certainly have the ability to ruin a wonderful day. We came here to enjoy ourselves. Can we not place another wager—just a small one?"

"Oh, all right," he relented. "But this time I shall have a say in which horse is chosen. Come." He stepped from the carriage. "Let's move up the rail, so we can get a closer look at the flesh running in the next race. They'll be bringing them out soon. Afterward, we'll place our bet."

"Want to try it again?" Ian asked, once Veronica had joined her brother, the two walking up the way.

Leah was busy watching the ceremony in which the purse was presented to the bay's owner. "I'll have to see the horses first."

"They're coming into the ring now," he informed her. "Pick the one you favor. Then I'll choose mine. Fair enough?"

"Fair enough," Leah said.

By the time the Whitcombs returned, Leah was still scanning the field. Her choice lay between a sorrel and a roan. They were both fine animals, equally matched. "I'll take the roan," she announced finally.

"The sorrel for me," Ian said.

"Betting again, Miss Kingsley?" Veronica asked, gaining the carriage.

"Why not?" Jonathan piped in. "Obviously she has an eye for good horseflesh, where you don't."

"The black was in the lead most of the time."

"Yes, but it didn't win. Hope our choice for this race makes a good show or we're dashed."

Again the trumpets sounded, heralding the start of the second race. "Same terms, Miss Kingsley. My horse against yours, not the entire field," Ian reminded. "Same wager also."

"Agreed," Leah returned, feeling quite confident.

The starting gun sounded, and as before the line of horses raced past the carriage. The sorrel and the roan were neck and neck, moving up in the pack as they rounded the first curve. Around the course they went. As one moved forward, the other soon overtook him. Neither seemed able to gain the advantage.

Finally, the pair rounded the last curve, heading into the home stretch. Their whips striking hard and fast, the jockeys urged their horses onward. First the roan was ahead by a nose, then the sorrel. Closing her eyes, Leah felt she couldn't watch. She relented, however, and peered through her lashes.

Less than a length to the finish line, the roan had pulled to the fore. Unbelievably, the sorrel expelled a burst of speed to win by a nose. Leah's shoulders slumped in defeat.

"Pay up, Miss Kingsley," Veronica said, the Whitcombs' own horse having lost. "Ian has won."

Leah's gaze immediately snagged Ian's. "We'll attend to the particulars later," he said, taking pity on her. "Right now, if everyone else is in agreement, let's head back to London."

"What shall we do then?" Veronica inquired.

"Since Miss Kingsley hasn't had the opportunity to do so, we can take a quick turn through Hyde Park, then it's on to Sinclair House for some refreshments," he responded.

"That sounds fine," Jonathan said, having instructed his driver to head back to London. Once everyone took their former places, the carriage was set into motion. "Perhaps we could even enjoy a parlor game later. Do you like charades, Miss Kingsley?"

"Charades?" Leah asked, and spied Lord Whitcomb's nod. "I suppose the game is enjoyable for some." She was thinking of her own pretense and not the sport, then prayed she never got caught. "In truth, I'm not very good at it."

"How about twenty questions?" Jonathan inquired.

"Even worse, I fear."

"We could always discuss politics," he quipped, and Veronica groaned.

"You men have a place for such talk," she said. "Please keep it at your club."

"Speaking of clubs, that reminds me," Jonathan said. "I saw Covington at White's, night before last. I cornered him and learned his mood stems from financial difficulties. His father's accounts were apparently in a shambles. I mention this, Huntsford—and ladies—because I know it will go no further. He did intimate he feared he might have to sell the house on Hanover Square. He didn't say how, but he was able to retrieve some money. It may not be enough to keep his family in London, though. I really feel sorry for the chap. He's like a man possessed. I offered to help him out, but he refused. Pride, I suppose."

"You said you were strapped," Veronica stated. "Where would you get the money?"

"That is none of your affair, dear sister. What's hidden will stay hidden from you."

The conversation turned to other things, and as Leah halfway listened, she pondered Jonathan's words.

The money Arthur had retrieved—was it from the sale of Balfour? If so, that meant he knew about their father, that he had acted with John Kingsley in an attempt to destroy the Daltons. Then again, the solicitor may have acted alone, delivering the proceeds from Balfour's sale, never telling Arthur from what source the money had come.

Leah wanted to get at the truth. Still, she feared in doing so she might end up with nothing. Knowing she couldn't risk losing Anne's allowance, she decided to let the whole thing die.

What difference did it make if Arthur was behind the Dalton's woes? Learning that he was wouldn't change their present circumstance. Nothing would. Except, that was, for John Kingsley's money. In a few months, she would have enough savings hidden away. And when she did, she'd be away from London, away from England, and away from Ian Sinclair. For some reason, the latter of the three made Leah feel utterly miserable.

Before long, the carriage turned into Hyde Park, near Speaker's Corner, then made a wide arc, looping toward the park's center. Other conveyances, their occupants enjoying the bright spring day, lined the avenue running parallel to what Ian said was the Serpentine River. Soon the Whitcombs' carriage exited onto Knightsbridge, then the horses trotted east along Piccadilly. Reaching Berkley Street, the driver headed the team north, until they were finally at the Square.

"Ian," Veronica said, the vehicle pulling to a stop. "Why don't you and I plan to have supper out tonight, then go to the theater. We never have any time alone together."

"Sorry, Veronica, I have more book work awaiting me this evening. Perhaps another night." Ian stepped from the carriage, then helped Leah out. "Are you coming in?" he asked the Whitcombs.

"No, I think not," Veronica stated. "I need to go along home and get ready for this evening. Since you cannot make it, Jonathan will be escorting me to the theater."

Leah noted Lord Whitcomb's surprised look. That he hadn't planned on doing anything of the sort was apparent. Then she remembered her unsettled debt. Thinking that Ian might want immediate payment once they were alone, she scurried up the steps and into the house. In her haste, she nearly collided with Simmons, who'd just stepped to the door. "Excuse me," she said, rushing toward the other set of steps.

Through the open portal, she heard the carriage pull away from the curb. Ian's footsteps followed her inside. Leah was halfway up the stairs to the gallery, when she heard him say: "Simmons, any messages while I was out?"

"Not for you, sir. But a letter has come for Miss Kingsley. It is here, sir, on the tray."

Hearing the butler's words, Leah clutched the banister for support. *The children.* Something must have happened to one of them. Little Peter, she thought, her emotions welling within her.

Dear God! Give me the strength to see this through.

The words tumbled through her mind as she prayed she

wouldn't succumb to the hysteria spiraling up inside her. She had to have the letter.

Turning slowly, she gazed down on Ian. His hat, gloves, and cane had been handed off to the butler. Clasped in the fingers of his right hand, the envelope tapped steadily against his left palm.

"From your Irish bounder, I suppose?"

CHAPTER
10

Leah was paralyzed with fear. By the look in the earl's eyes, she knew she was doomed.

"Well, Miss Kingsley, what do you have to say?"

"The letter could be from my uncle," she stated, trying desperately to retain her composure.

"The postmark reads *Leeds,* which is southwest of York," he countered, coming to the foot of the stairs. "Did your uncle take a detour en route to India?"

"Hand it to me, then, and I shall discover who the sender is."

Ian mounted the steps, latched on to her arm, and guided her up to the gallery. "To the sitting room, Miss Kingsley, where we can talk."

"There is no need for us to talk," she insisted, trying to catch hold of the letter, which was just outside her reach. "Loose me!" She pressed her heels against the marble floor and skidded along beside him.

Dragging Leah for several yards, Ian finally halted their progression. "Move or I'll carry you."

"Sir, whether the letter has come from my *Irish bounder,*

as you so uncivilly call him, or not, your withholding my mail is unconscionable. It is a matter of privacy. I demand you hand it over." Pray he didn't open it, or all would be lost!

"And I demand to know how he learned you were here."

"I have no inkling. From one of my uncle's servants, perhaps."

"My suspicions, Miss Kingsley, are that you informed him of your whereabouts."

"Impossible. I've not been from your mother's or your sight since I've been here."

Ian's gaze shot to the corner. "Milly!" The girl jumped and the feather duster fell from her hand, striking the table beneath the picture frame she'd been cleaning. "Have you ever posted a letter for Miss Kingsley?"

"N-no, sir, I haven't."

"Did she ever ask you to?"

"N-no, sir—n-never."

"Nor have I asked anyone else in your employ," Leah said confidently. "Go ahead. Inquire if you must. The answers will be identical to Milly's. Besides, you have no assurance the letter came from him."

He released her arm. With his fingers poised over the wax seal, he asked, "Shall we take a look?"

No! her mind screamed as her gloved hand caught a piece of the envelope. "I'd never be so bold as to rifle through your correspondence, sir. I ask the same courtesy from you."

Ian studied her. She was both determined and angry. He noticed how her eyes flashed like fiery emeralds. He behaved shoddily, he knew. The reason: He'd been provoked by the thought of Leah's being held in another man's arms. Any endearments, whether written or uttered, should come solely from him, not from some faceless Irishman, who, in Ian's estimation, wasn't deserving of her. Still, he realized there was only one remedy. Slowly he relaxed his grip.

Leah pulled the letter from his fingers. "Thank you," she whispered on a relieved sigh.

"You're welcome," he said just as she started to turn away. "But I again warn you, Miss Kingsley. Don't seek to trick either my mother or myself. The repercussions, should you do so, will not be to your liking." With that he strode across the gallery and into his study. The door banged closed behind him.

Leah stared at the panel for a moment. His warning, she knew, wasn't to be taken lightly.

In her room, Leah's trembling fingers tore through the seal, and she pulled the letter from the envelope. Quickly she scanned Terence's bold handwriting. As she'd suspected, Peter was ill.

> . . . those in charge at the orphanage are unwilling to call in a specialist, so a local practitioner is caring for him. I am not at all certain of the man's qualifications. While in York, two days past—Mr. Jones was kind enough to allow me leave to see Peter, carrying me there himself in his cart—I had heard talk that this Dr. White is more into his cups than not. I fear, sister, things may worsen, and we might lose our little brother if he is not given the medical attention he needs. His lungs are so very weak . . .

Leah's heart twisted in pain. Her brother may soon falter at the edge, teetering between life and death. Should he drop from the precipice into that dark void, she didn't know how she'd bear yet another loss. Why must her family be made to endure so much misfortune?

Punishment for her sins and her father's, she supposed, thinking it was unfair Peter should suffer because of their wickedness. Terence Dalton could do little to set right his wrongs. Judgment was already upon him. But if she were to repent, confess her transgressions openly, maybe her brother's life would be spared. Briefly, Leah fretted over whether or not she should seek out the earl and throw herself on his mercy, begging for clemency.

The repercussions . . . will not be to your liking.

Ian's statement rang inside her head, and Leah knew

wrathful words and instant retribution would be her sole reward should she toss herself at his feet, the truth pouring forth. In Newgate, she could do Peter little good. She must act on her own and go to York. Any delay, and it might be too late.

Tears stung her eyes as she rose from the side chair and headed toward the clothes cupboard.

Tucked in the back, under some folded petticoats, she found the tattered stocking she searched for. Her ill-gotten bounty retrieved from its toe, she made a quick tabulation of her savings. This, plus the money she'd won from Lord Huntsford at the races, should be enough to pay her passage to York and hire a specialist for Peter. Even Dr. Bridges, the Daltons' family physician, would be far better than the charlatan the orphanage retained.

Leah knew she had to get to a coaching inn, though she was at a loss as to which one. The cabby she hired should be able to direct her. She rushed back to the door, where she snatched up the articles she'd dropped upon entering the room, and stuffed the money and letter into her reticule. After turning the key, she jerked the door open. A loud gasp fled her lips.

"Mercy!" Leah's hand settled over her pounding heart. "You startled me."

His fist raised ready to strike the wood, Ian stared down on her. Slowly, his hand fell to his side. "Going somewhere?"

"For a walk in the gardens," she blurted out, grabbing at the first thing that came to mind.

His shoulder meeting the doorframe, he crossed his arms over his chest. "I suppose you need your reticule for such an adventure?"

"I didn't realize I still held it," she said, eyeing him carefully. "What is it you want?"

"I came to apologize for my actions earlier. To accuse you as I had was excessive. On seeing you now, perhaps my decision to ask for your forgiveness was a bit premature. You were planning to escape the grounds, were you not?"

"I said I was going into the gardens. I wanted to see the flowers, as well as take in some fresh air. After all, the atmosphere is a bit cloying, don't you think?"

"Not really, but if you insist on going outside, I'll join you."

"I'd prefer my own company."

Ian surveyed her a moment. "As you wish, but you won't be needing this." He took the parasol from her grip, leaned around her, and tossed it at the bed. "The sun's angle is such it can't possibly freckle your cute little nose. Nor will you be needing these." He relieved her of the reticule and gloves. Quickly, they followed the path of the parasol. "Especially your reticule—not in the gardens anyway. The shawl you might appreciate having." Pulling it from her hand, he swung it around her shoulders. "Now, if you're ready, I'll gladly escort you down as far as the gallery. Simmons can show you into the gardens."

"I can find my own way, thank you."

"What sort of host would I be if I allowed you to get lost? Take hold of my arm or stay in your room. Which will it be?"

Were she to slam the door in his face, he'd know she hadn't intended to seek out the gardens at all. Since he suspected as much already, she had no choice but to prove him wrong. From the corner of her eye, she spotted her reticule and memorized its position on the bed, just in case the thing was moved. Considering his reaction to the letter, she didn't trust him one whit.

"Since I want to see your mother's flowers, you give me little alternative but to comply."

His armed cocked, ready to receive her hand, Leah viewed it briefly. Finally, her fingers met the gray linen material covering his forearm. Hard sinews rippled under her touch, then as an inviting heat radiated through his sleeve, she bit back a groan. The man was merciless. Why couldn't he simply leave her alone?

Ian's hand settled atop hers. "Would you like to take something along to read while you're outside? That little selection you bought at the fair, perhaps? Go fetch it. I'll wait."

"I've packed it away," she said, praying he didn't insist she find it. "Besides, since this morning, I've lost my taste for poetry."

His comment about incest, no doubt. "Pity," he said, then his gaze hit the night table by her bed. "How about that book over there. What is it?"

"Mary Shelley's *Frankenstein, or the Modern Prometheus.*" Leah had found the book in one of Anne's cases and believed the story quite good. "You seem surprised," she said, noting his arched brow.

"I'd think it would keep you awake at night."

"Not really. I hold a great amount of sympathy for the monster. He is a gentle creature, scorned because of his ugliness. How can people be so cruel?"

"Fear and ignorance. Both inevitably lead to hatred. It is a human failing that has plagued mankind from the beginning of time. Do you wish to take the book with you?"

"No, I shall read it at night before I go to sleep."

At the mere mention of Shelley's book most women were reaching for their smelling salts. But not Leah. "A questionable decision," he commented, silently admiring her grit, "but, of course, it is your choice." He slipped the key from the lock, whisked Leah into the hallway, then secured the door from the outside. "Just in case you feared I might rummage through your things while you were outside," he said, pressing the key into her hand, then he urged her toward the stairs.

On a glance, Leah studied Ian as they traversed the corridor. He hadn't insisted she name the letter's sender, which surprised her. But then, he'd been certain the missive was from Anne's lover. Perhaps he felt he needed no confirmation on that point. His mind had been set. Yet he said he'd come to apologize for his behavior. Not many men would have been as considerate, especially when they felt they were being lied to. However, this man appeared to respect her privacy, and for that she was most grateful. Leah

146

wished he hadn't come knocking on her door when he had. Somehow, someway, she had to make her escape to York. Peter needed her.

Their feet meeting the floor of the gallery, Ian called out for the butler. Shortly, he appeared. "Show Miss Kingsley out to the gardens, will you, Simmons? She wishes to enjoy the tranquillity it provides." He released Leah's hand from his arm. "As always, supper is at eight. I shall see you then."

"I'd rather make an early evening of it," she said hastily as he started toward his study. "Can I possibly take in a tray in my room?"

Ian turned around. "There is the small matter on the loss on your bet which needs to be settled. I thought we might do so tonight after supper," he said, then fought to keep from laughing aloud. Apprehension and denial loomed on Leah's face. Too late, she regretted entering into the contest with him. But Ian promised himself she'd not rue the actual moment of payment. He'd leave her eager for another such match. "However, it can wait—for now," he said, deciding he'd keep her guessing. "If you'd prefer a tray in your room, I will be more than happy to oblige you. There will be other opportunities for us to resolve your debt. Enjoy the gardens, Miss Kingsley."

Leah gaped at him as he strode into his study, this time the door closing softly behind him. With the arrival of the letter, she'd forgotten all about the kiss. Another reason for her to escape Sinclair House, she decided, knowing she might never be able to resist him once their lips again met.

"Miss," Simmons said. "If you'll follow me, I'll show you the way out."

Leah traced after the butler. If there were only someway to break free of this place, she'd be gone in a flash. But after the earl's nearly catching her in the act of fleeing, his suspicions rightly compounding, she was certain her movements would be closely monitored. Her escape, she decided, would have to come at night.

She followed the butler down to the lower level, then on toward the back of the house, her fingers curling around the key in her hand. Pray he didn't renege on his promise not to rummage through her things. Leah hoped Lord Huntsford was a man of his word or all would be lost before sunset.

Once out in the gardens, she pretended interest in the flowers and ornamental shrubs, all arranged to create a dazzling display. Within her first turn along the path, she caught movement near a window. By its position on the house, Leah knew the glass panes belonged to the study. As she'd suspected, he watched her.

In a quandary as to what she should do, Leah thought of Peter. His blond image played in her mind while tears threatened. Frail and slim, he'd suffered enough in his short life. Why couldn't he have been strong and robust, the same as the others?

Leah knew she had to get to him, but at the moment, the risk was too great. She couldn't help Peter if she were imprisoned, which was exactly what would happen if she attempted a dash for freedom and failed. Even now, Ian Sinclair scrutinized her from the house. Likewise, once the order was given, his servants would undoubtedly be spying on her, too. With guards posted on all exits, she'd have no way out. Of course, she could dangle from her windowsill, praying the fall didn't kill her when she landed on the pavement below.

Sighing heavily, Leah realized her only hope lay in Terence. He'd have to take charge, seeing Peter got the care he needed. The money, however, would come from Leah. Tomorrow, with the excuse of needing another dress altered, she'd once again seek out Sally Foster.

Leah found herself at the back of the gardens. Unshed tears blinding her, she sank down onto a stone bench. A screen of roses sheltered her from the house and the prying eyes watching from within. "Oh, God, despite my sins, please let little Peter live, for he is innocent."

With that, Leah's sobs poured forth.

From the window in his study, Ian viewed the cover of roses, Leah's lavender dress showing through the breaks in the leaves. Knowing she'd taken refuge on the bench, he relaxed. When she'd first dropped from his sight, he'd been tempted to quit the house and search her out. If she really were determined to leave Sinclair House, as he suspected, she might have spied the gate at the garden's rear. A simple lifting of the latch would afford her entry into the mews. From there she could disappear into the streets, meshing with the crowds combing the sidewalks.

Obviously, she'd spotted neither the gate nor the carriage house, its stone walls hidden behind a thick curtain of ivy. The latter would give her no exit, its doors locked, but Ian had forgotten about the old gate. He'd have Simmons secure the wrought-iron portal as soon as she came inside. Or else next time she'd be gone.

Running his fingers through his hair, Ian silently berated himself for being so suspicious. Twice, while spying on her, he'd considered summoning Simmons, demand the extra key, then set a course for her room, where he'd search out the letter, once and for all certain of the identity of its sender.

Leeds wasn't that far from Kingsley's home, which sat to the south of York. Perhaps the bounder had taken up residence there, biding his time. Then again, the buck, knowing her whereabouts in London, may have come the distance of the Great North Road and was presently nearby, waiting for Leah to meet him. Maybe that was why she was so eager to escape the house!

There was only one way to find out, he concluded. The answers he sought lay in the letter. By reading it, he could still his concerns. Or provoke new ones. Either way, he had to know the truth.

About to pivot from the window, Ian saw Leah's head peek above the roses as she came up from the bench. Her fingers quickly brushed beneath her eyes, then squaring her shoulders, she walked toward the house. She'd been crying, he decided. For her lover, no doubt.

Once Leah entered through the back door, Ian sauntered over to his desk. If she cared that much for her Irishman, there was little he could do to change her sentiments. What he could do, though, was make certain John Kingsley's wishes were fulfilled. As long as his niece remained in the Sinclairs' protection, she'd not be afforded the chance to see the scoundrel whom her uncle so despised. This Ian promised himself.

Striding around his desk, he opened the door leading into the gallery in time to see the tail of Leah's dress disappear up the steps. Knowing she was headed to her room, he waited. A distant thumping of a door met his ears. On hearing it, he bellowed, "Simmons!"

The man came scurrying up the steps and across the gallery.

"Come in here," Ian said, thinking he hadn't seen Simmons move that swiftly in years. His tone upon calling the man, the earl decided, had apparently been most irritable. "There are some things I need for you to do."

Once Simmons had entered the study, Ian closed the door firmly. Ten minutes later, he opened it, and the butler existed.

"I shall see about the lock now," Simmons said most discreetly. "Several men will be posted around the house the night through. Should anything untoward happen, they will sound an alarm."

"Good," Ian countered, grinning.

"Anything else, sir?"

"Not at present. We'll see how the night goes."

"Yes, sir."

At the butler's slight bow, Ian watched as the man marched to the stairs, going in search of a lock for the gate. *By God!* He wasn't about to lose sleep over Miss Anne *Leah* Kingsley. This, too, he promised.

The next morning, after a fairly restful sleep, her tears coming only intermittently, Leah stared at the earl who was seated across the breakfast table from her. Dressed in what she now termed "his portrait garb," he appeared worn and haggard, especially for having retired so early. His mood didn't seem to be the best either.

She nibbled at her lower lip, wondering if she dared ask to be driven to the couturière's. She again hoped to engage Sally, the young woman posting the letter Leah had written to Terence just before she'd gone to bed last night. Her brother's missive was now naught but ash lying in the bottom of the fireplace in her room, a worry to her no more.

Her request formed in her mind, and she opened her mouth, but quickly closed it, her courage fleeing. By the looks of him, Lord Huntsford appeared ready to snap her head off at the least little word.

Ian glanced up from his bowl where he'd been chasing a stewed prune around with his spoon. He detested the fruit, believing it was meant for old men with weak constitutions. The description didn't fit him—yet!

"You look pensive, Miss Kingsley," he said, having caught her scrutiny of him. "Is something troubling you?"

"I was hoping I might ask a favor of you, but I hesitate doing so, since you seem to be in ill humor."

A damnable rotten mood was what he would call it. His gaze narrowed on her. Though no ladder had fallen against the house, no intruder had lurked on his doorstep, no alarm had been sounded during the night, he'd had little if any sleep. Just as he'd envisioned on the eve he'd first read John Kingsley's letter, cautioning the Sinclairs about Leah's suitor, Ian had indeed bounded from his bed at the least little noise, the sound sending him to his window to peer down on the street. A miserable night it was.

"Ill humor?" he questioned. "What gave you that idea?"

"Right now, your tone of voice."

"I apologize, Miss Kingsley, but I had a restless night."

"I'm sorry to hear that."

Was she? he wondered. "What is the favor you need?"

"It seems I continue to lose weight," she said, which wasn't a lie. Since coming to Sinclair House, she imagined she'd dropped nearly half a stone. "My dresses, I fear, are growing way too large. They were loose when I arrived, but are even more so now."

"Come to the point. What is it you need?"

"I was wondering if you could drop me by the couturière's, so I might have another dress altered."

"Just one?"

"Yes—why?"

"Because if you'd take all your gowns at once, it would save wear and tear on the horses—in this case *horse,*" he corrected. "Should I decide to take you, we'll have to use the phaeton, since Ferguson and the carriage are still in Bath with my mother."

"Could I afford the cost, I'd gladly take all my gowns together. But since the fees come directly from my allowance, to do so would cause too much of a financial strain on me. That is why I take them one at a time." Leah fell silent for a moment. She was willing to send her entire savings to Terence for Peter's care, but if she did so, she'd need additional funds to satisfy her account with the couturière. "Speaking of my allowance, your mother pays me once a week—uh, today is supposed to be the day."

"Since I'm unaware of where she keeps your money hidden, you'll have to wait until she returns."

"But I won't be able to pay for the dresses that are already in the shop. I promised to settle my account the next time I came by. That will be today—if you consent to take me." *Please say yes!*

Ian eyed her closely. "What do you do with all your money?" he asked, then noted how Leah's gaze hit the table. "Except for the book of poems, I've yet to see you spend any of it." She refused to look at him, fingers toying with the napkin covering her muslin skirt. "I guess you've been saving it for your alterations, correct?"

Her attention shifted back to Ian. "Yes. Your mother's couturière is very expensive."

"But she does fine work," he commented, thinking of how Leah looked in her new gown the night of the Carstairses' ball. "I'll lend you some cash." He named the figure. "Will that be sufficient for now?"

"I'm not certain," she said, hoping he'd offer more.

"Should you come up short just trek out to the curb. I'll be waiting for you there."

"Then you'll take me?"

"I will—at eleven."

"Thank you," she said, elated the money would soon be on its way to Terence. As she poked at her food, she prayed it wasn't too late.

Ian watched the play of her spoon. "You know, if you'd stop eating as though you were an injured bird, you wouldn't need your gowns refitted."

"You don't appear to be eating heartily, either," she said, noting his breakfast remained virtually untouched.

Ian studied his fare, then grimaced. "It's the prunes. I can't stomach the things."

"Neither can I," Leah said.

"Well there's only one thing to do—Simmons!" Ian called. In a few steps, the man was at his master's side. "Clear this away and bring Miss Kingsley and myself a decent breakfast, will you? I want some thick, juicy ham. What would you like?"

"Hot chocolate and some scones," she said.

"And some jam and butter," Ian added. "No fruit of any kind—except for the jam, that is. The countess isn't in residence at the moment. Miss Kingsley and I don't need to watch our waistlines," he said, patting his flat belly.

"Very good, sir," Simmons declared, clearing the table.

"Is that why we have fruit so often?" Leah asked. "Surely your mother doesn't fear becoming fat."

"She refuses to look matronly."

"I cannot imagine she ever would."

Ian grinned. "Nor can I. My grandmother looked one-third her age when she died two years past. She was seventy-five. Given that, heredity says my mother will remain quite attractive for some time to come. I suppose that is one reason why your uncle is so enamored of her."

"That, and the fact she has such an endearing personality," Leah said.

"I guess you're wondering where I derive my temperament?"

"I had questioned such," she said. "But I assume you are much like your father."

"His temper was far worse than mine. No, Miss Kingsley, believe it or not, I take after my mother. She was the only one who could tame Adrian Sinclair's moods. One word or one look from her, and the beast in him would gentle. Because of her, he purred more than roared. They were well-suited, and very much in love. Not often is a couple awarded such happiness. But it does occur every now and then."

"Are you hoping for the same with Veronica?" Leah asked, not meaning to do so. The words just slipped out.

Ian chuckled. "Still curious about the Lady Veronica's and my relationship, are you?"

Embarrassed, Leah couldn't hold his gaze. "Not really."

"Good. For the situation is still a mystery to me," he said, wondering why he kept the brunette dangling. The swing of the connecting door drew Ian's attention. Simmons entered the room. "Ah, our breakfast has arrived."

Once the plates were set before them, all attempts at conversation ceased. Catching hold of his knife and fork, Ian cut into his ham, his mouth watering from its delicious aroma. A piece meeting his tongue, he again pondered Veronica.

Not too long ago he believed they were well-suited, but he now knew he'd assumed wrong. He'd grown weary in his search for that special someone meant just for him. In his jadedness, he found himself willing to settle for companionship instead of love. But that was before he'd met Leah.

He'd made no commitment to Veronica, no reference to marriage had passed from his lips, not even a tender kiss was shared between them. Nevertheless, he imagined Veronica awaited his proposal. Ian felt a bit guilty about the situation. In fairness to her, he decided it was time he remedied the misunderstanding, making a clean break of it, so she could get on with her life and find a man who truly cared about her.

As to why he continued his association with Veronica and her brother, the answer was simple. He'd learned quickly not to press Leah too hard. Just the thought of being alone with him set her into a twitter. The Whitcombs afforded him the opportunity to be with Leah, while they unwittingly acted as chaperons. Keeping their outings in the form of a foursome was definitely to his advantage. That way he could orchestrate Leah's seduction in a slow and easy manner. Otherwise, she'd bolt.

Straight into her Irishman's arms, he decided, thinking about this new wrinkle presented to him just yesterday. The idea that the man might be in London annoyed Ian. *Damn!* Were he the unscrupulous sort, he'd find the letter—that's if it still existed—and read it. Although he'd been tempted, such underhandedness ran against his nature. For now, at least. Given the right set of circumstances, he might not be so noble in the future.

Perturbed, he attacked the ham with his knife, slicing through it with a vengeance. "I can tell you this, Miss Kingsley," he said, more determined than before to have Leah for his own. "There will be a wedding. And soon."

About to bite into the steamy buttered scone she held, Leah lowered it from her mouth. "As I recall, you said you were unsure of the situation. Have you since changed your mind?"

"Changed my mind? No."

Leah stared at him. "Well, do you or do you not plan to ask for the Lady Veronica's hand?"

"And as I recall, you said you weren't interested in my relationship with Veronica. Are you the one who has now changed her mind?"

"I was just wondering what you were going on about. First, you say you find the situation is still a mystery to you. Then you affirm you are going to be married and soon. I know it is none of my concern, but if you aren't certain exactly what it is you want, perhaps you should rethink the matter before you act too swiftly."

"I know precisely what I want, Miss Kingsley. It is simply a matter of getting it."

His tone had again grown surly, and Leah wondered at his swift change in mood. "You strike me as being the sort of man who always gets what he wants. But you sound as though you doubt your ability. Is that true?"

"I'm human, Miss Kingsley. And being such, I have a tendency to grow impatient when things aren't moving as quickly as I'd like. But you're right. I always win. This time, it will be no different." He cast her a wicked grin. "Speaking of winning, I believe you owe me something. Are you ready to pay up?"

Leah's eyes widened. "No!"

"Not reneging, are we?"

"N-no. I'm simply not ready, that's all."

"The longer it takes the more resistant you'll become. Why not just pay your debt and be done with it?"

"Because I'm not ready, I said. Can't you wait?"

Ian chuckled. "For now, yes. But I won't wait forever. Our lips will again meet in a kiss. Know it as the truth." As would their bodies, he decided, wondering just how he'd convince her to become his wife. The bit of ham he'd nearly mutilated because of his agitation over her Irishman dangled from his fork. "Eat up. It's almost ten. Remember we are to leave at eleven."

Feeling suddenly morose, Leah watched as he popped the morsel into his mouth. With the exchange, her own appetite had diminished considerably, nevertheless she obeyed his command. Biting into the once delicious-looking scone, she thought it had no taste. While she chewed, she listened as Ian ordered Simmons to have the phaeton readied and brought round from the carriage house. Wondering over his extreme moodiness, she wished she'd never come to London, never set foot in Sinclair House, never met the countess or her handsome son—especially the latter. If she hadn't ventured here, though, she knew there would be no hope of Peter ever recovering from his illness. At least this way, with John Kingsley's money paying for a qualified physician, he had a chance, one that would not have been afforded him otherwise.

The unappetizing scone nearly stuck in her throat as she attempted to swallow it. Quickly, she sipped some hot chocolate. From over the cup's rim, she spied the man across from her. An enigma, she decided, not understanding him at all. He hoped to marry one woman while desiring a kiss from another. Underhanded, devious, and irresistible —he was all of these. Again she wished she'd never set eyes on him.

As her cup settled on its saucer, Leah continued to peer at him through her lashes. Before her eyes, his body relaxed while a confident smile spread over his face. He appeared as though he'd just found the model solution to an exceptionally thorny problem.

Sensing trouble, Leah grew wary of him. "What, sir, has set you to grinning as though you were a cat that's just snared himself a mouse?"

"Am I grinning?" he asked innocently.

"Yes, you are."

"By your tone, I take it you don't relish me smiling. If not, I shall set to scowling whenever you are around. Better?" he asked, a dark frown settling on his face.

"It is not your smile that troubles me, sir. It is the thought that provoked it that has me worried."

"Ah, I see. You want to know what I was thinking, hmm?" His grin returned. "Sorry, but my musings are my own. However, I will tell you this. You should be thankful you're not intuitive enough to read my mind or you'd be blushing profusely, Miss Kingsley." His napkin settled next to his plate, and he rose from the chair. "If you'll excuse me, I need to change into something more suitable for our outing."

As Ian's long strides carried him to the door, Leah stared at his back. Whether she could read his mind fully or not, she was intuitive enough to know his thoughts had been about her.

Trepidation spiraled up inside Leah. Her life was about to take a quick turn. In which direction it would lead, she couldn't say, but it was Ian Sinclair who held the reins that governed her future. A frightening prospect, she decided, especially if he ever discovered her true identity.

Noting movement beside her, she looked up to see Simmons hovering close by.

"May I offer up anything else for you, Miss?" the man asked.

"Your prayers, Simmons," she said, rising from her seat. "I have a feeling I'll need them."

CHAPTER
11

The gelding's hooves clicked smartly against the pavement as Ian guided the phaeton along Oxford Street, again heading toward Berkley Square. Leah sat beside him, relieved the letter was now in Sally's hands, shortly to be posted. Soon Terence would have his instructions, along with the money meant for Peter's care.

Her parasol twirling with the gentle roll of her fingers, Leah smiled to herself. Sally Foster was truly a godsend. Rightly, when first spying Leah today, she'd guessed Leah was deeply troubled.

"What's wrong, Miss?"

"Someone near and dear to me is very ill, Sally."

"It ain't your Terence who's sick, is it?"

"No, it's his brother."

"The one who's in the orphanage," Sally inserted.

"Yes. He's gravely ill and in desperate need of a qualified physician who treats lung disorders. I must send a money letter to Terence. It's very important the funds get to him, so that he can hire a specialist, or else Peter may die. Could you post the letter for me?"

Apparently, Leah's expression had manifested some uncertainty, for Sally had lifted her chin a notch. "You can trust me, Miss. I might be poor, but I'm honest, I am. And that's the truth."

"I believe you, Sally. Just make certain the person to whom you give this is as honest as you are. My entire savings is in this envelope. If something were to happen to it, there would be no hope for Peter."

"I understand." Sally frowned. "If your Terence is in Leeds and you're here in London, how did you learn his brother was sick?"

"I received a letter from him."

"He sent it to the countess's?"

"Yes—her son intercepted it. He threatened to read it. Oh, Sally, I never felt so intimidated in all my life."

Upon Leah's explaining about the furor Terence's missive had caused, the young woman had quickly offered to act as an intermediary, Terence's letters sent first to her, Sally then delivering them to Leah.

"That way, you can be kept abreast of what's happenin' to his brother, no one bein' the wiser."

"But how will we work this?" Leah asked. "I cannot afford to have all my dresses altered. I'm in a pinch as it is now."

"If the countess or someone is willin' to bring you by, you can *pretend* to drop off a dress for repair. On Mondays and Wednesdays, Madame Lejeune usually takes her luncheon break between one and two o'clock—goes out with a gentleman friend, she does, her bein' a widow. In fact, that's where she was headed the other day, when you came in."

"Where is she today?" Leah inquired, wondering why the couturière hadn't greeted her the instant she'd come through the door.

"On an errand. She'll be back shortly, so we don't have much time to talk. Whenever you want to mail a letter, come by on the days I mentioned—'bout one-thirty, to be safe. Bring a dress with you, like you done today. I'll be here tendin' the shop while she's gone. Whenever a reply comes from your Terence, I'll bring the dress back round to Berkley Square, his letter hidden inside."

"Won't that cause suspicion? I mean—do you normally deliver gowns to your customers?"

"All the time. Of course, Madame Lejeune charges extra for the service. But my comin' by won't cost you nothin'—unless you'd like to tip me on occasion."

"I'd be more than happy to tip you, Sally. Especially since you are so willing to go out of your way for me. However, I fear I'm putting you at risk. Should we be caught, you'll undoubtedly lose your job."

"Pah! Ain't no loss at all," she insisted. "My beau and me decided it's time we got married. The weddin' is month after next. We'll be movin' to the west of England—his father is a tenant farmer, and Ben wants to leave the city and go back to the country. Not to worry 'bout me if we get caught. 'Tis you who'll be in the most trouble." She'd peered around Leah's shoulder through the window. "By the looks of that man out there, you'll be sufferin' mightily, you will. Who is he, if you don't mind my askin'."

"That's the Earl of Huntsford, the countess's son."

"The one who nearly read your letter?"

"Yes. He's the one."

"Married, is he?"

"No."

"Not a bad catch for a girl who's lookin' for a husband."

Leah had noticed the admiration in Sally's eyes. Decidedly all women gazed upon him in that special way. "I suppose not, *if* she's looking."

Their agreement made, Sally had fetched a pen and ink for Leah. Scratching out the return address on the securely sealed letter, Leah had replaced it with the one Sally quoted to her. A quick note had been scribbled on the envelope's back, instructing Terence to henceforth write her at the new address. Afterward, Leah had fished inside her reticule and withdrew a crisp bank note.

"Here, Sally." She'd handed her the money. "This should be enough for the postage. Keep whatever is left over in way of reimbursement for your trouble." She'd pressed the dress she'd brought with her into Sally's hands. "For when you receive a letter for me."

"Thank you, Miss. You're very generous. You'd best be goin', now. The earl, there, appears to be gettin' a mite fidgety."

Having noted through the window how Ian squirmed in the phaeton's seat, Leah had allowed herself to laugh openly. "He does seem a bit annoyed, doesn't he?"

"He does. And he just might come lookin' for you if you tarry too much longer. Besides, Madame should be back any minute."

"Please don't tell her I was here. I was supposed to pay something toward my account when I next came by, but I find myself a little short on funds. I'll come back later in the week."

"My lips are sealed. Uh-oh, he's comin' this way."

Before she could say a proper thank you to Sally, Leah had dashed out the door, meeting Ian in the center of the sidewalk. He'd looked surprised to see her, obviously believing she'd escaped him. Assisting her into the phaeton, he'd said nothing—until now.

"You appear quite pleased with yourself, Miss Kingsley. Did your fitting go that well?"

Leah continued to twirl her parasol. "Exceptionally well." She peered up at him through her lashes, biting her lip to keep from laughing uproariously. He was an unwitting accomplice in helping her sneak her mail through, which added to Leah's exhilaration.

Just as suddenly, though, guilt welled inside Leah to replace her merriment, as she thought about Peter. She looked to the roadway ahead.

By now, had Ian not prevented her from escaping Sinclair House, she'd be nearly to York, if not having already arrived. She hoped Peter would forgive her for not being there to see to his needs as she'd always done in the past when he'd fallen ill. Her heart was with him, even if she couldn't be there physically. Remembering his patience, something he'd gained for all he'd suffered in his few short years, she felt certain he'd understand.

Leah contemplated thanking the earl for stopping her

from charging off, her emotions insisting she go straight to her brother's side. Common sense dictated she be more prudent for all the children's sakes. She'd nearly forgotten that their futures depended upon her, and her alone.

Other than the few bills Ian had handed over to Leah when she'd stepped from the phaeton, only a couple of shillings jingled in the bottom of her reticule, her savings exhausted. Certainly, she could have journeyed to York, sneaking away at night, but if Peter's medical expenses exceeded the funds she'd laid aside, she would have no way of acquiring more in order to continue his care.

Then there was her plan to gather the children and flee England, starting their lives anew in another land. All her hopes were built on receiving Anne's allowance. She'd had no choice but to stay in London, especially when she was again short of cash.

Yes, she should thank Lord Huntsford for his timely intervention. Or else all would surely be lost.

"I doubt your smugness comes solely from a visit to the couturière's," Ian said, gazing down on her, his hands steady on the reins. "Something else must have triggered your complacency. I wonder exactly what it might be? Hmm—something devious, I'll venture."

Damn him. As always he'd hit the mark. "Wonder all you like, sir," she said haughtily, hoping by maintaining an air of insolence, she'd throw him off track. "There is nothing devious about it. My complacency, as you put it, stems from sharing in good conversation with a person of my own gender. With your mother gone, I miss having someone to confide in. I—"

"And I suppose you'd rather have a shop girl act as your confidant instead of granting the honor to me?" he announced, cutting her off.

"You are not a woman, are you?"

"No, but I am known for my patience—usually. I'm an exceedingly good listener and can be trusted fully. I inherited my mother's temperament, remember?"

"That may be, sir. But there are certain things a woman

can share only with another woman. So, unless you can somehow miraculously change your gender, I'll not likely be conveying my innermost thoughts to you."

Ian's deep laughter rumbled forth. "Ten sovereigns says you will."

Leah blinked. "I don't have ten sovereigns."

"No?" he asked, smiling down on her.

Leah knew precisely where his dialogue was leading: straight into another wager. But dared she risk it? Ten sovereigns was a lot of money—especially now. "You know I don't. If I did, why would I be borrowing money from you to pay the couturière?"

"Then what do you have that would be of worth to me?"

Temptation needled her. Never in a million years would she divulge her most private thoughts to this man. There was no way she could possibly lose to him. Not this time. "What would you like?"

Wickedly, his grin widened. "What are you willing to give?"

Spying the tantalizing gleam in his eyes, Leah slanted away from him and hugged the corner of her seat. "No more than another kiss," she snapped.

"That's two you'll owe me."

"I'll not forfeit this one, sir."

"Oh, but you will, Leah," he said softly as he leaned toward her. "Someday, all those words you now keep hidden away in your heart will be whispered solely to me, just as I will whisper the same to you."

Mesmerized, Leah could do naught but stare at him. Conversely, he made her feel weak and invigorated all at once. A sorcerer—that's what he was.

"Do we have a wager?" he asked, his attention still on Leah.

As though from a distance, she heard his question. "Yes," she said, not knowing she had.

A shout sounded, followed by the shrill neigh of a horse. His gaze jerking to the congested roadway ahead, Ian cursed. Captivated by Leah, he hadn't heeded their course. With a quick yank of the reins, he turned the gelding, avoiding the carriage that careened toward the phaeton. The action startled the horse. Eyes rolling, it reared, hooves pummeling the air. A sharp command broke through Ian's lips as he fought to control the beast.

From the corner of her eye, Leah spied a young man as he dashed from the sidewalk into the street. Leaping up, he caught the harness, attempting to bring the horse down. Hooves hit the pavement, but as the beast settled, his meaty shoulder struck the man's chest. The blow knocked the newcomer to the street.

Cursing anew, Ian tossed the reins at a second man who had run up to the phaeton. "Hold these and keep him steady," he commanded. The horse now under control, Ian stepped over Leah's feet and jumped to the ground. Gaining the injured man's side, he let loose another expletive as he squatted down, for he'd recognized the young man immediately.

A hackney driver, whose coach stood at the curb, hovered over both. "He's cracked his head a good one, gov'nor. Bleedin' bad, he is."

Ian slipped a clean handkerchief from his coat pocket, pressing it against the gash along the back of Arthur Covington's head. Then beside him he saw a flash of skirt. Leah stood just at his shoulder. "Tear off a length of petticoat, will you?"

Not more than a second after Ian had hopped from the phaeton so had she. Her heart had leapt into her throat upon recognizing their fallen savior. Now, staring down at her half-brother's pale face, Leah remained paralyzed.

"Leah—your petticoat!" Ian barked. "We need to bind the wound and stop the bleeding."

His sharp tone snapped her from her trance. She lifted her skirt and, with a hard tug, ripped one of the ruffles free. After handing the linen strip to Ian, she watched as he quickly wrapped it around Arthur's head. "Will he be all right?" she asked, finally finding her voice.

Ian secured the loose end of the makeshift bandage by tucking it into the bound cloth, then he looked up at her. "I don't know. We need to get him home." He turned to the hackney driver. "Help me carry him to the phaeton, will you?"

Grabbing Arthur's hat from the street, Leah raced ahead of the two men. Again in her seat, her half-brother was settled in next to her, his head nestled in her lap. "Where will you sit?" she asked Ian.

"I won't." After thanking the hackney driver, he climbed aboard the phaeton, took the reins from the man who still held them, then set the gelding into a fast trot, heading them all toward Hanover Square.

Briefly, Leah studied Ian as he stood in the cramped space beside her feet. As he expertly guided the horse along the street, she knew the accident would never have occurred had he been watching the roadway instead of her. Assured his balance was stable, she shifted her gaze to Arthur.

His resemblance to their father was uncanny. Twins, a generation apart, she thought, shaky fingers smoothing over his bandaged brow. Their sire's blood ran through them both, only now Arthur's was staining her skirt. As she stared down on her unconscious half-brother, any malice she held toward him disintegrated. Compassion filled her, and she offered up a prayer he'd again open his eyes. But not before she could slip away unnoticed, especially by him.

Like an ominous dragon, fate loomed up before her, ready to consume her with its fiery breath. She'd wanted to stay away from Arthur, wanted to be spared the indignity of meeting his family. But apparently it was not to be.

The phaeton swung around a corner, then it pulled to a quick stop. Leah looked up at the brick structure just beyond the curb.

"Get the door," Ian instructed, nodding at the entrance. Then, his legs bent, he lifted Arthur from the seat.

Leah hopped from the phaeton onto the sidewalk and scurried toward the entry. Under her hand, the knocker fell twice against the wood. Without waiting, she twisted the handle and shoved the panel wide. Striding past her, Ian walked into the darkened foyer.

"Direct me to his room," he said to the startled butler, nearly having run the man over.

"Up the stairs and—follow me, sir."

Watching as the butler and Ian angled themselves toward the steps, Leah moved through the doorway.

"Have someone send for a doctor," the earl ordered as he began climbing upward, Arthur cradled securely in his arms.

Leah noted a maid stood just below the stairs. Eyes wide, her neck craning, the young woman stared up at the two men as they wound the steps toward the second level.

"Get Dr. Smythe," the butler shouted down at her; she didn't move. "Now!"

The man's bellow bounded off the high ceiling in the foyer, and the maid sped toward the door, feather duster still in hand. Leah stepped aside as the girl ran past her, out into the sunshine.

"Crenshaw?" a female voice called from what Leah presumed was the sitting room. "What is all the commo—" Now at the doorway, the woman, dressed in deep mourning, suddenly clutched its frame, her gaze centered on the stairs. "Arthur?" Her free hand, fingers curling around a well-used handkerchief, flew to her mouth. "My Lord, what has happened to him?"

The woman, whom Leah guessed was Arthur's mother, had instantly gone pale. Arthur's hat fell from Leah's fingers as she rushed to Lady Covington's side. Steadying the woman, Leah assisted her into a nearby chair within the foyer.

"Oh, Ara—" Looking fully at Leah, she caught herself. "I'm sorry. For a moment, I thought you were—"

"Mother?"

At the front entry, Leah saw a young woman, dark blond hair peeping from under her black bonnet, hurrying toward them, with Arthur's walking cane in hand.

"Oh, Arabella," the older woman cried, rising from her chair. "What has happened to him?"

"I'm not fully certain," Arabella replied. "I was in the shop, looking at some crepe material; Arthur was outside, waiting for me. Someone came through the door and said there had been an accident on the street. By the time I got to the sidewalk, Arthur was gone. A man told me he'd been run down. Another said he'd been taken home. Where is he, Mother?"

"They've taken him upstairs."

"Who brought him home?"

"I believe it was Lady Huntsford's son. Dear God! First your father, now Arthur. I don't think I could bear to lose another of my family. What are we to do?"

"Come," Arabella said, gently urging her mother toward the stairs. "Let's go see to him. His injury may not be as serious as you think."

Having backed herself into the shadows near the sitting-room door, Leah surveyed the two women as they traversed the stairs. Indeed, Arabella was her sister, the shapes of their noses and chins being identical. Even the way she walked was somewhat similar to Leah's own gait, as was the square of her shoulders and the tilt of her head.

Knees shaking, Leah sought the chair that Lady Covington had vacated only moments before. In all the excitement, mother and daughter had paid little attention to the unknown woman who'd invaded the Covingtons' house, something for which Leah was exceptionally thankful. As she stared at the red stain on her skirt, she again offered up her prayers for him. For Arabella, too.

Strange how their lives ran parallel. First, it was the loss of their father, now each worried over a beloved brother. Leah hoped there would be no more tragedies. Both families had suffered enough.

The sound of voices drew her attention toward the front door. Still clutching the feather duster, the maid scurried back across the threshold, with a gray-haired man behind her. He followed the maid to the stairs, then up them, a black bag held firmly in his hand.

The gloomy atmosphere inside the house—its heavy drapes drawn, ornate mirrors covered, black crepe framing the doorways—suddenly became too much for Leah. She couldn't breathe.

Breaking from the chair, she scampered outside, heading

toward the phaeton. Her hands met the seat, where it protruded above the vehicle's side, fingers curling into the soft leather. As she supported herself, she drew fresh air deep into her lungs. The suffocating feeling subsided, and a soft sigh flowed from her. A second later, a pair of hands settled on her shoulders; Leah jumped, then spun around.

"Are you all right?" Ian asked, his tone one of concern. His eyes scanned her face as his hands reclaimed her shoulders. "You're so pale."

"I guess the excitement has finally caught up with me," she said in way of a half-truth. It was far more than Arthur's accident that had chased her from the house, but she couldn't tell him such. "I'll be fine in a moment." Wishing he wouldn't situate himself so close to her, Leah squirmed from the earl's grasp, then nodded toward the door. "How is he?"

Ian's hands fell to his side. "Once the pounding in his head has eased, he'll be fine. The doctor said he might have a slight concussion. The gash, though it bled a lot, is nothing to worry about."

"Then he has awakened?"

"His eyes opened before we got to his room. He insisted I put him down so that he could walk the rest of the way. I'm afraid he didn't quite make it. I managed to catch him before he fell."

Proud and independent—Arthur sounded as though he were much like young Terence in his temperament. "Lucky for him you were close at hand. Otherwise, he'd be sporting another bump."

Ian noted how the color had crept back into Leah's face. She looked far better than when he came upon her a moment ago. "I doubt he'd be too happy had he taken a second knock. He was not too pleased with the first."

"Does he blame you?"

"No. He blames himself for acting so impetuously. But it was my fault, not his. I'm just glad it wasn't worse than it is. He could have been killed."

"Lord Huntsford?"

At the call, Ian looked around. Arabella Covington walked toward him. Glancing back at Leah, he noticed she had turned away.

"I wanted to thank you for bringing my brother home so swiftly," Arabella said, now standing in front of him. "Arthur asked me to tell you not to worry over his mishap. He insists it was his fault, not yours."

"That's debatable. Had I been watching the street, instead of looking elsewhere, the entire incident wouldn't have occurred." He marked how Arthur's sister tried to peer over his shoulder at Leah. "Forgive my bad manners on not making the proper introductions," he said, stepping aside. "Miss Covington, may I present Miss Anne Kingsley."

On hearing the word *introduction,* Leah could have slipped through the crack in the sidewalk. Now, as she rotated to face Arabella, she wished the entire street would open up and swallow her.

"Miss Kingsley," Arabella greeted with a nod. "It is a pleasure to meet you, although, I dare say, I wish it had been under better circumstances."

"The same to you, Miss Covington," Leah returned, keeping her head down slightly, hoping that her bonnet would shield her face. "I do hope your brother recovers most rapidly, and without suffering any ill effects."

"From what the doctor has told us, he should be good as new in a few days." Arabella looked to Ian. "Thank you again, Lord Huntsford. Now, if you'll excuse me, I must see to my mother. She's still a bit upset. I fear too much has happened of late."

"My belated condolences to you and your family, Miss Covington," he said. "I shall come round in a few days to see how your brother is faring. Should you need anything— anything at all—please let me know."

"Thank you yet again, sir. Good day to you." Her gaze shifted toward Leah. "Good day to you, Miss Kingsley."

From beneath the rim of her bonnet, Leah watched as Arabella made her way back into the house. The door closed softly behind her.

"Let's be going," Ian said. After assisting a subdued Leah

into the phaeton, he rounded the vehicle and climbed aboard. The reins gathered, he set the gelding into a quick trot, then surveyed the street ahead.

Damn! He'd been behaving like a lovesick schoolboy. Forever in a stupor, he constantly thought about the woman beside him. Before he slaughtered all of London—pedestrians dashing for doorways, carriages crashing into each other and overturning—he had to put a stop to this nonsense. He was weary of waltzing around Leah. It was time he acted like the man he was—confident and direct.

Slow and easy had been his design for conquest. But no more. The strategy had just changed to an all-out assault, and the Delderfields' ball seemed a good place for him to make the first strike. Even now he could taste victory.

And the spoils would be, oh, so sweet.

CHAPTER
12

"You look beautiful, Miss," Milly declared, stepping away from Leah, the last of the gown's hooks secured.

"Think so?"

"Oh yes, Miss, I do."

Leah stared at her reflection in the standing mirror, amazed by what she saw. The amethyst silk creation, trimmed in black lace, emphasized the fullness of her breasts and the slim line of her waist, then flowed softly to her feet, brushing the tops of her slippers, their color an exact match to her gown. Tiny sprigs of violets dotted the crown of her upswept hair; curls caressed her ears, amethysts dangling from their lobes. Before the countess had left, she'd handed the earrings to Leah, with strict instructions she was to wear them the night of the Delderfields' ball.

Leah nervously smoothed her skirt. She dreaded going, dreaded walking into a room full of strangers whom she could barely abide. But most of all, she dreaded being in the company of Ian Sinclair.

These past several days, other than at mealtimes, Leah

had avoided him, she opting mostly to stay in her room, he his study. Yet she knew he was never far away.

Whenever she sought out the serenity of the gardens, he watched her from the cover of the house. Likewise, when their master was otherwise occupied, the servants kept vigil over her movements in his place, undoubtedly reporting to him at regular intervals. Obviously, he still believed she might seek to escape, rushing directly into her nonexistent lover's arms.

He could reckon whatever he wished. She was staying here, at Sinclair House, continuing to collect Anne's allowance. Unless, of course, little Peter's condition worsened. Then, she'd hasten to her brother's side, worrying about the consequences later.

She'd not heard back from Terence, but imagined she would shortly. Pray the money she'd sent him had gotten to him safely, and that Peter was now receiving the proper care.

"Go tell him I'll be but a moment more, will you, Milly?" Leah instructed as she turned from the mirror. The maid scurried toward the door. "And Milly." She looked over her shoulder at Leah. "Thank you for assisting me tonight."

"It was my pleasure, Miss," the maid replied, smiling shyly. "I hope you enjoy your night out."

"So do I, Milly," Leah murmured, certain the outing would be a disaster. "So do I."

Downstairs, Ian paced the gallery floor, his gaze switching from the clock to the stairs, then back again. His patience was ebbing, for he wanted to be at the front door, waiting, when the Whitcombs arrived. Otherwise, with Leah's tardiness, should Simmons be forced to permit them into the house, he felt certain Veronica would insist she pay call on his mother, seeing about the countess's health.

Sure calamity, he decided, desiring to protect Leah as long as he could, hoping to win her without mental duress. Later, should his new plan of action fail, he wouldn't be so inclined. However, that particular part of his scheme was reserved for last, it being the most devious and under-handed of all. He'd not use the ploy, not unless it became totally necessary, all other avenues having been exhausted.

Ian saw movement at the top of the stairs. It was Milly. "Is Miss Kingsley ready?" he asked.

"Yes, sir—well, almost. She told me to let you know she'd be but a moment more."

"Tell me, Milly," he said, exasperated. "Why is it a woman is always late?"

The maid's feet hit the gallery's marble floor. "I don't know, sir. Maybe because she wants to look her very best—especially if she's hoping to catch the eye of a certain man. When you see her, sir, I don't think you'll be the least disappointed. She's truly worth the wait."

Ian heard the rustle of skirts and looked to the top of the stairs. The moment he saw Leah, he realized how breathtakingly beautiful she really was. "You're absolutely right, Milly. She is *indeed* worth the wait."

Her shawl draped over her arm, Leah nervously descended the steps, with gloves, fan, and reticule in hand. As she drew nearer to Ian, she realized she had good reason to be in a twitter. Resplendently dressed in black evening attire, a white silk waistcoat hugging his lean belly, his stark white cravat tied to perfection, he was the epitome of every woman's dream. Leah wondered if she'd be able to resist him, something that was becoming harder and harder to do.

Please give me strength.

The fervent request, uttered in her mind, was sent heavenward just as his hand reached out for hers. Briefly, Leah hesitated, then her trembling fingers eased over his warm palm. His hand swallowed hers, and he assisted her down the last three steps.

"I was just about to come up after you," he said, looking down on her. "But I'm glad I waited. Watching you walk down these stairs was captivating. You're beautiful, Leah. No woman will outshine you tonight, as though she ever could."

As he spoke, his eyes had darkened from sapphire to a deep midnight blue. Leah felt suddenly breathless; heat rushed to her cheeks, while her stomach fluttered quite oddly. *Why did this man affect her so?* Her eyes cast away from Ian's as her hand pulled from his. "We'd best be going, before Jonathan and Veronica arrive."

"Yes, we'd better," he agreed as Leah headed to the second set of stairs. He caught up to her, then trailed her down to the foyer. "They don't know you are coming with me," he said, once they were on level ground. "Let me take the lead when we're asked about my mother's absence."

"Have you decided on a plausible ailment?"

He pulled the shawl from Leah's arm. "A severe headache, its effects having sent her to bed," he announced, draping the black lace covering over her bare shoulders. For a moment, he'd been tempted to kiss the creamy softness, but wisely he held the urge in check. "Does that sound acceptable?"

Leah glanced up at him as she drew on her gloves. "Yes. A headache sounds fine to me."

"By the way, I should warn you news travels fast in this town, especially among my peers. Mind yourself tonight, Leah, for the gossips are lying in wait, watching and listening, ready to spread the latest bit of slander. They thrive on scandal. It's their lifeblood. Without it they'd wither and die."

If Leah thought she was nervous before, she was now ready to bolt back up the steps. "I appreciate your telling me."

Ian caught her ironic tone. "You're welcome." The roll of carriage wheels sounded outside the door. The vehicle stopped. "Just stay close to me," he said, receiving his cane, hat, and gloves from Simmons, "and you won't get into any trouble."

"So you say," Leah offered as she pulled the edge of her shawl over her head; the long ends were tossed back over her shoulders.

At Ian's nod, the butler opened the door for the couple.

"Yes, so I say. Remember, stay close."

Not likely, Leah thought, as she stepped across the threshold, out into the night air. If she did, the scandalmongers would definitely have something to talk about, for the man was completely irresistible—tonight, especially.

The Whitcombs' carriage joined the long line of vehicles that had formed along the street where the Delderfields resided, all inching toward the torchlit entry.

"Why is there always such a wait?" Veronica asked, sounding perturbed.

"Perhaps, sister, it is because we have arrived during the main crush. Had you been ready on time, we would have gotten here a lot sooner, avoiding any delays."

The pair's squabbling was beginning to annoy Ian. When Veronica first spotted Leah, her look had soured considerably, while Jonathan's had brightened an equal amount. Once the man mentioned how glad he was that Leah could join them, his sister set to sniping at him, Jonathan giving back as good as he got.

"Miss Kingsley was a few minutes late, also," Ian proclaimed, hoping to quell their bickering. "But I've been told by a very reliable source that the end product is always worth the wait. I must say: *Stunning* is the word I would use to describe both the Lady Veronica and Miss Kingsley. Your tardiness becomes you, ladies."

"You see, Jonathan," Veronica said, her tone appearing less stringent. "Ian thinks it is acceptable for a woman to be late."

"I don't mind your being late," Jonathan returned, "but I do detest hearing your complaints about the hang up we are made to suffer because of it. However, I will agree with Huntsford. You are both quite attractive in your new finery. Possibly the prettiest two at the ball, I'll wager. Tell me, Huntsford, who is your source?"

Ian chuckled. "My maid, Milly."

"An astute young woman," Jonathan said.

"Definitely," Ian replied, his attention falling on Leah. "She knows beauty when she sees it, as do I."

With their carriage finally arriving at the entrance, a white-wigged footman came forward, lowering the steps. Ian and Jonathan descended to the sidewalk, then each waited to assist Leah and Veronica.

Leah was the first to rise from her seat; Jonathan quickly brushed in front of Ian. "Sorry, old man," he said, having trod upon the earl's foot.

An eyebrow arching, Ian looked down on the viscount. Old man, indeed. Gauging Jonathan's size and weight, he doubted the young pup could best him, whatever the challenge. Especially if it had anything to do with Leah. When she stepped down, Ian allowed Whitcomb to escort her to the door. Once Veronica's feet had found the sidewalk, he guided her up to the entry.

"I certainly wish your mother hadn't fallen ill," Veronica said, handing her invitation to the footman who stood guard at the door. "I imagine she's so very disappointed about not being able to come."

Ian passed the engraved card to the man, then watched as their names were checked off the guest list. "The Countess of Huntsford will not be in attendance tonight," he told the man. "She sends her regrets."

A line was scratched through Madeline's name, the word *ill* written beside it. The Delderfields were sticklers about a person who sent his acceptance, then didn't show. Most likely, the individual would never be invited again. Ian imagined that was why Veronica had made such a fuss about his mother's supposed illness. He just hoped one of the Delderfields didn't appear on his doorstep in the morning, seeking confirmation the countess had really taken to her bed.

After handing his hat and cane over to another footman, his name given for their retrieval later, Ian quickly led Veronica to the foot of the wide marble staircase, where they caught up with Leah and Jonathan, who were now stalled, waiting for the throng to ascend to the ballroom.

"I believe the Delderfields have expanded their guest list," Jonathan commented, pivoting toward Ian and his sister. "I don't remember seeing—Egad! Don't look now, but here comes old Rup and his *darling* mother." He rolled his eyes. "Mind that pink satin coat he's wearing. It's enough to set Beau Brummell to turning in his grave."

Like disobedient children intent on having their own way, the viscount's companions instantly glanced toward the door. Ian chuckled, while Veronica gasped. Leah could do naught but gape.

"It's the purple trousers," Ian remarked. "Had he worn puce, he may not have clashed as much."

"I told you not to look," Jonathan admonished. "He's spotted us. And he's coming this way, the duchess with him."

Rupert and the duchess reached the foursome, and polite greetings were exchanged all around. The duchess then introduced her son to Leah. "I had previously wanted to thank you for returning my mother's bracelet, but the occasion never presented itself," he lisped, ogling her through his lorgnette. "May I do so now, Miss Kingsley?"

"You're welcome, sir," Leah responded, the words nearly choking her. Since her savings were now depleted, Leah wished she'd had the nerve to keep the expensive trinket when first faced with the choice. What new harm could she have possibly suffered by adding another crime to her list? A hangman's noose already awaited her. "It was fortunate I spotted it when I did or the bracelet might have been lost."

"Yes, it certainly is," Rupert agreed, the words spraying from his lips; the foursome quickly took a step back. "And as your reward, dear girl, since we didn't have a chance to do so at the Carstairses' ball, I shall expect you to dance with me tonight."

"I believe Miss Kingsley's dance card is filled," Ian announced. "Perhaps another time, sir, at another ball."

Relief flooded through Leah the instant the earl's words left his mouth.

"Pity," Rupert stated. "I had so wished to hold the lovely lady in my arms."

As he cast the man a hard look, a cold smile crossed Ian's face. "Not this time."

The crowd began moving up the stairs, and Ian noted how

Rupert had situated himself directly behind Leah. His closeness irritated the earl. Positive the man would next attempt to fondle her derrière, masking his lechery in the guise of subtle little bumps, he purposely trod upon Rupert's foot.

"Sorry, old man," he said, repeating Jonathan's earlier apology, slickly gliding between Leah and the startled Rupert. "I hope I didn't ruin your slippers."

Rupert looked down on the pink satin shoe. "A small smudge, is all."

"My apologies, again," Ian offered, then followed Leah up the stairs, to the ballroom, where each guest was being presented.

As Leah waited her turn, she grew more nervous. She'd managed to slip through the last time at the Carstairses' ball, no one apparently having ever heard of Miss Anne Kingsley, much less having met her before. According to her uncle's letter, Anne hadn't been in the north of England very long, and even if she had, Leah doubted Anne was readily introduced around, John Kingsley being embarrassed by her alleged lack of manners. But there was always the off chance someone from York would be in attendance, and that someone may have indeed met the real Anne.

She prayed it wasn't so, then walking forward, she spoke in the footman's ear, for she lacked a formal name card to hand him.

"Miss Anna Kingston," he announced, his nasal tone ringing through the ballroom.

An understandable mistake, Leah deemed, the noise level around them being exceptionally high. No surprised gazes had shot her way as she stepped past the double doors, and she was grateful for the man's error.

The Whitcombs, then Ian, followed Leah, each of their names and titles being pronounced correctly. After Veronica had pointed out a set of four chairs, situated between two lush potted plants, the group moved around the room's perimeter, Ian and Leah in the rear.

"Changed your name, have you?" Ian inquired, chuckling.

"Yes, I have," she said truthfully. "The mistake matters not. No one here knows me."

"But there are plenty who would like to," he grumbled, having spied the wealth of masculine interest centered on her when she'd entered the ballroom. He'd identified several infamous rogues as being among the men who viewed her. "In the biblical sense, particularly."

Leah gaped up at him. "I'm certain you are mistaken, sir. No man has ever made any improper advances toward me before." *Except you.* "I doubt any of them shall do so now."

"Given the chance, they will. Don't let their suave manners fool you, Leah. They are a randy bunch, all eager to make a conquest."

"Much like you, I suppose?"

"Not quite," he declared, knowing even if he received her virginity tonight, he'd gladly marry her tomorrow. "There's a difference—a huge difference. Take it as truth."

They'd reached the chairs, and Veronica quickly seated herself in the second one to the right. Grabbing Leah's hand, Jonathan claimed the seat next to his sister, urging Leah into the chair closest to the plant. Ian had no choice but to take the remaining chair beside the second plant, fully opposite Leah.

Because of the arrangement, Leah was forced to converse with Jonathan, while Veronica chatted away at Ian. What about, he couldn't say, for his attention remained on Leah.

Then the earl noticed the approach of a young gentleman. He stopped in front of Leah, introduced himself, then took up the conversation. The first man was soon joined by another, then another, until a full half-dozen swains were circled around her, blocking Ian's view entirely. Directly, the group had grown to a solid dozen. Soon Leah's crystal laughter rose upward, deep chuckles following in its wake, and Ian's jaw clenched.

"You seem perturbed," Veronica said. "One would think Miss Kingsley's gaining so much attention is not to your liking."

Ian shifted his concentration toward Veronica. "I promised my mother I would keep a watchful eye on her. From the looks of it, the task may prove troublesome."

"Certainly, you don't plan to chase after her the night through, do you?"

"If need be."

"Heavens, Ian. First it was this mysterious man from Ulster who kept you glued to her side, now it is these young gentlemen at the ball. Perhaps it is your age, but you are forever playing the roll of an anxious father. Can you not relax your guard for once? The young woman is entitled to have some enjoyment in life. And so am I."

With the marked reference about the age difference between Leah and him, Ian grew testy. "Physically, Veronica, at the time of Miss Kingsley's birth, I may have been capable of siring her—though just barely. But I am not her father, nor do I think of myself as such. Far from it, in fact." Music filled the ballroom, proclaiming the first dance of the night. Slipping his gloves from his pocket, he donned them, then came to his feet. "Excuse me."

Having come halfway out of her chair, a stunned Veronica fell back into her seat when he turned away from her.

Trying to figure out which young man would be granted the first waltz, Jonathan included, Leah saw Ian shouldering his way to the fore of the group. *Choose one!* she demanded of herself. The silent command came too late.

"Gentlemen," Ian greeted, extending his gloved hand toward Leah. "There will be other opportunities for all of you. As it is, Miss Kingsley's first dance belongs to me."

A protest trembled on Leah's lips, but on spying the determined look in the earl's eyes, she knew her objection would receive a dismissal. Her hand slid over his palm, whereupon he urged her from her seat. The swains parting to form a path, Ian led her onto the dance floor.

"That was exceptionally rude of you," she snapped, gathering up her skirt so she wouldn't trip as they waltzed. The action, though probably not necessary, relieved her of having to place her hand on his shoulder. The least amount of contact between them the better. Now only their hands were linked. "How could you be so impolite?"

181

"Quite easily," he muttered, his fingers spanning her small waist. Deciding she stood too far from him, his hand slid to her back; he pulled her to him, then whirled her into the crowd. "Since I am the one who escorted you here, I am the one who gains the pleasure of the first dance."

Her feet keeping perfect time with his, Leah felt suddenly overpowered by Ian. His masculine aura radiated around her, its magnetic force inviting her closer. Strangely, she wanted to nestle against him, feel his special energy flowing into her, its potency giving her new life.

Fighting against the temptation, she tried to slant away from him, but the pressure of his hand drew her nearer and nearer. Several censuring glances came their way, their owners obviously outraged by the couple's immediacy, Leah and Ian's bodies nearly touching. "Why are you doing this?"

"Doing what?"

"Making a spectacle of us. You warn me about the gossips, yet you're the one who is bent on fueling their suspicions, which will surely start them all to clacking. Have you no concern for my feelings?"

"More than you know," he returned, wanting all her sentiments centered explicitly on him, first and foremost her love. "If they wish to talk about us, let them. The rumors will soon die down." *Once we are married, that is.*

Leah gaped at him. "If you care not about my feelings, what about Veronica's?" she asked, having noted the injured look on the woman's face when Ian had first spun Leah into the waltzing throng. "You're exceedingly callous to toy with her as you do."

"That will soon be rectified." If not tonight, then tomorrow, he planned to sever his ties with Veronica. He hoped they could remain friends, but he doubted it. "She'll soon have what she wants," he said, thinking of a particular man who would suit Veronica far better than he. An acquaintance of Ian's, Lord Winston was a widower without issue. Knowing the man should be out of mourning by now, Ian intended to direct him Veronica's way, certain they were well-matched. "By month's end, she'll be basking in the light of love. In the meantime, she'll just have to wait the moment of promise."

Remembering Madeline had mentioned that she thought her son would ask for Veronica's hand by the end of May, Leah glared up at Ian. It wasn't Veronica with whom he toyed, but *her!* "You're a cad, sir—a man without principle. Why a woman would want any involvement with someone such as you remains a mystery to me."

"Just say the word, and I'd be more than happy to unravel the riddle for you, Leah." Her eyes widened, and Ian chuckled. "What? Not daring enough to strip away the enigma? I promise you won't be disappointed by what you find."

Leah stiffened; her lips drew into a tight line. "You play games, sir. I'm not interested in being part of your sport."

"No?"

"No. As I said, you're a cad."

"In your eyes, maybe." Green fire flashed in their depths. "You speak of games—well, let it be known: Whatever game it is I play, I always win. Surrender, Leah. Don't fight the inevitable. It's a given that you'll lose to me."

Anger welled higher in Leah, but it was directed at herself, not at Ian. To struggle against him would be fruitless. She hadn't the strength to resist him. Still, she'd never admit it—not openly. And certainly not to him.

"There's no contest between us, so it is unlikely I'll lose," she snapped.

"Oh, there's a contest, all right. But the conflict is within you," he said. "Yield to your feelings, and the pleasures we find together will be unmatched. Give it up, Leah, and we'll both be the victors."

To Leah's disappointment, he'd mentioned nothing about love. Even if he'd uttered that magical word, expressed his desire to take her as his wife, Leah knew she'd have to reject him. For in the end, when he discovered her true identity— undoubtedly on the solicitor's return—he'd be the one spurning her. The situation was impossible.

The music stopped, and she pulled away from his arms.

"You dwell in your own fantasies, sir. It is time you sought reality. Go to Veronica. She is the woman you want."

As she started to turn away, Ian caught her arm. "I know who it is I want, Leah, and she'll be mine soon enough. As I said: I always win. It will be the same with you."

Breaking from his hold, she walked on stiff legs to her chair. Her admirers awaited her, each begging for the next dance. As the music struck up again, she saw Ian was headed toward the group. Pointing to the man nearest her, she allowed him to whisk her onto the dance floor.

The couple spun by the Earl of Huntsford, who now stood on the sidelines, and Leah's eyes briefly snagged his. Challenge showed in his gaze. He meant to have her at any cost.

I always win. It will be the same with you.

Hearing his words anew, Leah turned her head, intent on ignoring him. Fight him she would. But deep in her heart, she knew the battle was already lost.

CHAPTER
13

❧—————❨

Leah was whirled from the dance floor by her eighth consecutive partner since escaping the earl, then led to her chair. After a sharp bow, the young man quickly strode off into the crowd, his retreat no doubt hastened by the fact she'd virtually disregarded him. She felt bad about having treated him so shoddily, but in truth, she had more important things to consider.

Nearly falling into her seat, she snapped open her fan, then wagged it energetically. As the fast breeze cooled her cheeks, she glanced around. Her tension eased somewhat, for Ian was nowhere in sight.

On three separate occasions, Leah, and the swain with whom she'd waltzed at the time, glided by Lord Huntsford. He'd continued to hug the dance floor's perimeter, and on spying him, she'd promptly turned her head, the action meant as a snub. But Leah doubted it had had much of an effect.

Determined as he was, his pursuit of her promised to be relentless. Victory would be his, she knew. Still she vowed to stave him off for as long as she could. Equally as determined as he, she'd not allow herself to go down so easily.

Music filled the air once more, and a young man stepped forward. "Miss Kingsley, I believe this is my dance."

Long ago, on introducing her to each new swain as he approached Leah, Lord Whitcomb had corrected the mistake concerning her assumed name. Now, she wished her four remaining admirers would turn their attentions on someone else and leave her alone. By their eager expressions, she doubted they would. "Please, gentlemen, I'm simply exhausted," she declared, smiling at the group, playing the part of a simpering coquette. "Allow me to sit this one out, will you? If I don't catch my breath, I shall swoon."

Leah blinked as one particularly solicitous gentleman dashed off to acquire a refreshment for her.

"I'm perfectly fine," she told the lingering three, all having made earnest inquiry about her health. "A short rest, and I'll be ready to dance again."

Pretending to listen as each man attempted to outstrip the other in vying for her attention, Leah settled back, her fan waving more slowly.

Just beyond the plant, which separated one section of chairs from another, two female voices were engaged in a quick chatter. It wasn't until Leah heard *Lord Huntsford* that she actually took note of what they said. Leaning her ear closer to the greenery, she listened.

"I know for a fact Lady Halston's youngest son, Melvin, was in Bath. He returned just this afternoon. Lord Huntsford's carriage was seen by him, several times. The countess and her aunt were inside on one such occasion."

"Are you certain it was Lord Huntsford's carriage?"

"He said the earl's crest was clearly on the carriage and he swears he saw the countess inside. She's not here tonight either. She never misses a function at the Delderfields'. Never."

"The earl mentioned to someone she'd fallen ill—a headache, I believe."

"A ruse, I tell you. She's in Bath, and the two of them are alone in that house. Scandalous, I say. The way he held her when they were dancing—something illicit is surely going on between them."

"But the Lady Veronica says she expects Huntsford's proposal by month's end."

"Well, that makes it all the more wicked of him. Imagine prancing his harlot around in front of his peers and his future bride—the man is an absolute rogue. I doubt he'll be faithful to Veronica. Six months, I tell you, Frances, and he'll have a mistress—possibly Miss Kingsley, herself."

"She's John Kingsley's niece, is she not?"

"Yes. At least that is what the countess has said."

"Wasn't there a scandal in the Kingsley family sometime back—nearly twenty years ago?"

"Few know about it, but indeed there was. Kingsley's brother James was serving in the King's Regiment. He'd been assigned to the Ulster Province in Ireland. Fell in love with the daughter of one of those anarchists who is constantly striving for a free Ireland. Imagine any of them wishing to break from the Crown. They could never rule themselves, illiterate and rancorous as they all are. Anyway, Kingsley's brother resigned his commission and married the little rustic. It is even said he took up the fight against British rule—a traitor, if there ever was one."

Laughter erupted from the second woman. "Then she is of low birth, a common Irish slut. The earl will weary of her soon enough. He'll toss her into the gutter where she belongs, most likely before he marries. The Lady Veronica has nothing to worry about, being as educated and well-bred as she is."

"Perhaps not. But I'll wager you this: When they leave here tonight, returning alone to Sinclair House, he'll take the strumpet straight to his bed. Meanwhile, he flaunts his whore in front of us. It is all so sordid, I tell you."

"When will you understand, Gertrude, that he is simply using the little baggage? Look how he and Veronica dance together. By the way he gazes into her eyes, I say he is madly in love with her. Kingsley's niece is merely an itch he feels he must scratch. Oh, look Gertrude, there is the Lady

Seymour. I saw her watching Huntsford and his whore earlier. Let's go seek out her opinion on the matter."

"Scandalous, I tell you, Frances. Simply scandalous."

Nearly from the first, as Leah listened, a sick quiver had settled in the pit of her stomach. The rustle of skirts announced that the two women had escaped their chairs. Once she was certain they were gone, she gazed around the plant and searched the dance floor. Leah felt the blood drain from her face on spotting Ian and Veronica. Indeed, the earl smiled down on the brunette. To anyone who viewed them, they appeared to be madly in love, just as the gossiping Frances had said.

An itch he feels he must scratch. Was that all she was to him? Leah wondered, imagining the pair would soon escape to the gardens, to stroll in the candlelight with the other couples, love kindling in their eyes.

"Miss Kingsley—Leah? Are you all right? You're as white as a sheet."

She looked up to see Jonathan standing beside her. Then from the corner of her eye, she caught a flash of pink. Rupert was headed toward her, his lorgnette pasted to his face. "Yes, I'm fine." She popped from her seat, then swayed on her feet. "Excuse me, will you?"

Pushing through the men who surrounded her chair, she hurried around the ballroom, to the double doors, then out into the hall. On her swift exit, she nearly collided with a footman.

"Is there a place where I might seek privacy?" she asked. "I fear I'm feeling a bit faint."

"This way, Miss." Quickly the footman guided her down the corridor and through another set of doors. Leaving her on the settee in the sitting room, he inquired: "Should I fetch someone for you, Miss?"

"N-no. I'll be all right in a moment. Please. I'd like some privacy, if you don't mind?"

He inspected her closely. "If you insist, Miss. I'll be back shortly to check in on you."

When the doors closed behind him, Leah breathed deeply. Anger whirled up inside her; her head no longer swam.

An itch, was it? Well, she wasn't about to let him scratch it. Veronica could have the pleasure of easing his distress. It certainly wouldn't be her.

Leah sprang from the settee to pace the floor. What a fool she was! Because her heart was already forfeited to him, she'd believed all his rubbish about winning and losing, not fighting the inevitable. Stupidly, she'd nearly handed him the victory, little more than a volley of words passing between them. Well, the battle lines were now drawn. The next time she saw him, she'd fire a scathing verbal cannonade, delivering him a broadside. Scuttled, he'd sink into the depths, never to be raised. The arrogant knave.

The doors opened.

Thinking it was the footman, Leah pasted a smile on her face and turned around. At once she frowned. "What do you want?"

"I've come to offer you a proper thank you, dear girl. One I'm certain you'll enjoy."

Closing the doors, Rupert strode toward Leah.

"Maybe one of us should go see about her," Jonathan said to the four men who milled beside him.

Ian and Veronica had just returned to the area, the waltz finished. "See about who?" he inquired, looking for Leah.

"Miss Kingsley," one of the swains said. "She turned white and dashed from the room. We haven't seen her since."

"How long ago?" the earl questioned.

"Five minutes—no more—just before old Rup made his appearance here," a second would-be suitor told Ian.

"That's probably what sent her packing," yet another young admirer commented. "Merely the sight of the odious fop is enough to chase any young woman off into the night."

Through narrowed eyes, Ian searched the room, looking for the tell-tale pink coat. Cursing, he brushed past Veronica.

"Where are you going?" she called.

Headed for the double doors, Ian didn't respond.

* * *

"Unhand me, you fool!" Leah cried, forearms braced against Rupert's chest, attempting to stave him off.

After a minute or so of waltzing around the furniture, trying to escape him, she'd found herself trapped against a gilded *secrétaire* cabinet, standing at the far side of the room. The ruby stickpin gracing his cravat flashed in her eye. Were it a jeweled dagger, she'd plunge it straight into his black heart.

"Loose me, I say!"

Leah's leverage slipped; her glove snagged, then suddenly her fist struck Rupert's fleshy jaw. Instantly, her hands were slammed against the glass behind her head. By the force of the blow, she was surprised the panes didn't break.

"Now, now, Miss Kingsley," Rupert lisped, his body pressing against hers. Harsh fingers banded her wrists as he attempted to grind his hips into Leah's, but his flabby belly prevented full contact. "Give me a kiss—just one little kiss—and I shall let you go. It's that simple."

The words sprayed from Rupert's mouth; Leah's head jerked to the side, her eyes squeezing closed. "Never!" Feeling his wet lips against her cheek, she felt at once nauseated. "You salacious bastard," she said, gritting her teeth. "Get away from me!"

"Not likely," he muttered. "Not till I have what I want."

Somehow Rupert's belly bounded up; his groin gyrated against Leah's pelvis. She attempted to scream.

Rupert rammed himself against her. "Cry out, and it will be your last mistake."

Along with his words, did she hear the door open?

As he began rotating again, his turgidness now evident, even through her gown. Leah felt ill; her stomach rolled uncontrollably. "I'm going to be sick."

"I've heard that one before. Relax and enjoy it, dear girl. I surely will."

Were those footsteps coming her way?

A whimper trembled in her throat, then bled through her lips as he began a thrusting motion. This time Leah believed she truly might faint.

"You licentious son-of-a-bitch!"

The growled words bounded into Leah's ears just as Rupert was jerked away from her. "Ian?" she whispered, her eyes flying wide.

"Get out, Leah," he ordered, his hard gaze on her attacker. "Old Rup and I have a few things to discuss."

"Really, Huntsford, nothing is amiss," Rupert said, backing toward the opposite wall away from the earl. "She threw herself at me. Can't blame a chap for taking advantage of the situation, can you?"

"Get out, Leah," Ian bade her again, "and shut the doors behind you. Now!"

Fleet of foot, she bolted around the furnishings, toward the doors.

"Actually, Rup," she heard Ian say, "had I been in your place, I might have done the same."

Surprised by his statement, Leah slowed her pace and listened carefully.

"I thought you'd see it my way, Huntsford. After all, the girl is nothing more than Irish rabble."

"Irish rabble, hmm? Doesn't deserve to be treated with any respect, I suppose?"

"Not her kind."

With Rupert's words, Leah's fingers met the door handles. A spot of red glittered at her wrist. Rupert's ruby stickpin! Plucking it free, she tucked the gem inside her glove, shaking it to her palm. Payment for his lechery, she decided, then stepped from the room. Seeing movement to her side, she gasped. "Oh, it's you," she said, recognizing the footman who'd shown her into the sitting room.

"Miss," he greeted her, moving from his station beside the doorway. He took hold of the ornate handles, drawing the panels to. The latch clicked. "I'm certain the earl will be only a moment," he said, then moved back to his previous spot.

Her ear close to the door, Leah studied the servant. Standing at attention, he cut a fine figure dressed in a royal blue coat and white breeches, stockings and powdered wig to match. A hard thud sounded beyond the panels; Leah swore the floor shook beneath her feet. She saw the footman's lips twitch. He again stepped from his post.

"I believe the earl is coming now, Miss."

True to the man's word, the doors were jerked inward; Ian strode into the hall. With a flick of his wrists, the panels closed behind him. "You may want to keep the room sealed for a while," he said to the footman.

"As you say, sir." The man took up a stance directly in front of the doors. "Anything else that needs to be done, sir?"

"No. Everything is in its place." Ian slipped a crisp bank note from the pocket of his waistcoat and tucked it into the footman's palm. "Thank you."

"Glad I could be of service, sir."

The two men exchanged a quick nod, then Ian latched on to Leah's arm and guided her down the corridor.

Her knees wobbling, Leah attempted to gauge Ian's mood. "Where's Rupert?" she asked as they neared the ballroom.

Ian's eyes remained centered on the way ahead. "Taking a nap."

Leah's mouth worked several times, but nothing came out. Then she noticed his right hand. The glove was missing, and his knuckles blazed red. Her laughter bubbled forth. When she looked forward again, she saw they were headed toward the stairs. "Where are you taking me?"

"Home."

"But my shawl and reticule—they're still in the ballroom. And what about Jonathan and Veronica?"

"The Whitcombs can gather your things when they leave."

Now down the steps, Ian stalked past the footman who held his hat and cane for him; Leah skipped beside him, trying to keep up with his pace.

"How will we get home?" she asked, the front door behind them.

Ian kept a tight hold on Leah as they traversed the sidewalk, then the two stepped from the curb. Rounding the back of a carriage, its driver dozing, he pulled her into the street. With a quick look up and down the thoroughfare, he spotted a hackney.

The earl's shrill whistle split the air, startling Leah, along with the nodding driver. Staring at him, she noted the tic jumping along his jaw. "Are you angry with me?" No response came her way, and Leah grew exceptionally nervous. "You didn't believe him, did you?"

His chilled gaze settled on her. "I told you to stay close to me, but you wouldn't listen. He could have ravished you, Leah. Had his way with you over and over—"

"Stop it!" Her hands briefly covered her ears. She didn't want to hear such talk, didn't want to think about what might have happened. "No harm really came to me. I was feeling ill. The footman—the one at the doors—he led me to the sitting room and said he'd check in on me shortly. I don't know how Rupert got in. I suppose he followed me when I left the ballroom. Besides, you came. I wasn't harmed."

Unknowingly, his fingers tightened around her arm. "Yes, I came. But what if I hadn't? And what if the footman never checked in on you as he'd promised? What then, Leah? Do you think you could have fought the bastard off?"

"N-no."

Tear-bright eyes shimmered up at him as horses' hooves clomped in his ears. Ian wanted to take her in his arms, hold her close, but the hackney rolled up beside them. "Seven Berkley Square," he said, then helped Leah into the vehicle. Seating himself next to her, he pulled the door shut with a thump.

Silence surrounded the pair as they traveled the short distance to Sinclair House. Soon the hackney turned the corner. The wheels rumbled a bit farther, then halted.

Stepping down from the conveyance, Ian helped Leah alight. His wallet was slipped from his pocket, several bills pulled from inside. He handed them up to the driver.

The man's eyes rounded with surprise. "Thank ye, gov'nor," he said, tipping his hat.

Ian's ears were robbed of the words, for he was on the doorstep, fast after Leah. He caught up to her at the foot of the stairs.

"What's your hurry?" he asked, again snatching her arm.

Pointedly, Leah looked at his hand. "I'm going to bed."

"First, we talk."

He escorted her up the steps, across the gallery, and into the sitting room, the door closing behind them. Several lamps burned on a low wick, illumining the area.

"Find a seat," he said, releasing her, whereupon he took a stance by the fireplace, then removed his remaining glove.

Leah surveyed him as he propped his arm on the mantel. By the look in his eyes, she knew he wouldn't be put off. On rubbery legs, she managed to make it to the settee.

Trying to remain calm, she slipped the fan from her wrist, her gloves from her hands, allowing the ruby to fall into one of the lax fingers. "What is it you wish to discuss?" she asked, refusing to look up.

"Us."

Green eyes snarled blue. *"Us?"*

"Yes, us."

Leah frowned. Then enlightenment filled her. His itch that he wanted scratched, she surmised. "What could there possibly be to discuss?" she asked haughtily. "Especially when there is nothing between us."

Ian noted her insolent tone. "There is plenty between us." After all his planning, his strategy cunningly and carefully devised to break down her defenses and capture her heart, he decided the best course was a straight one. "It seems, Miss Kingsley, that I've fallen in love with you."

Blinking, Leah gaped at him.

"Close your mouth, Leah." At his command, her jaw snapped to. "Now, my question is: What do we do about it?"

"D-do about it?"

Ian strode toward her, then seated himself next to her on the settee. "Yes, Leah." He took hold of her left hand, her fan and gloves held in her right. "What do we do about my having fallen in love with you?"

A flurry of emotions spun around inside her: Joy, excitement, hope, fear, dread, and sorrow all mixed into one. Stunned by his confession, she didn't know what to say.

"Well? Do you have any suggestions?"

"I don't know what's to be done," she said, still locked in a mental turmoil. *Dared she believe him?* "N-nothing, I suppose."

Ian shot her a surprised look. "Nothing?" On her slight nod, deep laughter rumbled from his throat. "Search your heart and mind, Leah. Tell me how you feel—what you think we should do."

Run away together, she thought. Find a secluded place where the world and its realities could never touch them, could never displace the magic she felt whenever he was near, could never come between them, as she knew it eventually would. She loved him, loved him with all her being. If only—

Liar! Imposter! Thief!

As the words ricocheted through her mind, piercing her heart, she realized there was no hope for them. Why did he have to admit his love? Why couldn't the words have been left unsaid? Just knowing he truly cared about her made the situation all the more difficult. Their love, along with all its joyful promises, could never be. Misery filled her, and she moaned dejectedly.

"What is it, sweet?" Ian asked, marking the sorrow painted on her face. "Something troubles you. Tell me what it is."

Leah searched his exceptional eyes. She memorized the tenderness and adoration displayed in their sapphire depths, thinking he might never look upon her with such emotions again. If only she could be assured of his understanding, she'd confess all. Yet she feared that with the truth would come his withdrawal. His love would atrophy, to be replaced by censure, anger, and hate. "I-I can't."

Ian recognized she was frightened by something. "What are you afraid of, Leah?" he questioned softly.

Her agony escalated, and she shook her head. "I can't tell you."

"Has it to do with us?"

"Y-yes—no." Feeling as though she were dying inside, Leah pulled her hand from Ian's. "Oh, God! Please just leave me alone."

Ian was on Leah the second she bounded from the settee. As he spun her around, the fan fell from her fingers, clattering against the floor, her gloves dropping silently beside it. His hands gripped her shoulders. "You'll not escape me—not until you've told me what's troubling you." Her lips pressed tightly together, she refused to answer. "Has acknowledging my love upset you?"

Leah wanted desperately to be free of him. "Yes," she hissed, fighting against her tears.

Knifelike pain ripped through Ian's chest. "Then you don't return my sentiments."

Unable to look at him, Leah squeezed her eyes shut; she turned her head. *Yes, I return your sentiments. I love you!* She remained silent.

Ian was trapped in his own desperation. "Damn it, Leah! Look at me!" he demanded, shaking her. Her eyes flew open. Realizing how roughly he'd handled her, he eased the pressure on her shoulders. Then a thought occurred. "Does it have to do with your Irishman?"

"Yes," she lied, hoping he'd let her go.

Under a troubled brow, his eyes searched her face. "Are you in love with him?"

What was another lie after so many? "Yes."

He continued to study her. "Are you fully certain of that?"

Leah could no longer withstand his scrutiny. Casting her gaze downward, she attempted to turn her head. Ian's fingers were at once on the side of her face, his arm surrounding her waist. "What is it you want me to say?" she cried.

"I want the truth."

"I've given you the truth."

"Your eyes say otherwise, Leah. You're not in love with him."

"Yes I am," she insisted.

"No you're not." His hand cupped her cheek while his thumb lightly caressed her mouth. "Desperately, fully, wildly, you are in love with me, just as I am in love with you," he said, just above her lips. "You've been lying, Leah, and I shall prove it." Wet and hot, his mouth covered hers.

Hands pressed against his solid chest, Leah whimpered, trying to resist him. But, as his lips worked fervently against hers, her opposition quickly turned to acceptance. For this one moment in time, she wanted to experience the magic of his kiss, explore all it promised to offer, knowing it would never be so again. The fight drained from her, and she gave herself over to Ian.

Feeling her surrender, he groaned with want. Fire raged in his loins; his arousal growing almost painful. His lips left Leah's as he pulled back slightly. The arm surrounding her urged her closer while his hand slipped from her face, grazed her breast, then settled at her waist. "Open to me," he whispered, then his tongue lightly traced her lips prompting her to do so.

When she complied, his mouth again captured hers. His tongue probed, while his hand eased over her hip, fingers splaying across her bottom to knead gently.

At his touch, desire sparked inside Leah, its flame instantly spreading outward; she trembled in Ian's arms as a moan of longing vibrated in her throat. Her hands glided up over his shoulders to the back of his head. Impatient fingers threaded through the thickness of his hair. Briefly, she marveled at its soft texture. Then she drew him closer, her tongue answering his, teasing and withdrawing.

Ian quaked under her new womanly play, sweet and naive as it was. Wanting her even nearer, he shifted his hips against her, his hand pressing her to him.

A small gasp escaped her as Ian dragged his mouth away from hers. She was lifted into his arms, swung around, then laid on the settee. The cushion indented as he edged his right knee between her legs, pinning her skirt to the upholstery. Frowning, she stared up at him, a questioning look in her eyes.

Ian viewed the light flush on her cheeks, noticed how her

eyes were dilated with passion. The fire inside him burned higher.

"It's hot in here," he said, then shrugged from his coat, tossing it to the floor. His waistcoat and cravat followed; studs ripped from his shirt as he opened it. "Touch me, Leah," he implored. "Touch me here, above my heart. Feel how it races just for you."

Ian caught her hand when she wavered, placing it directly over his heart. Apparently, she needed no further prompting. Eagerly her fingers ran through the hair springing from the center of his chest. He smiled down on her. "Quit playing, and do as I asked."

Leah's hand stilled. "It beats quite rapidly," she said, marking his flesh was indeed hot.

"Because I love you—that's why my heart thunders so." His hand gripped the cushion near her shoulders, the other braced itself along the settee's back, then the knee centered between her legs slid downward, pulling against her silk skirt, as he leaned toward her. "I desire you, Leah—want you with every fiber of my being." Ian glided his foot along the floor; his hips now rested fully against hers. "Do you know what I'm saying?"

Despite the layers of material separating them, Leah understood all too well what he meant. His arousal was every bit as apparent as it was before. Gazing up at him, she nodded.

"And you desire me, too, don't you?"

Leah didn't know how to respond.

Ian released his hold on the settee's back and switched his position above her. His hips remained nestled against hers as he rested his weight on both elbows. His hands cupped her head, his hooded gaze boring down on her. "You desire me, don't you?"

"Yes."

"Why then, if you insist you love another, do you say you desire me?" Ian felt the slight shift of her head, but he wouldn't let her look away. "Answer me. Is it because you enjoy my kisses?"

His mouth swooped, and his lips played, devoured and teased. When he again lifted his head, not only did his heart race, but so did Leah's. He could feel its rapid flutter against his chest. *Damn!* He would force the words from her yet!

"Tell me why it is you desire me? The truth, Leah, the truth."

How could she fight him? She couldn't. "Because—" She hesitated.

"Yes? Because what?"

"Damn you!" she cried, tears suddenly flooding her eyes. "Because I love you." Her hands shoved against his shoulders, but she couldn't budge him. "You have your answer. Now leave me!"

"Never," he said, his thumbs gently wiping the moisture from around her eyes. "Don't cry, sweet. Don't you know how much I want you—how much you truly mean to me?"

The anger she felt at herself for confessing her love to him, for allowing him to force the truth from her, was instantly vented on Ian. "Want me, yes! But I doubt very much that marriage is on your mind—with me at least. Just as Gertrude—or was it Frances? Anyway, just as one of the old drabs implied: You have an itch you want scratched. Well, I won't be the one to ease your misery, sir. Not in a million years."

Ian jerked back a bit. A *V* formed between his eyebrows, marking his confusion. "Gertrude and Frances—who the hell are they?"

"You didn't want gossip tonight, but you managed to set the tongues to wagging."

"How?"

"By waltzing with me indecently close. I overheard what they were saying about you, about me, through the plant. They called me your whore. They know your mother is in Bath."

"How?"

"Someone by the name of Melvin spotted her. Unchaperoned as I am, they think you're taking me to your bed nightly—a last attempt at sowing your wild oats before you marry Veronica, I believe is what they concluded. When you're through with me, I'll be dumped into the gutter where I belong, Irish slut that I am."

Ian cursed vividly. "And that's what sent you packing off to the sitting room, I suppose?" She wouldn't answer. "Leah, don't you know by now I have no intention of marrying Veronica. I'll admit I considered asking her once. The reason was companionship, not love. Then I met you. Ah, sweet," he whispered, his lips blotting away the remnants of her tears. "When a man concedes his love to a woman, it can signify only one thing. Don't you know what it means?"

Yes, she answered in her heart. But it mattered not, for nothing could come of their love. Oh God. How she wished it could be otherwise. "I do, but—"

"But nothing!" Ian interrupted. "I love you, Leah, and I want you to be my—"

Just before the last word slipped from his mouth, the sitting room door opened; loud gasps sounded through the room. The earl tensed as three voices burst forth almost simultaneously.

"Ian?" Veronica cried, sounding hurt.

"Well, I'll be," Jonathan said, chuckling.

"Ian!" Madeline admonished, her tone sharp.

Staring down on Leah, her eyes wide with mortification, he was suddenly ambushed.

"Well, it appears the young pup has finally been exposed for the randy rogue he really is. What do you have to say for yourself, Huntsford?"

Recognizing the crackling voice, Ian closed his eyes and gritted his teeth.

Augusta!

CHAPTER
14

Ian slowly came to his feet as Leah quickly scooted to a sitting position. He turned to face the four intruders. "Good evening, everyone."

Veronica's eyes scanned his body, stopping specifically on the open shirtfront. With a small cry, she spun on her heel and fled the room, Leah's shawl and reticule falling from her hands to the floor.

"If you'll excuse me," Jonathan said, then followed after her.

"I hadn't expected you back so soon, Mother," the earl commented calmly.

"Obviously," Augusta answered for her niece.

Ian's eyes narrowed on the small woman dressed in widow's weeds. "I don't remember extending you an invitation to my home, Augusta. If you're wise, you'll trek out that door and take yourself back to Bath."

"Ian!" Madeline reproached. "Your aunt is here at my invitation. It is not for you to say she is not welcome."

"Isn't it, madam? The last I knew *I* owned this house, so it would seem that *I* have the exclusive right to say who comes and who goes within its walls."

"You evade the issue, Huntsford," Augusta asserted. "Whether I stay or leave is of no importance." She jabbed her cane toward Leah. "What do you intend to do about the young girl whom you've just sullied? That is the real question."

"Aunt Augusta, please," Madeline said. "Such discussion should be kept between Ian, Leah, and myself. I ask that you leave us for a bit. Simmons can show you to your room."

Augusta harrumphed. "Not likely." Her cane tapped beside her as she aimed herself at a chair. "I want to see how the knave tries to get himself out of this one. Maybe once, Huntsford," she said to Ian after she was seated, "but never twice."

"I can always have you tossed onto the sidewalk, the door locked behind you," the earl stated.

"You and what army, sir?"

Ian noted how she'd clutched her cane, readying it. Experience told him he'd be rewarded with a sound whack should he be foolish enough to approach her. Briefly, he celebrated the idea of whether or not to pick up the chair, Augusta in it, and heave the thing through the window.

"Ian."

Hearing his mother's voice, he dismissed the idea—for now. His attention turned Madeline's way.

"Augusta is right," she said. "The issue is . . . well, it's about—"

"My sullying Miss Kingsley, I believe," he stated, then saw the crestfallen look on his mother's face.

"Oh, Ian!" she cried, her hands wringing with anxiety. "I entrusted Leah into your care and you took advantage of my absence. You've ruined Leah's reputation and her name. Likewise, you've ruined ours. For heaven's sake, son, she's John Kingsley's niece! How will I ever explain this to him?"

"Does it need any explaining?" he asked.

Madeline's eyes widened. "Does it need—yes! I would think it does," she fairly exploded. "Your explanation, sir, and I want it now!"

"Hear, hear!" Augusta chimed in, thumping her cane.

Ian's gaze shot from his mother to the withered woman. The cane again stood poised and ready. How easy it would be to snap her scrawny neck.

Quelling the urge to follow through, he instead glanced back at Leah. Pale, she visibly trembled in the settee's corner, looking so very forlorn that he grew troubled over how she'd reacted when he'd confessed his love. Despite her own admission to the same, he felt positive his marriage proposal, had it been uttered fully, would have met with rejection.

Damn! He couldn't allow her to escape him. But his urgings were not enough. There was only one way to seal her fate. And the demand had to come from someone else.

"The explanation is simple, Mother," he said, his attention returning to Madeline. "I just couldn't help myself."

"Couldn't help yourself?" his mother cried, a cackle sounding from Augusta. "You've been taught prudence, sir. Yet you've thrown caution to the winds. How could you be so bold, especially since I trusted you so fully?"

Ian shrugged. "Much like the proverbial forbidden fruit, dangling in front of Adam, Miss Kingsley tempted me. I'm not perfect, Mother. The urge was too strong. I simply had to reach out, grab hold, and take a bite."

On hearing his rationale, Leah sat up. He was implying that she was to blame for this entire debacle. Forbidden fruit, indeed!

"Hope she tasted remarkably sweet," Augusta declared. "For things have certainly soured since."

"Aunt, please," Madeline groaned, then viewed her son. "Had it simply been Augusta and myself who found you, then perhaps things could have been kept quiet."

"Don't count on it," the woman said. For her interference, she received a sharp look from her niece.

"But Veronica and Jonathan were with us," Madeline continued. "I pity the girl for having been witness to your prurient exhibition. She was devastated by what she saw."

"I didn't know anyone would come bursting through the door. One usually knocks before entering a closed room."

"That's why locks were invented, Huntsford," Augusta snipped from her chair. "But apparently you were so caught up in your lust you forgot to turn the key."

Ian took a step toward the woman, but a sharp admonishment from his mother stopped his advance. Drawing a deep breath, he calmed himself. "I'm sorry if Veronica was somehow injured by what she saw," he stated, "but the fact is: We are no more than friends. I never committed myself to her, Mother."

"Even so, she *thought* you were going to offer a proposal of marriage."

"The term *marriage* never entered into any of my conversations with her. *You* were the only person to whom I mentioned the word in connection with Veronica. As for the rest of London, I can only assume Veronica was the one to spread the erroneous news about our forthcoming nuptials. Apparently, though, you passed the information along to Miss Kingsley."

"I did tell Leah when she inquired about your relationship with Veronica."

"And when was that?" he asked, looking back at Leah, noting she now sat at the edge of the settee.

"The second or third day she was here."

"That soon, hmm?" he asked grinning. Her gaze quickly skittered away from his.

"What does my telling Leah about you and Veronica have to do with anything?" Madeline snapped. "Unless we can persuade the Whitcombs to keep quiet about this, there is certain to be talk."

"Forget the Whitcombs, Mother. Talk, as you put it, is already making the rounds." He noted her questioning look. "It seems Gertrude and Frances, whoever the hell they are, were spreading the news at the Delderfields' tonight that someone by the name of Melvin saw our carriage in Bath. The word is: I've taken Miss Kingsley to my bed, the two of us enjoying an illicit love affair while you are away." He saw his mother blanch. "It is also stated I intend to dump my Irish slut into the gutter just before I marry the Lady Veronica."

"Well, when the cat's away—"

"Quiet."

The word erupted simultaneously from both mother and son. Lifting her chin and turning her head, Augusta harrumphed again.

"I had feared something like this might happen," Madeline said, wringing her hands anew. "I wasn't certain if Lady Halston's son saw us, but obviously he did. That's why I came back this evening, just in case he recognized the carriage. I intended to change and take myself to the Delderfields', with hopes of allaying any suspicions."

"Did you have to bring Augusta along with you?" Ian inquired. "Life would be far simpler if you'd left her in Bath."

"Unfortunately all her servants have deserted her. There was no one to see to her needs."

Augusta tapped her cane. "They were shoddy workers anyway. None of them will be missed."

"That is why I brought her with me," Madeline said, exasperation showing in her voice. "I had no other choice."

"A choice that will soon be amended," Ian stated.

"Oh, will you quit worrying over Augusta?" Madeline cried as she started to pace. "John will never speak to me again once he learns about this. I should never have gone to Bath—or at the very least, I should have taken Leah with me." As though she just remembered her, she rushed to Leah's side. Seated, she placed her arm around Leah's shoulders. "Oh, my dear, I'm so very sorry about what has happened. I thought I could *trust* my son." Her gaze snagged Ian's.

"He is not to blame entirely," Leah stated, then spied the twitch of Ian's lips. "I wasn't speaking of your seduction of me, sir."

"And I suppose you are now saying you didn't respond to my kisses—that you weren't as eager as I was to explore our desires further?"

"You were the one who led me in here, when it was I who said I wanted to go to bed."

A knowing smile split his face. "Go on."

A profuse blush spread over Leah's face as she realized how her words had sounded. "That is not what I meant, and you know it." She turned to the countess. "As your son said, there was already talk about the earl and myself."

"Then I am the one who is to blame," Madeline said. "If there were only something I could do!"

"I'll tell you how you can solve this muddle," Augusta piped in. "Yet I doubt any of you hold much favor in seeking my advice. From the way I've been dealt with since my arrival, I doubt also that I'll offer the solution once I'm asked."

Come on, Augusta, Ian's mind shouted. *For once in your life, cooperate!*

"Aunt Augusta," Madeline declared. "Can't you see we are in a fix here. Will you please stop interfering?"

Ian groaned inwardly. *Damn!* When was someone going to say the right word? The one he so desperately wanted to hear!

"All right, Madeline. I'll stop interfering. You won't hear another word from me on the subject. You won't even hear me say you should get the two married before the scandal spreads."

Trump and match! For the first time in his life, Ian considered kissing the old crone, but on spying her cane, he thought better of it.

"Married, you say?" Madeline inquired.

"Yes, married," Augusta snapped. "Once they are husband and wife, any talk about them will soon die down. But you didn't hear me say that."

"I'm not certain that's the answer. I'd have to have John's permission before—"

"You goosecap!" Augusta interrupted, banging her cane on the floor. "Were the man here, don't you think he'd demand that they be married immediately? I'm certain Kingsley won't object to your son being part of his family. It will give him an excuse to see you more often. But you didn't hear me—"

"I know, Aunt. I didn't hear you say that." Madeline looked to her son. "You realize what this means, don't you?"

Ian looked at Leah. His expanding emotions lifted from his chest to swell in his throat. Swallowing, he said, "I presume it means that Miss Kingsley and I are to be wedded."

"Since you have ruined Leah's reputation and our name," Madeline said firmly, "I shall expect you to fulfill your duty, sir."

He noted Leah's dazed expression. She appeared to be having difficulty absorbing the full meaning of what was just said. God help him when it all clicked in her mind. He'd be hard-pressed to quell her anger. She may never forgive him for tricking her as he had. "As you wish, Mother," he said, finally.

Augusta's cackle filled the air. "What? No objection, Huntsford?" She studied Ian briefly, then her eyes narrowed. "Used me, didn't you? Should have known what you were up to when you didn't take immediate exception to my suggestion. I'll give you this one, you young pup. But next time, I'll be ready."

Ian returned her stare. "It is unlikely there will ever be a next time, Augusta."

"Well, I have an objection," Leah announced, finally gathering her wits about her. She popped up off the settee. "I'm sorry, but I cannot marry your son, Lady Huntsford."

"Leah, what are you saying?" Madeline asked, coming up from the settee also. "Your reputation—the Sinclair name —unless something is done, and done quickly, we shall all be ruined."

"That may be so, but I cannot marry him."

"Is there something about Ian that you cannot abide?"

In desperation, Leah wanted to blurt out the truth about herself. But she'd quickly be sent to Newgate, her siblings suffering all the more because of it. What a fine mess this was. "No, there is nothing about your son that I cannot abide," she said, then spied Ian's quick wink. She turned on him. "Why don't you say something?"

"What is it you want me to say?" he asked. "You already know how I feel."

At present, yes. But once the truth was out—Leah refused

to think about that now. "Please, Lady Huntsford, believe me when I say it is better your son and I don't marry."

"Why, Leah?"

"Because, it just is."

"I'm sorry, my dear, but you've given me no sound reason as to why the two of you cannot be married. Since John is not here, I must act in his stead. Tomorrow, I shall contact the bishop. Within the month, you and Ian will be husband and wife."

Ian caught the brief flash in Leah's eyes. She was going to run. As determined as she looked, in the three consecutive Sundays on which the banns must be read, she would undoubtedly accomplish the feat.

"I have a far better idea," he said, gathering Leah's gloves and fan from the floor, pressing them into her hands. His own discarded attire was retrieved and draped over his arm. "Mother. Miss Kingsley. Go pack a change or two of clothing—something warm, but not too warm. Simmons!" he bellowed. The man instantly appeared in the doorway. "Have the carriage readied, the top up. I want it around front within a half hour." After the man dashed off, he turned to Augusta. *"You* stay put. I'll deal with you when we've returned."

"Returned?" Madeline asked.

"Yes, returned."

"And where, son, are we going at this late hour?"

"Scotland."

"Scotland?" she and Leah both cried.

"Aye, Scotland," he said, affecting a native burr. He stepped close to Leah. Catching her chin, he tilted her head and looked deeply into her captivating green eyes. "More precisely, my lassie fair, to Gretna Green."

Two days later, Leah found herself standing in a small church in Gretna Parish, Dumfries County, Scotland, with Ian beside her. A light rain fell on the ancient stone building, the grayness of the day paralleling her misery. She shook uncontrollably as she whispered her vows, while Ian's were spoken with far more verve.

At first, Leah hoped to escape, but was warned against it. Constantly held under a watchful eye, she attempted a different approach. But all her cajoling, pleading, whining, and fitful outbursts of anger during their arduous journey north, the group stopping for brief respites at inns along the way, had done her little good. Even when she'd reminded both mother and son that she and Lord Huntsford barely knew each other, their association spanning a few short weeks, she was quickly cut off. The countess remained firm: Leah and Ian would marry.

On their arrival to Gretna Green, the earl had insisted they'd not be married by a lowly coupler, but would stand before a man of the cloth. And so they did.

Presently, hearing the minister pronounce them husband and wife—Madeline wiping her joyous tears; Ferguson gripping his doffed hat most respectfully—Leah was turned toward Ian.

Luminous sapphire eyes gazed down on her, warm hands cupping her face. "I told you, my love, I always win," he whispered just above her mouth. "You are now my wife. Forever and always, I intend to keep you near me."

As Ian's lips took hers, sealing their marriage vows with a flaming kiss, Leah knew his special promise was meant only for the moment. Her heart ached unmercifully as a different pledge filled her memory.

I can forgive almost anything—apart from lies and deceit. . . .

CHAPTER
15

At her bedroom window, Leah stared down on the park in Berkley Square, pondering the night ahead. Although married, she was still a virgin, a situation that would soon change. If things were different, she'd be eagerly anticipating the time when Ian came to her bed. But considering the lies that stood between them, she dreaded the moment instead. In the end, their night of love would only cause her more pain.

Sighing, she remembered the minutes just after their nuptials. Her new husband had suggested they all travel to Falcon's Gate, his estate being at most a five-hour jaunt from Gretna Green, where they would spend a few days. But Madeline had insisted, most adamantly, that the group return to London immediately, where Leah and Ian would face their detractors straight off. Her mother-in-law's wishes were acceded to, the newlyweds, the now dowager countess, and Ferguson departing from the small church under a heavy Scottish mist.

Below the window, a carriage wheel squeaked as it rolled along the pavement. Closing her eyes, Leah groaned, for the sound reminded her of their first stop at an inn.

There Ian had walked through the door into their prospective room and aimed himself directly at the narrow bed, intent on testing it. Planting his taut backside on the mattress, he'd proceeded to bounce up and down. The ropes strained against the wooden side rails while a horrible groaning filled the air. Leah's face had glowed red.

"Sorry, not tonight, love," he'd said, bounding back onto his feet, striding toward her. "Maybe tomorrow night." Capturing her chin, he'd gently kissed her lips, then looked at the innkeeper. "My bride will take this room. You may find me another."

When the door had closed, she'd heard the innkeeper say: "The beds are old, sir. Not exactly made for the undertakings of young, energetic newlyweds."

With the man's comment, Leah had nearly sunk through the floor. Still she'd gained a reprieve—not simply once, but twice. For on the second night, the bed was found to be little better, if not in fact worse.

Under Ian's inspection, the thing barely held his weight, and had he insisted they share it, she could only imagine the horrendous crash that would have sounded during the wee hours, the inn's peacefully slumbering guests startled awake.

Tonight, however, she would not be so lucky. The beds at Sinclair House were sturdy. Whether it was in her room or his, Ian would make her his wife.

A fist struck the door; Leah jumped, her eyes flying open. Milly, she decided. Having arrived at Sinclair House less than an hour ago, Leah had requested she be allowed to rest, a hot bath to be sent up well before supper.

"Come," she called, gazing out the window again. The door handle turned; the latch released. When Leah looked around, she was surprised to see Ian.

"I thought you were going to rest," he said from across the way.

"I'm too tired to rest. If I lie down, I might not get up for weeks."

Mischief danced in his eyes as he grinned. "Sounds intriguing."

"To you, perhaps."

At her cool tone, his smile faded. "The water is nearly ready for your bath. In the meantime, a Miss Foster is here to see you—something about returning your altered dress."

Leah's heart somersaulted. Knowing Sally had received a letter from Terence, Leah prayed the news about Peter was encouraging. "Where is she?"

"In the foyer. Simmons is eyeing her most unpleasantly. I suggest you go down and attend to whatever it is she wants before he chases her out onto the stoop."

Leah angled herself toward the door. "The man is a pompous old—"

"Tsk, tsk," Ian said, catching her arm just as she passed him, his finger falling over her lips. "No profane words are allowed from my wife's sweet mouth, only utterances of jubilation and praise."

"I have no such predilection at the moment," she stated, slipping from his hold.

"But you will later—after the house has stilled for the night."

His meaning didn't escape Leah. As she rushed from the room, Ian's chuckles followed her down the hallway. Decidedly, she'd find no reprieve tonight. But then, considering her attraction to her husband, Leah wasn't fully certain she wanted one.

"Well," Augusta said across the dinner table, "the girl doesn't look any different." Her gaze shifted. "And you, Huntsford—you look a bit tense. Am I to take it the marriage hasn't been consummated?"

At Augusta's question, Madeline gasped, Leah's fork clattered against her plate, and Ian's wineglass nearly shattered in his hand.

Until that moment, Leah had been enjoying her meal. Terence's letter had conveyed he'd gotten the money, engaged the Daltons' former family doctor, and that Peter was slowly improving. A specialist might not be needed after all. Looking up from her plate, she met her husband's gaze.

Ian noticed his wife's discomfiture, her cheeks stained red. "Augusta, I will tell you this just once," he stated.

"Whatever occurs between my wife and myself is our affair, and ours alone. Seek to intrude again, and it will be your last such attempt."

The woman harrumphed, then jabbed at a potato with her fork.

"I understand you received a delivery from the couturière, Leah," Madeline said. "Have you finished with all the required alterations or do we need to take the rest of your dresses by?"

The woman's switch of topic was an obvious attempt to direct the conversation elsewhere. "There are two dresses still in the shop," Leah said. "I need to pay my account with Madame Lejeune. I imagine by now she thinks I've run out on her. While you were gone, I borrowed some money from your son. If I could have my allowance, I'll repay him and settle my account."

"I'm afraid that will be impossible now," Madeline said.

Leah frowned at her. "Why? My uncle said I was to have an allowance."

"That was before you married, dear. Your husband is now responsible for your debts. The matter of whether or not he grants you an allowance is up to him."

Alarm streaked through Leah. Her plans for herself and the children were suddenly crumbling around her. "But the couturière—the debt for her services was incurred before I married your son," she said, hoping her mother-in-law would relent.

"I'm certain Ian won't mind paying the small amount you owe."

His chuckles caught Leah's attention. "Sounds as though she thinks I might be niggardly with her," he said to his mother. Then his gaze settled on his wife. "Tomorrow, Leah, I shall go round and open accounts in all the finer establishments. The proprietors can send the bills directly to me. How does that sound?"

Awful, she decided. She needed money, not credit. With no funds, she couldn't possibly escape him, couldn't possibly flee to another land. She and the children were doomed. But more immediately, she couldn't even post a letter to

Terence. And should extra money be needed for Peter's care—Lord help her, she thought.

"Would it be too much to ask that I be allowed to have some cash—just in case I'm in a store where you don't have an account and I see something I like."

Ian perused his wife. She still might run, he decided, knowing she was uneasy about their sudden marriage. But why? She claimed she no longer cared for her Irishman, so what was making her so edgy? "Undoubtedly, I'll be with you whenever you're out," he announced finally. "But I'll grant you a few sovereigns a week, just so you don't feel impoverished."

"Really, Ian," his mother said, "couldn't you be a bit more generous."

"Whatever she wants, Mother, I'll gladly buy for her. All she need do is ask."

"Well, I wouldn't be too generous with the girl," Augusta proclaimed, "or you might find your coffers are soon emptied. And don't be wasting your money on altering her gowns. She'll be splitting the seams in them soon enough— that's if the two of you ever get down to business."

Ian's head slowly pivoted her way. He raked his gaze over the woman, stopping at her scrawny neck. Apparently, his mother noticed the small tic pulsating along his clenched jaw, for she suddenly rose from her chair.

"Aunt Augusta," Madeline chimed in as her napkin settled beside her plate. "Perhaps you'd like to come along to the sitting room with me. You can enjoy your nightly glass of sherry in there."

"I'm not done eating," the woman grumbled.

"Oh, yes you are," her niece insisted, urging Augusta from her seat.

"Fine, then. The meat was overcooked anyway and the peas are still raw." Her cane tapped beside her as she headed for the door. "Really, Madeline, you should hire yourself some competent help, starting with a new cook."

"Do you want dessert?" Ian asked Leah once Augusta was out the doorway.

"No."

"Let's say we take a turn in the gardens, then."

"Must we?"

"It's that or seek the privacy of our room. I'll not go near the sitting room."

"I'll get my shawl," she said, coming to her feet.

Ian chuckled. "You won't need a shawl, Leah. It's a warm night. Should you get chilled, I'll lend you my coat. Or better still, I'll wrap you in my arms."

Leah pressed her lips into a tight line. She had hoped to escape to her room and quickly burn Terence's letter, not having had time to do so before supper. Her anger stemmed not from the letter, for it was well hidden, but from Ian's dictatorial manner. "You are starting to annoy me, sir," she said, making her way to the door.

Ian's long strides carried him to her side. "Why?"

"Because you continually reject whatever I say. I am not a child who needs to be given constant direction. I would appreciate it if you'd allow me to make my own decisions."

They were now on the gallery, heading toward the stairs. "You refer to the shawl, I suppose?"

"That, among other things."

Ian trailed her down the steps, then on toward the back of the house. "What are the other things, Leah?" he asked as they stepped through the door into the gardens.

A balmy breeze flowed over Leah, the heady scent of roses filling her nostrils. Just as he'd said, the night air was warm. As she meandered along the path, Ian captured her hand, wrapping it around his arm.

"What other things were you speaking of?" he inquired again.

"From the moment I arrived here, sir, you have been issuing me orders. When I wanted solitude, I was forced to accompany you to Kingston-upon-Thames. Then it was the races. And then—"

"Your anger over the latter is probably because you lost the wager, which you haven't paid yet. In fact, you owe me two kisses, I believe."

"Two?"

"Yes, the day I nearly ran us into that carriage—the day Covington was injured—we made a wager then, too. Remember?"

"About what?" she asked, genuinely having forgotten the bet.

"About whispering all those words you keep hidden in your heart solely to me. You told me you love me."

"But I haven't told all," she said, wishing she could avoid doing so altogether. "So that wager is not yet lost."

"But you will tell all. And soon. Then I shall collect on both bets."

Leah stared up at him. Pray she could slip away from him before the truth was known. She couldn't bear to see the condemnation in his eyes.

"I'm sorry, sweet. You were telling me about my always issuing orders to you. First, it was Kingston-upon-Thames, then the races. And then?"

"Then there was the Delder—" Leah caught herself. She didn't want to think about that particular night. "I have grown weary of being told what to do. Since coming here, my life hasn't been my own."

"And you resent the intrusion."

"Yes."

"Especially our being forced to marry, right?" he asked, knowing that was what most incensed her.

"Yes—especially that. Wouldn't you resent it?"

"I wasn't the one being forced, Leah. If you'll recall, I was on the verge of proposing to you at the very instant we were found. But if I didn't love you as I do, I'll admit: I wouldn't relish being coerced into a marriage I didn't want. I'd fight unto my last breath against any such imposition. In fact, I was almost tricked into wedding a young woman I couldn't abide. But I stood fast against her father's demands that I marry her. It was fortunate I did, for her lies were soon revealed. There is a difference between what I nearly suffered and what you face now. Had you not acknowledged that you love me, I'd understand your objection to our marriage. But you did confess your love, so I cannot fathom why you're making such a fuss about our union. Are you saying you aren't in love with me anymore?"

"I don't know," she snapped, adding another lie to her list.

They had reached the stone bench where not long ago Leah had sobbed out her misery over little Peter. Stopping, Ian turned her to face him. "Are you sure about that?" he inquired, his hands remaining on her shoulders.

Leah felt certain her tears might flow again, this time because of the hopelessness of their situation. Valiantly, she held them back. "What does it matter if I love you or not? We are married and naught can be done about it."

"It matters to me plenty," he said, then shook his head. "Leah, you know as your husband I have the right to expect submission from you. You know also tonight we will share a bed."

Unable to look at him, Leah dropped her gaze to her feet. "I know."

His hand shifting, his finger nudged her chin upward. "But you don't seem very eager to do so."

"We barely know each other," she said, feeling the gentle warmth of his hand once it had again settled on her shoulder. "We didn't have a courtship. I don't even know if I like you."

"Nevertheless, you love me, don't you?" She refused to issue a response. "Why do you forever try to hide what is in your heart? Do you believe by not saying the words aloud that it will make a difference? You can't change what is between us, Leah. Deny you love me, if you wish, but you're not fooling me. And you're certainly not fooling yourself."

Leah's heart felt as though it were breaking. *Yes, I love you!* The words screamed through her mind as unbidden tears sprang to her eyes. If she could only be assured of his forgiveness, she'd confess all here and now. The truth, she grasped, would merely spawn his hatred. It was useless to hope for anything else.

Her misery masked with anger, she struck out at Ian. "Oh,

why did you have to insist we go into the sitting room instead of allowing me to go to bed as I had requested?" she asked, wishing she could somehow rectify everything that was wrong. "If you hadn't, none of this would have happened. That is another time I wasn't allowed to abide by my own decision—a resolution I especially rue for not heeding."

Her words stung. Indignation erupted in Ian as he wondered why she so stubbornly refused to accept their marriage. She loved him. He was certain of it. "I thought the sitting room would be the safest place," he said, quelling his rising anger. He caught her questioning glance. "There were things I wanted to make known to you. Had I allowed you to flee to your room, it would not have been long before I sought you out."

"You would have found the door locked."

"Do you think that would have stopped me?" Ian saw how her shimmering eyes widened. "I wouldn't have harmed you. What happened next would have ended as it did. But instead of on the settee, it would have been in your bed. And in that location far more would have taken place. What would you have done, Leah, had they all pitched in on us and found us fully unclothed, arms and legs entwined, our bodies melding, as though we were already husband and wife? Had you gone to your room, I wouldn't have been deterred. In fact I would have been less concerned about the servants listening at the door and more dogged in my quest to make you mine. I'd have made love to you, Leah, just as I will tonight."

There was no way around it, Leah knew. Still, she dreaded the prospect. Not because she didn't want him, but because she was afraid of sacrificing herself to him. Not her body, but her soul. Perhaps it was foolish, but she believed she could eventually forget him. Yet once they had lain together, once she had realized the full extent of his passions, her own rising to meet his, once they had shared fully in their mutual love, she knew she could never erase him from her memory. The pain of his loss would only worsen when the time came for her to leave. And she would leave, well before he knew of her deception, for she couldn't stand to see the look of loathing he'd cast upon her.

By her expression, Ian felt certain she planned to reject him. "Do you doubt my words?" he asked. "Do you hope I won't demand my husbandly due? If so, you are mistaken. Tonight, when the household has stilled and everyone is asleep, I shall come to your room. Be ready. And don't think to lock the door either." He patted the small pocket in his waistcoat. "I retain the extra key. Tonight, Leah, our marriage will be consummated. I won't be put off. Do you understand me?"

"I understand you are issuing orders again."

His hand glided from her shoulder, fingers splaying at the nape of her neck. "I am your husband, and, by your own vow, you will obey me. You'll not be disappointed, love. I promise you won't." Then he urged her toward him. "I'll seal it with a kiss."

Leah pressed her hands to his solid chest, ready to stave him off. But the kiss was over before it had begun. Surprised, she stared up at him.

"Do you wish to return to the house with me?"

The placidness of his voice made it sound as though they had never engaged in their discussion. "What about your aunt?" she asked, equally as poised.

"I intend to seek my study until it is time to come to you. If you like, you can visit in the sitting room with mother and the *ever-endearing* Augusta. When they retire, you may take yourself to your room."

"If you don't mind, I'd prefer to stay in the gardens a bit longer."

"No, I don't mind. Until later, love."

Another quick kiss fell on Leah's lips, then Ian released her. As she watched him walk up the path, she considered taking flight. A gate stood somewhere at the back of the gardens. Were she to find it—

"If you are hoping to run, the gate is locked," Ian called over his shoulder. "And I must warn you. Should you decide to scale the wall, be careful you don't fall on the guard I've posted in the mews. He may not be very understanding about your dropping in on him that way."

Damn him! Leah railed silently. He was too shrewd by far. Then she wondered, when the actual time came for her to flee, if she'd ever escape him.

No longer wanting to stay in the gardens, Leah stalked up the path to the house. Once on the gallery, she heard the study door close, then viewed the sitting room. Light shone from inside the area. Madeline and her aunt were apparently still visiting.

Leah didn't particularly desire Augusta's company, but at the moment, she preferred the woman's scrutiny over the alternative. She'd not go to her room until it was absolutely required. Even then she wasn't sure she could muster the courage.

"So, the new Lady Huntsford has decided to join us," Augusta said from her chair just as Leah came through the door. "Why aren't you in bed with your husband?"

Leah's feet skidded to a halt. Her gaze raked over the woman. "I believe Ian stated how he felt about your constant intrusion into our personal lives. If you didn't grasp what he said the first time around, I shall repeat his words, except they are now coming from me. Whatever occurs between my husband and myself is our affair, and ours alone. Do you now have a full understanding of what that means?"

"You forgot the part about my seeking to intrude again and it will be my last such attempt. Apparently, you don't retain the same urge to do me bodily harm as does your husband."

"Remain at Sinclair House much longer and that may change," Leah announced, then looked to Madeline. "I shall bid you good night."

As she turned away, her mother-in-law sprang from the settee. "Leah," she called, then quickly caught up to her just outside the door. "I'm sorry if she's upset you."

"It's not your fault."

"Yes it is. I should never have brought her back with me.

But the error will soon be corrected. Tomorrow, Augusta and I will be returning to Bath. Maybe then you and Ian can find some peace."

Under different circumstances, Leah probably would have objected to Madeline's leaving. But after tonight, she doubted it really mattered if she were alone with Ian or not.

"I imagine Ian will be relieved once she is gone," Leah said. "I must confess: I also will breathe easier."

"Well, you must admit she did find the solution to our problem."

Leah wished more than ever that Augusta had kept her advice to herself. "I suppose she did," she responded, then took a deep breath. "I wanted to apologize for what happened. I hadn't intended for anything to occur between your son and myself. You've been so good to me—well, I'm embarrassed by my actions."

"Don't fret, Leah. Ian has said it was his fault. It is I who should apologize for my son's actions. He knew better. But let's not think about the past. It's the future that you must consider. He loves you, Leah. And if I'm not mistaken, I believe you feel very much the same. I'm certain everything will work out for the two of you. Just be willing to give it a chance. My only concern is John's reaction once he discovers what has transpired. Perhaps I should see if there is some way to get in touch with him—an address where I might write him. If he learns the news beforehand, he won't be taken aback on his arrival home."

"Please don't trouble yourself about informing my uncle," Leah pleaded, knowing she needed time to plan her escape. She needed money, too, but she had no idea how she'd cull even so much as a farthing. Except for the postage, she'd not bilk Ian of any of his finances. She'd defrauded him enough as it was. "Since it is your son whom I've married, I'm certain he won't object. Had it been someone else, then, yes, it would be only fair that you should write him. Let's wait and surprise him. I'm certain he will be overjoyed."

"Sort of a welcome-home gift—is that what you're suggesting?" Madeline asked.

"Yes—exactly."

"How delightful, dear. I will consider it. Now, if you will excuse me, I shall inform Augusta about our heading back to Bath in the morning. Good night, Leah."

Once the dowager countess had returned to the sitting room, Leah took herself toward the stairs. The door to the study was still closed. She hoped it didn't open for hours to come, if ever again.

Upstairs in her room, after Leah quickly set a match to Terence's letter, sweeping the ashes into the back of the fireplace, she paced the floor. The lamp on the table near the window burned on a low wick, lighting her way. Her hands wringing, she was in a quandary as to what she should do.

Maybe if she cast herself through the glass panes, hitting the sidewalk below—no! She wasn't that desperate—yet. But as the moments passed, Leah found she was becoming more and more despondent.

The window continued to beckon. Staring at the draperies, she dashed toward them. The cords released, the heavy satin dropped across the lace curtains, concealing the glass. Afterward, Leah vowed to think of her self-destruction no more.

Down on the gallery, the clock struck ten, then eleven.

Be ready.

Her husband's words kept tumbling through her mind until finally, with an agonized groan, Leah walked to the clothes cupboard. Searching through the things inside, she found a muslin nightdress, a double row of ruffles edging the high-necked collar, a string of ribbons lining its front. Prim and proper she might appear, but the gown would afford her the feeling of security—until he stripped it from her.

On another groan, Leah readied herself for bed.

Past midnight, she heard footsteps in the hallway. She held her breath. The light treads traveled by her room. Two doors opened and closed down the corridor. Knowing the footfalls belonged to Madeline and Augusta, Leah grew more tense. Why she had been foolish enough to come to Sinclair House in the guise of Anne Kingsley she would never fully understand. Stupidity, she supposed. That, and impetuosity. What a fool she was for thinking she could carry off such a charade. Especially when it now promised to spell her demise.

Her hands still wringing, Leah continued to pace. *Just get it over with!* her mind finally screamed.

It was then that Ian's light knock sounded on her door.

CHAPTER
16

Leah's feet were rooted to the carpet near the table by the window. She wanted to run, but knew she couldn't. The time had come. There would be no more reprieves.

"Enter," she called in a weak voice, then watched as the door opened slightly. Instantly, she closed her eyes and prayed. "Allow me the ability to stand against him so that I won't be completely, totally lost to him." But as the inaudible words crossed over her lips, she realized her request was no more than a futile utterance. Except for her virginity, she already lay forfeited to him.

Her eyes again on the door, Leah watched as Ian wedged himself through the narrow opening. Gray linen trousers and a white silk shirt, open to mid-chest, punctuated his casual manner. His gaze fast upon her, she settled back against the panel, the latch catching hold. Shifting the glasses he carried into the hand holding the wine bottle, he felt for the key, then secured the lock.

The firm click resounded in Leah's ears; her breath caught in her chest as her knees suddenly wobbled. Somehow, she returned him stare for stare. Then his deep blue eyes lazily drifted over her unbound hair, trailing its length to her waist. Leah stood perfectly still as his gaze jumped to her nightdress. As he viewed the densely woven material from head to foot, her face, fingertips, and toes exposed, his lips twitched.

"Something amuses you, sir?" she asked, her shoulders squaring. He merely grinned. "What thought has tumbled through your wicked mind? Tell me."

"Christmas."

"Christmas!" she cried as she viewed the wine bottle, thinking he was foxed.

"Yes, Christmas," he repeated, his grin widening. "You look like a tidy little package all tied up in ribbons and bows—the kind one is tempted to shake while trying to guess what's inside. I'll enjoy unwrapping you, sweet. The mystery of what lies beneath that gown has me intrigued."

Leah felt her cheeks flame with embarrassment, then heard Ian chuckle.

"Some wine?" he asked, holding up the bottle and glasses. Slowly, he sauntered toward her. "It might calm your nerves."

If she guzzled the contents of the entire bottle, Leah doubted her quaking could be stilled. On second thought, by ingesting as much wine as possible, she just might be fortunate enough to pass out. "Some fortification would be nice."

His brow furrowing, Ian eyed her as the cork popped. Wine flowed into the glasses sitting on the table beside them. "You sound as though we are ready to do battle instead of making love. Are you planning to fight me, Leah?"

"N-no," she responded, grasping the wineglass as he handed it to her.

She quaffed the sweet liquid. The base of her empty glass hit the table, and as she reached for the bottle, Ian snared her wrist.

"Whoa. You don't want to dull your senses too much. Your pleasure will be lost."

"I want some more."

Ian noted that her words were not a request, but a demand. He studied her face. "Another glass and that's all," he said, easing his grip on her wrist.

Leah poured the red liquid to the rim, then downed the second glass nearly as quickly as she did the first. She set the crystal goblet on the table. "Delicious," she said, then giggled.

"Think so?" Ian asked, certain the wine had swirled straight to her head. Her small tongue darting, she licked the film of liquid from her lips, and he swallowed the groan of longing that trembled in his throat. Along with it, he swilled his own wine, then placed his empty glass beside Leah's. His eyes met hers. "It's time, sweet."

The pleasant giddy feeling fogging her brain evaporated, his words having had a sobering effect. "So soon? I thought we might talk."

"We've talked enough. It's time I unwrapped my gift."

His long fingers traveled to her throat to deftly untie the first ribbon. Leah swallowed hard. The second bow was disentangled. Her heart pounding in her ears, she weaved to and fro on her feet. The third ribbon was unwound, its loops falling free to reveal the cleft between her breasts. Then as Ian's fingers caught the fourth ribbon, her hand met his. "Must you go so fast?"

"I could try the feat with my tongue. It may delay the inevitable. Then again, it may not."

Vividly, Leah imagined that warm, wet sliver twirling close to her breasts. She shivered at the delectable thought.

Ian noticed her reaction. The image created by his words, he decided, had excited her. He grew more confident. "Is that what you desire, Leah? Should I tackle those ribbons with my tongue?"

She blinked. "N-no."

Laughter rumbled in his throat. "Then I will reserve the privilege for when there is nothing between us."

Ian's fingers worked beneath Leah's, the ribbon quickly coming undone. Then taking her wrist, he moved her hand aside. Desire flamed in his loins as he glimpsed a hint of what lay beyond the gown's rift. The knuckles of his free hand penetrated the opening and lightly grazed her soft curves; again he watched for her reaction.

Biting back a whimper, Leah felt her head swim, but her lightheadedness wasn't from the wine. His touch was what sent her reeling.

The remaining ribbons were untied to her waist. Eager to see her fully, Ian took hold of the ruffled collar, parting the gown at her throat. Slowly, he edged the material down over her shoulders. "Incredible," he pronounced as his palm cupped one perfect globe. A tiny tremor whispered through Leah's body at his touch. Then as his thumb gently teased the rosy peak, he waited for the expected response.

Under his tantalizing play, her nipple grew taut. Sensation radiated throughout Leah. A moan filtered through her lips. Closing her eyes, she allowed each new feeling to expend itself, then was amazed when it sparked to life anew.

"Do you enjoy this?" he asked huskily.

"Yes," she whispered, and her other breast was plied in the same way as was the first. The magical sensations doubled, until she felt she might swoon. "Why do you bedevil me so?" she questioned, her eyelids parting.

"Am I tormenting you?"

"Yes."

His thumbs stood motionless. "Do you want me to stop?"

"No."

His thumbs again began their erotic play, and Leah's eyes fluttered shut. Basking in the knowledge that he was master of her emotions, Ian watched her changing moods. Delight painted her face, as did frustration.

No longer satisfied with simply manipulating her swollen crests, he wanted to taste them as well. His head dipped and his tongue flicked against one hard bud, then his mouth suckled gently. His lips left the wet, glistening crest to capture its erect twin, ministering to it the same as he did the first.

With this new attack on her senses, excitement twirled

through Leah. Certain she might spin away from him, she grasped his shoulders and held fast. The sinew beneath his shirt beckoned. She caressed his hard flesh, marveling at the rippling brawn, then her hands glided across the slick silk to the nape of his neck. Fingers threaded upward into his rich, thick hair, urging him closer.

At her prompting, Ian's ministrations intensified. He drew her taut flesh deeper into his mouth, sucking like a ravenous babe. The breath hissed between her lips, and Ian quickly eased off.

She'd grown far too sensitive for such rigorous play, he realized. Later, when she had become well-versed as his lover, and he as hers, all constraints would be broken, their unbridled passions seeking and reaching new pinnacles, boundless ecstasy their reward. For now, because she was yet unschooled in the ways of a man and a woman, didn't fully understand the gratification that would come with their joining, he intended to seduce her with tenderness.

His desires now shackled, his tongue streamed lightly up over her breast, stopping at the curve of her throat. His lips nibbled above the erratic pulse as his hands met her slender waist. "What else do you want, sweet?" he asked, one hand sliding over her hip, cupping her enticing little bottom.

"I-I don't know. You are the one who is supposed to be so clever about all this. You tell me."

Fingers splaying, he kneaded her derrière through the muslin. "Better still, I'll show you." He pulled her firmly against him. "I want you. Do you know what that means?"

His hard arousal made itself evident as Leah felt the gentle glide of his hips against her belly. At Balfour, having helped oversee the breeding of the ewes when they were in season, she certainly wasn't ignorant about what transpired between a male and a female when they mated. But those were sheep. She and Ian were not.

"Do you know what that means?" he repeated.

"Y-yes."

While his large hand continued to fondle her bottom, exploring fingers urging her ever closer to his shifting hips,

Leah conceived that the act of mating was far more tender between humans, far more enjoyable as well.

Anticipation rose inside her as she envisioned the enchantment of their first joining, Ian's sapphire eyes looking lovingly upon her, passion having darkened their color to indigo. Then, in her mind's eye, his masterful lips captured hers in a hungry kiss just as his hard body moved above her. Eager to have her, he positioned himself between her spread thighs, his adept hands having inflamed her desires, making her as impatient as he. On his gentle probe, they would at last be one, his erect member easing deep inside her.

The image of Ian's body thrusting and withdrawing, her own meeting his ardently, swelled in Leah's mind. Fire sparked low in her stomach as a sultry wetness flowed from her, her secret place suddenly tingling with want. She groaned when the hand at her waist shifted, then edged lower to finally burrow between her thighs, where his fingers stroked gently. Was this real or just part of her fantasy?

As Ian continued his exploration, the material beneath his hand grew damp. Wanting to be free of the barrier that kept him from touching her fully, he was tempted to rend the gown from her body. But he quelled the urge, knowing the action would frighten her. Instead, his hand grew bolder. Skillful fingers found what they sought, attending the small bud solely. He watched as the first signs of pleasure illumined Leah's face. "What do you want?" he asked, his fingers stilling to a feathery touch.

Ian's hoarse voice broke through her reverie. Realizing the luscious excitement she felt stemmed from Ian's mastery of her, she again trembled in his embrace. Unknowingly, she moved against his hand, seeking again the full enjoyment it gave.

"What do you want?" he asked anew. His fingers pressed against her and quickened their pace. "This?"

Leah's breath caught in her throat. Unable to speak, she nodded her reply.

"Then it is time we made love," Ian said, and swept Leah into his arms. He strode the short distance to the bed where he placed her in the center of the downy mattress. Quickly, he was beside her, his leg hugging her thighs. His head resting on the palm of one hand, he smiled down on her. "I shall now unwrap the rest of my gift."

His right hand began gathering the material, and Leah felt her gown work upward from her ankles, over her shins, to her knees. Embarrassment and expectation spun through her simultaneously. His leg lifted, and the fabric skimmed across her thighs to her hips, then settled at her waist. Afterward, his warm palm met her bare belly, and his little finger toyed in her curls. Leah lurched convulsively.

"Easy, sweet. You enjoyed my touch before. Do you now fear it?"

"No."

Under his hand her stomach muscles remained taut. "Then why do you tense?"

"You bedevil me again," she accused.

Noting the position of his little finger, he smiled. So close, yet so far, he decided, knowing exactly what she desired. "Soon your torment will end. But first comes your unveiling." He shifted onto his knees, and Leah was quickly relieved of the gown. Gazing down on her, he avidly explored each inviting inch now revealed to him. "I had anticipated beauty, but nothing as wondrous as what meets my eyes."

The wadded nightdress was pitched through the air, landing on the floor at the bed's foot. Then Ian jerked his shirt over his head, tossing it in the same direction.

Fascinated, Leah studied his broad shoulders. Their hard sinew tempted her; her hands ached to touch him. She scanned the crisp curls springing from the center of his muscular chest, fingers suddenly tingling. Inquisitively, her gaze trailed the narrow shaft of dark auburn hair darting down over his taut belly past the indentation of his navel. A strange heat radiated through her as she noted the firm bulge below his waist. That he was sizable was evident. But exactly how sizable she could only imagine, the gray linen swathing his lean hips and powerful legs hindering her view.

Beside her, impatient to feel flesh against flesh, Ian swiftly disrobed. His boots hit the floor, stockings floated after them. Trousers and undergarments followed, then he eased back onto the mattress and stretched out beside her. Her face, he noticed, was averted.

"Look at me, Leah." When she didn't obey, his finger met her jaw, and with a gentle nudge, he urged her around. "Afraid of what you'll see?" Her teeth played along her lower lip, no response coming forth. "Don't be frightened of my nakedness. Glory in my body, the same as I do in yours."

Held under his intense scrutiny, Leah grew terribly nervous. Not fully conscious of her actions, she reached outward. Fingers curled in the silk coverlet, and she dragged it toward her, intending to conceal her nudity, but Ian quickly captured her wrist.

"No. You won't hide yourself. Once unwrapped, a gift should be displayed, especially one as precious as you. But *this* gift is for my eyes only."

"But I feel so—"

"Vulnerable?" he asked as he leaned over her, his hand on her waist. He saw her nod. "Then it is time I made you feel something else entirely. Kiss me. Ease my torment." His manhood pressed against her hip. "And I'll ease yours. Ecstasy will be our reward."

He heard her whimper of agreement, and his mouth, hot and wet, claimed hers. Wine never tasted so sweet as it did on Leah's lips, and Ian feasted hungrily, savoring the intoxicating flavor. At his urging, her lips parted, and their tongues met. Coyly, each drove and dodged the other, mimicking the ritualistic motion that was to come.

Dizzy from the thrusting play, Leah again gripped his shoulders. The smoothness of his warm skin amazed her as unhampered fingers caressed the rippling muscle beneath, fondling each hollow and rise. Excitement and fear swirled through Leah as she became fully aware of his strength.

His large hand glided upward from her waist to capture her breast. Expert fingers kneaded gently, his palm grazing her nipple. Though tender now, power resided in his hand

—both hands!—the mighty force capable of breaking a thick limb. Or her neck. Misery filled Leah; a groan fled her throat as she wondered what he'd do to her when he discovered her true identity.

Ian heard the piteous sound, felt her stiffen beside him. His hand stilled as his mouth deserted hers, then sluiced across her cheek to play at her ear. "What is it, sweet? Am I hurting you?"

Not yet, but you will.

Tears stung her eyes as the words tumbled through her mind. "N-no."

He drew back to gaze into her shimmering emerald eyes. "Then what is it?"

Leah returned his steady look. Just this once, she wanted to experience fully what it meant to be his wife, know completely the ecstasy he had promised her. Her arms tightened around his shoulders, drawing him nearer. "Make love to me, Ian," she whispered. "Make love to me, and passionately."

At her request, Ian's hand contracted reflexively on her breast. "This is your first time, Leah. I'll surely injure you if—"

"No—please do as I ask." Leah noted he remained hesitant. Her hand caught his, forcing it from her breast across her stomach, then lower. "Please," she pleaded, pressing his palm intimately against her.

As Leah's hand rubbed against his own, Ian remained outwardly still. But inside his heart thundered. Fire seemed to scorch his veins. His manhood throbbed unmercifully. Then Leah's thighs opened. Unable to resist her invitation, his fingers slid into the satiny folds, exploring tenderly. Then one met the erect bud to rotate gently. "Passionately, you say?" he questioned, feeling as though he might burst with need.

Tingles of delight rippled through Leah, Ian's hand working skillfully. Her hips rose, seeking something more. "Oh, yes."

"Then so be it," he growled as his face sank toward hers.

Clasping his head, Leah received his fiery kiss, her tongue darting and retreating, playing with his own. Under Ian's mastery, all sensation centered on her lips, then quickly radiated throughout her core. His hand shifted. Fingers probing, one entered her, searching for her maidenhead, then slipped past. Hot moisture streamed from her as he explored her fully, thrusting and withdrawing, his thumb circling, fueling her pleasure. Still she was not satisfied.

Leah finally realized what she wanted. Her joy was not complete unless Ian shared in it as well. Fingers unwound from his hair, then drifted down his neck, smoothing over his furred chest, past the rippling contours of his taut belly, at last finding what they sought.

Ian's whole body shook uncontrollably as her cool hand grasped his swollen member. With a tormented groan, he tore his lips from hers. "Woman, it is you who now bedevils me," he growled as his hand covered hers. He showed her the motion that pleased him. When Leah found the rhythm, his hand left hers. Explosive joy jolted through him as she worked her magic on him. His eyelids squeezed shut, he savored each unerring stroke. Then, when her thumb boldly teased the slick crown of his manhood, his breath hissed between his teeth. "Enough," he rasped moments later.

"I've disappointed you," she said, releasing him.

"Hardly," he countered, an odd chuckle escaping his throat. He levered himself up on one hand, the other reclaiming her. "Open to me." He urged her thighs apart. "Wider, sweet," he said, his knuckles grazing her curls.

His delicate touch sent her heart to fluttering. Obeying his command, Leah felt him shift. Ian was at once above her. His knees settling between her legs, he leaned over her. Hands sank into the down mattress, one on each side of her shoulders, as he supported his weight.

"Close your eyes, Leah." Questioningly, she stared up at him. "You want passion, and so you shall have it. Whatever I do I do for you, for me, for us. Now close your eyes and enjoy the moment."

His darkened gaze held the promise of fulfillment. Desiring that it be hers, Leah again obeyed him. Eyelashes flittered downward, then as the mattress dipped, she felt him sink nearer.

His lips brushed her forehead, grazed her cheek, then touched the tip of her nose. Briefly they played on her own before sliding to her chin, then lower to the curve of her throat, where they nibbled at the tiny pulse.

He moved downward. Delicious fire streamed through her as his tongue quickly laved the nipple of one breast, then moved on to the other. Soon his lips trailed to her navel, his teeth nipping lightly at her stomach. Tiring of the distraction, his mouth charted a new course, progressing lower and lower, until his lips skimmed her curls.

At this new assault, Leah's fingers coiled in the linen pillowcase. She drew breath shallowly as expectation soared inside her. A moan trembled on her lips, Ian's fingers again gliding into her folds.

"Easy, love," he whispered, stroking her lightly. Then spreading the dewy petals, he gazed at her virginal beauty. "Relax and take pleasure."

The touch of his tongue nearly sent his wife catapulting from the mattress. Ian's hands caught her thighs. Pressing them wide, he continued to torment her until at last her hips rose to meet him. The musky taste of her sparked new fire in his loins. Pain throbbed at his core, the lusty itch inside him growing unbearable. Were it not for his promise to see to her own gratification first, he'd be deep inside her, seeking his own release. As Leah's fingers curled in his hair, urging him closer, he forgot about his needs, for her pleasure was actually his.

Delirium encompassed Leah as she quavered on the edge of rapture. It eluded her, and a groan of frustration lifted from her throat. It was then that Ian's play grew more urgent. She burned with the passion he had ignited deep within her. Her head lolled on the pillow, fingers threading through his hair. Open to him, she allowed him whatever he sought. His tongue swirled and probed, then teased vigorously, incessantly. The sparks erupted higher, blazing into an inferno, its overwhelming heat rushing through her body.

A soft cry sounded in her throat as the first spasm struck. She arched, and Ian avidly tended her, allowing the waves of ecstasy to run their course. When she went limp, he rose above her.

The intolerable heat Leah once experienced had turned into a pleasing sort of warmth. Languid eyes opened to see Ian hovering just above her. A smile traced her lips as her finger touched his chin. "Incredible." She breathed deeply, certain no feeling could ever compare to the one she just experienced. Then she wondered how she could possibly leave him, though leave him she must.

"It's not over yet, sweet," Ian announced huskily. Fingers delving, he noted she was still wet. Under his exploration, she opened to him, allowing him access, and the throbbing in his loins increased. His weight resting on one hand, his arm shook as he positioned himself. Checking his urgency, he eased into her until he reached her maidenhead. "It will hurt," he warned.

Feeling the crown of his manhood nestled inside her, Leah was impatient to experience this new form of pleasure. "But ecstasy will follow, won't it?"

"God, yes," he rasped, then captured her lips in a hot, wet kiss.

Ian pushed against the barrier, then drew back and, with a quick thrust, broke through. A subdued whimper flowed into his mouth, Leah stiffening beneath him. His kiss deepened, giving her time to adjust. Then when he thought she was ready, he edged upward. Warm satin enveloped him as he filled her completely.

"Gratify me," he said, now gazing down on her. His hand tunneled beneath her hips, drawing her closer. "Give me the pleasure I seek."

"Gladly."

Ian's breath caught when she rotated against him, tempting him further, then like a taut wire, his control snapped. Each thrust nearly sent him over the edge as he buried himself, then withdrew. No woman had ever excited him as did Leah. But then, no woman had ever claimed his heart. Not until now.

Her silky thighs cradling him, her slender hands stroking his back, she lured him to completion, her hips rising to meet him stroke for stroke. Desiring that she share in his ecstasy, he kneaded her alluring bottom, then clasped her nearer. Soon her eyes widened. Pleasure streamed across her flushed face, her caressing spasms enticing him to join her. His heart swelling, Ian couldn't resist. With a guttural cry, he gritted his teeth. Rapture embracing him, his rich seed spilled at the rim of her womb.

Moments later, when his breaths came more easily, he rolled to his side, bringing Leah with him. "Incredible," he uttered, smiling at her, his finger tracing the soft line of her jaw. They lay in silence for a long while, each studying the other, then Ian said, "I love you, Leah. No woman, except you, has heard those words from me. No woman, except you, ever will. I know our wedding wasn't exactly what one might call traditional. I suppose you've felt as though you've been victimized by all that's happened. But know this. I'll never fail you. You are now and always the only woman I will ever love."

A bittersweet feeling swirled inside Leah at his confession. Claimed by guilt, she was unable to hold his gaze.

"Look at me."

Slowly, she obeyed his soft command.

"I want to know what is in your heart. Be honest, and tell me."

Gripped in so many lies, she nearly forgot how to speak the truth. "I'll lose our bet if I answer," she hedged.

"Then lose it. Or better yet, I absolve you of our wager. Just tell me."

Leah couldn't resist his request. "I love you, Ian Sinclair. Love you with all my heart. Despite my claims to the contrary, I have always loved you. I think I have since the moment I first saw your portrait—arrogant as your image might be."

Relief washing through him, Ian chuckled. "Then why did you forever run from me?"

"You came on a bit too strong for my liking."

Mirth sparkled in his eyes as his hand skimmed over her

shoulder. "Virgin that you were, I suppose I frightened you."

"Yes, you frightened me," she answered, knowing her fear stemmed not because she was once a virgin, but because of his possible wrath.

His fingers grazed the trail of silken hair, traveling down the tempting curve of her back. "Would I frighten you now if I told you I desire you again?" His hand grasped her firm bottom, dragging her toward him. Hard and hot, his manhood teased her belly. "Or do you think, by what we've just experienced, you've gotten over your fear of me?"

"Let's not think about what was in our past." *Nor about what is in our future.* "There is only now, Ian. Whatever you desire, it is yours."

"Then so be it," he growled anew. Anxious to be inside her again, he pressed Leah back onto the mattress.

Afterward, still basking in the rapture they'd shared, Ian curled around Leah, holding her close to his chest. "Good night, love," he whispered.

She glanced over her shoulder at him. "The lamp— shouldn't we extinguish it?"

"No."

"No?"

"That's what I said. I might awaken and want you again."

"Can't one make love in the dark?"

"Not if one wants to see the ecstasy on his lover's face."

Near dawn, Leah awakened. Noting her husband still slumbered peacefully, she crept from her bed. Gathering her nightdress from the floor, she donned it, then walked toward the table by the window.

Extinguishing the lamp's flame, its soft light having disclosed their joy several more times during the night, she drew back the heavy drapery and stared through the lace curtains. Pink streaked the sky above the houses opposite the small park. The new day promised to be beautiful, nearly as beautiful as was the preceding night.

Ian. His name winged through her mind as she remembered the wondrous lovemaking they had shared. She'd surrendered to him, body, heart, and soul. Truly, she was forever lost to him. The thought of leaving him nearly destroyed her. How could she possibly give him up when she loved him with every inch of her being? An impossibility, but it had to be done.

She had to escape him and soon. But to do that, she needed money. Without the necessary funds, she couldn't conceivably care for the children. Still she refused to abandon her siblings. Oh, if there were only some way she could stay, gathering the children to her, Ian accepting them willingly, her heart would be filled with glorious contentment. But for that to happen, she'd have to confess. Unfortunately, the truth was now her enemy. Despite his claim never to fail her, she knew that to be inaccurate. He'd not forgive her for her deceitfulness.

As the sun peeked above the housetops, golden light streaked through the curtains, casting a lacy pattern on the table beside her. Leah was intrigued by the fascinating design. Then, she spotted the gloves she wore on the night of the Delderfields' ball. They were yet tucked behind the lamp where she'd placed them prior to packing for their trip to Gretna Green.

Snatching them up, she felt the fingers. The ruby. It was still inside. Until now, she'd forgotten all about it.

With a quick shake, Rupert's stickpin fell into her hand. She examined it carefully. As the ruby glittered in the sunlight, she decided it was genuine. Worth a small fortune, she surmised.

"What are you doing, sweet?"

She thrust the gem back into the glove, then set the thing aside. Slowly, she turned to gaze at her husband. His head propped against his hand, the sheet hugging low against his lean hips, he looked so inviting. "I was watching the sunrise," she said, then smiled.

He grinned in return. "Come back to bed." He lifted the sheet. "I want you beside me always."

As she walked toward him, she wished that were true. At the bed, she pulled her nightdress over her head. It fell from her fingers as she slipped under the cover.

Hooded eyes looked down on her. "That's better," he said, his arm curling around her waist, urging her closer.

"I thought you were asleep," she said, her finger touching his chin, brushing lightly against the rough stubble that had appeared overnight.

His head dipped while his lips opened. He caught her finger, drawing it into his mouth. His tongue played briefly, then he released the digit. "I was asleep, but then I missed you." Shifting his weight, he bore her back against the pillow. "Don't ever leave me, Leah."

"I won't," she said, feeling the instant sting of tears. *At least, not in my heart.*

"Good," Ian breathed, then his lips took hers in a searing kiss.

As Leah eagerly gave herself up to his desires yet again, the ruby stickpin flashed in her mind's eye. A new plan was starting to form. How she would get the money was no longer a mystery to her. She knew precisely what she needed to do.

"Ian," she said much later. "You're mother is right, you know. We need to face our detractors at once. Is there a party this week?"

His fingers played lightly across her stomach, dipping into her dewy curls, then lower. He marveled how Leah automatically opened to him. Already she was as eager as he. "The Alcotts have a soiree tomorrow night, I believe."

"Then we should make a point of attending."

As he watched his hand, he frowned. "Are you certain you want to do this?"

"Yes," Leah stated emphatically, wishing it could be otherwise. "To delay will only make things more difficult." His touch grew bolder. Knowing she would miss him, she felt as though her heart were breaking. "It must be done," she said, referring not only to their attending the soiree, but also to her inevitable abandoning of him.

"Couldn't we wait a week or two?"

"No." Her plan was set. All she had to do was implement it. "It must be done now, Ian."

"You're right," he agreed, not thinking in the least about

239

their detractors, the soiree, or anything else except Leah and the endless joy she gave him. Effortlessly, he centered himself between her thighs. "We'll do it now."

Once again, Leah willingly gave herself to Ian, basking in the glory of their love. Only the here and now existed for her, for them. There would be no tomorrows, she knew, for soon she would be gone.

CHAPTER
17

Three weeks after the Alcotts' soiree, the London party circuit clamored with the news: A thief was in their midst. Fingers pointed as speculation rose. One of their own was attempting to strip the peerage clean.

Secreted away in the corner of the gardens at Sinclair House, Leah inspected her bounty. The jeweled letter opener alone, which she'd foisted from the desk in the Alcotts' study, would fetch a hefty price. And the solid-gold snuffbox she'd lifted from Lord Nevins—the pompous boor—was surely worth a goodly sum.

Leah laughed as she remembered, while waiting in the hallway outside the Chatwells' ballroom for Ian's return with their refreshments, how Lord Nevins had snorted a pinch or two of snuff. The gold box was quickly set aside on a nearby commode as his dozen or so stout sneezes were caught by his lace-trimmed handkerchief. Offering his apologies to those nearest him, sniffing loudly as he did so, he'd turned back to retrieve the box, only to find the article was gone. And so was Leah.

The other objects she'd pilfered, stowing them in the

pocket she'd sewn under the ruffle of one of her petticoats, stashing each one away in her special hiding place once she'd felt it was safe, probably weren't of much worth. But every penny counted.

Either way, she'd have to wait until she was far from the city walls before she sought the proper agent to fence her illicit gains, one who was most discreet.

Studying her cache, Leah sighed, for she was certain she'd have to continue her thievery. Luckily, according to Terence's latest letter, received just yesterday from Sally, Peter was still improving. The money she'd dispatched for his care had been sufficient, a limited amount remaining, so she had no worries over needing to send more. But the booty she'd already acquired wasn't enough. In order to make her escape, the children with her, she must double the amount of her loot, if not triple it. The risk became greater each time she wrought her larceny. Inevitably, Leah knew she'd be caught.

The piece of carved ivory she'd purloined from the Bosworths settled next to the other articles, Leah wrapping the sum in a length of linen, dropping the cloth into a roomy leather pouch. Placing the bag into the hole she'd dug, the excess dirt scattered throughout the gardens, she scooted the heavy rock over the opening.

Dusting off her hands, she rose from her knees. Upon turning, she gasped.

"What in heaven's name are you doing out here?" Ian asked, just having come upon her. "I've been looking for you for a good twenty minutes."

Leah swallowed what she believed was her heart. "I-I was just having a look-see. The area seems so very bleak back here. I thought perhaps some shade-loving flowers might brighten it up a bit."

Ian spied the high color on her cheeks, noted the dots of perspiration on her upper lip. Was it from exertion, nervousness, or simply the heat of the day? "I'll talk to the gardener about it," he said, thinking it was the latter.

Leah's knees wobbled. Now what? "If you don't mind, I'd

rather do something with the area myself. I do so enjoy working with the soil and being outdoors."

Stepping nearer, Ian slipped his hands around her waist and pulled her close to his hips. "What else do you enjoy, sweet?"

Through her skirt and petticoats, Leah felt his manhood burgeoning against her. Her hand met the crisp hairs on the center of his chest. Today he wore his portrait garb. "Is that all you ever think about?" she snapped, her nerves still jangled from nearly being caught with her illegal goods. She was certain he hadn't been watching her for more than a second. Otherwise, he'd be poking under the rock. "It's only been an hour or so since . . . since—"

"Since we made love?" She didn't answer. "That was in our bath, Leah. I'm eager to experience whatever delight might unfold elsewhere. Why don't we slip behind the tree and see what comes of it?"

"You're insatiable, sir. I ask you again: Is that all you ever think about?"

"That, and food."

"Keep eating as you have been, and you'll soon grow fat."

"Not if I get my proper exercise. But you seem intent on impeding me from doing so."

As he spoke he began backing Leah toward the tree he'd mentioned. She just now noticed the direction they were taking. She dug her heels into the soft ground, but to no avail. "What do you think you're doing?" she cried, her hands shoving against his sinewy shoulders.

"You don't want me to get fat, do you?"

They were now at the corner of the ivy-covered walls behind the ancient tree. Leah's back hit the rough bark, Ian leaning into her.

"The servants—someone will see!" Leah insisted.

"We're secluded enough. This tree makes two of you. Besides, you said you enjoyed the outdoors. What better place than here?"

A strangled growl met his ears as his hands fumbled with her skirt and petticoats, drawing them up between them.

His wife's displeasure was apparent. But that would soon change. His fingers searched for the slit in her pantaloons which was hidden between her thighs. Breaching the opening, he found what he sought.

"Damn! If the style should change and a woman's underpinnings sewn closed, a man will be at a veritable loss," he commented, his hand eagerly priming her.

The play of his fingers excited Leah. In a breath's time, she was wet and ready. "Damn you!" she scolded, her hands gripping his shoulders as he lifted her. "You always get what you want."

Releasing his hard member, Ian smiled wickedly. "Always," he proclaimed.

Then he was inside her.

Several hours later, Leah's back came up from the center of the silk coverlet. Shaking her head, her long hair brushed against bare hips. She stretched languorously.

Lying on the bed beside her, his hands clasped behind his head, Ian watched his wife's catlike movements. Thank God he hadn't tossed her out on the doorstep as he'd considered doing the first day she'd arrived. He'd once called her a stray, but he now knew she was of the finest pedigree. If not by ancestry, then simply by the fact that she was Leah. Perfection in every way, he decided, certain their children would be exceptional as well. As he gazed at the lustrous flaxen waves covering the silken skin of her back, glimpsed the soft curve of her hips, spied the satiny roundness of one breast, he again sensed the first stirrings of desire.

Damnation! He assumed he'd grown far too old to maintain this sort of stamina. At thirty-three, he felt more like he was seventeen. Far be it for him to complain. He was, after all, enjoying himself immensely. Then as Leah glided to the side of the bed, he caught her arm. "Where do you think you're going?"

She glanced over her shoulder at him. "We have a party tonight, remember?"

Ian hissed a curse. "You're starting to sound like Veronica."

Leah's gaze narrowed on him. "And what does that mean?"

"You are forever engrossed in what party you'll be attending next. We've made our required appearances. Why can't we just stay in and enjoy our evening together *alone?*"

"Because we've told the Moncreiffes that we're coming."

Ian dragged her back across the silk coverlet. When she was again at his side, he released her arm and gripped her waist. "You know I hate these functions, despise more than half the people who attend them. The only reason I am in London for the Season this year is because I wanted to find myself a suitable wife. I've found her. And I didn't even have to leave my own house to do so."

"But you did have to leave Scotland," she interjected quickly.

"Yes, I did. In a few weeks, madam, we shall be returning there. For now, can we not give up these pretentious duties, popping from one house to another, smiling congenially at all those we meet while wishing to hell we were someplace else. Let's just stay here—please?"

More than ever, Leah needed to be at the Moncreiffes' ball, especially if, as Ian said, he intended to return to Scotland soon. Maybe she'd be fortunate enough to acquire three or four articles tonight. Their hosts' home was reported to contain many valuable items, a collection of priceless jade in particular. Maybe she could end her thievery in one fell swoop.

Rolling onto her knees, Leah straddled Ian's hips. "A bargain, sir," she said, pressing intimately against him. "You go with me tonight, and when we return, I shall repay you by acting as your paramour. Whatever you desire of me, I shall do."

A smile teased Ian's lips. "You're already my lover, sweet. Why do I need a paramour?"

"Use your imagination, Ian. Are there certain things you might attempt with another woman that you certainly wouldn't try with your wife?"

Several things shot through his mind. His blood burned from the images he conjured up. Then he suddenly snapped to. "But you are my wife, Leah. I doubt I'd be able to forget that."

"After we've returned from the Moncreiffes', I won't be your wife. If need be, I'll veil myself. As your woman of mystery, whatever you desire, I'll do."

"What about now?" he asked, feeling himself growing rock hard. "Could you possibly give me a sampling of what I might look forward to later?"

Leah slowly shook her head. "Tonight, after the ball."

As she lifted herself away from him, Ian grumbled under his breath. Then, without warning, her head dipped, her lips meeting his manhood. "Christ, woman!" he said, hissing, then grabbed for her, but caught only air.

Several feet away from him, Leah turned. "Tonight, Ian. After the ball."

As he lay there staring up at the canopy over their bed, Ian decided the Moncreiffes' ball didn't seem so unappealing after all.

The melodies of a waltz floated through the Moncreiffes' ballroom, the gaily colored crowd spinning in time to the music. Ignoring the happy throng, Leah watched her husband closely from a quarter of the way around the room.

He was still engaged in conversation with four of his mother's acquaintances. The women had cornered them both nearly five minutes ago, first inquiring on Madeline's whereabouts, then subtly questioning them on their sudden marriage.

As the inquisitive females edged closer to Ian, his answers apparently being of greater interest to them than her own, Leah had sidled away, then deserted him altogether. Now, as she skirted the dance floor, she gave her husband one last look, then slipped through the doorway into the corridor, wondering where she might find the jade.

Traipsing along the marble-floored hallway, opening doors as she went, Leah pretended confusion. So far she had found the study, the sitting room, and the library, all of which she quickly crossed off her list of possibilities. As she shut the door to the latter, she was confronted by a footman.

"May I help you, madam?" he queried, gazing down his long nose at her.

"I seem to be at a loss, sir," she said, batting her lashes, playing the part of a simpering fool. "I cannot for the life of me find the privy."

His eyebrow arched as he cleared his throat. "There is a water closet below on the first floor, madam. I assume you are unattended?"

Leah blinked. "Unattended?"

"Your maid—she's not with you."

"No. She is ill."

"Wait here, and I shall fetch someone to assist you?"

"That won't be necessary. Please just show me the closest way. I shall see to myself, thank you." Suspicion sparked in the man's dark eyes, Leah registering such. Undoubtedly, because of the thefts, he'd been instructed to question anyone who was found outside the immediate vicinity of the ballroom. Fearing he might sound the alarm, she wriggled, her feet quickly hopping into an agitated dance. "Well, are you going to show me the way? Or do you wish for me to have a mishap, here and now?"

Red from embarrassment, the man waved his hand in front of him. "This way, madam."

Leah followed him down the hallway to the back staircase. Along the way, she noticed there was yet another door she hadn't looked behind. Talk of Lord Moncreiffe's having added another piece of the priceless jade to his collection had been the topic of conversation among several of the guests. While eavesdropping, she'd discerned the trove was kept in a special room. Perhaps it was the one she'd just passed.

"Down the steps and to your right—you'll find what you seek behind the first door to your left," the footman said, reaching the top of the stairs.

"Thank you." Leah lifted her skirt slightly, her hand catching the banister. "I am forever in your debt."

His gaze searching the ceiling, the man again cleared his throat, and Leah proceeded down the stairs. Once she rounded the narrow landing, she descended two more steps, then stood in place, her feet tapping, at first loudly, then lighter and lighter. To anyone above, she hoped it sounded as though she were still descending. Her simulated treads stopped, and she listened, wondering if the footman was still there. Leah released her trapped breath when she heard his long strides carrying him back down the corridor.

On tiptoes, she quickly retraced her steps, then reaching the top of the stairs, peered down the long hallway. Except for the footman, his back presented to her, the corridor was empty. Her skirts hiked, she dashed to the door she'd spotted. Releasing the latch, she looked inside, then slipped into the lighted room, the door closing quietly behind her.

Leah's breath caught as her eyes searched the area. Antiquities abounded in glass cases, all relics from a bygone era. Her gaze glanced off the cabinet containing a Roman urn, on to another holding a small Grecian statue. Although she suspected these artifacts, like the others displayed, were of great worth, all were far too large to hide on her person. Then she spotted the jade.

Rushing to the glass case, she studied the intricately carved pieces. Each being the product of a long-dead artisan from some unknown dynasty, the finely crafted sculptures were probably the illicit spoils from Britain's Opium War with China. All were obviously authentic, and all were quite valuable. Their beauty, Leah accepted, was unmatched.

Incredibly, the case's key was still in its lock. Her brow furrowed as she viewed it. Careless of her host to leave the thing so handy. Anyone could easily slip into the room, the treasures quickly purloined, the thief vanishing into the night. Too easily, Leah decided, wondering if she might have walked into a trap. Remembering the old adage about a gift horse, she dismissed her fears. Her trembling fingers rose, aiming for the key. Leah froze as she heard the door open behind her.

"You there!" a man's voice bellowed. "What are you about?"

On shaking legs, Leah turned toward the man, who was now striding toward her. Under silver eyebrows, his hard blue eyes bore into her.

"L-Lord Moncreiffe," Leah said, breathing deeply, her hand covering her chest. "You startled me."

"I should hope so," the man said, now standing in front of her. "What are you doing in here, madam?"

Think, her mind demanded. *Find a plausible excuse.* "I-I was admiring your collection, of course."

"Admiring? Is that all?"

Oh, why had she attempted this dangerous scheme. She knew she'd get caught. Unable to speak, she nodded her reply.

"Who gave you permission to enter this room?"

"W-why no one," she squeaked.

"Yet you took it upon yourself to snoop about my house without first seeking my consent."

"I'm sorry, sir, if I've overstepped the bounds of propriety. I had heard about your collection from several of those who are in attendance tonight. I have a penchant for antiquities, but I didn't wish to trouble you, especially when you were so busily engaged with your guests. In fact, I was unable to find you at the time. I didn't think my coming in here would present a problem. I certainly apologize if it has."

Lord Moncreiffe looked past her at the cabinet. Relief showed on his face when he saw nothing had been disturbed. But, when he glanced back at Leah, his gaze hardened again.

"If you haven't heard, madam, there is a thief lurking about London these days—a thief who has invaded all the finer houses. Because no one enters many of these homes without an invitation, it is a given this larcenist, whomever he or *she* might be, is a member of the peerage. Considering you've stolen in here as you have, I am of a mind that *you* are this thief."

Leah felt certain she had met her doom. Deciding she'd not go down so easily, she mustered as much bravado as she could, squared her shoulders, and looked the man in the eyes. "I beg your pardon, sir. You accuse me falsely. I expect an apology."

"Instead, madam, I shall summon a constable."

"Lord Moncreiffe," a woman called. "You are mistaken if you are accusing the Lady Huntsford of being a thief."

Leah thought she recognized the voice. Looking past her host, she now noticed how several guests hovered near the door. One broke from the pack and stepped forward. It was Rupert's mother.

"Your Grace," Lord Moncreiffe stated, the jewel-draped duchess having gained his side, "I'm certain this young woman planned to steal my jade. If you don't mind, I shall attend to seeing she is arrested without interference from you."

"Is anything missing?" the duchess inquired.

Moncreiffe inspected the glass case again. "No."

"Then I would say you don't have any proof."

"Were we to check the guest list of all the houses that were robbed, I will wager her name is upon each and every one," he said of Leah.

"As was mine, sir," the woman countered. "As was yours, also."

"But neither you nor I were caught where we shouldn't have been."

"Perhaps not. But then, Lord Moncreiffe, you don't know who has been in here prior to the countess or who might come in after we depart, especially since you leave the door unguarded and unsecured. And look here." She pointed to the glass case. "You've left the key in its lock. Your carelessness is abominable. It would serve you right, sir, if you were robbed blind."

"And I say I have caught our thief."

"Twaddle," the duchess said, moving next to Leah, a protective arm surrounding the younger woman's shoulders. "Had the girl possessed such a inclination, she would have snatched up my bracelet the moment it unknowingly fell from my wrist at the Carstairses' and been off with it, no one the wiser. Instead, on finding it, she chased after me and returned it immediately. Does that sound like the workings of a thief's mind—especially, Lord Moncreiffe, when alone my bracelet is worth more than the price of all those green carvings of yours added together?"

Moncreiffe studied the duchess, then inhaled deeply. "It is debatable about the worth of your gems versus my collection of jade, Your Grace," he said with the release of his breath. "But, by what you've just said, no, that does not sound like the workings of a thief's mind." He looked at Leah. "I apologize, Lady Huntsford, for accusing you unfairly. However, henceforth, should you desire to see something of interest to you, please ask first. Especially until this larcenist is caught. Now, if you wish to view my collection, you may join with the others as we all take a turn about the room."

The tension drained from Leah's body. Had it not been for the duchess she'd soon be in the custody of a constable, her husband's censuring look following her out the main entry. "I accept your apology, sir. And I shall very much enjoy seeing your collection."

The man bowed. "My pleasure, madam."

Leah and the duchess quickly fell into line with the others at the door. Once Lord Moncreiffe explained his error to all, they began their guided tour.

Moving slowly along, Leah studied the duchess from the corner of her eye. Obviously, she knew nothing about her son's confrontation with Ian or she wouldn't have so readily come to Leah's aid. "Thank you, Your Grace," she whispered, while their host droned on about the Roman urn.

Dangling earrings struck against her many necklaces as the duchess turned her head toward Leah. "Think nothing of it, child. Despite Lord Moncreiffe's accusations, I knew you were innocent of any wrongdoing. Everyone is on edge lately, Lord Moncreiffe included. Stupid of him to leave his collection unattended as he did. But I must agree with his statement. Until the thief is caught, we all should be most careful about what we do, lest we be falsely charged."

"I understand fully," Leah said softly, then pretended interest in her host's monologue about his assorted treasures. To again risk being caught was madness, pure and simple. This time her luck had held, though it was unlikely to do so in the future. Yet what choice did she have but to continue her thievery? She needed money—desperately so.

While she wished otherwise, stealing seemed to be her only recourse. Next time—and there would indeed be a next time—she'd be far more careful when she made her attempt.

As the group moved around the room, Leah began to comment on Lord Moncreiffe's statements, adding information about each of the eras from which a certain artifact was derived. By the time the small party had completed their tour, her host seemed to be most impressed with her knowledge. His suspicion of her had evaporated.

"You truly are interested in antiquities," the man said, the assembly having vacated the room, Lord Moncreiffe locking the door behind him. He motioned for a footman, then instructing his servant to stand guard, he traversed the corridor toward the ballroom, with Leah beside him. Just outside the entry, he stopped and turned to his guest. "I again apologize for my accusation, Lady Huntsford. With all this worry over there being a thief in our midst—well, I—"

"Think nothing of it, sir. I fully understand your concern."

"What concern?" Ian asked, coming up beside them.

"I'm afraid, sir, I accused your wife unfairly."

Gazing down on Leah, Ian frowned. "About what?"

"It's not important," she stated, wishing her host had kept his mouth shut.

"Oh, but it is, madam," Lord Moncreiffe declared. "I owe your husband an apology also."

Gritting her teeth, Leah listened as the man explained the events that had transpired, again offering his regrets over his error to the earl and the countess alike. Smiling her acceptance, she watched as her host again took himself off into the ballroom.

"So you've been snooping, is it? I'd wondered where you were off to."

"I wasn't snooping," Leah defended. "I had heard about the marquess's collection. I simply wanted to see it."

"Leaving me alone with those ogresses in the process," he

said about his mother's friends. "I thought I'd never get away from them. When I did, you were gone."

"I shall make it up to you."

He escorted her toward the stairs. "Indeed you will, madam."

"Where are we going?"

"Home."

"Already?"

"It's nearly one in the morning, Leah."

"But my reticule."

Ian patted the small lump just under his coat. "It's safely tucked away."

Outside the entry, the pair waited on the step. Soon a footman routed the phaeton up the drive. Once his wife was seated, Ian climbed aboard.

As they quickly traveled the streets toward Berkley Square, Leah lightly chewed her lower lip, wondering at her husband's haste. "Are you angry Lord Moncreiffe found me where I shouldn't have been?"

Ian's head whipped toward her. "Why should I be angry?"

"I was afraid I had caused you embarrassment."

"Embarrassment?"

"Yes, why else would you have left the party in such haste?"

His chuckle filled the air. "As I recall, sweet, we struck a bargain. I fulfilled my part by escorting you to the Moncreiffes', now it is your turn to execute your part." Under his expert hand, the phaeton turned the corner. Sinclair House stood only a few yards away. Reining the horse to a stop, he then turned to her. "Or do you now hope to renege? If so, I won't let you."

With her nearly having been caught filching the jade, Leah had forgotten all about their pact. Remembering the terms, she felt a quickening deep in her stomach. Then Ian's head lowered toward hers.

"I won't let you," he repeated softly just before his lips captured hers. Long moments later, he pulled back. "Let's say we seek out our bed and see what mysteries unfold."

Enveloped in the blush of desire, Leah smiled up at him. "Gladly," she whispered, then allowed herself to be led into the house.

When the gallery clock struck four, Ian still lay awake, his slumbering wife curled close against him. His lips brushing the crown of her silken head, he smiled to himself. Despite her attempts to make him forget she was his wife, not for a moment had he done so. Nevertheless, he couldn't help but marvel over what they'd shared.

As promised, she'd pretended to be his paramour, her ingenuous play eliciting responses beyond his wildest dreams. In all his intimacies with the opposite sex, never had he enjoyed such ecstasy. All women paled in comparison to his beloved. Only she could evoke the rapture he'd experienced. Only she could offer the hope of its ever happening again. Intuitively, Ian was certain the overwhelming pleasure he'd known would once more be his, simply because of Leah.

Ian's heart swelled as he basked in the knowledge he'd found her. Now that she was his, he vowed never to let her go. Nothing could ever make him turn from her. Nothing would ever come between them. Only death would ever separate them. Even then, should he go first, he'd not desert her, his spirit lingering beside her, until she would at last join him.

"Ah, sweet," he whispered, holding her closer to him. "I love you so. And nothing can ever change that."

His eyes drifting shut, Ian soon slept, comforted by the fact that Leah would always be beside him.

"I'm so happy your mother has returned," Leah said, several days later as she and Ian traveled in the phaeton toward Madame Lejeune's. Tucked inside her reticule was another letter to Terence, while one of Anne Kingsley's old dresses sat in her lap. "I did miss her."

"Well, I didn't," Ian said, negotiating a turn.

Leah gaped at him. "Ian—surely you don't mean that."

"I do."

"Why?"

"Things were different while she was away."

"What things?" Leah asked, confused.

"Modesty is acceptable when in public, madam. But when you are in my bed, I expect something else entirely."

Pink painted Leah's cheeks. "But I'm afraid she might hear us," she defended.

"Precisely. Although I love my mother, I do not wish to have her under the same roof with us. She's ruining my pleasure. That's why we'll be leaving for Scotland at week's end."

Leah felt the blood drain from her face. "Ian, you don't mean that, do you?"

"I do. So if you're thinking to have that dress altered, I suggest you either hold on to it or, when the repairs are made, have the thing shipped to Falcon's Gate. For *that,* sweet, is where you'll be." The phaeton stopped in front of the couturière's. "I'll await you here."

Her teeth worrying her lower lip, Leah wondered if she'd gathered enough goods so she could take flight. She'd nabbed a few more trinkets at the Favershams' last night, Madeline insisting they all go to the ball. But she doubted her latest gains were worth much.

Week's end, she thought, realizing she couldn't possibly journey to Scotland with him. Escaping from Falcon's Gate would be far harder to achieve, the nearest town undoubtedly being miles away. London was her only option. But why did it have to be this soon?

Misery filled her upon knowing she must leave Ian. Once, she was certain she could handle their parting when the time came. But now, she wasn't so sure.

"What's wrong, Leah?" Ian asked. "You look as though you've just suffered a terrible loss."

"I have," she whispered, the reality of what it meant to forfeit Ian eating at her soul. She loved him, even more so than she loved the children, which was great in itself. Oh, why did it have to be this way?

Ian's brow arched. "It's not as though she's passed on, Leah. My mother will come at regular intervals to visit us.

You'll see her often enough. In the meantime, you'll have me to keep you company."

Obviously, he'd misunderstood her. Still he had no way of knowing what she'd actually meant. "Can't we stay in London a bit longer?" she asked, looking up at him. "Just a few more weeks?"

"Sorry, love, but I must be getting back to my estate. There is much to be done. I've neglected it long enough. Now run along and see to your repairs. I'll be here when you're finished."

Long fingers captured her chin, and Leah received Ian's light kiss. Slipping from the phaeton, the dress clutched close to her chest, she scurried toward the shop's entry, absently thinking about Ian. Several yards from the door, the bell jingled as the panel opened inward. Arabella Covington stepped from inside, Arthur trailing a step or two behind her.

"Why Miss Kings—I stand corrected. It is now Lady Huntsford, I hear," Arabella said, smiling. "May I offer my congratulations to you and the earl on your recent marriage."

"Thank you," Leah returned, rebounding from her surprise. Then she was at once staring at her half-brother.

Arabella looped her arm through his. "Arthur, this is Miss Kingsley—Lady Huntsford, now."

He tipped his hat in greeting. "I know your uncle," he said, his tone cool.

By the way he inspected her, Leah was certain he was searching to see if in someway she knew something about the Covingtons. "Really? He never mentioned such. But then I am not acquainted with everyone my uncle knows. I haven't met any of his clients. Do you have business with him?"

"No. Of course not," he answered abruptly. "We met here in London at a party."

"I see." Arthur didn't respond, and Leah forced herself to say something, the silence between them becoming most tedious. "Well, I'm happy you are now recovered, Lord Covington."

"I am, Lady Huntsford, thanks to your kind intervention."

"Think nothing of it, sir," she countered, believing his manner was less stiff. "I was glad I could be of help."

"Oh, but I do think of it. My sister told me you were most concerned about my mishap. Foolish of me to have dashed into the street that way, but then I've never been noted for being exceptionally cautious."

"It was your concern about my husband and myself, as well as those who were close at hand, that got you injured. As far as I am concerned, you were and are a hero. I just wish you didn't have to suffer for it."

At her praises, Arthur's face reddened slightly. "Well, I'm quite stout now, ready for my next adventure. If you'll excuse me, I'd like to speak to your husband."

Arabella's soft laughter filled the air. "He never could take a compliment," she stated, her brother having rushed off toward the phaeton. Then she grew serious. "I won't keep you, but I wanted to ask a favor of you."

"If I can be of help, certainly."

"Please tell your husband that his kind show of concern was greatly appreciated. I'd do so myself, but Arthur knows nothing about the earl having paid his medical bills. Nor is he aware of the contribution your husband made in way of extra cash to see us through these difficult times. Arthur is so very proud. I doubt he would accept Lord Huntsford's charity in the same way as do my mother and I. Just tell him we cherish all he's done for each of us."

"I will," Leah said. Her husband's generosity amazed her, for not everyone would be so kind. But then not everyone was Ian. Another reason why she loved him as she did. "Is your mother doing better?"

"Yes, much better." She looked toward the phaeton. "Arthur appears ready to be on his way, so I'll say my farewell. And again congratulations on your marriage. You are most fortunate to have found such a wonderful man. But then, I suppose you already know that."

Staring after Arabella, Leah fought against her tears. Yes, she appreciated how wonderful Ian was, and that's what made leaving him so very difficult. *At week's end.* Fumbling with the doorknob, she realized the time for her to go was upon her all too soon.

A half hour later, at Sinclair House, Ian reached around Leah and opened the front door. In the foyer, he caught her arm, turning her toward him. "There aren't any parties tonight, are there?"

"No. Not tonight."

"Then, since I didn't do so before, I'd very much enjoy taking you to the opera."

"Really?"

His wife had been so very quiet on their drive home, her brow furrowed as though she were dissecting a thorny problem. Noticing how her face had brightened, he smiled. "Really."

"Could we ask your mother to join us?" she asked, thinking this might be her last chance to ever be with Madeline. Once they were again home, Ian would be the focus of her attention. Tomorrow, before the sun's first rays hit the rooftops, Leah planned to be gone. "Please?"

"Yes, we can ask. But don't be surprised if she has made other plans."

"I'll go up and see if she's done so."

"Whoa," Ian said, again catching her arm. Leah looked at him with questioning eyes. "A kiss, madam. Right here."

Rising on tiptoes, Leah brushed her lips against his cheek on the exact spot where he'd indicated. "Satisfied?"

"For now."

"Then you have changed, sir."

"The foyer, madam, is no place to toss up your skirts. Later, when we are in our room, the full truth will be known."

"And what truth is that?"

"You'll discover I haven't changed a bit."

After tomorrow, he was bound to change, his hurt soon turning to hate. She couldn't bear to see such a virulent look in his eyes. That's why she wanted to slink off into the night, while Ian was still peacefully asleep.

"Go ask your question," he said. "I'll meet you in our room."

"First, a kiss, sir. Right here."

Noting where her finger lay, Ian was more than willing to oblige. His lips took Leah's in a ravenous kiss. Moments passed, then his head slowly lifted. "Go, before Simmons finds us lying here naked on the floor."

Leah rushed to the stairs, then lifting her skirts, attempted a fast trek up them. Immediately, her head swam, an episode that had come upon her with regularity in the past several days. Just as quickly, the dizziness passed, and Leah raced the steps again.

Behind her, Ian followed at a slower pace, allowing the effects of his wife's kiss to wear off. Halfway to the gallery, he heard the knocker fall against the front door. As it sounded again, he turned and retraced his steps. "I'll get it," he shouted, hoping to save Simmons a trip. Then he jerked the panel wide. Surprise instantly lit his face. "Damnation man! What on earth are you doing here?"

"It's a long story, Huntsford. One I'd strongly like to forget. Mind if I come in?"

Realizing he was blocking the opening, Ian moved aside. "Forgive me. I just hadn't imagined seeing you this soon."

"I hadn't counted on being back this soon."

Removing his hat, John Kingsley strode across the threshold.

CHAPTER
18

"It's good to see you," Ian proclaimed while closing the door. He debated whether or not he should tell Kingsley that he and Leah were married, then decided to let the man relax a bit before delivering the news. Taking Kingsley's hat, cane, and gloves, he set them on the stand. "Come. Let's go on up. I'll ring for some refreshments, then you can tell me all about your trip."

"It was a veritable disaster," Kingsley growled, climbing the steps, the earl beside him.

"It sounds as though you had a bad time of it," Ian commented as he and Kingsley started across the gallery to the sitting room. "How about a brandy, John?" Ian shifted directions toward the study instead. "It might help soothe your nerves."

"A good idea, Huntsford," he returned. "I'd rather my mood lightened before I see your mother. She is here, isn't she?"

At Kingsley's anxious query, Ian smiled to himself. He wondered if he and Leah would soon be present at another wedding.

Shut inside the study, he waved Kingsley toward the chair at the front of his desk, then headed to the side table and the brandy. "Yes, John, she's here." He lifted the crystal top from the decanter and poured two fingers' worth of the golden liquid into the waiting glasses. "She'll be both surprised and delighted to see you, I'm sure," he said, now beside his guest. One glass handed over, he aimed himself around the desk and seated himself, where he raised his own glass in salute. "To your health."

"And to yours, sir," Kingsley replied.

Both men sipped their brandy, then Ian asked, "What happened that you are back in England so soon?"

Kingsley swilled some more brandy. "As far as I'm concerned, I should never have left."

Ian's eyebrow arched in query.

"A storm hit, and we were shipwrecked off the coast of Africa. A horrible incident, it was. We came ashore close to a native village. Luckily, the chaps were friendly enough, else we might have been made part of their evening stew. Even more fortunate for us, the French settlement of Saint-Louis stood nearby. We had to wait for a supply packet to carry us back to France. From there, my man Farnsworthy and I headed on to England. The poor fellow refuses to set foot on a ship again. He is now traveling overland to York. It was an abominable experience. I don't relish the thought of leaving England's shores again myself."

"Is Victoria aware of your mishap?"

"I've sent word to our queen that I've arrived in London. I await a reply, whereupon I shall give her or her representative a full report. Should she request I attempt the journey again, I believe I'll beg off, asking she find some other chap to take my place. A knighthood would be nice, but the distinction isn't worth any further strain on my nerves, not to mention the threat it would again pose to my life. Next time, I might not be so lucky."

Ian chuckled. "Then to say India is not high on your list of places to visit wouldn't be far off the mark."

"Not at all, sir. Not unless I can get there by land."

"Well, I'm happy you are safely back in England. When mother and Leah hear about your harrowing adventure, I know they will be equally as happy."

The man's brow furrowed. "Leah?"

"I meant Anne," Ian said, thinking the use of his wife's middle name may have confused him.

"Anne?"

"Your niece, John. Have you forgotten who she is?"

"Hardly. But I doubt the ungrateful chit cares one way or the other where I am or what's happened to me. To be truthful, I feel much the same about her."

Ian bristled. "Perhaps you're being a bit too judgmental. If you'd allow yourself the opportunity to know her better, you might find she's not as disagreeable as you think."

"She's every bit as disagreeable as I think—just like her father was." Kingsley's frown deepened. "Forgive me, Huntsford, but how is it you know about Anne. And my trip to India—I wasn't aware you knew about that either. I didn't have time to write your mother before I left—a case of too many things happening at once, my niece's elopement being one of them."

Confused by Kingsley's words, Ian stared at him. "Elopement?"

"Yes, elopement."

"I'm sorry, but I'm at loss as to exactly what it is you're saying," Ian said, his confusion deepening. "Let me get this straight. Your niece eloped prior to your leaving York?"

"That's precisely what I'm saying. I was preparing to send the chit south into your mother's care when I got word she'd run off with that detestable Irishman who'd followed her from Ulster. Good riddance to the girl, I say. She was a lost cause from the moment she came into my care."

Ian fought to deny what he'd just heard. Surely, the man was mistaken. Too much sun aboard ship, perhaps. "Are you certain about this?"

"Certain as I'll ever be."

A cold feeling overtook Ian. "You're positive your memory hasn't failed you?"

Kingsley stared at his host. "The appalling events I suffered didn't cause me to lose my faculties, sir. I remember exactly what happened. I was sitting in my office when my coachman came rushing in with the note Anne had left behind, announcing her elopement. I'm not daft, man. Should you need confirmation on this, I'm certain my man Farnsworthy will be glad to give it. Miss Dalton, also."

What felt like a knife twisted in Ian's gut. "Miss Dalton?"

"Yes. She was there, running on about her deplorable situation."

Ian suddenly bounded from his chair. Striding to a nearby cabinet, he jerked open the doors and rummaged through his files.

"What is this all about, Huntsford? Why are you so interested in my niece?"

"Because, sir, I am supposedly married to her."

"Married? Why that's impossible!"

"This Miss Dalton," Ian said, finding the two documents he searched for. "What is her full name?"

"Let me think," Kingsley stated. "Before his death, her father was a client of mine. Her mother's maiden name was Balfour. That I know. But the children—"

"Is her first name Leah?"

"Yes—that's it. Leah Balfour Dalton."

Anger flamed inside Ian. *Liar! Betrayer! Cheat!* His jaw clenched as his fingers curled around the marriage certificate, crushing it in his hand. He cursed vividly.

Kingsley came to his feet, then made his way to Ian's side. "What is it, Huntsford? What's all this talk about marriage to my niece? It's impossible, I say."

"Agreed," he affirmed, his burst of temper now curbed. He handed the marriage certificate over to the solicitor. "Read the signature aloud."

Taking his spectacles from his pocket, the man perched them on his nose, then straightened the crimped paper. "Anne Leah Balfour Dalton Kingsley." He looked up at Ian. "I'd say you've been duped, sir. But how?"

"Recognize this?"

263

Kingsley caught hold of the second piece of paper. "This is the letter I was writing to your mother when—why, the girl ran off with the thing."

"Explain," Ian said.

"I was late leaving for Hull. I had just finished this letter of introduction when I received word about Anne's elopement. I thought I had scrapped the thing. Undoubtedly, she retrieved it."

"How?"

"I left Miss Dalton in charge of seeing to Anne's luggage. Paid her a tidy sum, too. She was supposed to have instructed the private coachman, who was to ferry my niece to London, to dispose of Anne's possessions. After learning the chit had eloped, I ordered her clothing be distributed to the poor. But apparently—"

"She found a use for Anne's things herself," Ian finished for the solicitor, disbelief still rippling through him. He felt like a doomed man lashed to a sinking ship, the black waters of destruction swirling around him, sucking him under. Leah. The only woman he ever fully loved. She couldn't be an impostor, couldn't have tricked him. But the facts indicated otherwise. "My question is why, Kingsley?" he asked, trying to keep a clear head. There had to be an explanation, one that would free him from this nightmare. "What would make her pose as someone else?"

"Perhaps because of her circumstances."

"What circumstances?"

"She was rendered destitute—a situation caused by her father's death. I had to sell the Dalton family home. Four of her siblings are in an orphanage in York. The oldest boy works for a smithy in Leeds."

"Leeds?" he queried. The letter she'd received was not from her Irishman, but her brother!

"Yes, Leeds. That's where the Daltons hail from. Or should I say just outside. What are you going to do about this?"

In his mind, Ian sank deeper into the eddy that threatened to swallow him. He closed his eyes and inhaled deeply. "I don't know."

"You've been hoaxed, man. Impostor that she is, I suggest you have her arrested."

Hoaxed was right, Ian decided, his eyes hard upon the solicitor. "Arrested?" he questioned, forcing himself out of the dregs of his misery. Breaking free, he felt a cold fury rouse inside him. Lies! All lies! "I just might do that. But first, I want you to tell me precisely what you know about this Leah Balfour Dalton—anything—everything. I want it all."

Before heading back to his desk, Ian snagged the decanter from the side table. Brandy sloshed to the rim of his glass. Quaffing half of the liquid, he fell into his chair.

"Now, start talking," he told Kingsley.

"There's not much to tell. Her mother died, then her father. Because—"

"How did they die? And when? Give me details, John. I won't settle for anything less."

"At the end of February, her mother fell ill. I don't know the cause. Within a week, Mrs. Dalton had succumbed. Her father died in a riding accident nearly on the same day."

"Riding accident?"

"Yes, he was thrown from his horse. Killed instantly. Indeed, a tragedy. Anyway, Terence Dalton's debts were numerous. I had no choice but to sell the house and grounds. As I said, four of her siblings were sent to the orphanage in York. Her brother, Terence, is working for a smithy in Leeds—Jones, I think the man's name is. To be near the children, Miss Dalton sought employment at a local inn not far from the orphanage. I believe she worked as a scullery maid."

Scullery maid? She was too refined for that sort of work. "When you say house and grounds, I assume you don't mean a croft and patch of sod. The family once had money, correct?"

"They were not as wealthy as you, Huntsford. Nor would Balfour compare to Falcon's Gate, but, yes, they were not in want."

"So what happened?"

"The man's debts were numerous. I sold Balfour and paid

them all immediately. Had I waited, more debts would have been incurred. As a result, Dalton's children would have been sent to the workhouse. I had little choice but to act as I did."

Ian studied the man sitting across from him. "You're not telling all, Kingsley. I can see it in your eyes."

Before the solicitor could answer, the door opened. "Ian —oh, I'm sorry," Leah apologized, embarrassed by her sudden intrusion. "I didn't realize you had a visitor."

His attention centered on his wife, the earl felt a frigidness encase him. "That's quite all right. Come in, madam. I believe you know our guest."

From her position by the doorway, Leah inspected the back of the man's gray head. Slowly, he turned around in his chair. Recognition instantly took hold; Leah's heart stopped. *Dear God—no!*

Her gaze jumped to her husband's face. Cold, censuring eyes stared back at her. *He knows!* And he hated her. Hated her with as much passion as he once loved her.

Her fingers gripped the doorframe for support, a sudden lightheadedness overtaking her. The children! Ian! Everything was lost. The room spun before her eyes as she felt the blood drain from her face. It wasn't supposed to be like this. Her knees wobbled, a gray sort of haze creeping in around her.

Fighting against the encroaching blackness, she blinked; a pitiful whimper trembled in her throat, for she couldn't keep the unwanted invader at bay.

From a great distance, she saw her husband vault from his chair. His curse split the air just as she crumpled to the floor in a dead faint.

CHAPTER
19

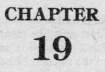

"What's happened to her?" Madeline cried as she rushed along the upstairs corridor toward her son. Her gaze skipped beyond Ian. "John? What on earth are you doing here?"

Having scooped Leah up into his arms, Ian had quickly crossed the gallery, climbed the steps, and now strode toward their room. "We'll explain in a minute, but first, the door."

Skipping ahead of Ian, Madeline twisted the handle and pushed the panel inward, whereupon her son crossed the threshold, then aimed himself at the bed and placed Leah in its center.

"Get the basin," he ordered, nodding at the night stand, his mother now beside him. "When she awakens, she'll undoubtedly be sick."

Lifting the pitcher, Madeline thrust the china bowl into his hands. "She's fainted, then? But why?"

"From the shock of seeing me," Kingsley stated, hovering at the bed's foot. "I took her by surprise."

"You've taken us all by surprise, John, especially when we thought you were on your way to India, if not already there,"

Madeline stated. "But that doesn't explain why she fainted."

"That's exactly why she fainted. She thought I was in India."

The hum of voices intruded on Leah's peace as she rose from the depths of darkness. She moaned.

"Explain later, John," Madeline said, then plunged a clean washcloth into the pitcher. "I have no time for your roundabout babble."

Another moan escaping her, Leah's head rolled on the pillow, then her eyelids fluttered open. Bewildered, she was unable to conceive what exactly had happened to her. Then the first wave of nausea struck. The basin was thrust her way; a cool, damp cloth blotted her brow. Her stomach settling, she slumped back against the pillow. From the corner of her eye, she saw Ian set the basin aside.

"Feeling better, dear?" Madeline asked, leaning over her.

The cool cloth gently wiped across Leah's face. "Yes, but how did I—" Her gaze shooting past her mother-in-law, she spied her husband's impassive expression. Eyes shuttered, he stared back at her. So unfeeling, she thought. "Oh, God—I'm sorry. Truly, Ian, I didn't mean for this to happen." Tears welled, then several spilled from the corner of her eyes, sliding into her hair. "Please, if you'd just let me explain."

"Though I doubt it will make much difference, have at it," he said.

At his flippant tone, Madeline swung toward him. "Can't you see she's upset?" She looked to her daughter-in-law. "Explain what, dear? What's troubling you so?"

Held under the woman's compassionate gaze, Leah felt her throat close with emotion. She, too, would turn against her, once the truth was out. Biting her lower lip, Leah found she couldn't speak. The self-condemning words remained trapped inside.

"Before you again attack your son, Madeline," John said, gaining her attention, "there is something you should know. Perhaps you won't be so sympathetic to the girl once you've discovered what it is. The young woman before you, the one who threw herself on your mercies, presenting herself as Anne Kingsley, is *not* my niece."

Stunned, the dowager countess switched her attention back to Leah. "Is this true?"

"Y-yes."

"Who are you, then?"

"Please believe me," Leah beseeched, grasping Madeline's hand, "I didn't want to lie to you. I didn't want to involve you at all. But, under the circumstances, it seemed as though I had no other choice. I—"

"Unlikely," the solicitor stated. "As for her name, it is Leah Balfour Dalton."

"Sinclair," Ian added, his gaze at last shifting away from Leah. "You saw the marriage certificate, John. I presume my *wife* and I are still legally wedded?"

At his question, Leah's heart lurched. Then she understood why he'd asked it. He wanted to disclaim her. Wanted to discard her as though she were yesterday's slop. She couldn't blame him for feeling as he did, not after the way she'd deceived him.

"Between my niece's name, she did sign her own. You appeared before a man of the cloth, who under the law is an agent for both church and state. Yes, you are legally wedded, but I see no reason why you can't seek an annulment. If not an annulment, then a divorce. I'm certain one would be granted, given she's an impostor. But a case like this never seems to escape notice. No matter how quiet one tries to keep the proceedings, a scandal always manages to result. Besides a civil case, you may also have a criminal suit on your hands, especially if she has defrauded you of money or property."

Once the man's legal advice had been given, Ian swung his gaze back to Leah. "It seems, John," he said, watching for her ensuing reaction, "you too were defrauded. When she fled York with your letter, she also carried a bank draft with her." He saw Leah grow tense. "Until almost a month ago, you paid exclusively for her care."

Deep lines etched Kingsley's brow as his gaze speared her. "Not only did you pass yourself off as my niece, thrusting yourself on these unsuspecting people as you did, but you broke into my desk and stole the bank draft. Your thievery will not go unpunished, young woman. I shall summon a constable immediately."

Leah's lethargy quickly dissipated. Anger taking its place, she came up off the bed. Rounding the end bedpost, she bore down on the man. "Have me arrested if you will, sir, but first I shall have my say. You speak of deception and lies, when it is you who helped perpetuate the greatest lie of all. Had you the decency to answer my questions, to state the truth about my father when I requested it, I probably wouldn't have been forced to act as I did. But no! You continued to protect him, continued to protect his other family, while my siblings and I were made to suffer."

Leah noted Kingsley's surprise, then continued: "Yes, I know about them. They still have a fine home, don't they? They still are together, able to console one another in their time of grief. I've seen them, Mr. Kingsley. In fact, I've been in their home. Dismal it was, black crepe hanging everywhere. But at least they are given the chance to mourn, unlike we Daltons. No, they don't know who I am. I wasn't about to ruin them as I'm fairly certain you helped my half-brother ruin us. I'm not that heartless, sir."

The look in Kingsley's eyes told Leah she hadn't missed the mark. He and Arthur *had* acted as a team all along.

"You accuse me of being a thief. Well, in my estimation, you are no better than I. You've stolen my birthright, stolen what little solace my siblings and I could find in one another. Instead, you made certain we were tossed from our home without even so much as a farthing in our pockets. Young Terence and I were left to worry over our next meal, while the others were shipped off to that horrid orphanage."

"I was simply following instructions," the man defended, unable to look her straight in the eye. "You can't blame me for any of this."

"Can't I? Then you can't blame me for what followed."

"The fact remains. You took money that didn't belong to you. A crime has been committed, and you—"

"You're right, sir," she interrupted. "A crime has been committed, and it was aided and abetted by you. Remember little Peter, Mr. Kingsley? Remember how I told you he was too weak to bear the dampness and dreariness in that orphanage? Well, just as I had predicted, he fell ill. Had it not been for your precious money—money I used to find him the proper medical care he so urgently needed—he would have died.

"That money, Mr. Kingsley, was part of the fee my father paid you to keep his illicit little secret quiet. As far as I'm concerned, *that* money didn't belong to you. It belonged to my family, and I used what was given to me solely for them. Impeach me if you will, but you, sir, must bear part of my guilt. Were you honest, you'd carry all of it."

Kingsley sighed heavily. "You speak of honesty, young woman. Well, in my profession, I am honor bound not to disclose any information I have about my clients. That is why I couldn't tell you about your father. I really had no choice in the matter.

"However, I ask that you forgive me for the inconvenience I have caused both you and your family. As far as my bringing any charges against you, you may rest easy on that account. You were right, madam. The money you took was rightfully yours. I wish now I had been more sympathetic when you first approached me. Perhaps the events that transpired since would not have come about.

"It is now up to the Sinclairs whether or not they wish to prosecute you—that's if any law has actually been broken. As for myself, I think I shall seek out the earl's study. I am in much need of another brandy." He turned toward mother and son. "Madeline. Huntsford. Excuse me, if you will, please." Then turning on his heel, he strode from the room.

Ian released his mother's shoulders. Twice she'd tried to break into the conversation, her son having held her back. "Go with him," he said. "I'd like to speak to Leah alone."

"As you wish, son." She looked at her daughter-in-law. "I—I—" She also emitted a heavy sigh. "I'm sorry, dear. At the moment, I don't know quite what to say."

Leah watched as Madeline placed the washcloth on the night stand. Then the woman walked out into the hallway, the door closing quietly behind her. Left alone with Ian, Leah dreaded the harsh words to come. Yet, surprisingly, endless silence met her ears. Her nerves fraying, she could take no more. "Say what it is you have to say, and let's be done with it."

"It is you who needs to explain, madam. Not me."

Unable to do so before, she finally caught Ian's gaze. No emotion showed in his eyes. She could explain all she might, but she doubted it would do any good. "Did you understand anything that I said to Mr. Kingsley?"

"Most of it. I assume your father was a bigamist, and that Arthur and Arabella Covington are actually your brother and sister. At Kingston-upon-Thames, when Jonathan was talking about the Covingtons, making reference to how much you resembled Arabella—that's what sent you chasing off across the green, isn't it?"

"Yes. I couldn't bear hearing about them, knowing my brother and sisters were in an orphanage, knowing young Terence was laboring for a smithy, when the Covingtons were all safely tucked in their fine house, still close to one another. Until just now, I wasn't fully certain that Arthur was involved, though I had suspected as much. I don't blame my half-brother for our misery, for the fact that the Daltons are now paupers, struggling to survive. Undoubtedly, he was as ignorant of our father's bigamy as I was, only he discovered the truth first. I suppose he wanted to protect his family at all cost. It was the same with me. We did what we had to do. Our father is to blame for all that has happened, as is Mr. Kingsley. They are the ones who are at fault. But it is my family that is made to suffer."

Ian felt empathy for his wife, but that didn't excuse her for the deceit she'd played on him. "Why didn't you tell me about this?"

"And what would you have done, Ian? Taken pity on me? Accepted me for who I really was? Given me shelter? Helped pay Peter's medical bills? At our first meeting, you warned me you could forgive almost anything except lies and deceit. The moment I left York the game was set. Because of my situation, I had no choice but to play it out. I risked too much to do otherwise."

I can forgive most anything . . . apart from lies and deceit, that is.

As his own words rolled through his mind, he knew now it was his threat that had chased her up the stairs on her first night at Sinclair House, fear written in her eyes. In truth, she had good cause to be frightened of him. Lies and deceit. Admittedly, there was something in his character that wouldn't allow him to abide either. Something that refused to allow him to do so now.

"You never gave me the opportunity to say yea or nay on the matter, madam. You hid the truth from me and with malicious intent."

"Malicious?" she questioned. "If it is considered malicious for one to protect one's own family, then yes, that was my intent. If you are saying I acted without conscience, then you are wrong. I didn't want to involve myself in any of this. Had I been offered another choice, one promising that I could again reunite my family, I would have gladly taken it. But I was given only one choice, Ian. I was forced to take it." To Leah, he seemed unconvinced. "Tell me. If I had told all that first night, would you have offered me your assistance?"

"I don't know."

"Considering the way you are reacting now, I sincerely doubt you would have, especially when I meant nothing to you then." He remained stolid, unforgiving. "Oh, what is the use," she said finally. "You've judged me and have found me guilty. Nothing I say or do will change that."

"I'm giving you the chance to explain. You owe me that much, considering."

His eyes, she noticed, were now glacial. "What is the point, Ian. As I said: You've judged—"

"The point, madam," he announced coldly, "is I am due an explanation. I want the truth—all of it. Now!"

Rage dwelled inside him, Leah knew. Only by a thread

did he keep his fury leashed. Swallowing hard, she fought to stave off her fear. "Where do you want me to start?"

"At the beginning—start with your family, if you must. Maybe then I will gain some understanding as to why you did what you did."

Unable to withstand his frigid glare any longer, Leah turned from him and walked to the window. Peering through the lace curtains, she looked down on the park. Small children with their nurses still played among the greenery, the blond-haired girl who reminded Leah of little Emily being one of them.

Drawing a deep breath, she began her tale, relating it in a quiet monotone. She spoke of her days at Balfour and of her siblings, describing each. She told of Peter's condition, her father's long absences, her mother's flightiness and how, because of it, Leah had become the mother-figure to all. She related how Elizabeth Dalton had fallen ill, how through Mr. Kingsley, her father was to be summoned. "She died with her beloved husband's name on her lips."

Then came the notification a week later that her father had been killed. Leah spoke about the family's confusion over not knowing where their father was buried or why the information was kept from them. Next, she related the sale of Balfour, the children being sent to an orphanage, young Terence's finding work with a smithy, and she at an inn. She told of the innkeeper's lechery; how in anger, she'd stormed the solicitor's office; how Kingsley had refused to answer her questions; how after the man had left, she'd rifled through his files, searching for an answer.

"I needed to know why this had happened to us. Armed with the address on Hanover Square, the letter to your mother, the bank draft, and Anne's clothes, I journeyed to London. By saving the allowance your mother gave me, I planned to later gather the children and flee England, well before Mr. Kingsley ever returned. But from the start everything seemed to go wrong—almost everything, that is. I found the answer I sought about my father soon enough. I didn't have to look far," she said, then fell silent.

Long ago Ian had quietly moved to the corner chair. From there, he'd listened as she related her story. His elbow resting on the chair's arm, his forefinger curling over his upper lip, he viewed her back. "How so?" he asked finally.

Thinking about the first time she'd seen Arthur, Leah snapped from her reverie. "That day we first went to the couturière's together and you asked to be dropped by White's, you met Arthur in the doorway. Upon seeing him myself, I knew instantly who he was. He could be my father's twin. I asked your mother about him, and she told me the details about the late Lord Covington's death. I knew then my father was a bigamist and that Arthur was my half-brother."

Ian watched as she slowly turned toward him. Unshed tears shimmered in her eyes. Seeing them, he hardened his heart. "Why were you so interested in the address at White's?" he asked, just now remembering her chatter about it.

"I was more interested in St. James's Street than in White's. I inquired because I wanted to get my bearings. When you stated the number, I didn't have to look any further. White's was where we sent our letters to my father. Then as fate would have it, Arthur appeared." A short laugh erupted from Leah. "Fate always seems to be intervening where I'm concerned."

"Is it?"

"Yes. Peter's illness for instance. From my allowance, I had managed to set aside a tidy little sum, then I learned he'd fallen ill. The letter you thought was from Anne's Irish bounder was in fact from young Terence."

"I'm aware of that now."

"Yes, I imagine you are. Anyway, I sent all the money I had to Terence, so he could find a physician to care for Peter. The doctor who served the orphanage was no more than a drunken sot. Because of Peter's special needs, I couldn't risk having the man attend him. Fortunately, our former family doctor took the case. In Terence's last letter to me, he said that Peter is much recovered."

Ian studied her a moment. "Did you use someone in this house to get your correspondence out?"

"No. I didn't lie to you when I said no one here was involved."

"Then who, madam, assisted you?"

"It was Sally Foster, the shop girl at Madame Lejeune's."

"I suppose that is why you were perpetually taking a dress by to have it altered?"

"It was," she admitted. "My letters were hidden within the gown. Sally would then post them for me. After Terence's letter arrived here, I arranged for Sally to henceforth receive his correspondence. She'd bring his letter by under the guise of returning an altered dress." Leah decided against telling him how she'd slipped from the shop that long-ago day. What purpose would it serve? "Sally didn't know who I was. She simply thought she was helping two lovers who were being kept apart."

"Such as the day we arrived back from Gretna Green," he said.

"Yes."

"Devious, but most effective, madam."

"I couldn't go without knowing about Peter or the other children. Their welfare is very important to me."

"Important enough to risk being hanged?" he asked. "That's what might have happened had Kingsley not relented and instead had you arrested."

"I'm aware of that. More than once I imagined myself sitting in Newgate, awaiting the day of my execution. I wasn't a fool as to what the consequences might be were I to get caught."

"Weren't you?"

"I knew the risks, Ian." Including that her heart would be broken one day. "Believe me I did."

"Tell me this: When you said you loved me, was that also a lie?"

Her throat choked with her own tears. "No. I have and still do love you."

His gaze raked over her. "That's hard to believe, madam. Of course, your concept of love might differ from mine.

Obviously, it does, especially since our marriage is based on naught but a series of falsehoods."

"If you remember, sir, I told you I couldn't marry you, but you forced me into it anyway."

"But you didn't say why, did you?"

"No."

"Yet you had several chances in which to do so, including during the ceremony. Remember, madam? 'If either of you know any just cause why you may not lawfully be joined in this marriage, speak now or forever hold your peace.' Even before God you chose not to tell the truth."

"He is well aware of my sins. At the time, adding one more lie to the list didn't seem to matter."

Leah jolted back a step as Ian came up out of the chair. Fury blazed in his eyes as he aimed himself at her. Abruptly, he caught himself. Veering off, he headed back the way he came, fingers raking through his hair.

"Damn it, Leah. Didn't you know your masquerade would eventually be exposed? Kingsley was bound to return sometime. When he did—" He caught himself as a sudden dawning took hold. He spun toward her. "You were going to run, weren't you?"

Leah nearly withered under his accusing stare. "Y-yes."

"When?"

Her throat closing again, she couldn't respond.

"When?" he shouted, then saw Leah jump.

"Before dawn, tomorrow."

Ian felt as though he'd just been kicked in the gut. "Tomorrow?" He saw her nod, then he roared with laughter.

Leah's eyes widened. *He's gone mad.* The thought frightened her, and she backed nearer to the window.

"Fate, madam, seems to have tripped you up once again," he announced after he'd quieted. "Tell me this: Since you didn't have any funds, your illicit savings spent on your brother's care, how in hell do you think you could have escaped England, when you couldn't even have made it from London to York?"

Leah's knees wobbled. "I have other resources."

"What resources? The minute we married, Mother cut off

your allowance. Other than a few shillings here and there, you've sought no money from me. You couldn't have possibly found the funds you needed to make good your escape." *Damn her.* Did she know the agony he'd have suffered had she slinked off into the night, never to be seen or heard from again? "Unless," he said, composing his next words carefully, hoping to strike back at her, "you were planning to sell your body to the highest bidder along the way. Considering your acquired expertise in bed, whoever the knave is, he should be well satisfied with his acquisition."

Leah stiffened. "I am not a whore."

Ian shrugged. "Liars, cheats, thieves, whores—they all fall into the same category. Mark my words: With no money, you'd be selling your body soon enough. Truly, sweet, you'll keep your clients happy. I found enjoyment in you once. Maybe old Rupert would be willing to pay a tidy sum for the privilege of being your first customer. You could always seek him out and make the offer."

Like a knife, his words cut into her heart. Obviously, he wanted to hurt her, and he'd accomplished the feat with ease. Tears of anger masked her tears of pain. "How dare you speak to me like that. What we had was exceptional. I'll not let you defile those memories with such low talk. It is unforgivable."

"Yes, what we *had* was exceptional. But that is now over. It is you, not I, who defiled those memories with your lies and deceit. That is what is unforgivable, madam. Now tell me straight off. What are these other resources you spoke of?"

Leah's teeth nibbled at her lower lip. Undoubtedly when she told him, he would kill her. Did it really matter? Everything had come to ruin. The children were lost to her, as was Ian. "I—I—really Ian, you don't want to know," she said, cowardice striking.

"Oh, but I do—unless, of course, you are about to tell me you're the thief who's been working the party circuit." Before his eyes, she blanched. Fingers forked through his hair as his harsh curse exploded around them both. "For the life of me, I cannot believe this! *You* are the thief?"

"I had no choice."

"Damn it, Leah, everyone has a choice!" he fairly yelled. "Obviously, you don't have enough sense to make the right ones." Her hands clasped tightly together, she stared at the floor. Exasperated, Ian studied her at length. "Where are the things you took? Or have you managed to sell them?"

"No, I haven't sold them. I thought it would be better if I waited until I was away from London before I found a buyer."

"Well, at least you had enough sense to do something right. Where have you hidden your spoils?"

"Under a rock in the back of the gardens by the tree where we, uh—"

"I get the picture."

"I couldn't think of any other way to come up with the money. I didn't want to take yours. It didn't seem fair."

"And why the hell not? You've managed to wreak havoc with everything else that was precious to me." He saw her confused look. *My marriage for one!* he felt like shouting. "My good name, Leah," he said instead. "If word of this ever gets out, the Sinclairs will stand in ruin. My mother will never again be invited to another party. London is her home; these people on whom you practiced your thievery are her friends. Do you think she could possibly survive the scandal once they learned the truth?"

As she gripped her hands tighter, Leah's nails bit into her hands. "I didn't mean—"

"I didn't mean," Ian mimicked harshly. "But you did it anyway, didn't you? Start making a list of everything you took and of what belongs to whom. Then get yourself ready. Perhaps we can still salvage something out of this mess."

"What do you plan to do?" she asked, watching as he strode to the door.

"First, I'm going out to the gardens to find your little stash. Then, madam, you are going to return each and every piece to its rightful owner."

"Me?"

"Yes, you. Should you get caught, it will be your neck, not mine."

"Wouldn't it be better if we just leave things as they are. No one knows I'm the thief."

"Probably. But that's not what *you* are going to do. Ready yourself. I'll be back shortly."

Leah stared at the door for a long while after it had closed. Considering what Ian had just insisted she do, she doubted he gave a fig about his *good name*. If she were caught replacing the items, the Sinclairs would stand in ruin, as he'd said. Then, again, maybe that was exactly what he hoped for—her getting caught.

Maybe he wanted her arrested. Maybe he wished to see her carted off to Newgate. Maybe he desired to watch as the trapdoor swung from beneath her feet, her neck snapping as the rope jerked with the force of her weight. Punishment for her treachery, she surmised.

Certain that was his intent, Leah vowed to be extremely careful.

"Thank God you didn't get hold of Moncreiffe's jade," Ian said, seating himself beside Leah. "I can't imagine how you'd pull that one off." His jaw set, he guided the phaeton away from the curb. "Who's next?"

The couple had just paid call on the Chatwells. While traversing the hallway, Leah had pretended to have accidentally dropped her reticule. Quickly, she'd stooped, slipped Lord Nevin's gold snuff box from inside her sleeve's deep cuff, then on rising, kicked the thing under the commode where the man had last seen it. After a brief visit, whereupon Leah and Ian had expressed how very much they enjoyed the Chatwells' party, the pair took their leave.

As Leah reviewed their visit, she was thankful the Chatwells' ballroom and their sitting room were on the same level. Sneaking up a flight of stairs to return the item to its general locale would have been risky indeed. *Too* risky for her liking.

"We are to be at the Alcotts' by three," she announced, checking their schedule of appointments.

Since last evening they had been making the rounds, Ian requesting in advance they be received by each of Leah's victims. All had graciously invited the Sinclairs into their homes.

"What is it that needs returning there?" he inquired dully, having grown weary of the whole mess.

"The jeweled letter opener."

"Where does it go?"

"The study."

"Hand it over," he said.

Leah stared at him. "But I thought you said that I was to return all the articles. Are you now saying you're going to replace this one yourself?"

"I doubt, madam, the Alcotts plan to receive us in their study. It would be better if the article were found in the vicinity of where it was last seen, appearing as though it were simply misplaced and not stolen, correct?"

"That's what we agreed."

"Well, do you plan to demand a tour of their house?"

"No."

"Then hand the thing here. I'll think of something to get Alcott into his study. Later, he'll find it under his desk."

Not wanting to put her husband at risk, Leah hesitated. "I am the one who took it, Ian. I should be the one to put it back. I could slip it between the cushions, just like I did with the piece of ivory at the Bosworths'. Someone will find it eventually."

"I imagine someone would, madam. Especially when he sat on it. Hand it over." Leah did as requested. Switching the reins into one hand, Ian quickly stuffed the letter opener, point down, into his boot. His cuff straightened, he asked, "How many more after this one?"

"The Alcotts are the last."

"Then, except for the letter opener, everything has been returned."

Leah bit her lip. "There is still the ruby stickpin."

Ian's head jerked toward her. "What stickpin?"

"It's Rupert's. I didn't steal it," she defended quickly. "When I was trying to fight him off, the thing apparently caught in my glove. I didn't find it until after I was nearly out into the hallway." She watched as his hard gaze swung back to the street. "I'll pay a call on the duchess and her son myself. You need not come with me," she said, knowing how much Ian despised the man.

"It's not necessary."

"Don't you want me to return it?"

"I know several charitable institutions that could use the proceeds from its sale. That's where old Rup's stickpin will do the most good." He directed the phaeton around the corner, then pulled it to a stop in front of the Alcotts'. After helping Leah from the vehicle, he escorted her up the stairs. Inside the house, the butler led them to the sitting room. Just before reaching its doorway, Ian whispered down on his wife: "Smile, madam. You are about to come face-to-face with the first of those whom you cheated."

An hour later, the couple exited the house, pleasant farewells said to their hosts.

"Well, did you manage it?" Leah asked, once the door had closed.

"I did," Ian responded, descending the steps, Leah beside him. "The letter opener now rests under his desk. But your thievery cost me a pretty penny, madam."

"How so?" she asked, allowing Ian to help her into the phaeton.

"I had to invest in a sugar-beet farm in Massachusetts."

"Massachusetts?"

"In the American colonies—or what used to be the colonies." Ian climbed aboard and took up the reins. "Lord Alcott's brother resides there. Thinks the product will do well." He set the horse into motion. "If not, I've just lost a small fortune."

"Did you have to go that far? All you had to do was kick the thing under his desk."

"It is the price I'm willing to pay to protect my good name."

Relieved the ordeal was over and that Ian's *good name* was still intact, Leah sighed. "Now what do we do?"

"We go home and pack."

"Pack? Where are we going?"

"Scotland. We'll leave before nightfall."

Leah gaped at him. "You're still taking me with you?" she asked finally.

"You sound surprised."

She was. "I thought—well, when you asked Mr. Kingsley about whether or not we were still legally wedded, then hearing his answer, I assumed you planned to have our marriage dissolved."

"Our vows said 'Until death do us part.'"

Dared she hope? "Are you saying you've forgiven me?"

"No, I'm not saying that at all."

"What are you saying, then?" she demanded, wanting desperately to know where she stood.

"Sit back, madam, and listen," he ordered, "and I'll clarify everything for you. First, I want to know if you are pregnant."

Leah's gaze snapped to his face. "Would it change anything if I were?"

"Between us, no. But I will want you to have the proper care if you are. An heir is important to me."

But she wasn't, Leah realized. "I'm not pregnant," she said, not fully certain one way or the other if she was.

"Good. Second, when we arrive back at Sinclair House, you will pack your belongings, and your belongings only. You may take your new gowns. I've repaid Kingsley for what your deceit has cost him. His niece's clothing, and the like, are to be given to the poor, just as he'd instructed. Last night, he reaffirmed he wouldn't press charges against you, so you have no worry there.

"Third, we will remain married. As Kingsley said, an annulment or divorce is seldom kept quiet. For mother's sake, I'll not risk a scandal. So until one of us dies, we'll stay husband and wife. But that doesn't mean we have to live together."

"Didn't you just tell me that *we* were going to Scotland?"

"I did. Now hold your tongue and listen." Her jaw clamping tightly, Leah fell back against the seat, and Ian continued with what he was saying. "There is a small cottage at the edge of my estate. That is where you will take up residence. Everything you need will be provided for you. However, you will never set foot in my home. Falcon's Gate is, and will always be, off-limits to you. So don't even attempt to come near the house or you'll be turned away." Briefly, he took his eyes from the roadway to look at her. "Do you understand what I've just told you?"

Misery encasing her, Leah kept her gaze cast down. "I understand you are banishing me because you no longer want anything to do with me. Wouldn't it be far simpler to allow me to just go my own way? Or do you want to make me suffer?"

"Suffer?" he questioned. "How is providing you with a home, food, and clothing for the rest of your life making you suffer? Isn't that what you wanted all along? Isn't that why you perpetrated your lies and deceit, masqueraded as someone else, just so you could acquire those things?"

What about love and companionship? Leah questioned in silence. Those were far more important to her than any of the physical trappings he could provide. And the children. Would she ever see them again?

"Answer me!" he barked.

Leah started. "I did it not for myself, Ian, but for the children. I want to have my family together again. They've endured so much." Pausing, she drew a deep breath, then plunged ahead. "Do you think they could come live with me?"

"No. They are not my concern, madam. So do not ask again."

While she spoke tears had gathered in Leah's eyes. With his answer, one fell to her skirt. She understood his anger at her, understood why he wanted to hurt her. She deserved his punishment. But Terence, Hope, Kate, Peter, and Emily were all innocent of any wrongdoing, and Leah couldn't quite fathom his cruelty toward them. "Ian, please reconsider. I—"

"I said no."

The phaeton halted before Sinclair House. Once Leah had alighted, she stood gazing up at the majestic structure, certain after today she'd never see it again, then she slowly climbed the steps.

Lingering on the doorstep a moment, she viewed the small park. As always, children played within its boundaries, their nurses close at hand. Leah searched for the blond-haired girl, who was now familiar to her. But on this day, she wasn't among the others. The same as with Sinclair House, Leah knew she'd not see the sweet little child ever again, but at least she had a home and a caring family to gather around her, unlike Leah's own siblings.

"Are you coming?" Ian asked, from inside the door.

When she crossed the threshold, Leah found she could no longer curb her tears. Brushing past Ian, she ran to the stairs, then up them, her sobs raining down on the foyer.

They've endured so much.

Hearing his wife's words again, Ian slowly climbed up to the gallery behind her.

CHAPTER

20

**Falcon's Gate
Selkirk, Scotland
July 1841**

Warm sunshine beat down on Leah's back as she pressed the wet soil around the small rosebush she'd just transplanted. Moving it from the rear of the freshly whitewashed cottage, she'd given it a more prominent position near the front entry.

Rising from her knees, she blinked rapidly, fighting off her dizziness. The giddy feeling was upon her constantly with any sudden move. Her head clearing, she stood back and admired her handiwork. The small garden she'd been putting in to brighten the cottage and yard was finally taking shape.

In the three weeks since Ian had nearly booted her from his carriage, his harsh look his only goodbye, Leah had worked herself continually. It was the only way she could take her mind off her loneliness, off the children, off Ian.

Inside her new home, the two large rooms and loft sparkled with cleanliness. The rustic furnishings gleamed from a good polishing. While outside, the grounds had been cleared of dead growth, new flowers taking its place.

Later, when the sun had sunk lower and it was cooler, she planned to repair the old gate, its hinge having come loose that morning as she carted away some pruned limbs. Dumping the litter at the edge of the small creek just across the lane running to the cottage from the main road, she'd inspected the large oak branching over the dirt track. A rotted limb jutted toward the gate, creaking in the light wind that had fondled it.

Hearing its forlorn groan now, Leah viewed the thing again. Thinking it was a hazard, she felt certain the limb would soon fall. If she could find a way to scale the tall trunk, she'd next attack the thing with a saw. She simply had to keep busy.

Gathering her hand tools and the shovel, Leah strode toward the wheelbarrow parked by the fence. The sound of rolling wheels and trotting hooves captured her attention, and she looked up the lane toward the road. A passing carriage, she decided, wondering if it could be Ian. She'd glimpsed him several times over the past three weeks as he'd headed into Selkirk or back. But that's all she ever caught of him—a glimpse.

Expectation rose, and she held her breath and waited. The sound grew closer, then to her surprise, she saw a vehicle turning from the road. Frowning, Leah stared at the sporty little buggy occupied by a woman and a child. Then suddenly from nowhere, a furry little dog darted into the lane to yap excitedly at the wheels as he ran alongside. Wiping her hands on the skirt of her black muslin dress, Leah waited for the pair to pull up beside her.

With a soft command from the woman, the horse was reined in. But the gelding jerked back, the buggy wobbling, as the small dog sped around the vehicle, his quick barks coming as fast as his stubby tail wagged.

"Merlin! Behave!" the woman ordered sharply. The shaggy dog at once skidded to a stop beside the buggy. Falling back onto his haunches, his pink tongue lolled as he panted actively. "Good boy," she said, the horse and buggy again under control. Then she looked at Leah and smiled. "Good afternoon. I had heard we had a new resident in the area, so

I thought I might stop by to say hello and to welcome you. My name is Alissa Braxton, and this is my daughter, Megan."

"Hello," the little girl said, smiling shyly. She looked up over her shoulder. "Mama, may I play with Merlin?"

"Yes, dear. Just don't go too far. We won't be staying long."

The little girl leapt from the buggy, then skipped up the lane, the gray-and-white dog bounding after her.

"You must excuse Merlin," Alissa said, once she'd alighted from the vehicle. "He is such a bounder. Has no manners at all. But then he is much like his owner— mischievous and free-spirited. Of course, he has a tendency to pout, too. Especially when things don't go his way."

A striking beauty, Leah decided, watching as the woman came toward her. Dressed fashionably in a lilac day dress, and with rich, mahogany hair peeking from beneath her matching bonnet, she clearly hailed from the upper class. Garbed in her old togs, Leah felt quite dowdy.

The woman's striking blue eyes surveyed her closely, and Leah realized she was being assessed. Then a pleasant smile was aimed Leah's way.

"I do hope I'm not imposing on you," Alissa said. "Perhaps I should have sent word around first instead of just dropping by."

"Forgive me," Leah said finally. "I so rarely see anyone, I've forgotten how to behave." Other than one of Ian's footmen, who came by twice weekly, to see if she needed anything or to post a letter for her, she saw no one. "Leah Sinclair," she said, returning the smile. "Might I offer you some refreshment?"

"No, not today. My son will be waking soon from his nap. His father, though he tries valiantly, just doesn't seem to have the ability to quiet little Zachary. I fear their temperaments are too much alike. Besides, he will be hungry when he awakens, so I cannot stay. Another time, maybe."

"How old is your son?"

"A little over three months."

"But you are so slim."

The woman's light laughter bubbled into the air. "I wasn't three months ago."

Leah glanced up the path at the dark-haired little girl. Her huge green eyes were nearly the color of Leah's. "And your daughter? What is her age?"

"Seven."

The same age as was Peter, Leah thought. "You live close by, I take it."

"At Hawkstone—the estate next to Falcon's Gate. My husband, Lord Ebonwyck—Jared—and Lord Huntsford are old friends. We visit quite often with each other, though only once since Ian's return from London."

Leah wondered if Lady Ebonwyck's courtesy call was no more than a sudden desire to have a look-see at the banished wife. "Oh, really," Leah said coolly.

"Yes. He seems to have become a recluse of sorts. Despite Jared's and my attempts to draw him out, he refuses to come by and see us. Well, I really must be going now." She turned and looked up the lane. "Megan—come, dearest." Her gaze swung back to Leah. "I do hope you'll allow me to visit you again."

Before Leah could respond, the small dog came dashing down the path and through the gate. Round and round Leah he sped, yapping loudly. Then he stopped and sat back on his haunches, a front paw waving in the air.

"Yes," Alissa said, "Merlin is much like his owner. Right now, I think he's thirsty."

"Wait, and I'll get him a drink," Leah said, but the two Braxtons had stepped up into the buggy. Under Lady Ebonwyck's expert hand, the horse was turned around in a tight circle and pointed up the lane. "What about your dog?" Leah cried.

"He's not our dog," Alissa called, with a wave. "Merlin belongs to Ian."

Hearing a pitiful whine, Leah looked down on the shaggy-haired Merlin. His paw still waved in the air. "Come on, then. Let's get you something cool to drink."

Water from a dipper sloshed into the earthenware bowl,

then Leah headed for the door where Merlin waited. Setting the bowl on the stone step, she squatted down beside him. As he lapped eagerly, Leah's fingers tousled his shaggy head. "You're a cute little thing."

With that, Merlin's tongue left the bowl and quickly licked along Leah's cheek, then thrust itself back into the water to lap some more.

Wiping the wet trail from her face, Leah smiled and shook her head. Then she remembered Alissa's words.

You must excuse Merlin. . . . But then he is much like his owner . . . he has a tendency to pout, too. Especially when things don't go his way.

Undoubtedly, the woman had come by to have a firsthand look at Ian's ostracized wife. But, in her own way, she had also delivered a message to Leah.

"Is that what he's doing, Merlin—pouting?"

The dog's yip of agreement pierced her ears, and she laughed.

"He's become a recluse, has he?"

Two yips rose upward.

"Good. I hope he is as miserable as I am."

A mile away, Ian stood by his bedroom window, staring in the direction of the cottage. He wondered how Leah fared, then chastised himself for caring. Like a sharp spike, the pain inside him drove deeper each day. Rage and melancholy were the only two emotions he ever felt. *Love!* He thought it was to bring one joy, not agony. Damn her for causing him this much misery!

Still, he was tempted to march out to the stables and have his stallion saddled.

How many times had he ridden Woden toward the cottage, wanting to see her, but then again, not? Nearly reaching the crest of the hillside, Leah's little house sitting just on the other side, he would turn the stallion around and head home again. By repetition, the beast knew his way, Ian no longer needing to give him guidance. Before the earth was permanently scarred, between house and cottage, he had to put a stop to these jaunts.

Woden could rest today, he decided, his urge to ride out quickly checked.

Maybe Alissa was right. Perhaps he was being stubborn, making himself suffer needlessly. On the day his two closest friends had visited him, he'd told both Jared and Alissa Braxton all that had transpired since he'd last seen them. Anticipating sympathy, he'd gotten a lecture instead. Never did he expect to hear Alissa call him foolish, but she had.

"I would think, Ian, you, of all people, would be a bit more understanding," she'd said. "Love isn't very easy to come by. And certainly, once you've found it, you don't toss it away as quickly as you have done. Stop being so foolish. I'm certain you can find a way to forgive her. Allow your pride to stand in the way, and you might very well regret that you have."

"I'll never forgive her deceit," he'd returned.

"Then it is your loss, my friend."

He hadn't seen Jared or Alissa since. His loneliness, however, was eating away at him, destroying him slowly, and he imagined he'd soon relent and drop by.

The days were bad, but the nights were far worse. After hours of tossing and turning in his large bed, sleep would ultimately come. But just as surely, sometime before dawn, he would reach for Leah, only to snag the air. Instantly, he'd awaken, wondering where she was, then it would all come crashing in on him again.

Rest eluded him, for once he'd stirred, he couldn't fall asleep again. He spent long hours pacing the darkened hallways in search of peace, both mentally and emotionally. At one time, he was content within these old walls. But now the place seemed extensive, looming, hollow, with no satisfaction to be found inside. What amazed him most was that Leah had never been here. No memories of her resided at Falcon's Gate. Still it seemed as though there should be.

Perpetually, as he strode the black corridors, he was haunted by the look in her wide green eyes when he'd left her standing in front of the cottage. Her unshed tears shimmered in the bright sunlight. "Goodbye, Ian," she had said, yet he hadn't had the decency to even bid her farewell.

Her last words to him perpetually attacked him when he least expected them to do so. A sad ending to a perfect beginning. Or so he had thought.

Then there were her other words, uttered while they traveled from the Alcotts' to Sinclair House their last day in London. They, too, would strike him at the most inopportune times. He could still hear her sobs as she ran up the stairs, his edict given.

They've endured so much.

All she had ever wanted was for her family to be together again. Maybe if he granted her that, he could forget her. The peace he sought would be his, and he could get on with his life, her ghost finally put to rest.

Positive that was the answer, he moved from the window out into the hall. "Duncan!" His shout echoed through the vast house. Growing impatient when the man didn't appear immediately, he strode the corridor toward the stairs. "Duncan!"

"Yes, sir," the thin man gasped, running up the steps. "Something wrong, sir?"

"Sorry, Duncan," he said to his butler, "I hadn't realized you were downstairs."

"Quite all right, sir. I've been getting a bit lax on doing my exercises, anyway."

Ian arched an eyebrow at the man. At seventy, Duncan was still spry, but it would seem a rocking chair would suit the man far better than a stint of calisthenics. Then, perhaps not. "Send someone down to the stables. I want the coach readied and around front in a half hour. Afterward, you will help me pack."

"Pack, sir?"

"Yes, Duncan, pack."

"Where are you going, sir? If you don't mind my asking, that is?"

"To Leeds, where I hope to find a smithy named Jones, then from there, I will be on to York and the orphanage."

"Orphanage, sir?"

"Yes, Duncan, to the orphanage. Maybe, then, I'll get some sleep."

The steady cadence of horses' hooves broke the interminable silence within the coach as the Earl of Huntsford, along with his charges, traveled ever closer to Falcon's Gate.

In the seat opposite Ian, blond heads swayed rhythmically, while four sets of wary eyes, ranging from gray-green to deep emerald, stared back at him. Beside him sat the oldest of the group. The sandy-haired Terence remained as stonily mute as did the others.

The trip from northern England had been a long and tiring one. With each passing mile, the children had become more excited, the topic of their constant chatter being Leah. At the continual mention of her name, Ian grew more tense, until he felt as though he would surely explode.

Then, when the coach had turned off the main road, leading from York to Selkirk, to begin executing the final leg of the journey to Falcon's Gate and the cottage, Ian explaining such, Hope, Kate, Peter, and Emily began bounding up and down on the seat, each squealing with glee. Ian, his mood surly, had erupted angrily, barking his command that they be still. For the past half hour, except for an occasional cough from Peter, not a sound had escaped any of them.

Their stares plagued Ian, and his guilt mounted. The conditions at the orphanage were deplorable. Far worse than he could have ever imagined. Seeing the place firsthand, he understood why his wife so desperately wanted her siblings away from there. Still, Ian would not forgive her for the deceit she'd played on him, refused to pardon her for planning to desert him without so much as a word. Had she cut out his heart, it would have been far more merciful an act on her part. At least then he would feel no pain. But that didn't excuse him for having behaved the way he had toward the children. They were innocent of all that had transpired between Leah and himself. Knowing such, he sighed.

"I apologize for losing my temper," he said. "However, if you want to surprise your sister, as we all agreed to do, then you must be very quiet, especially since we have less than a furlong to go." Before his eyes, their expressions changed to that of expectation, then of joy; smiles lit their faces. "Now, drop the curtains, so she won't see who's inside. We'll be making the turn shortly."

His words obeyed, Ian leaned his head back against the seat and closed his eyes. Soon, he thought, certain once Leah was reunited with her siblings, his anguish would cease.

Leah was busy weeding the fence line when she heard the rumble of wheels on the main road. Stilling the hoe, she wiped her brow with the back of her hand, then watched and waited.

A coach appeared. Making a wide arc, it turned and lumbered down the lane toward her. Not recognizing the vehicle, she leaned the hoe against the top rail and slowly made her way toward the gate. Leah's heart somersaulted when she saw the markings of the crest.

Ian.

Smoothing her hair, then her skirt, she waited for the horses to be reined in. She knew she looked a fright, but she cared not. Anticipation grew inside her as she wondered why he had come. The shuttered coach sat still for the longest time. She trembled slightly, thinking he may have changed his mind.

After what seemed an eternity, the door opened. A blond head appeared. At first Leah felt certain she was hallucinating. Then, with an excited cry, she was out the gate.

"Terence!" Her arms were flung around his neck just as his name escaped her lips. Her brother returned her hug with a strength she didn't remember. "You've grown," she said, smiling up at him. Her fingers felt the brawn in his shoulders and arms. "You've become a man."

He blushed slightly, then grinned back at her. "That, sister, I have."

"The others—are they with you?"

Terence stepped aside. There in the doorway stood Hope. She bounded to the ground, followed by Kate, then Peter. All three rushed toward Leah and her open embrace.

"I can't get down," little Emily said, peering over her shoulder at the big man who kept to the shadows.

Staring at the child, her lower lip poised in a pout, Ian bit back a groan. Damn if she didn't remind him of Leah. On a swallowed curse, he snagged Emily from behind and stepped from the coach. The moment the child's feet hit the solid ground, she was off at a full run, and Leah scooped her up into her arms to twirl her around.

"Oh, Leah. That nice man brought us back to you," Emily said, hugging her sister's neck as though she'd never let go.

Holding Emily close to her, Leah looked at Ian. Tears of joy and gratitude glistened in her eyes. "Yes, dearest. That nice man did, didn't he? And I thank him for being so very kind."

"There is no need to thank me, madam," Ian said, his tone cool. "You have what you've always wanted. My duty done, it is now finished between us. Good day to you, and goodbye."

Stunned by his words, Leah watched as he climbed back into the coach. Several bound bundles were tossed out onto the ground. "Ian," she called, but the door thumped to with finality.

Once the coach was turned around, Leah watched its progression up the lane, her joy having turned to sorrow. He was wrong. She didn't have what she'd always wanted—not entirely.

"Where's he going, Leah?" Emily asked.

"Away."

"Will we ever see him again?"

"I don't know, dearest. Perhaps." She set Emily down. "What do you say we go see your new home?"

Terence's arms were filled with several of the bundles that Ian had thrown from the coach, and Leah bent over to snag the last. Her head swam as she rose from her waist. Once the dizziness subsided, she directed the children through the gate and up the walk.

He'd be back all right, Leah decided, now positive her suspicions were correct. And the day of his return would be the day the footman had announced to his master that it appeared Lady Huntsford was with child.

"My mother will be arriving at Falcon's Gate in just a few days. In her honor, I'm planning a dinner party," Ian announced to his hosts three weeks later. Both he and Jared stood by the fireplace in the sitting room at Hawkstone, sipping their brandies after an excellent supper. Alissa sat in the chair nearest them. "I've also invited the Whitcombs up from London. You'll enjoy Veronica and Jonathan, though their bickering does tend to get a bit tedious at times."

"Veronica?" Alissa asked. "Is she the one who—"

"Yes. She's the one."

"But I would think she'd be most unforgiving about the way you treated her."

"Apparently, Veronica is not one to hold a grudge." Unlike himself, he silently confessed. "I wrote to her, apologized for my behavior, explained that Leah and I are now separated, and invited both she and her brother to Falcon's Gate. The Whitcombs replied they would be delighted to come."

"Are you certain you aren't creating more problems, Ian?" Alissa asked. "You *are* married, and to give the Lady Veronica any hope that there could be something between the two of you seems highly unfair."

"Is it?"

"Yes, it is."

"Well, then, maybe I should clarify something, Alissa. For the moment, I am married, *but* that may soon change." From the corner of his eye, he saw movement near the doorway. "The dinner party is next week. I'd like very much for the two of you to join in the celebration."

"Me, too, Uncle Ian?" Megan asked, entering the room.

He chuckled, then winked at his godchild, who had undoubtedly come down to say good night to them all. "That will be up to your papa and mama."

She looked to her parents. "May I go?"

"We'll see, sweet," Jared answered. "Right now, you need

to give kisses round to everyone, then go along up with Mary so she can put you to bed."

"Will Zachary be going to the party?" she asked.

"Probably," Alissa said. "Now do as your father has said."

Noting Alissa's light blush, Ian bit his lip to keep from chuckling. He'd been told by Jared that she was caring for Zachary herself, refusing a wet nurse when the babe was born. Under the circumstances, she had no choice but to bring her son along. Ian mused how nice it would be if Leah . . . The thought was quickly brushed aside.

"Well, then," Megan announced. "If Zachary can go, then so shall I."

"Princess," her father said with mock sternness. "You will do as you're now told. Hugs and kisses, then to bed with you."

Megan skipped to Ian's side. Reaching down he scooped her up. After her kiss fell upon his cheek, she said, "If you invite me, personally, Uncle Ian, they cannot make me stay home. Remember that."

"I'll remember," he responded, then over the child's head saw her father roll his eyes. Setting Megan on her feet, he watched as she went first to Alissa, then Jared, kissing them both good night. Once at the doorway again, the maid taking her hand, she curtsied. Mary ushered her from the room. "She's certainly a charmer," he commented, chuckling.

"Thanks to your spoiling her as you do, she is," Jared said, after sipping his brandy.

"She's my godchild. What else do you expect?"

"As my friend, I would hope you'd be a bit more supportive."

"Something I had hoped from you," Ian countered in reference to Leah. He raised his glass in salute. "You'll find no sympathy here, friend."

As Ian quaffed his brandy, he missed the quick look that was exchanged between his hosts. He lowered the glass. "You should be grateful Megan is able to speak her mind, Jared. Especially when a year ago, she couldn't even talk."

"I *am* grateful, Ian. Had it not been for my wife, who, as I recall, played me false in the beginning also, Megan would still be mute. What perplexes me is you knew Alissa wasn't Agatha Pembroke—God rest the woman's soul—yet you held your tongue. To me that is the same as conspiring."

"That was different."

"Oh, is it now?" Jared asked.

"Yes. Alissa had good reason to do what she did. She thought she'd killed Rothhamford, the odious lecher. She knew no one would have believed her when she told her story: The bounder attacked her, and she acted in self-defense. A young actress being persecuted by the likes of Creighton—she'd have gone to the gallows."

"You mean Rothhamford's father, the earl."

Ian stared at Jared. "You know the story better than I, sir. You know also that she had no choice but to pose as someone else so she could flee England. And it was through her love and understanding that your daughter is now well."

"Strange," Jared said, "how you can see one set of circumstances so clearly. Yet you are completely blinded when it comes to another. Your wife's situation is not all that different from what Alissa's was. Both felt threatened. Both did the only thing they knew to do at the time. If either of them had been given another choice, each probably would have taken it. But, then, I wouldn't have met Alissa, and you wouldn't have met Leah. Think about it, man. Leah would still be a stranger to you."

"I wish the hell she was," Ian growled, slamming his drink onto the mantel. Brandy sloshed onto his hand, but he ignored it. "Thanks for the hospitality. I shall show myself out."

Lord and Lady Ebonwyck stared at each other as the front door forcefully slammed shut.

"You've done wonders with this place, Lady Huntsford," Alissa said, stepping down from the buggy several days later. "I am truly amazed."

"Call me Leah."

"Only if you'll call me Alissa."

"Agreed." Briefly, Leah fought with the gate. The hinge had been repaired, but now there was a problem with the latch. Finally, it gave way, and she allowed the marchioness, Megan, and little Zachary, who was being held by a young maid, entry. "May I offer you some lemonade?"

"Water for me," Alissa said, taking her baby from the maid's arms, "but lemonade would be nice for Megan and Mary. I'm nursing Zachary myself. I learned early on I have to be very careful what I ingest so it doesn't affect him or we walk the floors at night. Don't we, love?" she cooed, her finger brushing his pink cheek.

"He certainly is a beautiful little boy," Leah said, peering over Alissa's shoulder. "All that dark hair—and his eyes. Such a deep blue."

"Yes, but they should be turning green soon. See the tiny specks?"

"Now that you mention it, yes."

"My husband's eyes are nearly the same color as yours, Leah. But they are an exact match to Megan's." She turned to her maid. "Mary, go fetch the blanket from the buggy and spread it in the shade here, so we can lay Zachary on it."

Leah heard the familiar groan. "Not here," she said, looking up at the old oak. "That limb might give way, and I wouldn't want anyone under it when it does. I keep forgetting to ask to have it removed. Over here." She pointed toward the house. "This tree is sturdy. Though not as large, it should provide plenty of shade."

While Mary returned to the buggy, Leah and her visitors moved closer to the cottage.

"I had heard your brothers and sisters are living with you," Alissa said. "Megan would so like to meet them, if she could."

"Surely. Terence. Children. Come out here, will you? We have visitors," Leah called. Her siblings appeared at the door, then one-by-one came outside. "This is Lady Ebonwyck and her daughter, Megan. And this is Megan's little brother, Zachary." She switched the introductions.

"This is Terence, Hope, Kate, Peter—he's your age, Megan —and, of course, Emily."

"I'll be six in December," Emily proclaimed, her chin lifting a notch.

"That is a wonderful age," Alissa said, "but five is very nice, too."

"You all have green eyes, just as I do," Megan declared. "That should make us friends right off."

"May we go play?" Hope asked.

Leah nodded. "But stay within the yard."

"Do you have a ball?" Megan inquired.

"No," Kate responded.

"Some dolls?"

"No," Hope said.

"We have an old barrel hoop and a stick," Peter chimed in.

Megan looked over her shoulder at Alissa. "Doesn't Uncle Ian like his wife's brothers and sisters? He brings me toys all the time."

Upon Leah's hearing the child's words, her heart twisted painfully.

"That was impolite of you to say such a thing, Megan," Alissa reprimanded softly. "Apologize to your new friends."

"I'm sorry," she said, looking at each one. "But I think it's awfully mean of Uncle Ian to behave so."

"You are probably right, Megan," Alissa stated. "However, we don't say such things so openly."

"Tell you what," Terence declared. "Your Uncle Ian gave us a cart and pony. If it is all right with your mother, and if Leah agrees, I'll harness it up and give you all a ride in the back field."

"May we, Leah?" her siblings asked.

"Mama?" Megan inquired.

"I see no reason why not," Alissa said, "but it is up to Lady Huntsford."

"If you are very careful, Terence."

"I'm always careful."

"I know. And very helpful as well." She depended on him a lot lately, especially with the recent onset of nausea that affected her so often. "When you are through with your ride, we'll all have some lemonade."

The children danced up and down excitedly, then Terence said, "Come along, everyone. Peter, you can help me harness the pony."

The children rounded the cottage, heading to the small stable, and Alissa offered to help Leah with the lemonade. With Mary attending Zachary, the blanket spread under the little shade tree, the two women entered the door. Leah heard her guest gasp in delight.

"The wildflowers—the chintz curtains—it looks like an English garden," Alissa said. "How very lovely, Leah."

"Probably the place reflects such because I am English," her hostess replied.

"So am I."

"Do you miss England?" Leah asked, gathering the lemons.

Taking a knife, Alissa began slicing the fruit. "Not really. I hail from London. Too much noise and congestion. But I do miss the theater."

"Ian had promised me a night at the opera," Leah said, squeezing the lemons into the pitcher of fresh water. Adding sugar, she stirred the mixture. "Unfortunately, that never came about." She placed the pitcher on a wooden tray, then gathered some cups for the children to use, afterward setting the whole aside for later. Two glasses of lemonade in hand, one for herself and one for Mary, Leah headed toward the door. "Let's go on out where it is cooler."

Standing near the rear fence, Alissa sipped the water she'd drawn for herself. "Peter seems small for his age," she commented, watching the happy little group traverse the field in the cart.

"He's been ill since birth," Leah said sadly. "He is one of the main reasons I did what I did."

"I am aware of Ian's side of the story, Leah. If you feel you need to tell me yours, I'd be glad to listen. And I'll not judge you either."

Leah studied the woman closely. "No, I imagine you would be exceptionally fair."

"Sometimes if we talk about things, it helps."

Leah hesitated at first, but then allowed herself to open up to Alissa. Her entire story finished, she sighed. "That is why he hates me so, why he has banished me to the cottage. From what he's said, he'll never forgive me. I suppose I can't fault him for feeling as he does, but I had hoped he'd be a bit more understanding."

"I'm surprised he hasn't been more understanding, considering your story and mine are quite similar. In fact, Ian was my champion, protecting me from Jared's discovering who I really was."

"Who you really were?"

Smiling, Alissa said, "Let's find a cool spot and sit down, then I'll tell you my story."

Once seated on the grass under a tree by the rear fence, Lady Ebonwyck began her tale. She told Leah about how as an actress in London she'd been accosted by a member of the peerage; how she defended herself with a pressing iron, cracking Rothhamford's head; how she'd fled Covent Garden to the safety of the boarding house where she lived.

"My landlady, who also had been an actress helped me disguise myself as Agatha Pembroke, one of her boarders. The woman was a governess by trade, working only with special children. Unfortunately, she died earlier in the evening, and Eudora—she was my landlady and dearest friend—knew Jared was coming for Agatha that night. Megan had been mute from the time her mother was killed in a fire at Hawkstone."

"I thought you looked too young to be Megan's mother," Leah said.

"Yes, but she now calls me mama. Anyway, Eudora knew I had to escape London or else I'd be charged with Rothhamford's murder. I was certain I'd killed him, but later discovered I only wounded him. Jared was my only hope of escaping. I used him to flee England. However, Ian was aware I wasn't the real Agatha Pembroke. He'd met the woman himself. Yet he kept my secret."

"Why?"

"He told me once that he knew I was good for Megan, that he saw an improvement in his godchild, and he wasn't about to destroy the inroads I had made with her." The rest of her story unfolded, Leah listening with care, until Alissa finally said, "It was through Jared's and my love and understanding, coupled with Ian's help, that Megan is able to speak. And it is because of Ian that Jared and I are as happy as we are. That is why I cannot understand Ian's inability to forgive you, Leah. Jared treated me nearly the same way when he found out who I really was, but as I said: Ian was my champion. He forced Jared into finally seeing the truth. Your husband is being most stubborn about all this. Too stubborn, in fact."

"I suppose it is because the shoe is now on the other foot," Leah offered. "What your own husband once felt, Ian is now experiencing himself."

"I believe it's called pride," Alissa said. "Men have the knack to wear it, just like a woman wears her Sunday best. Except they sport it the week through. I'm certain he still loves you, Leah. It is simply a matter of him rediscovering that particular truth for himself." She looked to the field. "The children are coming in. I guess we should get their lemonade ready."

"Thank you, Alissa, for being so understanding. I do feel better having talked with you."

As Leah started to rise, a wave of dizziness overtook her. Her stomach lurched, and she fought to keep the lemonade down. She thought she had conquered it, but when she came fully to her feet, the nausea struck again. She rushed to the corner of the yard and relieved her stomach.

"Are you all right?" Alissa asked, having traveled after Leah to assist her.

"Yes." she returned after wiping her mouth on a handkerchief Alissa had handed her. "I'm fine now."

"Does Ian know?"

"Know what?" Leah asked, pretending ignorance.

"I'm not stupid, my new friend. I've gone through this myself. Does Ian know you are carrying his child?"

Leah gazed at Alissa at length. She sighed. "No, I haven't told him."

"Are you going to?"

"No."

"And why not?"

"If he decides to come back to me, it will because he loves me, not because I carry his child. Right now, I don't have to contend with his censuring looks, his snarling comments. Should he force me to come to Falcon's Gate, I'd not be able to withstand his coldness. He still abhors me. Until that changes, I'll not allow myself to feel any more pain than is necessary. It is bad enough as it is."

"You know you can't hide it from him forever."

"Yes, I know. When the day comes—the day his footman breaks the news to him—that is the day I'll face him. Not before. Not unless, by some miracle, there should be a reconciliation between us." Leah caught Alissa's hand. "Promise you won't tell him either."

Blue eyes studied green. "I will keep your secret, Leah. But only if you promise not to jeopardize yourself or your child. You work too hard around here. Give me your word that you'll get more rest, and I'll give mine that your secret will be kept safe."

"I work as hard as I do to keep my mind off things, but, yes, I promise to ease off a bit."

"More than a bit, Leah—a lot."

"A lot, then. I give you my word."

"And I give you mine."

Their pact made, the two women made their way to the cottage where they served the children lemonade and cakes. A half hour later, Alissa announced that she must be going, for little Zachary was starting to stir from his nap.

"You take good care of yourself, Leah," she said as she headed toward the buggy, with Mary, Megan, and the baby already inside. "I'll be coming round to make certain you do."

"You are welcome to do so, anytime."

Alissa hesitated briefly, and Leah thought she had wanted to tell her something important. Apparently, Lady Ebonwyck decided against it, for she smiled instead, then waved her goodbye.

As Leah watched the buggy roll up the lane, she wondered what Alissa had been about to say. Intuition told her it had to do with Ian. In truth, Leah was glad Alissa had held her tongue. Leah was miserable enough as it was.

CHAPTER

21

Dark clouds grouped on the horizon, eclipsing the sinking sun. The air was inordinately still. Worry etched Leah's brow as she viewed the rising thunderheads, for the children were overdue.

The group had planned a trip into Selkirk and a visit to the market. But Leah's bouts of nausea had been more severe than usual today. Begging off, she'd insisted the children go without her, but only if they promised to return before supper. Once Terence had hitched the pony to the cart, the remaining Daltons scrambled aboard, and all excitedly headed into town. Now, with the storm approaching, she wondered if they'd make it safely home before the wind and rain struck.

A distant rumble caught her attention, and Leah hoped Terence would be wise enough to seek shelter. But, as she remembered, there weren't too many sites along the way affording refuge to a traveler. The closest house to the cottage on the road to Selkirk stood miles away. If they were past that point, Leah was certain Terence would continue to journey homeward.

Lightning flashed, thundered cracked louder. Lifting her

skirt, Leah dashed through the gate and up the lane to the road, where she looked in the direction of town.

Disappointment filled her when she didn't see the cart and its occupants. Hoping the group might be just around the bend, she ran ahead to the curve to view the long, straight stretch. Still the road remained empty.

Her teeth nibbling her lower lip, Leah waited another several minutes, but to no avail. The storm drew ever closer. Finally, she decided to seek help. If Peter got drenched in a cold Scottish rain, he would again fall ill. Knowing she couldn't risk that happening, she headed toward Falcon's Gate.

"Lady Ebonwyck," Veronica said from her place beside Jonathan on the settee in the sitting room, "with two children, how on earth have you managed to maintain your exceptional shape?"

"I watch what I eat, for one," Alissa replied. "But even more so, with two children to watch over, I have no time for idleness."

"She also has a husband to look after," Jared said, perched on the chair's arm beside his wife. "As one might expect, she is kept quite busy."

Standing near the fireplace, Ian noted Alissa's soft blush. Jared's meaning wasn't lost on him, and he chuckled. "Besides that, Veronica, she is younger than you."

"But your daughter—"

"Megan is my stepdaughter. My husband was a widower when we met. Megan prefers to call me mama, thus I gladly allow her to do so."

"I see," Veronica said. "That explains why you look so young."

"Age has nothing to do with it, Veronica," Madeline said, ensconced in a chair to the right of the Whitcombs. "Much of what we are can be traced to heredity. I imagine Alissa's mother was very young-looking and in excellent shape before her passing. All you need do is to study your own mother, especially if you resemble her—which you do, dear—and you'll see yourself twenty years hence."

"Well, sister, if the dowager countess is correct, you should be rather plump," Jonathan asserted. "As I recall, you, even more so than Mother, have a great fondness for chocolate. Considering such, it may not take twenty years for you to round out. I'll give it ten."

A picture of Veronica's mother emerged in Ian's mind. Not an appealing sight, he decided. Then briefly he wondered what Leah's mother looked like. Just as quickly, he shoved the unwanted thought aside.

"If that is the case," Veronica snapped, "since you take after father, you should be quite bald by the time you are thirty."

"But not fat," Jonathan returned.

Ian shook his head. "We are not here to bicker, but to enjoy a pleasant evening. Call a truce, you two, and allow the rest of us to relax."

A clap of thunder sounded, rattling the windows. "What ho?" Jonathan said, coming up off the settee. He strode to the window and inspected the sky. "It seems the storm is nearly upon us." Then his gaze settled on a point near the end of the driveway. He turned to Ian. "It appears, old man, you have a visitor."

The knocker hit the front door sharply. When Leah didn't receive an immediate response, she let the thing fall again, this time harder. The wind escalated, and her eyes searched the sky. Rolling clouds fomented above her. Lightning flashed, and another blast of thunder vibrated through her. Just as she reached for the knocker again, the door opened.

"I need to see Lord Huntsford," she said to the elderly man who peered at her questioningly. "It's extremely urgent."

"I'm sorry, but Lord Huntsford is unavailable at the moment. He is entertaining guests. Perhaps you will consider calling at another time."

Leah glared at the man. "What is your name?"

"Duncan."

"Duncan, I am Lady Huntsford. Tell my husband I wish to see him immediately."

"I'm sorry, milady, but my master has given strict orders you are never to be allowed inside this house."

"I'll wait here on the doorstep, Duncan. Just do as I've asked."

"I'm again sorry, but he left word I was not to disturb him."

She viewed him suspiciously. "Disturb him, is it? Well, if you are too squeamish about doing so, stand aside, and I shall disrupt his tranquillity myself."

A loud crash split the air as lightning struck not far from the front door, startling both Duncan and Leah. Seeing her chance, she quickly slipped by the dazed butler, dashing into the house.

"Where is he?" she demanded, but the man remained tight-lipped. Ian's familiar voice sounded around the corner to her right. "Never mind. I shall find him on my own."

Her feet tapping quickly against the marble floor, Leah kept just ahead of the laggardly Duncan. As she passed each room, her eyes scanned its interior. Ian's voice rose again, followed by a feminine reply. *Veronica.* Leah rushed ahead toward the sounds. In a few strides, she skidded to a halt in front of the door.

All conversation ceased when she stepped into the room. Leah's gaze first hit upon Alissa. Concern showed on her friend's face. Then she looked to the handsome man who hovered beside Alissa. Jared, Leah decided. Madeline caught her eye next. Trepidation showed on her mother-in-law's face. Undoubtedly, they all were aware she was coming.

Leah's attention skipped toward the window where Jonathan stood. By his expression, he had been the one who had broadcast the alert. Then she spotted Veronica, who glared her disdain. Finally, mustering her courage, she forced herself to face Ian.

"I need to have a word with you," she said. "It's very important. Otherwise, I wouldn't be here."

His cold gaze raked over her, then he looked to Duncan. "You were told *not* to let her in."

"I'm sorry, sir, but she slipped past me."

"Please, Ian. I need your help."

"What is it, Leah?" Alissa asked, while Ian remained stolidly silent.

"You know each other?" Ian asked, his surprise evident.

"Yes," Alissa replied. "I've paid call on her several times." Again she heeded Leah. "What's happened?"

"The children," she said, her gaze finally breaking loose from Ian. She'd get no help from him. "They've gone into Selkirk and haven't returned. The storm—I fear they'll be caught in it. Should Peter get wet, he might fall ill again."

"And you want me to go out searching for them, getting myself soaked in the process, correct?" Ian asked. Damn! Why couldn't she have stayed away? He'd thought the ache within him had ended. Then she had to appear. "I'm afraid not, madam. If you haven't noticed, I have guests."

"Ian," his mother said at last. "Your wife has asked for your assistance. Entertaining us is not as important as finding her siblings."

"Not to you, perhaps. But it is, in actuality, a matter of what is important to me." He looked at his wife. "Go home, madam. The children are probably there waiting for you. I'll wager anything you've made this trip for naught."

His words hurt. He was so unfeeling, she decided, tears burning her eyes. Thunder boomed again. "I can understand your malice toward me, Ian, but for the life of me, I cannot understand why you despise my siblings so. But, then, I suppose you are not the man I thought you were. I'm sorry I interrupted your little gathering. I'll not bother you again."

His body held tensely, he watched as his wife ran from the room. Her quick footfalls carried her to the front door, then he heard the heavy panel slam behind her.

Once frozen in her chair, Alissa now bounded to her feet. "You fool," she castigated, startling everyone, especially Ian. She rushed to the window. "She'll not make it. The storm—it's about to break."

"I'll go after her," Jared said, coming up behind his wife.

"She doesn't have far to go—a mile at the most. She's

capable of making it on her own," Ian stated. *By God, she'll not have her way this time!* "From what I know about her, a little wind and rain shouldn't deter her. She's far more resourceful than anyone thinks."

Blue light streaked just beyond the panes. Jared pulled his wife to safety, the loud crack still ringing in their ears. Then a blast of wind struck the huge stone structure. The house trembled on its foundations.

"A little wind, you say?" Alissa inquired.

Ian noted the sarcasm in her voice. He had the good grace to cast his eyes downward.

"I swore I'd not tell you—not unless I thought Leah was putting herself in jeopardy. I can no longer keep that promise. She's not on her own, Ian. There is someone with her."

His attention again on Alissa, he felt his gut constricting. "Are you saying what I think you're saying?"

"Yes. She's carrying your child."

He cursed with verve, then aimed himself at the sitting-room door. Striding through the hallway, he doffed his coat and unwound his cravat, tossing the pair at Duncan as he passed him.

Once he gained the front entry, he jerked open the door. Stinging rain pelted his face and body, while at his feet, the droplets shot off the floor. Dipping and weaving, the tree-tops whipped wildly in the wind. Lightning popped all around, the resounding thunder echoing through the house. *Leah.* Her name traveled through his mind, and he berated himself for not stopping her.

A hand settled on his shoulder. Jared stood behind him. "You can't go out in this."

God, what have I done?

The question ripped through Ian as he shrugged from Jared's hold. "The hell I can't," he snarled, then at a fast lope, he took off up the drive toward the road.

The wind assailed Leah as she slid down the lane toward the cottage, rivers of water running beneath her feet. Soaked and chilled, she prayed the children had made it home before the rain broke.

Blinking the moisture from her lashes, she spied a small light dancing beyond one windowpane. Relief washed through her. Thank God. They were all safe.

I'll wager anything you've made this trip for naught.

Her wet hair lashing her, she gritted her teeth, then cursed herself for having gone begging to Falcon's Gate. Afterward, she cursed Ian for having turned her away.

At the gate, she saw Terence making a dash for the cottage. Undoubtedly, he'd been in the stable, attending to the pony and cart. With a wave she caught his attention.

"Did Peter get wet?" she shouted, fumbling with the old latch.

"No, we made it just in time."

"Good," she yelled, still struggling with the gate.

"Wait," Terence called as he changed directions to spring across the yard toward her. "I'll help you."

Relaxing, Leah dropped her hand from the latch. Above her a horrendous groan sounded, followed by a loud crack. *No!* Her feet slipped in the mud as she tried to run.

"Leah!"

Terence's horrified cry met her ears just as the rotted limb struck her.

She felt herself falling, then everything went black.

"Get inside," Jared ordered as his carriage was pulled up beside Ian. "Do it, man, before you drown."

Ian saw that both Jared and his coachman, Mr. Stanley, were perched on the driver's seat. "What? And ride in comfort?" Ian asked.

"Well, do somethin' afore we all drown," Thom Stanley snarled.

Ian was beside both men in a flash. "Go!"

The whip snapping, Mr. Stanley set the bays into motion and the covered carriage sped off.

"No sign of her?" Jared asked.

"None." At the most, his wife was only five minutes ahead

of him. "She's probably at home, safe and dry," Ian said, thinking she was certainly swift of foot.

"Hope she is, my friend. Hope she is."

As the carriage slipped around the final bend, Ian spotted Terence emerging from the lane. At a hard run, he came toward them, waving his arms.

"Pull up," Ian ordered when they were nearly beside him. In the mud, the vehicle slid past Terence. "What's wrong?"

"It's Leah!" Terence called, running back to them. "A tree fell on her."

The words hit him with agonizing force. *God no!* At once Ian bounded from the seat, Jared behind him. "Where is she?"

"Down by the gate. I couldn't get the limb off her. I don't know if she's alive or—"

Cursing, Ian loped down the muddy track leading to the cottage, Jared and Terence directly after him. On reaching Leah, Ian hunkered down on one knee. He lifted the muddy strands of hair from her face. His trembling fingers smoothed over her head, then came away. He stared at the red film as it washed from his hand. "She's bleeding."

Damn his own soul for having forced her back out into the storm.

As the words streaked through Ian's mind, he felt his composure slip. For Leah's sake, he had to remain calm. "It looks like the gate took the brunt of the limb's fall," he said, taking hold of his emotions. "From what I can see, she's not wedged. With care, I think we can pull her out."

"Is she still alive?"

"She's breathing, Terence," Ian said, gazing up at the shivering lad. "You're sister is a fighter. I doubt anyone or anything could keep her down." Pray that was true, he thought. "Now, Jared, break those dead branches away, so she won't get snagged. Terence, you can assist me as I pull her free."

The hard rain still pummeling them, the men quickly went to work. While Ian again checked Leah for any injury to her neck and upper back, Jared snapped the rotted debris from the downed limb, tossing it away. Terence hunched beside Ian, awaiting his command.

"All clear," Jared informed.

"Terence, watch the movement of her body," Ian ordered. "If you spy anything that appears out of sorts, alert me."

"Understood."

"Ready?" Ian asked, gripping Leah at the apex of her arms and torso. At Terence's nod, Ian slid her with ease from under the fallen limb. Once she was free, he quickly checked her lower back and legs. "Nothing seems to be broken." Then Ian slowly turned Leah over.

Like a limp doll, her headed lolled against his arm as he cradled her. So pale, he thought, his hand smoothing over her cheek. As he stared down on her, the ache in his heart became unbearable. His eyes stung, then his tears, mixed with raindrops, fell on her face. "Oh, God, Leah. What have I done to you?"

"She has suffered a severe concussion," Dr. Drummond said nearly an hour later. He turned from the earl's bed where Leah lay to look directly at Ian. "Other than the gash on her head, plus a few scratches here and there, I can see no additional injury."

After their arrival at Falcon's Gate, Mr. Stanley had immediately set out for Selkirk and the doctor. "Will the child survive?" Ian asked Drummond, his gaze remaining fixed on Leah. She was so pale.

"That depends on your wife. Right now, I don't know what to expect. The blow was serious. Outwardly, she suffered only a cut. But what it will do inside her skull, I cannot predict. All we can do is wait. When and if she awakens, I'll have a better understanding of her prognosis."

"*If* she awakens?"

"I'm sorry, but I cannot promise you she'll even do that."

His eyes closing, Ian curled his fingers into tight fists. His harsh expletive was heard by all who stood in the room.

"Instead of cursing your Maker, young man," Dr. Drummond admonished, "I suggest you start offering Him your prayers." The man looked to the room at large. "I believe someone here offered me some hot tea when I arrived."

"Me, sir," Duncan said, hanging near the door.

"I think I'll take you up on that. This dampness has chilled me to the bone." His hand settled on Ian's shoulder. "Should there be any change, I'll be downstairs."

His attention on Leah, her damp hair spread about his pillow, Ian nodded.

"Is there anything I can do?" Alissa asked, coming up behind him.

"Bring her back to me." Then glancing at Alissa, he noted the film of tears that brightened her blue eyes. "I remember a time when I stood beside you, keeping a constant vigil," he said, referring to when he and Jared had squared off in a duel. Jared had been shot, Ian's gun never fired. But that was another story unto itself. Right now, his concern was for Leah. "Pray, Alissa, that all turns out as well," he finished, the memory locked away.

"I will, Ian. With all my heart, I will."

Then Jared was next to him. "The rain has let up. Should I have Mr. Stanley go round and fetch the children? You promised Terence you'd send for them."

A long breath flowed from Ian's lips. "I suppose. Tell Mr. Stanley for me that, if it is still raining when he gets to the cottage, he is to make certain Peter is covered and kept warm. Should the child become ill again, Leah would never forgive me." A hollow laugh erupted from him. "As though she would now."

"She loves you, Ian," Alissa said, as Jared exited the room to find his coachman.

"I wonder if that's really true." His gaze was again riveted to Leah. "She withheld the news about our child—not that I blame her. Now I might lose both of them."

"She didn't tell you because she wanted some sort of assurance you still loved her. Otherwise, she feared you'd demand her return only because she was the mother of your heir."

Pain caused by his own guilt streaked through him. "Her fear was for naught."

"You still love her, then?"

"I've always loved her, Alissa. From the day I first saw her standing at the foot of the stairs at Sinclair House, gazing up at my portrait, I knew we were meant for each other. She called me arrogant. And that I've been. Despite what she did, despite what I've said or how I've behaved, despite everything, I've never stopped loving her."

"Son," Madeline said, coming away from the foot of the bed where she'd stood listening quietly, "don't torture yourself so."

"Torture myself? At this moment, I'd gladly suffer all the torments of hell if it would help set right the wrongs I've done to Leah! A trusted friend once called me a fool. That is mild to what I now call myself. She told me not to let my pride stand in the way. I did. She said I might very well have regrets. I damn well do. If Leah should die—"

"Ian, please," his mother implored, "you must have hope."

"Hope? Yes, she should be here momentarily." Both women stared at him as if he'd gone mad. He sighed. "I know what you meant, Mother. I was just thinking of the children and how they will react to seeing Leah this way. To them, I'm the nice man who delivered them to their beloved sister. How can I possibly face them when I was the brute who turned her away when she sought help?"

"Why don't you change into something dry, son? Afterward, a brandy might calm you some. Alissa and I will stay with Leah."

"I know you mean well, Mother, but I'll not leave her. In fact, I want to be alone with her. Please. Allow me some time with her by myself."

"Come, Madeline," Alissa urged. "Let's do as he's asked."

The dowager countess studied her son. "Yes, you are right, Alissa. Remember, Ian, you must have hope."

"I'll remember."

His attention again on his wife, he heard the soft closing of the door. Regrets streamed through him as he scanned

Leah's delicate features. So many days lost, so many hours spent in utter misery, all because of his damnable pride! If he could change the recent past, he surely would. But time only moved forward, never backward, he knew.

Leaning close to her, his lips brushed her forehead, then settled on her own. Why had he been so arrogantly unforgiving? What did he gain from it, other than more grief?

On a heavy sigh, he straightened. Dragging a chair closer to the bed, he sat down, then burrowing his fingers under her limp hand, he lifted it and pressed it to his cheek. "I've been so very wrong, Leah. Come back to me. I couldn't bear it if I lost you yet another time. Please come back."

The hours passed slowly as Ian kept a constant vigil. Except for the children, Ian barely remembered who came or at what time, his attention always remaining on his wife.

Each of her siblings were allowed to visit at regular intervals. All would talk to her, sharing stories of their past. While Ian listened to each one, his empathy grew. That they loved her, possibly even more than their own parents, was quite evident. Leah had been their rock, their citadel, their sanctuary. Without her, they'd be lost, just the same as he.

With each visit, he understood more and more why she had fought so hard to secure a future for the Daltons, even risking the gallows in her attempt to do so. The ties that bound this family together were stronger than any imaginable. Ian prayed they would not be severed.

"She's so still," little Emily said.

Her wide, green eyes, so much like Leah's, looked up at Ian as she sat on his lap. "She's sleeping, Emily," he said quietly.

"That's how my mama was. But Leah told me she had died. If Leah dies, Ian, does that mean I won't see her anymore, just like I don't see my mama? My papa, too?"

Ian thought his heart had just been ripped from his chest. Tears formed in his eyes as he rocked the child. "Hush, little one," he whispered, not certain how to answer her.

"Why do you cry?"

"Because I love her, Emily."

"I do, too."

"Then let's say a little prayer for her. If God knows how much we both love her, perhaps He will allow her to stay with us."

"If God doesn't let her stay, where will she go?"

"To Heaven, to be with your mama and papa."

Emily frowned. "Where will I go?" Her eyes widened. "Not back to that place where I had to go before?"

"No, Emily. Never back there. You, along with your brothers and sisters, will stay here with me," Ian said, knowing he could not turn them away.

After Emily's careful examination of him, she said, "I think Leah would like that."

Ian felt her body curl against him. Her little hands folded together, then her lips moved as she offered up an inaudible prayer. Holding Emily close, he tendered his own request, sending it toward the heavens once again.

"She told me you were married," Terence said, on his next visit, Emily now safely tucked in bed, "but I don't understand why she stayed at the cottage while you lived here."

From his chair, Ian contemplated Leah's brother. Accusation flashed in the lad's eyes. "Because, Terence, I had been acting like a fool," he responded, waiting for the next barrage. As expected, it soon came.

"She'd not be lying here, near death, had you protected her the way a husband should protect his wife. Why did you marry her if you didn't want her around?"

"How much did Leah tell you about why she traveled to London, about what she did while she was there, and about her marriage to me?"

"Very little," her brother said. "I knew only that she was inquiring about our father and that, in doing so, she was using an assumed name. I didn't learn she was married until after she'd written me, saying she was in Scotland. Once we were at the cottage, she just talked about how glad she was we were together again."

"That's understandable. She missed you all a lot. But since she didn't acquaint you with any of the particulars about what happened these last several months, I'll leave it up to her, when she awakens, as to whether or not she wishes to do so."

"Don't you mean *if* she awakens?"

"I understand your malevolence toward me, Terence. The blame for Leah's condition lies strictly on my shoulders. But I won't allow you, or anyone else in this house, to imply that she might die—not when around me."

"Best pray, sir, she recovers," the boy threatened. "For if she doesn't, your life will be worth little."

"I know that, lad. Believe me, I do."

At three in the morning, Alissa slipped into the room. Dr. Drummond had just left. As he'd examined Leah, his extended sigh didn't sound very encouraging to Ian. Then the man had simply shaken his head and ambled on toward the door.

"Any change?" she asked.

Ian felt Alissa's hand on his shoulder. "None. She just lies there, while I keep listening for each breath."

"I presume you plan to spend the night with her?"

"I'll not leave her."

"Then you need to eat something, Ian," she said.

"I don't want anything, not in the way of food."

"Something to drink, then?"

"No!" he snapped, then caught her hand and squeezed it. "I'm sorry, Alissa. Besides that of knowing Leah will recover, the only thing I desire right now is to be left to my own thoughts. You understand how I feel, don't you?"

"Yes—very much so. If you need me, I'll be just down the hall."

"I remember saying nearly the same thing to you."

"I, too, remember, dear friend. Like you, I wanted to be left to my own thoughts, to be with Jared by myself." Her fingers pressed his shoulder. "I'll check in on you later."

After Alissa left, no one else disturbed him. Knowing her,

Ian felt certain that she sat just outside the door, turning everyone aside who sought entry, allowing him his privacy.

For long moments, he sat silently and stared at Leah's face. Then he leaned forward, telling her what was in his heart.

"Please, love. Open those beautiful eyes of yours and let me gaze into their familiar green depths. Leah, wake up."

Only her soft breaths answered him, her eyes remaining shut.

Undeterred, he kept up a constant dialogue, until he could think of nothing else to say. He'd begged, he'd pleaded, he'd threatened, but to no avail.

Releasing a long breath, he sat back in his chair and rested his head against its upholstered back. The first light of dawn streaked the sky beyond the window. A new day. He wondered what it would bring.

Both hands met his face, and he massaged his eyelids, then his temples. His fingers slid down to his chin, then dropped away. Afterward, he rested his arms on the chair's. Closing his eyes, he promised himself it would be for only a little while.

Shortly, he dozed.

From the blackness that encased her, Leah slowly came swirling upward toward the light. Staring at the bed's canopy for a moment, studying the designs on its wooden inlaid panels, she frowned, then looked around the room. Where was she? Then she spied the slumbering man beside her, his chair drawn close to the bed.

For a while, she scanned the angles of his handsome face. His dark lashes rested lightly on his lower eyelids. The stubble on his unshaven jaw matched the thick auburn locks atop his head. Even in sleep, he looked worn and weary, and she wondered why. Drawing a long breath, he nodded. As she watched, his lashes separated. Sapphire eyes examined her, then he quickly jerked to attention.

"Leah?" Ian questioned, leaning forward. His heart raced

with joy as he took hold of her small hand, his lips eagerly caressing each finger. "Thank God, you've finally awakened. I thought—never mind what I thought," he said, smiling. "Welcome back." He marked her curious inspection of him. "What's troubling you, love?"

Ian's heart stood still when she asked, "Do I know you?"

CHAPTER
22

"Unfortunately, Huntsford, we know little about the workings of the mind," Dr. Drummond said. "Your wife's amnesia could resolve itself in a few days or it could last indefinitely."

"That's what you told me three weeks ago just after she awoke," Ian snapped. Through the window of his study, he watched Leah. She sat on the terrace in the sunshine, an open book of poetry resting on her lap.

"She may be suffering from some form of repressed hysteria, the shock of her injury being too much for her to absorb. Then again, the blow may have caused some damage to the brain itself. Whether her condition is permanent or not, I cannot say. Time—"

"I know. Time alone will tell," Ian said, cutting Drummond off. Why didn't she know him—her siblings— somebody on God's green earth? He drew a shaky breath, then released it. Still he watched Leah. "Our child—is everything all right there?"

"As far as I can tell, the babe is fine. Physically, your wife is exceptionally fit. I don't expect any problems during her pregnancy." He retrieved his bag from the desk top.

"I'll be round in a few days to check in on her. Don't forget: Nothing negative about your wife's past is to be related to her. Learning she engaged in what is usually considered criminal activity might be too much for her to digest."

In order to help Leah, Ian had told Dr. Drummond all he knew about her past, her siblings filling in the rest. "What if she begins recalling things—little fragments here and there?" he asked, turning from the window. "Without having some idea of what's happened previously, the bad, as well as the good, she won't know where these pieces fit into her life. She'll undoubtedly be wondering what it all means."

"In my opinion, we have a delicate situation here. As I told you, I have treated only one such case before. Although he had no recollection of it, the gentleman was informed he'd killed his wife and child. Unable to bear such a horrendous thought, he took his own life."

"Leah's infractions are in no way comparable. I doubt she'd act as melodramatically."

"I agree. Thievery is not the equivalent to murder. But we have no way of knowing how she will react when faced with the truth about herself. Although I doubt she would attempt to take her own life, she may try to escape what she cannot accept."

"Are you saying she might run?"

"It's a possibility. In talking with her, I've ascertained she possesses high moral standards. This knowledge of right and wrong is not necessarily part of her memory, but part of her character. You can tell her she's a thief, explain she acted with the best of intentions, but I doubt she'd believe you. Because of their resemblance to her, she cannot deny her relationship to her siblings, but she has no memory of them. She has no understanding of how much she loved them or to what lengths she was willing to go in order to protect them. The truth thrust upon her all at once, her need to disallow the verity of these events may become stronger than her need to remember them."

"These events—if she starts remembering and begins

asking questions, what am I suppose to do? Lie to her? Tell her I'm unaware of what she's talking about?"

"In that case, use your own judgment. Just be careful not to upset her. It could have disastrous results if you do." The man sighed. "She may remember nothing, Huntsford. Have you forgotten that?"

"No. I haven't forgotten. For Leah's sake, I hope you're wrong."

"I do, too. If, however, her memory is gone forever, that doesn't mean she can't build new memories. The two of you will simply have to start over. She loved you once, so I'm certain she can learn to love you again. Does that ease your mind any?"

Ian couldn't imagine staring at a black void where his past should be. It would be hard to accept. He thought Leah felt very much the same. "Some," he answered, turning to view his wife again. "What would ease me more is if she could be the way she once was."

"Time will tell," Drummond said.

Weary of hearing the banality, Ian ignored the man.

"I'll be back in a few days," Drummond repeated. "In the meantime, I suggest you get some rest. You look like hell, Huntsford. Wearing yourself down won't in the least help your wife or your child."

Again not responding, Ian heard Drummond's footsteps carry him to the door, then out. Rest. It eluded him even more so now than it had before. His guilt was what kept him awake at night. That, and the vacant look in Leah's eyes each time she gazed at him. Her lack of recognition had nearly destroyed him. He wanted her back. Still, he feared what would happen once her memory returned.

An end to their relationship, Ian guessed, knowing she had every right to despise him after what he'd put her through.

Instead of his hoping she regained her memory, maybe he should be praying she didn't. The ghosts of her past held at a distance, she'd have no reason to hate him. As

Drummond had suggested, they could start afresh. She loved him once. Surely, the emotion could dwell in her anew.

Lies all over again. Only this time he would be the one who promoted them, not Leah. And in the off chance she did regain her memory one day, he imagined her reaction would be similar to his own. Tit for tat, as it were. Ian knew he couldn't allow that.

No, if they were to start afresh, Leah had to be aware of the truth, remembered or not. For now, he'd not press the issue, thereby affording her the opportunity to heal. In the interim, he'd offer her his love, his understanding, his support, hoping, when she did regain her memory, she'd not be so eager to spurn him.

He viewed Leah with anticipation, wishing it would be just that simple. In truth, he was uncertain whether his newly demonstrated devotion could possibly make a difference. Raking his fingers through his hair, he emitted a derisive snort, knowing time alone would tell.

On the terrace, bathing in warm sunshine, a copy of Byron's poems laying unattended on her lap, Leah stared off into the distance. Questions abounded in her mind, none of them being answered. All she knew was what she'd been told. The rest was a blank.

Terence, Hope, Kate, Peter, and little Emily were said to be her siblings. That they cared deeply for her was evident, their affection and concern being unmatched—except perhaps by that of Lord Huntsford. No matter how hard she tried, she remembered none of them. Because of it, a sadness lingered in her heart.

It was as though she were staring at a huge gray wall. Try as she would to scale the barrier, hoping to peer over its top and view what lay beyond, she could never reach its pinnacle. Her constant struggle seemed hopeless, for the barricade went on endlessly, and Leah wondered if her past would be forever hidden from her.

Sighing, she closed her eyes and pictured Lord Huntsford, the man who was said to be her husband, the man who was said to have sired the child she carried in her womb. The slight roundness of her belly attested she was pregnant, as did her bouts of nausea. But how, when, or where the babe was conceived eluded her. She could only hope the wee thing had been created in love.

The earl's image remained as Leah opened her eyes. Virile and handsome, Lord Huntsford positively intrigued her. From the first moment she'd spotted him, she knew in her heart of hearts he was somehow special to her. But how special, she didn't fully know, not until he'd announced they were married. The news was as much of a shock to her as her inquiry had been to him.

Do I know you?

When she'd uttered those words, his look of hope had turned to one of devastation. After he'd searched her eyes carefully, he'd bounded from his chair and stridden to the door. Once in the hallway, he'd shouted for Dr. Drummond.

Later, when she had recovered from her own shock, he began to explain who she was and what had happened to her. "You've had an accident, Leah—that's your name, sweet. You took a hard knock on your head. It's affected your memory. With rest, everything should soon come back to you. In the meantime, I'll be here beside you."

As Leah remembered, sincerity had evinced itself in his eyes, along with the light of love. But even now, his gaze conveyed what she believed was an expression of guilt, coupled with regret.

At one time, she'd been startled awake by the abrupt opening of the door. Ian had come up out of his chair to face the intruder.

"Jonathan and I are going back to London," the attractive brunette announced.

Veronica was her name, Leah thought. Yes, that's what **Lord Huntsford had called her when the woman had** entered.

"A safe journey to you both," he'd returned, then dismissing the woman, he'd again reclaimed his seat.

Over these past weeks, his devotion had been unwavering. He loved her, yet something troubled him. Leah could see it in his eyes, and she couldn't help wonder if something had struck a wedge between them. A disagreement or an argument, perhaps?

She'd never been bold enough to ask about their relationship. Even if she brought up the issue, she doubted she'd receive a straight answer. Just how she'd been injured still remained a mystery to her, for no one seemed willing to discuss it. They all tiptoed around her, apparently fearing they might somehow upset her. In Leah's mind, the question was why.

Uneasiness erupted inside Leah. The feeling swelled. Instinctively, she sprang from her chair, the book hitting the slate, then she dashed across the terrace, and into the gardens.

As she scampered along the path, heading aimlessly away from the house, she drew breath fast and hard, attempting to fight off the urgency roiling inside her. This sudden desire to bolt overtook her at the strangest times. Yet she never could decide if she was hurrying toward something or away from it. The sensation faded, and Leah slowed her pace. If she could only remember. . . .

Leah started when a loud yap sounded from the small dog that had bounded from behind a bush. Round and round her feet, Merlin ran. Finally, he settled on his haunches in front of her.

"Scared me you did, you little vagabond," Leah said. When she was on the terrace, the small dog had become a companion to her, usually lying at her feet. "Where have you been these past three days?" Merlin's pink tongue lolled while his forepaw waved in the air, and she squatted beside him. "Thirsty?" she asked, her fingers ruffling through his shaggy hair.

You're a cute little thing.

In her mind, a door opened. A white-washed cottage with

a thatched roof flashed inside her head. Flowers bloomed in a small yard. Merlin sat on the doorstep, lapping water from an earthenware bowl. Then the door slammed shut.

Blinking, Leah slowly rose to her feet. She stared at the little dog. Dared she hope he would understand? "The cottage, Merlin—do you know where it is?"

His quick bark sounded.

"Could you take me there?"

He yapped, then scurried toward the woods beyond the garden.

Thinking she might be crazy for following, Leah nevertheless tracked after Merlin. After fighting her way through the trees, she emerged into a field. Once across it, she faced a hillside and another stand of trees.

All the while she'd journeyed, the small dog had cut back and forth, then ran around and around, but always he led her onward. Presently, he sat at the top of the hill, waiting.

Her skirt lifted high, Leah trudged up the slope. "If you've led me on a merry chase, Merlin, I shall never forgive you," Leah announced only yards from the hill's crest. Reaching it, she stood motionless.

There below her was the cottage from her vision. But why did she remember it?

"Come on, boy. There has to be an answer down there somewhere," Leah said, then descended the hill.

Once beside the fence, she called out, but no one answered. Hiking up her skirt, she scrambled over the top rail, Merlin scooting under the lower one, then they both crossed the yard.

The front door stood before her. She knocked, but received no response. "Anybody live here, Merlin?" she asked.

His head tilted as he whined, then he set to scratching at the weathered wood.

"If you say so," Leah said, then released the latch and pushed the panel wide. She surveyed the dimly lit interior.

Withered flowers hung lifelessly over the rims of crocks, jars, and other makeshift vases. A film of dust covered the furnishings and floor. Empty drawers lay cocked in several chests. Beds were stripped of linens, mattresses left askew.

"It appears, Merlin, someone vacated this place in a hurry." Looking down on the small dog, she noticed how he panted heavily. "You're thirsty, aren't you? Let's see if we can find you some water."

Merlin shot out the door and around the side of the cottage. Following, Leah spied him beside the stone circuit marking the well.

"Go on and drink, boy," she said, having drawn the bucket upward on its rope, setting it next to Merlin. "I'm going to explore a bit."

As Leah rounded the small cottage, she studied all that met her eyes. Nothing seemed in the least familiar to her. She had hoped that upon glimpsing her past, then finding the cottage, everything would fall into place, her memory finally returning. But the wall remained. The barrier seemed to loom ever higher, and she wondered if it would ever come tumbling down.

Emerging from the back of the cottage, Merlin now beside her, she observed a mangled gate, a rotted tree limb resting atop it. Felled by the winds, she surmised, shrugging. Having searched the yard, she decided to reenter the cottage.

Inside, she inspected each piece of furniture, then climbed to the loft to have a look around. Again, nothing triggered her memory, and Leah felt certain she'd journeyed here for naught.

Back on the first level, she concluded they should head back to Falcon's Gate. "Come, Merlin. Let's go along home. There's nothing here for us."

At the door, she jumped as an explosive greeting cracked in her ears.

"Damn it, Leah," Ian snapped, having come out of nowhere. He'd seen her spring from the terrace, but by the time he'd reached the gardens, she was gone. He'd been searching for her ever since. "You had me scared half to death."

Clinging to the doorframe, she stared at him. *Damn*

it, Leah! Damn it, Leah! The words ricocheted through her head, while in her mind, she saw Ian coming toward her. Fury blazed in his eyes. He looked as though he could kill her. Abruptly, he caught himself and veered away from her, fingers raking through his hair. *Damn it, Leah . . .*

The door to her memory closed again.

Noting she'd gone pale, Ian was at once beside her. "What's wrong, love. Are you ill?"

Leah blinked, then searched his face. "No. I saw you coming at me. You were angry. It was in a bedroom, I think. It looked like an English garden. You said: Damn it, Leah—the same way you did a moment ago. I can't remember anything else."

Sinclair House, Ian thought, knowing she referred to the time when he'd just learned of her deceit. Of all things for her to have recalled, it had to be that. "Do you remember anything else?"

"The cottage. I had only a glimpse of it in my mind. That's why I came here."

"How did you ever find it?"

"Merlin led me through the woods and across the field."

Quelling his urge to shake her, along with his dog, Ian released his breath. "Don't ever run off like that again, madam. Next time, I might not be able to find you."

"How did you know I was here?"

"A lucky guess."

"Then the place belongs to you?"

"It does. Now, come. Let's head back to the main house."

"Why do I know about the cottage?" she asked as he guided her toward the fence where Woden awaited them both. "Was I here once?"

"Since you live at Falcon's Gate, it is a given, at one time or another, you would have been here." He helped her over the fence, then bounded the top rail himself. "Up you go." Assisting Leah sideways onto the saddle, he mounted directly behind her. "Home, Woden."

As the big stallion started up the lane, Ian's arms around

her, his hands steady on the reins, Leah gazed up at him. "Can't you give me more information? It would, after all, be nice to know *something* about myself."

Not now, he thought. Especially when he'd wanted to have more time with her before her memory returned. In that space, he'd hoped they could build a new friendship, a new love. Though he never intended to withhold the truth from her, he couldn't afford to come out with it this soon.

"We'll talk about it later," he said finally. "Presently, I ask you to enjoy the scenery."

"If you won't answer me on that question, will you please answer me this: Where does this road lead?"

"This way leads to Falcon's Gate," he replied, nodding in the direction they were going. "Back the other way is Selkirk."

"Scotland—correct?"

"Yes, Leah. Scotland." He studied her a moment. "As I recall, I had acquainted you on your whereabouts before."

"I've been acquainted on many things. But I don't know if any of what I've been told is true. I have no memory, therefore I must rely on everyone else to provide the information I seek—though, I dare say, not much is given. That's what makes me so angry."

"Understandable—considering your disposition."

"Are you saying I have a temper?"

"A wee one—nothing that can't be tamed."

"What about you? Do you have a temper?"

"It has been known to erupt, now and again, with provocation."

"Then I must have provoked you," she said.

"If you're referring to your flash of memory, I told you already, Leah, I won't discuss it. Not now."

"When will you discuss it?" she asked, determined to have the truth, but he remained silent. "Why won't you talk about it? Don't you understand what I'm going through? Or do you even care?"

"I care, Leah," he said, looking down on her again. "Probably more than you'll ever know. For my sake, and yours, don't press me any further."

This cursed wall! Why couldn't she break through it? Then a thought occurred. "Has Dr. Drummond forbidden you to speak to me about my past?"

Exasperation showed on his face as his jaw clenched. "Leah, I—"

"Please, Ian, tell me that much."

Blue eyes studied green. "He mentioned we should be cautious. Too much information all at once could be harmful."

"Harmful?" she questioned with a frown. "How could knowing about myself possibly be harmful? Unless—"

"Enough!" Ian stated firmly. "The subject is closed. Understand?"

Lips drawn tight, Leah stared at him. "You *do* have a temper, sir."

"Provocation, madam. That's all it takes, remember?"

"I wish I could," she said forlornly.

"Everything will come back to you soon enough. Just be patient."

"I suppose I have no choice, especially when I'm purposely being kept in the dark."

"We're home," Ian responded, thankful they were. Silence enveloped Leah as he turned Woden down the drive. As still as she was, he suspected her mind whirled with speculation.

Leah's thoughts were indeed spinning. She must have done something awful for Dr. Drummond to have ordered her past to be concealed from her. Murder? Larceny? What?

Unable to find an answer, Leah decided that she was looking for trouble where none existed. Smiles on their faces, her siblings seemed quite content. Given his wealth and status, her husband appeared to want for naught, except, perhaps, a fully functioning wife. So what could possibly be wrong?

Yet, because of that one quick flash of memory, Leah suspected things weren't always as serene as they were now. Fury had once teemed in his eyes. If she could just remember what she'd done, she'd have her answer.

Woden was reined in at the front entry. Dismounting, Ian reached up, and his hands spanned Leah's waist. "Come, sweet."

Her fingers met his shoulders as he easily lifted her from the saddle. Briefly, she marveled at his strength, then wondered if she might have done so before. Once her feet touched the ground, she attempted to turn away, but Ian held fast to her waist.

"I know you want to remember everything all at once. But don't rush it, Leah. Give yourself some time. It will all come back to you eventually. By what you've said, the process has already begun."

Leah searched his face. He seemed apprehensive about her remembering. Something troubled him deeply. "What if my memory doesn't return? What if I'm able to grasp only snatches here and there? Am I to be left permanently fumbling around in the dark, not fully aware of who I am or what my life was like? And what about us? Except for your angry look, I cannot fathom what sort of relationship we had. It's not fair for me to be kept ignorant of these things. I have to know."

"I understand. I promise I won't allow you to wonder forever. I can't tell you everything about yourself, but when the time is right, I'll tell you all I do know, especially about us."

"When?"

"Soon, Leah," he said, his knuckles softly grazing her cheek. "Soon."

Leah felt his hold relax, and she expected him to free her, but as though he'd forgotten something, his grip again tightened.

"Should you by chance regain your memory all at once, I want you to know something. No matter what went before, no matter what has passed between us, I love you, Leah. I love you from the depths of my heart. Don't forget that—ever."

His light kiss brushed her lips, then he released her. Stunned, Leah stared after him as he led Woden to the stables.

No matter what has passed between us . . .

CHAPTER

23

Several days later, Leah was ensconced on the terrace. Her siblings played nearby, but she paid them little heed. Still fuming over her mother-in-law's refusal to apprise Leah about the particulars of her past, she felt like socking one of the Sinclairs straight in the nose—mainly Ian. But if he were unavailable, she was certain Madeline would do.

They were much alike, mother and son. No matter how hard she tried to pry an answer from either of them, both remained tight-lipped. Undoubtedly, the two had formed an alliance, agreeing never to reveal what they thought might prove harmful.

Harmful to whom? Leah wondered, her mood growing more surly. Maybe they were not trying to protect her, but themselves. Either way, something was amiss, and she vowed to discover what it was.

Feeling a nudge on her arm, Leah looked to her side. His lips tinged blue, Peter stared at her through watery eyes as he gasped for breath. Without hesitating, Leah jerked him across her lap and, with a quick chopping motion, beat her hands up and down against his back. Shortly, he coughed, expelling the mucus from his throat. His airway now cleared, he breathed deeply and pushed to his feet.

"Are you all right?" Leah asked, noting his color had returned.

"Bright as a new penny," he said, grinning.

Leah frowned. "How did I know to do that, Peter?"

"It's what you've always done when I had trouble breathing."

"I suppose I acted from instinct, for I cannot remember ever assisting you in such a way." She smiled gently. "I'm sorry, Peter, but I can't."

"You taught me how to help him," Hope said, she and Kate having come to check on their younger brother. "When we were at the orphanage, I had to do it quite often."

"And I helped her," Kate stated proudly.

Her stomach forming into a knot, Leah stared at the girls. "When were you ever in an orphanage?"

Her three siblings exchanged glances. "We're not supposed to tell you," Peter informed finally.

"Why not?"

"Because I asked them not to," Ian stated from behind her. As expected, his wife swung toward him, accusation written in her eyes. For now, he ignored her. "Feeling better, Peter?" he inquired. Seeing the boy's nod, he said, "Then the three of you go along and play. I believe your sister wishes to speak to me privately."

The trio skipped from the terrace, heading toward Emily who sat on a blanket playing with the doll Ian had presented her.

Leah's gaze raked him from head to foot as she rose from her chair. He was dressed casually in a white flowing shirt, black trousers and boots to match. His lack of conformity bespoke arrogance, she decided, then was certain, somewhere in her past, she'd concluded the exact same thing before.

"I want far more than to simply have a private chat, sir," she stated, her siblings safely beyond earshot. "I want answers, and I want them now. Should you refuse, let it be known, I'll seek them someplace else."

"Such as?"

"The orphanage for one. Since you've stated the children and I hail originally from Leeds, I'd think that would be as good a place as any to start my search. Wouldn't you?"

At length Ian eyed her, then he released a long breath. This time she'd not be put off. "Let's adjourn to my study, and you shall have your answers."

Ian led the way while Leah followed. Now seated in a comfortable chair opposite his desk, she waited for him to situate himself. Once he did, he asked, "What is it you want to know?"

"Everything, sir, but let's begin with this orphanage." She edged forward in the chair. "Why didn't you tell me the children had been sent to such a place? Was this something recent? How—"

"Leah, be still," Ian ordered gently. "One question at a time. Right now, just sit back and listen." Amazingly, she obeyed him, and he began, "You were told your parents were both deceased, but what you weren't told—simply because we want to keep unpleasant things away from you for the time being—is that they passed on just this year. Your mother fell gravely ill at the end of February. Your father was in London at the time, and in his attempt to reach her side before she died, he suffered a fatal mishap along the road north to Leeds. It is believed his horse stumbled; your father was thrown. His body was found by a passing mail coach the next day."

Leah felt a bit guilty. Not remembering her parents in the least, she experienced no remorse. She imagined that would change the instant her memory returned. For now, she was simply interested in the facts. "How did my siblings end up in an orphanage? Were there no relatives we could rely on?"

"They apparently were unwilling to help. From what I've learned, your father's debts outweighed his assets. In order to keep you and young Terence out of the workhouse or away from debtor's prison, your family home was sold, the proceeds paying the creditors. You and Terence sought employment while Hope, Kate, Peter, and Emily were placed in an orphanage in York. However, you were unable to find a suitable position, so you came to London, where we met. I was there for the Season."

"How did we meet?" she asked, eager to know.

"You carried a letter of introduction from your father's solicitor—John Kingsley." Ian waited and watched for a reaction. None. "He is also a family friend—to the Sinclairs, that is. As I was saying, we met when you came to London. In short order, we fell in love, married, then at my desiring to return to Falcon's Gate, we traveled on to Scotland. After our arrival, I collected Terence from his labors as an apprentice to a smithy, then together, he and I retrieved your siblings from the orphanage. And here we all are."

Leah studied her husband. He wasn't giving her much detail, but at least she was receiving some answers. "My accident—how did that come about?"

Ian tensed slightly. He chose his words carefully. "There was a storm. You got caught in it while searching for the children. A rotted limb fell. You were struck."

A picture of the mangled gate flashed through her mind. "It happened at the cottage. But what was I doing there?"

How could he execute this answer without being accused of total deceit? "You'd given Terence and the others permission to go into Selkirk for the day. The cottage lies between here and there. What better place to seek refuge in a storm?"

She thought of Merlin sitting on the doorstep on a bright sunny day. "I have other memories of the place. They have nothing to do with a storm. I must have gone there quite often."

"Yes, you were often there."

"Did the children play at the cottage? Was that why I remember it?"

Ian grew more cautious. "They played there," he said, then fell silent.

"You're not willing to tell me any more, are you?"

"For the time being, no. I've answered your question pertaining to the orphanage, plus some. We shall now give it a rest."

Leah's eyes narrowed on him. "A rest, you say? Why? Is it

because you fear I might learn something about you—about us—that you wish to keep secreted from me?" He held his tongue, and Leah was certain she'd hit on something. "I say you are indeed afraid of my discovering something about our past."

"The past is dead, Leah. Neither of us can change what has happened in our lives, so why worry over it?"

"That is easy for you to say, especially when you remember yours so well." She popped from her chair. "Good day to you," she bit out, then headed toward the door.

Ian was on her before she'd gone so much as three steps. "There is much in my past I'd like to forget," he said, capturing her arms. "Sometimes, I wish it would simply be wiped free. At least, then, I'd not have to suffer the torment of knowing the mistakes I've made. The past is unimportant. It is the future I worry over, and how it will be for us, for our child. You loved me once, Leah, with great passion. That is what I desire again."

"How can I offer you such when I don't remember what it was like between us?"

"Tell me, this: When a babe is born, can he or she recall what has happened while in the womb? If so, why, as we mature, do we forget these things? Or could it be simply that as we grow we gain our remembrances?"

"I don't know anything about that. Don't you understand? I can see no farther back than the day I awakened in your bed."

"Then think of yourself as a newborn babe, Leah." He drew her closer. "Start building your memories now. Start building them with me."

Leah stood frozen as his head lowered, then hot and moist, his mouth covered hers. Temptingly, his tongue glided along her lower lips, and though the action set her stomach to quivering in the strangest way, she refused to allow him entry.

Noting how stiffly she held herself, Ian soon lifted his head. His gut twisted, fear glutted him. She despised him, he surmised, staring at her long and hard. "My error, madam. I had hoped we could begin anew."

"How can we begin anew when you refuse to help me now?"

Releasing her, he turned away. "I have my reasons."

"Which are?"

If he confessed how he'd rejected her, how she'd really come about her injury, then he'd have to tell all, Leah's deception included. Drummond still believed that if she learned anything detrimental about herself, it might send her over the edge. Ian was beginning to doubt the good doctor's wisdom, but who was he to argue with the man. What he did know was that Drummond had better damn well be right!

"I cannot say," he answered at last. "Believe me, if I could, I would."

Leah studied the linen-covered back that was presented to her. "I'll remember, Ian. Someday, my past will come back to me. And when it does, I may not forgive you for the way you've treated me. You speak of our future. Well understand this: We may not have one."

Ian heard the door open. *Just tell her!* his mind shouted. Then the panel closed with what he imagined was the sound of finality.

From the window in Ian's room, Leah watched her husband as he agilely kicked a ball across the back lawn toward a marked goal, with Peter and Terence as his opponents. To the side sat Hope, Kate, and Emily. Between their enjoying a pretend tea with their dolls, the girls cheered their brothers' efforts as the boys sought to steal the ball away from Ian. Though she imagined he was quite skilled at this game called football, he nevertheless allowed the boys every opportunity to filch the ball from under his feet, giving them a chance at victory, when in fact, he could easily win.

I always win.

Leah blinked on hearing the words in her head. No pictures had flashed in her mind, just Ian's voice, and she questioned what the phrase meant and when he'd said it, if he ever had.

She'd not been very kind to him these past several days, ignoring his greetings whenever they'd met. Taking her cue, he'd begun to cut a wide path around her whenever he'd noted her approach. He'd granted her some distance, never encroaching. In one way, she appreciated his doing so, but in another, she wondered if he'd given up on her.

For some reason, the prospect didn't sit well with Leah. Instinct told her that this is where she wanted to be, here at Falcon's Gate, with her siblings and her husband. Because of his kindness and devotion, not to mention his masculine good looks, she understood why she'd initially fallen in love with him. Were it not for his refusal to tell her about her past, she could easily fall in love with him again. His silence was what threatened to keep them apart, nothing else.

Leah felt again the first twinges of anxiety welling inside her. The attacks were coming more frequently. With each siege, her desire to run became stronger. She remembered her vow to seek answers elsewhere if none were given to her here. Leeds, York—they were good places to start her search. And then there was John Kingsley, her father's solicitor . . .

The urge to flee Falcon's Gate to ferret out her past grew stronger. She simply had to know who she was. Devising a quick plan, she felt certain she could easily slip away during the night. To journey back to England, she needed money. Nibbling at her lower lip, she glanced about the room. Though she'd been occupying the huge bedroom, it was in fact Ian's. Except for a few articles of clothing, he'd not removed his possessions. She looked at the large chest across the way. Maybe he kept some coins in there.

She went to the chest and began rifling through the drawers, working from bottom to top. Shirts, cravats, stockings, and incidental articles of clothing were all that she found. She stared at the top and final drawer. Her last chance, she decided. Pulling it open, she stood on tiptoes and stared over its rim.

Silver paper caught her eye. In her mind, she saw green ribbon binding a small package. Just as quickly it was gone. Lifting the wrapping from the drawer, for she hoped something of value might lay inside, she dropped back on her heels. She pulled the edges of the paper aside, then examined what she found.

A brooch, centuries old—at least, that's what she thought on first glance. Then, again, it could be a replica.

A maypole flashed in her mind, streamers dipping and weaving. Sapphire eyes gazed at her in reverence. Ian, she decided as she drifted further into her vision. *"Mince pies,"* she heard him say.

Across a field of green, banners flapped in the wind. Trumpets heralded. Knights rode on valiant steeds. A joust? Is that what she saw?

A moonlit balcony danced in her mind's eye. The scent of flowers wafted around her. Incredibly, she thought she heard herself crying, then her sobs subsided.

"No more tears, then?"

It was Ian who asked the question.

Her own voice echoed in her ears. *"No more tears."*

"Is there anything else you need?"

From afar, she saw herself gazing at his mouth.

"How about this?"

Heat seared through Leah's body as she relived his kiss. Her knees wobbled, but she dared not move for fear the door to her past would slam shut again.

Then her vision skipped to a room, its trappings resembling an English garden. A small package veiled in silver paper, tied with green ribbon, sat on a silk-covered bed. In her mind, the paper and ribbon fell away to reveal the brooch she held. With it was a card.

Affectionately, Ian.

Leah quickly searched through the wrapping in her hand. The card appeared. It was all true! She remembered, but what did it mean?

Closing her eyes, she leaned against the chest, allowing her mind to float free.

She was at once in a glittering ballroom. Swathed in shimmering amethyst silk, she waltzed alongside a gaily dressed crowd, Ian holding her in his arms.

"You're a cad, sir—a man without principle. Why a

woman would want any involvement with someone such as you remains a mystery to me."

"Just say the word, and I'd be more than happy to unravel the riddle for you, Leah."

"You play games, sir. I'm not interested in being part of your sport."

"No?"

"No. As I said, you're a cad."

"In your eyes, maybe. You speak of games—well, let it be known: Whatever game it is I play, I always win. Surrender, Leah. Don't fight the inevitable. It's a given that you'll lose to me."

Leah's memory streamed to a small church. Rain fell outside its stone walls.

"I told you, my love, I always win. You are now my wife. Forever and always, I intend to keep you near me."

She was in the bedroom again, Ian with her. He was angry, very angry. His words slammed into her again.

"Tell me this: When you said you loved me, was that also a lie?"

"No. I have and still do love you."

"That's hard to believe, madam. Of course, your concept of love might differ from mine. Obviously, it does, especially since our marriage is based on naught but a series of falsehoods."

"If you remember, sir, I told you I couldn't marry you, but you forced me into it anyway."

"But you didn't say why, did you?"

As Leah leaned against the chest, she felt suddenly ill. What had she done to make him so angry? She held her breath and prayed the answer would come. It did, and with force.

From a distance, she saw Ian spring from his chair. Fury blazed in his eyes as he came at her, then abruptly changed directions, fingers raking through his hair. *"Damn it, Leah. Didn't you know your masquerade would eventually be exposed?"*

Masquerade . . . masquerade . . .

The word echoed through her head. Her mind spun

wildly. Then like a wellspring, her past came flooding in on her.

"My God—Ian."

Feeling the blood drain from her face, she stumbled toward the bed, the brooch clutched tightly in her hand. Certain she might faint, she fell upon the mattress.

It all came back to her at once.

Violent winds whipped through her mind as she envisioned the storm and her frantic attempt to return to the cottage. She relived the worry she'd suffered over the children, thinking they'd be caught in the tempest. She experienced again the relief that streamed through her when she saw the light in the window. Again she heard the limb crack, then watched in horror as it fell toward her, her feet slipping in the mud as she attempted to get away.

Leah!

Terence's terrified yell echoed in her mind. Then she remembered all had gone black. When she'd awakened, Ian sat beside the bed. Unshaven, he looked weary and worn. Leah wondered if he'd chased after her in the storm or if Terence, fearing his sister might die, had gone for him. Did it really matter?

The devotion and gentle concern that Ian had displayed toward her seemed to say he'd forgiven her for her past sins. He looked upon her with love in his eyes, and she was gladdened by the knowledge that he did. Still, beyond that light of genuine affection lurked a glimmer of guilt. Regret, too. Did he fear, for having turned her away, that she might not be so willing to forgive him?

Should you by chance regain your memory all at once, I want you to know something. No matter what went before, no matter what has passed between us, I love you, Leah. I love you from the depths of my heart. Don't forget that—ever.

On remembering those words, Leah rose from the bed. With a quick glance through the window, making certain Ian was still on the back lawn, she headed toward the door. As she descended the stairs, her feelings for Ian renewed themselves tenfold. Her cheeks flamed as memories of the passionate moments they'd shared enveloped her. Indeed, their child had been conceived in love.

Leah's pace quickened as she made her way through the house, then onto the terrace, ever closer to Ian. She was now halfway to her destination. Her heart swelled with anticipation. If need be, she'd travel the world just to be again at his side.

From the corner of his eye, Ian saw movement. Leah came toward him. Briefly, he studied her. Even at this distance, he felt as though there was something different about her. His heart stopped for an instant, then tossing the ball at Terence, he cut across the lawn toward her.

Ten paces from each other, they both halted their progression, each searching the other's face.

Wondering if he should accept what he saw as being genuine, Ian dared not move.

Leah spied the question in his eyes. She could no longer remain silent. "Ian—I love you. I truly do."

On her lips, the words seemed almost a whisper, traveling toward him on the light breeze, yet in his heart, they rang loudly, joyfully. Nothing had ever sounded so sweet.

In an instant, they were in each other's arms, their lips meeting in a ravenous kiss, each starved for the other.

"Oh, Leah," Ian said, finally tearing his mouth free. "I've missed you so."

"And I've missed you, Ian. More than you can imagine."

"I can imagine. Truly, I can." Sincerity lit his eyes. "Welcome back, love."

"It's good to be back. Whether it be in mind, heart, or body, I shall never leave you again."

"You're right, madam. Henceforth, you won't get five feet from me. Should you attempt it, I'll be on you in a flash."

An impish light danced in her eyes. "Promise?"

With her query, Ian emitted a groan. Then suddenly he realized they weren't alone. "I believe your siblings are wondering what's going on," he said, then eased her from his embrace.

Looking at her brothers and sisters, she noted how they stared at her questioningly. She smiled, then winked. "Well, what's wrong with all of you? Don't you know your big sister? She certainly remembers you."

With shouts of glee, they all surrounded her. Hugs and kisses were exchanged with Leah. Afterward, all of them teary-eyed, they gazed at each other. Their joy no longer able to be contained, their laughter rose into the air. It was then that Merlin broke from the shrubbery, to run around their feet.

"Come here, you little vagabond," Leah said. Hunkering down, she ruffled his hair. "You're the one that started my remembering. For that, you deserve a big bone."

Merlin's tongue cut a path across Leah's cheek, then he yapped loudly.

"Come," Ian said, drawing Leah up to his side. "A celebration is in order. Let's all head to the house. You, too, Merlin."

The Daltons streamed across the lawn to the terrace, Merlin at their heels. Following more slowly, Leah looked to Ian. "Your mother will be wondering what all the commotion is about."

"When she learns its cause, she'll be delighted."

Leah's teeth worried her lip. "I fear I wasn't very nice to her lately."

"She told me that you'd questioned her about your past—even mentioned she thought you looked to be on the verge of violence when she refused to cooperate."

"I fear, sir, there is a wicked streak that runs through me. It is at times hard to control."

Picturing Leah in his bed, her long, flaxen hair the only raiment she wore, Ian felt his blood stir. "By wicked, do you mean playful, madam?"

"That's a strong possibility, sir. You'll just have to wait and see."

Having reached the French doors, Ian wished fervently he'd confined the celebration to a mere two. Then as he watched his mother and wife embrace, he was gladdened they were all together.

Welcome back, love, he thought anew, knowing no man could be as happy as he. He'd found that special someone his mother had insisted he'd one day meet, and in his heart he gave thanks, for he couldn't imagine his life without Leah.

The flame burned low in the bedside lamp as Ian and Leah lay cuddled close together. Their desire satisfied, they basked in the afterglow of their lovemaking.

"I believe I've won our wager," Ian said, his voice still husky.

Leah lifted her head from his chest and gazed into his wondrous eyes. "What wager?"

"The one made on the day I ran Covington down. Remember? I wagered that all those words you keep hidden in your heart would one day be whispered solely to me. As I recall, you just did that. You owe me a kiss, Leah."

At Ian's reference to her half-brother, Leah felt no animosity at all. In fact, she wished all the Covingtons well. "As I recall, you released me from that wager, sir. Therefore, I owe you nothing."

He frowned. "Hmm—you must be mistaken. Probably that blow you suffered caused some minor difficulties with your memory. You owe me a kiss."

"There's not a thing wrong with my memory, sir. It is you who is addled."

"I'll admit I'm still a bit dizzy from the rapture I just experienced, but I haven't lost my wits completely." He rolled her onto her back and hovered above her. "Now pay up, madam."

"And if I don't?"

"Then I'll keep you in this bed until we wither away."

"Were it just the two of us, I don't think I'd object."

Ian's hand smoothed over the slight roundness of her belly. "The wee babe does need his nourishment." He sighed. "I guess Duncan will just have to bring our food and drink up here."

"You wouldn't dare let the man see us like this, would you?"

"You lost the wager, Leah. All you need to do is give me a kiss. If you continue to refuse, then I'm willing to wait you out. Duncan can come and go as he may. Your obstinance is for naught, love. In the end, you know I'll win. I always win—always."

Leah noted the mirthful twinkle in his eye, his abiding affection shining just beyond. How glad she was that fate had sent her his way. She couldn't imagine ever being without him. Her fingers linking behind his head, she pulled him close. "In this case, my love, I think we've both won."

"Agreed, sweet. Now pay up."

EPILOGUE

Christmas 1841

Crackling flames danced beyond the hearth in the sitting room at Falcon's Gate where Lord and Lady Huntsford had stolen away to privately exchange their gifts.

Ian's eyes reflected the fire's warmth and the glow of his love as he gazed down on his wife's bowed head, awaiting her response.

Trembling fingers traced the wording on the document while Leah's eyes glazed with tears. Balfour—it belonged to the Daltons once again.

"Well, madam, have you nothing to say?"

With a joyous cry, Leah flung her arms around her husband's neck; quick kisses covered his handsome face. "Oh, Ian, how did you ever manage it? I thought Mr. Kingsley said the new owner refused to sell?"

Ian's arm tightened around his wife's thickening waist, but the roundness of her stomach made it impossible to hold her as close as he'd wanted. "It was simply a matter of numbers. When I hit on the right set, the man was more than eager to sign over the deed. By the new year, the premises will have been vacated and a caretaker installed. Are you pleased?"

"Very," she returned with a smile. Then she glanced at the settee and the hand-embroidered silk cravat and quilted satin robe on which she'd spent hours sewing. "You've outdone me, sir. By far, my gift to you seems paltry in comparison."

On that, their babe kicked.

His belly absorbing the tiny shock, Ian grinned. "Not so, love. You've given me more than I had ever hoped for, had ever dreamed possible. To think, in a few short months, I'm going to be a father." He saw the light of happiness fade from her eyes. "What's wrong, Leah?"

"I'm just thankful our child will be born on the right side of the blanket, that's all."

Ian knew she still harbored animosity toward her father. He hoped what he next divulged would take some of the edge from her anger. "There's something I've not yet told you, Leah—something we'll need to share with Terence. You will have to help me decide how we should approach the matter."

"He's been denied entrance to Eton, hasn't he? They found out about his parentage—discovered he's a bastard. Oh, I knew something like this would happen. Damn his eyes!" she said of her father. "He's left us nothing but a legacy of grief."

Ian kissed her brow. "Hush, sweet. Don't excite yourself. Let's sit, and I'll explain."

He guided Leah to the settee, where he brushed aside the cravat and robe, then urged her onto the cushion.

"What I have to say has to do with parentage all right, but I think you'll be relieved once you hear it." He folded himself down beside her and took her hand. "I received a letter from John Kingsley. At my request he did some checking into your father's background. It seems, Leah, that one Henry Terence Dalton Covington, alias Terence Dalton, married an Elizabeth Balfour six months prior to exchanging vows with the present Lady Covington. It is Arthur, Arabella, and their siblings who are illegitimate, not you and your siblings. The records will confirm this."

Relief flowed through Leah on hearing her husband's

words, then she asked, "Did Mr. Kingsley say if he learned why my father decided to marry two women?"

"The story that your father relayed to John, sometime back, was that, as with many in the peerage, he was expected to marry within his rank in order to combine both name and wealth. In your father's case, it was more a matter of money, for the Covingtons had apparently fallen on hard times. A marriage was arranged, one that was assured to ease his family's financial burden. Though your father held genuine affection for the Lady Gladys Preston-Davis, he didn't really love her. Then while on holiday in the north of England, he met your mother, fell madly in love, and married her within a matter of two weeks. They, too, found their way to Gretna Green, the same as we."

"Are you saying my mother knew he was a member of the peerage?" Leah asked, confused.

"That remains unclear. If she did, John wasn't aware that she knew. Your father may have used an assumed name from the beginning. He may have wanted to escape the pressures of his title and enjoy himself one last time before he married."

"You mean he wanted to sow his wild oats, don't you?"

"I was trying put it in a more tactful manner, but, yes, it's possible he intended such. But whether or not your parents were intimate before they married is of no consequence. The fact remains, your father took Elizabeth Balfour as his wife—his *first* wife."

"Well, if she did know, she certainly kept quiet about his being part of the peerage," Leah said, then considered the point. "Maybe she did know—all of it."

"What makes you say that?" Ian questioned.

"She never once objected to his being in London most of the year. If she was unaware of what was going on, then why didn't she demand he either move his business north, or his family south, so that we could all be nearer to each other? I know *I* would have."

"She wasn't you, Leah. True, she may have known all, but she may have simply been so much in love with your father that, in her eyes, whatever he did was never wrong."

Remembering how very amenable her mother was, Leah accepted Ian's explanation. "You may be right," she said. "Mother never was very assertive. And she fawned over my father continually—when he was around, that is." She sighed, then asked, "If he was already married, then why did he marry Gladys?"

"From what Kingsley said, your father realized that his impetuosity had in no way solved the Covington family's financial problems. Your mother was of common birth, daughter of a merchant, I believe?"

"Yes, she said her father was a silversmith and had once owned a shop in York. She was sixteen when he died. She'd lost her mother several years prior to that. But what does that have to do with anything? He married my mother, and he should have honored his vows. He was a bigamist, Ian. What in God's name would possess a man to conduct himself in such an immoral way?"

"In your father's case, he found himself in a fix. He was obligated to support your mother. Likewise, he was obligated to see to the Covington family's security. He could ill afford to tarnish his name and the title that would someday be his. Had he simply rejected Gladys, announcing his marriage to your mother, he would have had no way to support her. From what John gathered, your father took the risk. He married Gladys, then proceeded to lead a double life, both as Terence Dalton and Viscount Henry Covington. It wasn't until your mother took ill, and your father's subsequent death, that his duplicity was exposed. First Arthur came upon it, then you. Kingsley, of course, had been sworn to secrecy long before."

"Did Mr. Kingsley say how Arthur discovered the truth?"

"While going through his father's papers, he came upon a locked tin box. Inside was the deed to Balfour, a marriage certificate, and a miniature portrait of your mother. John Kingsley's card was also among the items. Needless to say, Arthur made a hasty trip to York. What ensued wasn't very pleasant, according to John. Arthur threatened to expose John's part in keeping the bigamy quiet. Faced with the possibility of ruining both their names, the two men came to an agreement."

"All at my family's expense," Leah stated, renewed anger trembling in her voice. "How can you abide the man? If he ever shows at Falcon's Gate, I shall personally slam the door in his face."

"John knows the harm he has caused and is overcome with remorse. Initially, he was unaware of your father's deceit. By the time he learned what was going on, he was in far too deep. The same as did Arthur, Henry Covington, regardless of his long-standing friendship with John, threatened to take Kingsley down with him should the truth be exposed. John had no choice but to keep silent."

"I shall never forgive him," Leah said of the solicitor.

"Why on earth not?" Ian asked, only to find his wife gaping at him. "Leah, had Balfour not been sold from under you; had you not gone to Kingsley to discover why; had you not thought to pose as his niece and come to London in an attempt to unearth your father's past; we would never have met. We wouldn't be sitting here now, my telling you all this. Whatever Kingsley's role, he was the catalyst that brought us together. Because he was, I am willing to forgive him anything."

Her husband was right. Had it not been for John Kingsley, things would have taken a very different turn. She couldn't imagine her life without Ian. Cold, lonely, and miserable, she surmised. Instead, her days were filled with warmth, companionship, and laughter, all because Ian was near. Knowing as much, Leah felt the first twinges of forgiveness.

"I've changed my mind. I'll not slam the door in his face after all," she said finally. "But only because he brought us together."

Ian chuckled. "At least you've taken a step in the right direction, sweet. Otherwise, if he and mother ever do marry, I'd hate to think of the battering his nose would take every time they came for a visit."

"Do you think your mother will ever remarry?" she asked.

"I don't know. She still misses my father. Their love was very special—a once-in-a-lifetime find. She warned me not to be so eager to settle for mere companionship when I finally chose my wife. I'm glad I heeded her advice. I fear, however, she will now be forced to settle for the exact thing that she cautioned me against."

"Companionship, and not love, you mean?" Leah questioned.

"Yes."

"At this stage in her life, maybe that is all she really wants. Besides, I saw how her eyes would light up at the mention of John Kingsley's name. It may not be the same as it was with your father, but I'm fairly certain she's fallen in love again."

"I hope so," Ian said. "But mainly I just want her to be happy."

"Tell me," Leah said, "how ever did you get Kingsley to reveal all this information about my father? I thought he was bound by ethics not to divulge anything about his clients."

"It was more my mother's doing than mine. She was the one who persuaded him to get at the truth and disclose both what he knew and what he had learned—something to do with spending Christmas at Kingsley Hall with him."

Leah laughed lightly. "A threat, was it?"

"It worked, didn't it? We have the information, and John has mother at Kingsley Hall. Fortunately for him, mother's anger over this situation has eased somewhat."

Briefly, Leah reviewed what she'd just learned about her father.

"Did Mr. Kingsley tell you where my father was buried?"

"In Nottinghamshire at Southwell Minster in the Covington family plot. The place is not far from Covington Court. Whenever you feel up to it, I'll take you there," he said.

"It will be awhile—if I go at all." She fell silent for a bit. 'Poor Arthur and Arabella," she said finally, genuinely sorry for the pair. "They will be devastated."

"*Poor Arthur* is more like it. As it is, he stands to lose a good deal more than Arabella. The title *Viscount Covington* actually belongs to Terence. I can only imagine how Arthur will react once he learns the truth. You did tell Terence about your father's bigamy, correct?"

"Yes. He knows, but the others are still unaware of it. I'd like to wait until they are older—that's if I tell them at all."

"Well, I think we'd best let Terence know the whole of it. Before we pull the rug out from under the Covingtons, Arthur especially, Terence needs to decide if he really wants the designation of viscount. Though he is entitled to it, I doubt his peers will be too receptive in welcoming him into the fold. Only Terence can decide what will be best for him."

"There's nothing to decide," a hard, low voice declared.

Both Ian and Leah looked to the open doorway to see Terence standing at the threshold. With a brief glance at Leah, Ian came to his feet. "Come in, Terence, and take a seat."

"I'll stand," he announced, entering the room fully.

"I presume you heard everything?" Ian inquired.

"Enough to know I have no desire to ruin my half-brother's life. My own, as well."

"Are you sure, Terence?" his sister asked. "You've just learned about this and have had no time to think it through."

"I've thought it through. Leave the Covingtons as they are. My plans do not include staying in England anyway," he stated. "I've had my nose stuck in books far too long. Adventures await me. I want to live them, not read about them."

Under a quizzically arched brow, Ian stared at the lad. "You'll finish your education first, then you may seek the adventure you desire. Understood?" Terence gave a quick nod of agreement, and Ian smiled. "Which reminds me," the earl said, slipping an envelope from the inside pocket of his coat. "Master Terence Dalton, you have been accepted at Eton. You will be expected for the spring semester, but only with the stipulation that you continue on to King's College."

"Oh, Terence!" Leah cried as she sprang from the settee to hug her brother. "How wonderful."

A commotion sounded in the foyer, cheerful voices rising

throughout the house. "That's what I came to tell you," Terence stated. "I saw Lord and Lady Ebonwyck's coach turn down the drive."

"Well, it appears they have arrived," Ian chimed. "Let's go greet our guests."

Later, when the house had settled for the night, Ian and Leah left the sitting room where they'd spent the last half-hour in quiet conversation.

As they made their way to the stairs, Leah gazed up at her husband, her arms linked with his. "So, I hear you've been playing Cupid, sir."

Ian blinked, then looked down on her. "Cupid? What makes you say that?"

"Alissa said they received a Christmas greeting from Jonathan. In passing, he mentioned his sister was seeing a Lord Winston. Isn't that the gentleman with whom you've been corresponding lately?"

"Come to think of it, it is."

"Well?"

"He's a widower. I simply mentioned he might look Veronica up when he was in London. Apparently, he did." As they turned the corner, Ian came to a quick stop. "Where did that come from?"

His gaze was riveted to the huge portrait of himself, which had suddenly appeared at the foot of the stairs.

"Why, Sinclair House, of course," Leah said.

"I know *where* it came from. How and when did it get here?"

"I missed seeing it, so I asked your mother if it would be too much of an imposition to have it sent to Falcon's Gate. It arrived three days ago while you were at Hawkstone. Duncan oversaw its hanging during our dinner."

Ian chuckled. "I wondered why he was so long between serving courses. And this is also why you insisted we say our farewells to the Braxtons in the sitting room instead of at the door. *Now* I understand all."

"I had hoped to surprise you."

"That you have." He and Leah had stopped at the base of

the painting. Ian carefully inspected his likeness, then said, "A rather arrogant fellow, I'd say."

"I say you have misread the artist's depiction entirely," Leah asserted. "Look at the tilt of the earl's head, the way he has positioned his body, and, of course, that mischievous light in his eyes. I'd say it bespeaks a zest for life."

"Zest, hmm? Are you certain?"

"Very certain," Leah whispered, her own eyes reflecting the love that was in her heart.

FROM AWARD-WINNING
AUTHOR CHARLENE CROSS COMES
A SWEEPING TALE OF
LOVE SET AGAINST THE PAGEANTRY
OF MEDIEVAL TIMES.

Splendor

by
Charlene Cross

POCKET
STAR
BOOKS

Available from Pocket Star Books
mid-October 1994

956

Marylyle Rogers

Marylyle Rogers delights with her thrilling, richly-woven medieval romances...

- ❑ HIDDEN HEARTS...............................65880-8/$5.50
- ❑ PROUD HEARTS.................................70235-1/$5.50
- ❑ CHANTING THE DAWN.................70951-8/$5.99
- ❑ DARK WHISPERS............................70952-6/$4.99
- ❑ THE EAGLE'S SONG.........................74561-1/$4.99
- ❑ THE KEEPSAKE................................74562-X/$5.50
- ❑ CHANTING THE
        MORNING STAR..................74563-8/$5.50

And Don't Miss...
CHANTING THE STORM
Coming in mid-April

Available from Pocket Books

POCKET
B O O K S

POCKET BOOKS
PROUDLY ANNOUNCES

SPLENDOR

Charlene Cross

Coming from Pocket Books
Fall 1994

The following is a preview of
SPLENDOR. . . .

Avranches Castle, Normandy
January 1153

Wanderlust ran in the veins of Rolfe de Mont St. Michel as though it were his lifeblood. The thought of marriage had never once entered his mind.

Not, that was, until four days ago.

The sinking winter sun at his back, Rolfe looked up at the gray stone fortress and its imposing tower. What he sought lay just beyond the castle walls. He had a quest, and by his knight's oath he'd not fail his mission, or Henry of Anjou could fail his.

Still, he'd not volunteered his services simply to ensure Henry's success. Rolfe had another motive. Revenge. He could almost taste its sweet reward. Miles d'Avranches would suffer for his cowardice. This Rolfe promised himself.

A frigid wind swept the barren hillside, sending a chill down Rolfe's spine. He raked back the strands of hair that had whipped across his face to settle them at his shoulder. Devoid of the protection of his hauberk, he again shivered as the cold air penetrated his clothing.

Catching the edge of his hood, Rolfe covered his head.

Four years had passed since he and Miles had last met, four years in which Rolfe had matured and hardened in both aspect and character. He was no longer the young knight-errant eagerly seeking wealth and adventure on his first Crusade. Though Rolfe doubted the weak-kneed Miles would recognize him, he nevertheless thought it might be wise to keep his face hidden.

His steed having strayed slightly from the path, Rolfe reined the great destrier in line with the procession of men, women, and attendants as they made their way up the lane toward the gates.

"Smile, Garrick," he ordered his companion on spying the man's pensive expression. "You look as though you're about to attend a funeral."

The statement drew a sharp glance from the grizzle-haired knight. He pressed his mount close to Rolfe's.

"'Tis a possibility," Garrick replied in a low voice. "What worries me is that it may be our own."

Rolfe chuckled. "You're becoming an old woman. Stop wringing your hands. Naught will happen to us."

"Had you a solid plan in mind, I might agree with you. As it is, we go in blind. I don't like it, my young friend. It is too dangerous."

"Have faith, Garrick. I know what it is I want to accomplish. It's just a matter of discovering how to go about it."

"Risky, I say," the older man grumbled. "Especially when there is only we two."

"The smaller our number, the less suspicion we draw. Now lighten your mood and pretend you are enjoying the day. We promised Henry we'd keep the barons occupied, and that we shall."

Garrick snorted. "I hope by *occupied* you have more in mind than our providing the entertainment at the wedding feast as we are baited by a pack of ravenous hounds. Should we get caught, that's precisely what we'll be doing."

Along with the others, the pair passed under the portcullis and into the castle. "Have no fear of that, Garrick," Rolfe reassured as he now carefully scanned the high walls of the inner courtyard. His gaze stopped on the comely young woman framed in an open window. "There'll be no celebration tomorrow. No nuptials either. Not without the bride."

Tomorrow was her wedding day.

Excitement bubbled inside Catherine of Mortain as she watched the activity in the courtyard below. The guests were arriving less frequently now, and she imagined this particular group might be the last.

Miles.

Her betrothed's name whispered through her mind, and Catherine's heart raced with anticipation. Proud, handsome, and well-mannered, he was the epitome of what she desired in a husband. For unlike most men—her father being the exception, of course—he seemed genuinely interested in her opinions. Complete agreement with her views was something else entirely, but at least Miles didn't chastise her for speaking her mind, something that was highly uncharacteristic for his gender.

Yes, in an age when women suffered from the curse of Eve's deceit, females considered to be the lowest of all God's creatures, Miles exalted his betrothed, honoring and respecting her. *That* was why Catherine loved him so.

"'Tis a cold wind blowing through that window. Come away from there, child. Else you'll catch your death."

A smile still playing on her lips, Catherine turned to see her nurse ambling toward her from the far side of the vast chamber. "But, Eloise, much is happening below. Can I not watch?"

"No," the woman said firmly. "Now come away from there."

"I'll marry only once, you know. Don't be so eager to ruin my pleasure."

Eloise brushed past Catherine, intent on shuttering the window. "You'll not marry at all should you take a chill," she stated, the stained-glass panes closing with a rattling thump.

"Oh, Eloise, you worry far too much. I have never been ill a day in my life."

"Good fortune has shined on you, 'tis true. But remember

there is always a first time for everything. Come along now. You are expected below to greet your guests. Your father awaits you."

"And Miles?"

"He's there, too."

Catherine studied her nurse. Eloise was akin to a mother to her, had acted in that very capacity since Catherine was twelve, when her mother had died. She valued Eloise's opinion and, in this situation, wanted desperately to win the woman's approval. "You still don't agree with my marrying him, do you?"

"'Tis not for me to say whom you marry or don't marry."

"That's not what I'm asking. You don't like Miles. Why?"

"He is not what he seems," Eloise grumbled.

Catherine thought to defend her betrothed, but her words died on her lips as Clotilde scurried into the room.

"M-milady," she said on an awkward curtsy, then fell silent.

Eloise's niece was painfully shy and equally plain. Catherine always felt the former in the girl was a direct result of the latter. Knowing Clotilde would say no more unless prompted to do so, Catherine smiled gently, then asked, "What is it?"

"I-I just came from the chaplain. H-he says the bishop has arrived along with several clerics. He will be meeting with them shortly, and he won't be able to hear your confession until tomorrow. He'll meet you at dawn in the chapel."

"Thank you, Clotilde. I know how difficult it was for you to speak to him on my behalf. Now, fetch my comb, will you?"

After Clotilde did as she was bade, Eloise quickly groomed Catherine's hair, then the three exited the women's quarters and descended to the great hall. Seeing the servants' strained expressions as they hurried about the huge room, Catherine instructed both Eloise and Clotilde to assist with the serving. Immediately the pair took up flagons of wine and began filling the empty goblets at one of the many tables.

Searching out Miles's whereabouts, Catherine saw he was

already seated in his place of honor at the head table. To his left, an empty chair between, sat her father, while Miles's father was ensconced to his right. Her heart tripping lightly, Catherine promptly sought her betrothed's side. But her pace slowed when she heard the raised voices as they swelled in subdued anger, particularly her father's.

"Don't attempt to convince me that Stephen is a strong and just king. If things stay as they are, England will not survive under his rule," he said. "His barons do naught but pillage and rape the land. Because of their lawlessness, I must keep my own estate heavily guarded. You know as well as I, Geoffrey, that a knight's pay is not meager of coin. I cannot say about your circumstance, but my coffers are fast becoming empty. Stephen has lost control, I tell you."

"You worry too much, William," Geoffrey d'Avranches countered. "Just because a few barons stand in disagreement with each other doesn't mean all of England is on the verge of civil unrest. Tempers flare, then they are quickly soothed. Stephen's authority is no less secure than it ever was. Besides, as two of his barons, we stand to gain far more than we ever have. Stephen is not as strict as was his predecessor."

"That is my point," William snapped. "He is weak and indecisive. As for the term *we,* you had best change that to the singular. I am content with what I have. But I fear you are not. Greed, Geoffrey, is part of Satan's scheme. Beware your immortal soul, my friend, or you may find it is lost."

Catherine noted how her future father-in-law's gaze had narrowed on her sire. "Milords," she said, her hands falling on her father's shoulders. "Such political talk is far too cumbersome, especially at a time like this. Our guests are enjoying themselves. And so should we."

"You're right, daughter," William declared. His large, callused hand patted hers. "The night is indeed for merrymaking. Come. Sit. There will be no more cumbersome talk, as you call it."

While her father spoke, Miles had risen from his chair. "And what, Catherine, do you know of politics?" he asked.

"I know that Stephen has a generous heart. Because he

does, he tries to please everyone at once. For that reason, he is perceived as being weak. Still he might be wise to take a stand. His position as king could depend on it."

"A stand? Against whom?" Miles asked. "Those who support him?" He chuckled. "Catherine, you are such a delight, but I fear your woman's reasoning is not very sound. No man would be so foolish as to make enemies out of his friends, especially Stephen."

Catherine frowned. Her "woman's reasoning"? He made it sound as though she were a dunce, simply by virtue of her gender. She felt Miles's touch. He lifted her hand from her father's shoulder, upward to his lips. His light kiss brushed over her fingers.

"Do not wrinkle your brow so, Catherine. It mars your exceptional beauty," he stated, his gaze penetrating hers.

Catherine was instantly captivated by the alluring look in Miles's dark blue eyes. Butterflies seemed to wing around inside her stomach, and she forgot about his disparaging remark. Instead, images of their forthcoming marriage bed flashed through her mind. Heat flamed from her neck upward to her cheeks, for Catherine knew her thoughts were anything but maidenly. Immediately she feared the consequences of such a fantasy.

Lustful was what the chaplain would say when she made her confession tomorrow. Ten days' penance, starting with her wedding day, would undoubtedly be her reward.

Was feeling desire for one's future husband really a sin?

The question rolled around in her mind. Knowing the castle priest was quite strict in his views, Catherine debated whether or not she should meet him at dawn. Though she desired to ease her conscience, thereby coming to Miles not only pure in flesh but pure in spirit, something told her she might be wise to forgo confession altogether.

From his position at a lesser table, Rolfe ignored the jovial throng of several hundred that feasted in the great hall and concentrated on the betrothed couple seated on the dais. The sable-haired bride-to-be, in particular, held his interest, had done so for the past half hour.

A waste of woman's flesh, sweet and soft, he thought in disgust as he watched Catherine of Mortain from over the rim of his cup. Certain she was the one he'd seen at the window, he decided she was indeed fair, but Rolfe wondered if she possessed all her wits. To marry Miles would be a grievous mistake. A cowardly husband would afford her no joy, only a passel of spineless sons, the same as their sire.

But the beautiful Catherine's future happiness was of no concern to him. What did concern Rolfe was the forestalling of tomorrow's nuptials. Opportunity was all he needed. He prayed the occasion presented itself, and quickly, else all would be lost.

Rolfe swilled his wine, then grimaced at its bitter taste. But the wine was no more bitter than the feelings he held for the comely Catherine's betrothed.

Memories of the road to Antalya filled the field of his mind. Heathen Turkish raiders swept down from the hillsides, catching the unsuspecting Crusaders off guard. At seeing the vicious pack, Miles fled, leaving Rolfe's father and older brother to fight one of the many bands alone. By the time Rolfe managed to battle his way to their side, lifeless bodies lying in the wake of his sword and ax, he discovered he was too late. His only family lay dead, bludgeoned and maimed.

Quickly Rolfe shut the door to the past. That the gutless Miles hadn't recognized him was no surprise. Though neither had continued on the sacred journey, each had gone his separate way. Still, Rolfe was determined to keep his distance, just to be safe.

A shadow fell over him, and Rolfe looked up to see that Garrick had returned. "Well?" he asked, once his companion was seated.

The knight lifted his cup and shielded his lips from prying eyes. "The talk is about the wedding and the bridale," he whispered. "It seems they are still unaware that Henry has invaded England."

"Even Stephen may not yet know he is about to be dethroned. But it shouldn't be long before he is faced with the truth."

"Aye," Garrick seconded. "Pray Henry is successful, for England's sake."

Both men lifted their cups in salute, then drank deeply. Grimacing anew, Rolfe wondered if everyone's wine was as foul as his. Then again, his mood might be the cause of the sour taste in his mouth. "What about the two women?" he asked. "Will we find any help there?"

"The plump one is the Lady Catherine's nurse—Eloise is her name. The younger one is Eloise's niece. The girl is pitifully plain and terribly shy. Of the two, I'd take my chances with her."

"If she is as shy as you say, I doubt I'll get within ten feet of her before she seeks to flee," he said, watching the girl in question.

"I've yet to know a woman who would willingly run from you. One glimpse of your wide, white smile and her heart will melt. She'll be wanting to thread her fingers through your tawny locks and press her lips to yours. With luck, her tongue will loosen as well."

Garrick's words drew a sharp look from Rolfe. The older knight guffawed. "There have been times, my friend, when I've missed the mark," he said, once Garrick had quieted. "I fear this may be one of them."

"If you wish to discover if that is so, I suggest you act now. She's headed behind the curtain to the kitchens."

Knowing this might be his only chance to glean the information he sought, Rolfe came up from the bench and was quickly away from the table. His gaze on the girl's aunt, making certain she didn't spot him, he strode the hall's perimeter. When he reached the curtain, he glanced at the betrothed couple. For some unexplained reason, the look of devotion that the sweet Catherine cast upon her future husband galled Rolfe. Dismissing the pair, he quickly slipped behind the barrier.

"Well?" Garrick questioned on Rolfe's return.

"Come. Let's make our way outside."

Once in the courtyard, Garrick asked, "Were you able to question the girl?"

"Aye."

"And?"

"In a few hours we'll gather our mounts and leave the castle."

"Leave?" Garrick inquired, a frosty mist showing on his breath. "Have you given up?"

"No. We'll position the horses in the woods. You'll await me there."

"And where will you be?"

"Here. I plan to return on foot."

"I'd think you'd draw suspicion, leaving then returning."

"Dressed in a priest's robes, I doubt anyone will question me."

"A priest's robes?"

"Aye. At dawn I'll be in the chapel, ready to receive the Lady Catherine's confession."

"Have you sought to tempt your betrothed by inviting him to your bed before the nuptials?"

Catherine stared at the priest, whose deep, clear voice resonated through her. When she'd arrived at the chapel a little before dawn, she'd found him instead of the chaplain.

"Your regular confessor has fallen ill," he'd told her. "Ingested something that didn't agree with him. He asked that I receive your confession. I hope, my child, that meets with your approval."

Undeniably she'd been relieved by the announcement, for this man's manner seemed less stringent than did the chaplain's. But his interrogation was coming ever closer to the one question she hoped not to answer. Catherine wondered if she would truly be so presumptuous as to lie should he ask it.

"Should I repeat the question?" he asked.

Catherine scanned his face, its angles and planes drawing together into what could be termed perfection. A fringe of tawny hair brushed his wide forehead as it peeked from beneath the linen coif that hid his tonsure. Instead of the pallid complexion that most men of the cloth bore, his skin was a healthy bronze. His gray eyes, as soft in color as a dove's breast, gazed at her through lazy, long-lashed lids. He was indeed handsome—too handsome for a priest.

"My child, your concentration seems to be straying. Shall I repeat the question?"

Catherine blinked. "N-no." What had she been thinking? "I—I've never sought to tempt my betrothed."

"You sound unsure."

Biting her lip, Catherine could no longer hold his gaze. "I've not sought to tempt him," she repeated.

"Not even in your thoughts?" he asked gently.

Again she stared at him. His eyes were clear, free from condemnation. She didn't know why, but she suddenly grew bold. "Is it really a sin to desire one's betrothed?"

"Then you desire him?"

How could she lie and seek the Lord's forgiveness at the same time? "Aye, I do." Then she blurted, "Please be merciful. I'll exist on bread and water for forty days if need be, but do not forbid the consummation of my marriage. I promise to be a good wife, obedient and submissive. I'll observe the days that we are forbidden to lie together, and when I am with child, I'll abstain altogether as the Church demands."

"You know the saints' teachings well," he replied.

Cynicism had sounded in his voice. As Catherine looked at him questioningly, a muffled squeal, coupled by a slight scraping noise, annunciated from behind the alter. Her eyes widened.

"Rats," the priest stated. Quickly his hand caught her arm, and he urged her from her knees. "Come, my child. Let us leave here before they overrun the place."

Catherine allowed the priest to guide her from the chapel. Soon she found herself outside in the courtyard. "Why have we come out here?" she asked, shivering.

"By your confession, you must do penance. You know that, don't you?"

"Yes, but—"

"You have requested leniency, and I shall grant you such. By doing penance as I prescribe, you will be allowed to consummate your marriage. Otherwise you will wait ten days. The bishop will be notified of such before you state your vows at the church door."

Catherine searched his face. "What is it that I'm supposed to do?"

"We shall go to the woods below the castle. There you will kneel and recite your prayers for one hour."

"One hour?"

"Yes. And you shall be humble, my child."

Hesitant at first, Catherine felt she had no choice. Gooseflesh had risen on her arms, and she was shivering uncontrollably from the cold. "I shall get my boots and a heavier cloak," she said, for she wore only her slippers, which were meant for indoors. But as she started to turn, he grabbed her arm, startling her.

"No, milady." His grip loosened. "As part of your penance you shall suffer from the elements. 'Tis this or a regular penance."

"As you wish."

Catherine followed the priest to the gatehouse. The guard looked them over when she requested passage out. After she explained her need and assured him that they would return in an hour, he ordered the gates opened.

As they traversed the hillside toward the wood, Catherine listened to the sound of the priest's robe as it slapped sharply against his legs, his long strides carrying him onward. She was hard pressed to keep up with him, skipping quickly along.

Once they'd reached the woods, she felt his hand again on her arm. Together they ducked the barren branches, traveling ever deeper into the forest. A sharp limb snagged her hair, and she cried out when she was suddenly pulled backward. The priest's deft hands hastily untangled her from the branch, and they continued on.

"Are we almost there?" she asked, fearing they might get lost.

"Nearly," came his reply.

In less than a minute they stood in a small glade.

"Is this the place?"

"Aye."

Expecting instructions from him, she received none. Then she heard the rustle of fallen leaves and branches breaking under a heavy foot. Horses, she thought, turning toward the sound.

Dressed in a hauberk, a man appeared, two destriers trailing after him. Confused, Catherine turned back to her confessor. Her eyes widened as he pulled the linen coif from his head. A wealth of tawny hair tumbled to his shoulders. "You're no priest!" she cried the second she realized he bore no tonsure. The priest's vestments were stripped from his body to reveal a knight's armor. Catherine felt her heart race with trepidation. "Dear God! What is this all about?"

"You are coming with us, my fair Catherine," Rolfe proclaimed.

"With you? Where?"

He caught her arm. "To England."

"But why?"

"'Tis a matter of politics."

Struggling against his hold, Catherine opened her mouth, but before she could scream, he shoved the coif inside. Her hands drawn behind her back, they were rapidly bound with a leather thong. A heavy cloak dropped across her shoulders, the ties secured, then she was cast upon the saddle, her abductor mounting behind her.

Miles!

His name tore through her mind, for she was certain she'd never see her betrothed again.

Look for

SPLENDOR

Coming from Pocket Books
Fall 1994